The options

"The Younglings you'll deal with are in danger," he said. "Once before you visited a world that was endangered—to save it. This world we have no power to save. Do you realize what that means?"

I was beginning to, and it wasn't a happy realization...

"It means that there are just three ways it can end," he told me gently. "The danger may not materialize; in that case your personal peril, which will be great, will be all you have to worry about. On the other hand, these people may be wiped out, and if so"—he paused, his eyes meeting mine, then forged ahead—"you will either share their fate or stand by, helplessly, and watch it happen."

"Watch it happen? Will it be sudden?"

"They are on the verge of a nuclear war, Elana."

FIREBIRD
WHERE SCIENCE FICTION SOARS™

The Ear, the Eye and the Arm   Nancy Farmer

Enchantress from the Stars   Sylvia Engdahl

Firebirds: An Anthology of   Sharyn November, ed.
    Original Fantasy and
    Science Fiction

House of Stairs   William Sleator

Interstellar Pig   William Sleator

Moon-Flash   Patricia A. McKillip

The Mount   Carol Emshwiller

Parasite Pig   William Sleator

Singing the Dogstar Blues   Alison Goodman

THE
FAR SIDE
OF EVIL

SYLVIA ENGDAHL

FIREBIRD

AN IMPRINT OF PENGUIN GROUP (USA) INC.

FIREBIRD
Published by the Penguin Group
Penguin Group (USA) Inc., 345 Hudson Street, New York, New York 10014, U.S.A.
Penguin Group (Canada), 10 Alcorn Avenue, Toronto, Ontario, Canada M4V 3B2
(a division of Pearson Penguin Canada Inc.)
Penguin Books Ltd, 80 Strand, London WC2R 0RL, England
Penguin Ireland, 25 St Stephen's Green, Dublin 2, Ireland
(a division of Penguin Books Ltd)
Penguin Group (Australia), 250 Camberwell Road, Camberwell, Victoria 3124, Australia
(a division of Pearson Australia Group Pty Ltd)
Penguin Books India Pvt Ltd, 11 Community Centre, Panchsheel Park,
New Delhi - 110 017, India
Penguin Group (NZ), Cnr Airborne and Rosedale Roads, Albany, Auckland,
New Zealand (a division of Pearson New Zealand Ltd)
Penguin Books (South Africa) (Pty) Ltd, 24 Sturdee Avenue, Rosebank,
Johannesburg 2196, South Africa

Registered Offices: Penguin Books Ltd, 80 Strand, London WC2R 0RL, England

First published in the United States of America by Atheneum Publishers, 1971
Second edition published in the United States of America by Walker Publishing
Company, Inc., 2003
Published by Firebird, an imprint of Penguin Group (USA) Inc., 2005

1 3 5 7 9 10 8 6 4 2

LIBRARY OF CONGRESS CATALOGING-IN-PUBLICATION DATA

Engdahl, Sylvia Louise.
The far side of evil / Sylvia Louise Engdahl.
p. cm.
Sequel to: Enchantress from the stars.
Summary: A young girl from an advanced civilization is sent as an observer to a planet
whose people have not yet learned to control their use of atomic power.
ISBN 0-14-240293-1 (pbk.)
[1. Science fiction.] I. Title.
PZ7.E6985Far 2003b
[Fic]—dc22
2004056339

THE
FAR SIDE
OF EVIL

o n e

The wind is howling through the trees outside, a cold, hateful wind. By standing on the bunk I can just barely reach the window. It's quite dark now, and the stars are brilliant, though they seem terribly far away. They, at least, are familiar and comforting, a reminder of home.

There is no use pretending that I am not scared. I am in prison, and I do not think that I shall get out. Oh, I'm not guilty of the charges against me; I'm not at all what my captors think I am. They know nothing of my real identity beyond my first name, Elana, and the fact that I seem surprisingly young to be involved in a sabotage plot. They would be even more surprised if they knew the truth.

It is very funny, really. They think that I'm a foreign agent, and I am. Only I'm the agent not of their political enemies but of a civilization far in advance of theirs, an interstellar federation. I am not a native of this planet.

If they knew that I wasn't born here on Toris, they would probably be more certain than ever that I have hostile intentions; and that is ironic. After all, we of the Federation visit the worlds of Younglings—peoples who are not yet fully mature—simply to study them; and as an agent of the Anthropological Service, I am bound by the Oath to hold those peoples' best interests above all other considerations. Furthermore, I am a prisoner not for having harmed anyone but because I'm trying to prevent a horrible disaster that is threatening this world as the result of our presence. What I'm doing may not work, and if it doesn't—well, if it doesn't, a whole Youngling civilization may be wiped out. And if it were not for the surveillance camera that is hidden in the ventilator, I'm sure I would break down and sob, for I have never felt so alone. I cannot reach any other agent, even telepathically; they are all too far from me. There is no one to help, and the responsibility is all mine.

My cell is a cubicle no wider than it is high, absolutely bare of anything but the rigid bunk and the heavily barred slot of a window above it. (There is another bunk, but it's folded back against the wall, for I am in solitary confinement; I see no one except when I am taken out for questioning.) The metal door is solid and has an electrically controlled panel, through which my food is passed—when I'm given food, that is, which isn't often. In the center of the ceiling is a huge naked bulb that burns day and night without respite. It doesn't have the intended effect on me any more than my interrogator's harsh spotlights do, since the sun of my home solar system is brighter than this one's and my eyes are relatively insensitive to glare. To see the stars, however, I must cup my hands around my face and press close to the window.

Out there, out beyond this isolated and sorely troubled planet, lies a universe of countless worlds: fascinating worlds with their own civilizations, their own heart-lifting beauties, their own sorts of terrors, griefs, and joys. I may never visit them again. But they are there, and somehow knowing that gives me courage. Life is *not* all evil and ugliness, even here on the planet Toris! Though the men who have imprisoned me are a rather sorry lot, they are not really representative of their race, which is, like all Youngling races, a promising one. And as I stand here looking out at those glittering stars, I can't help wishing that the Torisian people knew of the universe that is waiting to be explored. It's harmful to Younglings, of course, to find out that there are human beings more advanced than themselves; I am sworn to keep that secret even at the cost of my life. So I cannot tell them how things are. But what would I say to them, if I were free to speak?

I would tell them that they are a good people, better than they know. They have a big future ahead of them, a future among the stars, which I shall not jeopardize by revealing anything to my captors. At least we of the Service hope they have a future. The disaster I am trying to prevent is not their only peril; they face a larger danger, and from that we are powerless to save them. Our science has discovered much that they have not yet dreamed of; still, we don't have enough knowledge. That is why we have come. If—well, if things go badly for them (and they look bad now), we hope at least to learn something that will help to save other worlds.

But our work here may be all for nothing—worse, it may backfire. If I fail to fool my captors, if they guess that I am not the saboteur I'm pretending to be, then the Torisians will be in trouble for which we are to blame. That's a chilling prospect. I can't stop shivering, and it's not merely because this cell is kept so miserably cold.

They have been trying to make me answer their questions by a method that, from my study of the ways of Younglings, I judge to be the traditional one. (There was a time, before I was fully trained, when such barbarism would have shocked me; I am older and wiser now.) Their failure to obtain any information is a matter not of heroics on my part but of defenses they don't know I have. I did tell them that much, because I just couldn't resist the temptation and I knew that they would not believe me. "You can't *force* me to cooperate," I warned. "The human mind can't be forced. You can't even hurt me if I decide not to be hurt." My interrogator laughed and declared that I would shortly learn otherwise. But he is ignorant; the human mind has all sorts of powers that he would scoff at. I'm aided by those powers: telepathy and psychokinesis, plus some other skills that are very useful when it comes to dealing with pain. What has been done to me so far has been a bit scary, but it has not posed any serious problem.

However, I think that fairly soon I shall swallow my pride and start putting on a good act for them. If they were to discover that I really am impervious to their present techniques, they might experiment further, and I am not at all eager to have that happen. Up till now they have shown restraint because they want to keep me in good shape for a public trial. But if they should abandon that idea, well, there are things they could try that I would find disconcerting, to say the least. I have some impressive powers, but I'm not free to use them all. I am sworn; I cannot use any form of self-protection that would reveal that I am alien.

I try not to think about that. I try not to look ahead at all, for the thing that frightens me most is the likelihood that if my ruse succeeds I will be stuck in this prison for years and years, for the rest of my life, maybe. I know that I shall not tell them anything; I know that they will not kill me until I do, except perhaps by accident. Even if they do threaten to kill me, death is something I have faced before. I am experienced in such matters, and I know that facing it is a kind of terror I can handle. But to be locked up here forever on a Youngling planet, when I have been trained for the stars . . .

Of course, it may not come to that. This planet may be doomed in any case by the natural laws I was sent to learn about.

There is a small chance that my own people will eventually be able to help me. They will try. Only they cannot do it if it means harming any Younglings, either through violence—which is contrary to our principles—or through disclosure. So I may be in for a long ordeal, and if I am to withstand it, I must find something to occupy these dismal hours between interrogations. I shall record the whole story of this ill-fated mission, I think. The only way open to me is through a rather difficult mental discipline, one in which I was recently trained; it's a real challenge. (You "store" the words in your subconscious mind so that you can "read" them back later, quickly, without thinking them through—a little like memorizing long passages under hypnosis, except that you have full control over what you're doing.) I need that kind of a challenge! I need it to keep my mind off other things. Things like the fact that I may never again see my home or the man I'm to marry . . . that disaster may hit Toris at any moment and that if it does, it may be partly my fault . . . that my interrogators may come up with some ghastly new tactic tomorrow . . .

And I have another need. The current game they are playing is having its effect on me. Confession, they tell me, is the best route to peace of mind; and that is less ridiculous than most of their assertions, though I'm certainly not about to buy peace of mind for myself at the cost of harm to this world. They have an unbelievably far-fetched statement written out for me to sign; they have shown it to me a number of times, and my laughter has been not forced but genuine, because the list of my alleged "crimes against humanity" is hilarious in the light of my true mission. But each time, back in my cell, that laughter has turned to silent tears. While their ideas about the human mind are primitive, they are right, I suppose, in their conviction that everybody feels guilty about something. In my case it is true, anyway.

I tried, not long ago, to do a very dreadful thing. My attempt did not succeed, but if it had I would have a terrible load on my conscience; I would deserve whatever punishment fell my way. Yet if by some miracle it becomes possible, I shall try the thing again, for if it is not done, the people of Toris will have little chance to survive.

For me, the mission began one sunny afternoon in a top-floor office of Anthropological Service Headquarters, on the planet where I was born. (Its star is unnamed on Torisian charts and is very distant.) It was the day of my graduation from the Academy, and I was frantic, for I had received no word about what my assignment was to be. My name hadn't appeared on any of the rosters that had been posted. Only that morning, however, I had had a call from the secretary for the Executive Staff. I was to see the Personnel Director. Not my adviser or some other Academy official, but the Director himself.

My case was, to be sure, somewhat extraordinary. Unlike my classmates, who were to take the Oath that evening, I already wore the Emblem; I had been sworn several years before, during a mission to the Youngling planet Andrecia. It's rare for a student to be invested prior to graduation, but rarer (and illegal) for anyone but a sworn agent to visit a non-Federation world. Since I'm the daughter of a Service family and had gotten myself involved in a mission commanded by my own father, I had been allowed to commit myself sooner than usual.

The Oath is an extremely serious business; you give your life to the Service, totally and without reservation, renouncing your allegiance to your native world. The conditions aren't made easy; they're designed to discourage people who might take lightly our position with regard to Younglings, for it's vital to the Younglings' welfare that we refrain from exerting any sort of influence on their civilizations. Your job as a field agent is to study them and sometimes to protect them, but not to play God. It's a fascinating job, one worth sacrifices. Only it's an awesome responsibility, and you go through a great deal to qualify.

It's not enough for you to be intelligent, and proficient in controlling your psychic powers, and willing to work hard. It's not even enough for you to be willing to die rather than bring harm to the Younglings, though that is necessary and not a mere figure of speech. You must also have a special sort of empathy: an ability not only to understand the Youngling viewpoint but to feel it. What's more, you must be able to face things that aren't pleasant, things that the ordinary Federation citizen never sees. War, poverty, disease, filth and violence and hatred—these are facts of life on Youngling worlds. As an agent, you encounter horrors that are unimaginable by the standards you grew up with. And although you are not permitted to take any action with respect to them, neither are you meant to become insensitive. There are some people who could harden themselves, who could see such things and not mind; but if you are that kind of person, you just aren't chosen.

It's a career that doesn't attract many recruits. It means giving up all but occasional use of our natural psychic abilities, forgoing the more impressive ones—those that set our species apart from the Younglings—entirely. To some, that would be like wearing chains to live among the paralyzed. And after all, we of the Federation have plenty of other challenges open to us, things concerned with developing still greater powers of the mind that our science has just begun to investigate; our lives need never be dull.

Yet the Service is what I have wanted all my life,

and even learning the truth about it, as I did on Andrecia, didn't dampen my enthusiasm for long. If there are dark things to be seen, well, there are wonderful things, too; on the whole the exploration of the universe is incomparably thrilling. Which is fortunate, because the Oath is irrevocable, and I would hate to be stuck in a desk job at Headquarters.

On graduation day, I entered the Director's office glad to be through with my studies and desperately eager to hear where I was to be sent. My fiancé, Evrek, who had been two classes ahead of me, was away on an expedition. Besides, before we could marry, we both had solo trials to complete; so we would have to wait a while longer to work as a team in any case. Meanwhile I was more than ready to get back on a starship, preferably one bound for uncharted regions.

Though I hadn't met the Director before, I wasn't nervous about the interview and I found him easy to talk to. All the men and women who hold top positions in the Service seem to have that odd combination of strength and warmth that is so characteristic of my father: the ability to inspire trust. Besides, Service people are a close-knit fellowship—much closer than outsiders would imagine, considering that we come from all over the galaxy and have widely diverse backgrounds—and we have no formal rank. We're bound to obey the orders of those over us, such as instructors, the Executive Staff, a starship commander, or the Senior Agent on a field mission; but these people aren't surrounded by protocol, and socially we're all peers.

The Director sat not at his desk but near the windows, and I was offered a comfortable seat facing him. "What do you hear from your father?" he asked, pass-

ing me a steaming cup from the hot-drink dispenser beside his chair.

"Not too much," I said. "He's still away, command-
ing a survey mission."

"I know. I'd give a good deal if he weren't, because
I need him; right now I need all the top-level people I
can pull in." He sighed, then continued, "However,
we're here to discuss your own assignment."

I started to make some conversational remark but
stopped short, sensing the seriousness of his mood. He
was worried, preoccupied; it didn't take a telepathic exchange to tell me that. Apparently, I had not been sum-
moned for a routine pep talk.

"You've had previous field experience," the Director
said slowly. He gave me an appraising look, and I
guessed that he had been through the whole file on the
Andrecian affair. "It's an impressive record, Elana. And
as you probably know, your rating at the Academy is
good. It's more than good."

He hesitated as if not quite sure how to proceed.
He was leading up to something, I realized. Service supervisors don't usually compliment you on your
record; if it's good, it speaks for itself, and in any case
they have better ways of boosting your self-confidence.

"Is it too good," I asked, "to qualify me for a survey
team?" An unwelcome thought had crossed my mind.
The Service might want me to go right into graduate
work. Not that I wasn't planning to get an advanced
degree eventually, for scholarship is important in the
Service; we are, after all, anthropologists as well as
field agents. But I had expected to wait until Evrek and
I were ready to start a family, which wouldn't be for
some years after we were married.

The Director smiled somewhat apologetically. "We—well, we have something rather special in mind for you," he admitted. "We wouldn't want your first regular assignment to be an anticlimax."

"Special? Not another intervention case?" I asked, astonished. As a rule, the Service doesn't intervene in the affairs of Younglings, for the evolution of human races is a natural process that just can't be tampered with. Only in the rare instance where a planet is in great danger—where it's threatened by invasion, as Andrecia was, for example—do we step in; and even then our action has to be indirect.

"No," he told me, "not intervention, but something equally important."

Equally dangerous, too, I judged, from the buildup he was giving the job. Of course, all fieldwork is potentially dangerous. Whether or not we encounter overt hostility from the Younglings we are in contact with, our commitment to prevent disclosure at all costs can get us into some appalling fixes. We're unarmed, after all, and we're not allowed to use powers that would reveal our true origin.

"We need an observer," the Director went on. "Many observers, in fact, for we must have as many independent opinions as we can get."

"And you think I'm well suited to do this observing?"

"In some respects you are ideally suited. In the first place, you bear enough physical resemblance to the Younglings involved to pass unnoticed among them." That's always a factor; Service people are of all races, and only a small percentage can disguise themselves as natives of any given planet.

"More than that," he went on, "you're qualified by your unique background. You have proven yourself trustworthy under stress, yet you are still inexperienced enough to give us a fresh, unprejudiced report. Sometimes a beginner will spot something the experts miss."

There was a pause. I was well aware that he had not yet told me the whole story. All survey teams observe. That's what they exist for, and it is not considered "special." "There must be a catch," I said. "It sounds too easy."

"Too easy," he lashed out, "or too insignificant?"

I blushed, caught off guard. They are good psychologists, the senior staff people; you cannot hide your feelings from them.

The Director got up, abruptly, and walked toward the tall windows through which filtered white sunlight was streaming. "Our primary mission," he mused, "is to add to knowledge, knowledge that may or may not have any sort of direct benefits. Slow accumulation of data, expedition after expedition, year after year—it's not a very dramatic business. Rarely do tangible results show up, and when they do, their usefulness isn't always apparent—"

He broke off, turning back to me. "That's the one thing that worries me about you, frankly. You got off to an unusual start. On Andrecia you were thrown into a situation where you could accomplish something immediate and concrete. I was speaking lightly, a moment ago, about not wanting your next job to be an anticlimax. It will be; your whole career may be anticlimactic in the sense that you may never again have such an opportunity. Are you prepared for that?"

With a forced laugh I answered, "I guess I can do without any more opportunities to come so close to getting myself killed."

"More agents are killed in survey work than in spectacular rescue missions. Your mother, if I remember correctly—"

"Of course. I just mean I haven't any burning ambition to—to slay any more dragons."

"You too are speaking lightly. But I think you know what I'm talking about, Elana."

I knew. And I must confess that it was something that had bothered me on occasion, notably during one dreary exam week when it had seemed as if no future assignment could possibly be worth the grind. Common sense told me that I could scarcely expect to save any more planets from invaders! Yet I had joined the Service not only to see the universe but to make my life count for something.

"Are you prepared for the fact that your work won't always be exciting?" he repeated.

I groped for words, then gave up and answered simply, "I am sworn."

"Touché." His hand rose to the pendant that he wore, as do we all: the multifaceted Emblem. "You are sworn, so it doesn't make a great deal of difference whether you're prepared or not."

I didn't reply. The cup, from which I had scarcely sipped, had grown cold in my hand. Settling himself again in the chair opposite me, the Director met my silence with a smile of sympathy and approval.

"Forgive me for testing you," he said. "I'll be honest. Given a free hand, I would put you to a harder test. You have exceptional aptitude for the job we do, but you need more seasoning, more discipline, and I would see that you got it through a long apprenticeship in routine work."

Holding my breath, I did my best not to show apprehension. Such an assignment, I realized, was just the type the Service would be likely to pick for me. They wouldn't send me on a grand tour of romantic worlds. Service supervisors operate on the theory that the rougher they make things for you, the more you will learn, and if you show promise, they sit up nights inventing ways to make life very rough indeed. The aim is not to break your spirit; actually, they want you to show initiative, even to rebel if you use good judgment about it—rebel against obstacles. The obstacles, if not automatically present, are arranged.

The system isn't as harsh as it sounds. If you're a person who enjoys being challenged (and if you aren't, you'll never make it through the Academy entrance tests, let alone graduate), you don't mind playing along. Besides, you discover that the things they put you through always make you feel *good*. They build you up, give you confidence. No doubt that would also apply to the kind of apprenticeship he had proposed, for your education doesn't stop when you leave the Academy; but I had been hoping for a more intriguing post.

"However," the Director went on, "once again something unusual has come up, something of unquestioned significance. So I'm going to contradict nearly everything I just said and offer you an assignment that will probably finish the job of ruining you for anything routine and tame."

I let out a sigh of relief, and the anticipatory tingle I felt wasn't at all unpleasant. He was saying, "I'm re-

cruiting every agent who can halfway qualify, because
it may involve the most important anthropological discovery of our era. No, don't smile yet," he put in
quickly. "Not till you hear more about it. It won't be an
enjoyable assignment; if you accept, you'll be plunged
up to your neck in something very distressing."

"*If* I accept?"

"This particular mission calls for volunteers," he
said quietly.

There was no need for him to spell out the implications; while all field jobs are risky, some involve more
risk than an agent is ordered to assume. But his strategy, of course, had been effective. Not that I was
pushed into accepting; if there had been the slightest
question about this being a job I would want, the offer
wouldn't have been made. Moreover, I could have
turned it down. I don't go along with the notion that
people aren't responsible for their own choices, or that
they are somehow not "free" because something has affected the odds. The Director's suggestion of routine
work as the only available alternative was entirely sincere; he was not threatening me. And though he may
have used shrewd psychology to hook me, he went on
to give me full warning.

"Elana," he said seriously, "the mission isn't an easy
one. As I told you, you'll be sent in as an observer. The
situation to be observed is, to say the least, explosive;
that in itself entails hazards. But there's something
worse: You will be *only* an observer, and you won't like
what you see."

He had become very grave and, I felt, heavy-
hearted. We hadn't communicated silently, for we didn't
know each other well enough to do so without need;

yet since emotion heightens telepathic sensitivity, I grasped more than had been expressed in verbal form. "The Younglings you'll deal with are in danger," he said. "Once before you visited a world that was endangered—to save it. This world we have no power to save. Do you realize what that means?"

I was beginning to, and it wasn't a happy realization. When you're in contact with Younglings you begin to identify with them, care about them. Younglings are *people*. You feel just as strongly about them as if they were your own race; if you're not a person who can do that, you are not selected to be a field agent. But it's painful. You are vulnerable to all kinds of hurts.

"It means that there are just three ways it can end," he told me gently. "The danger may not materialize; in that case your personal peril, which will be great, will be all you have to worry about. On the other hand, these people may be wiped out, and if so"—he paused, his eyes meeting mine, then forged ahead—"you will either share their fate or stand by, helplessly, and watch it happen."

"Watch it happen? Will it be sudden?"

"They are on the verge of a nuclear war, Elana."

Before I go further, I must say something about Randil, for because I want to be entirely fair, I think that I shall tell this story from his viewpoint as well as from my own.

This business of trying to look through someone else's eyes is a thing in which I've had practice. I've been asked to do it with Younglings, as an exercise in understanding Youngling viewpoints, but there is no reason, I guess, why it can't be done with a fellow agent. As I said, I want to be fair to Randil. I don't know what he'll say to justify himself if he ever gets back to the starship, but I think I know why he did what he did; perhaps in spite of all that's happened, I would be the best person to speak on his behalf. After all, I too have sometimes questioned Service policy.

And besides, I too know what it is like to be in love with a Youngling.

Randil is in love with a Torisian girl named Kari. That's not so astonishing. Kari is a lovable person, my closest friend here on Toris. We of the Service may be dedicated to our work, but underneath we have the same feelings everyone else has, and the Oath doesn't bar us from human relationships. Well, Younglings are human. The fact that they are of younger species doesn't put them below us as individuals, even though they don't have the control of psychic powers that our more mature Federation species do. And when individuals know each other, like each other, it's hardly extraordinary for them to fall in love.

It's hopeless, of course—between an agent and a Youngling, I mean. Hopeless because there is no future in it. The agent knows that from the beginning, but sometimes the Youngling doesn't. I was spared such a situation; though the man I loved on Andrecia didn't know my true identity, he was aware that I was not of his people and that I could not remain in his world. Randil hasn't been spared it. Kari is sure that he's going to ask her to marry him. Not that he has said or done anything to indicate it, but she can't help sensing that his love for her is serious, for there is telepathic contact between them.

Naturally, Kari doesn't know that it's telepathy. Younglings are unaware of their psychic powers and can't use them under normal circumstances. They can't communicate with each other except, rarely, in a most primitive and erratic fashion. But with us they can. It's a matter not of "reading" minds but of silent conversation; and though we don't converse with them deliberately, when you're in love with somebody, it's not easy to keep your thoughts strictly to yourself.

We have had training. We are not in danger of inadvertent disclosure or anything like that. It is emotion that unconsciously leaks through. All psychic abilities— telepathy, psychokinesis, or whatever—are closely involved with emotion; the stronger your feelings, the more power you have. Randil hasn't been able to conceal from Kari the fact that he would like to marry her, so she believes that it's just a matter of time. He couldn't tell her otherwise without jeopardizing his cover. I know how this is going to turn out. It is going to be very tragic for both of them.

But it will not be the most tragic thing that has happened to Randil. The fact is, if nuclear war comes to Toris within the next few days, the bulk of the blame will rest squarely on his shoulders.

Younglings who are facing the prospect of a nuclear war believe that it's a hideous thing, which of course it is. The sad part is that they think not merely that the war would be hideous if it occurred, but that they themselves, as a people, are to blame simply for having gotten themselves into a fix where they're threatened by it. They might be a little more hopeful if they could read the histories of the Federation planets.

I am not saying that the leaders who start such wars are not blameworthy. They are, and Toris has its share of them, if the one who has been conducting my interrogation is any sample. But Randil is not all wrong when he tells me that Younglings are peace-loving underneath. Most of them do want peace, and it's too bad that they blame themselves for being related to the troublemakers.

Randil, though, has not met my interrogator. He has not yet lost his illusions. He is used to Federation society, Federation standards, and he hasn't had any previous dealings with Younglings. So he goes to the other extreme and declares that no one could possibly start a war on purpose. That's a very dangerous assumption.

The unfortunate fact is that all worlds go through a phase in which the possibility of nuclear war exists. It's a well-known phase; it's even got a name: the Critical Stage. Most planets get through it with their civilizations intact, the war and other fatal courses of action having been averted. Obviously, all the Federation worlds did, and we also know of some advanced Youngling peoples that are out of danger.

A few, sadly, do not get through. I shall not describe what happens to them.

What makes the difference? Why does one planet come safely through its Critical Stage and another planet fail? We don't know. That's what we're here on Toris to find out.

We know *how* it happens. We know what the turning point is. But we don't know exactly why that point is or is not reached. And the reason we don't is that we have no records from the worlds that have failed.

If Toris fails, we will have records. That's the whole purpose of this mission.

The Director knew when he recruited me how hard that purpose would be for me to understand and accept—even harder than for most agents, because I had once been involved in a mission where action was taken. "We'll try to stop it, won't we?" I protested when he told me that we had no power to save Toris. "The war, I mean—we certainly won't just wait!"

"You know better, Elana," the Director said regretfully. "Besides, I told you that this job would not involve intervention."

I hesitated, mustering my self-control, judging all the angles as I had been taught to do. "I suppose you're going to tell me," I said finally, "that it would be interference in their internal affairs. But surely, if it's a choice between that and letting their whole civilization be wiped out—"

"Elana," he reminded me, "the hands-off policy isn't arbitrary; it's for the Younglings' protection. In following it, we put their best interests first, as we are bound by the Oath to do."

Hotly I retorted, "And it would be in their best interests to let them blow up their planet while we sit back and take notes? Is that what you're saying?"

He was equally forceful. "I will be blunt. Yes, I'm saying exactly that. Think, Elana! You suggest that we should stop their war. We can't stop it. We don't know how. We don't even know whether it's going to materialize; and if it doesn't, any tampering on our part would simply make matters worse."

It was true enough, I realized, that finding a way to help would be easier said than done. We couldn't stop the war by force; though the Federation has powers far superior to anything possessed by Younglings, one thing we do know is that the use of force does more harm than good. We also know that we can't reveal ourselves to Younglings without doing irreparable damage to the civilization involved. In the rare cases where we intervene, it is through a ruse of some kind, and that's not always feasible.

"We ought to at least make an attempt," I persisted. "I know why meddling is forbidden: Younglings advance only through solving their own problems, and their development is thrown out of kilter if we try to solve any of their problems for them. But isn't that pretty meaningless if they don't survive long enough to go on developing?"

"Of course. And the policy allows for that; it permits us to step in if we're sure that nothing else can prevent extinction of the Youngling race. That isn't the case here. Many worlds—most, in fact—manage to avert nuclear war on their own, and interference might very well reduce this one's chances."

"Yet some don't. Maybe nothing else *can* prevent these people's extinction! Suppose we saw an opportunity to act safely, to do something that wouldn't involve force or disclosure—would we break policy?"

"Don't torture yourself over a question that won't arise," he said gently. Leaning forward, he looked straight into my eyes. "It's not an easy one to grapple with; don't think that I haven't had sleepless nights over it myself. But on this mission you are not going to face such a choice."

That seemed like evading the issue. I didn't reply aloud, but silently I challenged him: *How can you be sure? Am I to pretend not to see it if it comes?*

If you did, you wouldn't be worth much as an agent.

I turned away from him, fixing my gaze on the bright arch of windows and, beyond, the towers of the city, seen through the sun-filter as shadowy, abstract shapes. Why, I thought privately, do we get ourselves into these things? When we could live here, here where everything is clean and comfortable and safe, and "nuclear war" is a reality known only to the ancients?

"There will be no conflict with policy," the Director assured me. "In order to figure out any sort of action, we'd have to know the key—the factor that keeps some worlds from diverting their energies into the normal channel instead of into destructive ones—and if we knew that, we'd also know whether intervention was justified. But we don't have that key. We don't understand the dynamics of the Critical Stage; that's precisely what we hope to learn from the mission."

"Critical Stage?" I said slowly. It was the first time the term had come up in our discussion, so I had to think back over several years of study to place it. "Isn't that the period just before a people begins to colonize space? When they've reached the point where they can move beyond their home planet, only they haven't quite taken the plunge?"

The Director nodded. "Do you remember what's 'critical' about it?"

"Well, if they're at the point where they have the technology to attempt space travel, they also have the technology to destroy their world, either by depletion of its resources or through a war of annihilation—and every case that has ever been recorded shows that a people will do one or the other, but not both."

"That's right. They've got to develop that technology, and the preparation for war helps do it. Which is all right, as long as it doesn't go beyond preparation. The natural outlet of the effort is the colonization of space, which all peoples must achieve in order to become mature."

"And establishing off-world colonies prevents all-out war itself from occurring?"

"Yes, if there's an ongoing commitment to the effort. That's the turning point. Once they're putting all their energy into it, they're out of danger." He sighed and added grimly, "The people of the world to which you're going haven't so much as orbited a satellite."

"I didn't know that there were any Younglings in Critical Stage—now, I mean. The cases I studied were all past history."

"The planet Toris," he explained, "was discovered only a short while ago. If we had found it sooner, we would have seen the crisis approaching; we would have had teams in there for years. As it is, we've got to work fast. We don't know how much time we have left."

I shivered. Implicit in that last remark was a warning that we would use all the time there was. If it ran out unexpectedly, there might be no rescue for the observers.

Wanting to change the subject to something more encouraging, I asked, "Who's to be Senior Agent?"

"There won't be one," he told me.

I stared at him. "But I thought that always, even for a two-person team—"

"Elana," the Director said, "there's one more thing you've got to know before you make a final decision. We're not setting this up in the usual way; it won't be a team. The agents involved will work independently." He hesitated before adding abruptly, "It will count as your solo."

"Solo?" That was a real shock. You don't do your solo till you've been on some team jobs, ordinarily. It's a scary business; you are left alone somewhere on the Youngling planet, no communication with your ship or with the other on-world agents permitted. "Am I ready?" I asked, a bit shakily.

"No," he admitted. "Not by the normal standards. But since the job is going to require you to work under solo conditions, it would be unfair not to give you credit for it."

"Will we all be separated, then? Without contact?"

"Yes, and your position won't be very secure," he warned. "You know the rules for solo. We don't help you. We keep the advance information we give you to a bare minimum; you're simply thrust into an unpredictable situation and forced to adapt to it. Well, in this case that's just what will be done, not as a test exercise but because we don't have any advance information. We've as yet received no reports from anyone who's been down to the surface of the planet! All we know so far has been learned from radio and telecasts picked up from orbit. Frankly, Elana, we've done too little groundwork to set up any cover reliable enough to be used by more than one agent; we can't afford to have everyone make the same mistakes."

I was horrified, and I suppose it showed. Willing though I was to accept danger, it was unlike the Service to start off with a callous assumption that agents were expendable.

The Director understood my concern. "That's the least of our reasons for isolating the observers, however," he continued, his smile warm and reassuring. "We have others, all part of a somewhat desperate scheme whereby we hope to make our handicaps work for us instead of against us. Don't worry, you'll have support."

I couldn't think of anything to say. It was all rather overwhelming.

You can still back out if you want to, he told me silently.

No, I responded, although inside I felt far from comfortable. Aloud, I added, "It's a chance to—to find the key, isn't it? I mean, if someday we do understand the dynamics, the thing that makes some Critical Stage worlds fail—"

"We could save other Younglings. But Elana, that may be an impossible dream. The key won't be anything simple. It will be buried in a mass of data that may take many years to collect and analyze. There's no guarantee that these people will embark on space colonization even if they come through the current crisis—and observation of one world won't be enough; we'll need cross-checks, comparisons."

"All the same, I guess it's worth a try." I stood up and, with as bright a smile as I could manage, asked, "How soon do I leave?"

"The day after tomorrow. You'll be briefed en route." He too rose and took my hand. "Good luck, Elana. You know, don't you, that we wouldn't send you if we hadn't plenty of confidence in you, if we weren't sure that you could handle whatever comes up?"

He meant it, and it was a comforting idea. But I am sure that the Director, in his wildest thoughts about what might come up, never imagined anything like the fiasco I am trying to handle.

That night I stood waiting outside the Academy's Great Hall, where the rite of investiture was to be held, feeling quite magnificent in my proud new uniform of silver-trimmed white. (We don't wear our uniforms except on very special occasions; I hadn't had one before despite the fact that, being sworn, I had been theoretically entitled to it.) I was happy yet also a bit wistful, a bit lonely. My classmates were walking on air, for the taking of the Oath is one of the most thrilling acts of an agent's life, a real high point. And though as a participant in the ceremony I was to renew my commitment with all the colorful pageantry I had previously missed out on, I couldn't share the same excitement.

My own big moment stood clear in my memory; it always will. The shadowy, mysterious Andrecian forest; the firelight; the solemn beauty of the ritual and, during the secret parts, the unaccustomed intensity of telepathic contact; the feel of the Emblem's chain being dropped over my head—and of course, the inexpressible elation. That can only happen to you once. For me it was long past, in space and in time, and I wasn't the same person anymore.

I wish Evrek were here, I was thinking. Would the next time we entered this Hall together be at our wedding? Would we ever be together at all? What if that expedition he was on ran into trouble? Or what if Toris . . .

Randil, a classmate whom I didn't know well, came up to me and said with enthusiasm, "I hear we're going to the same place."

"Toris?" I asked, incredulous. The Director had implied that he was not sending inexperienced new graduates to Toris, and I had certainly never heard of anybody going solo on his first mission. What's more, Randil had not even been trained for fieldwork; he was aiming for a scholarly career and had specialized in data analysis techniques. Was the Service that hard up for agents who could pass, physically, as Torisian?

"They're scraping the bottom of the barrel, I guess," he admitted, sensing my reservations. "But I did my Third Phase thesis on Critical Stage cultures, and when I heard that one had been discovered I wanted to see it firsthand. I suppose they agreed to send me because they think the research I've done will give me an edge in adapting to the society."

Sometime I would like to read Randil's thesis. I don't doubt that he did a fine job on it; Randil is brilliant. He is also very much in sympathy with the Torisians. But there's a danger in concentrating too hard on abstract theory, especially if you aren't taking the practical training to balance it. Most of us had been thoroughly educated in Youngling ways and Youngling attitudes, not just the attitudes of whole cultures but those of the sorts of individuals we would be likely to have to deal with. Although Randil, during his graduate work, would have visited Youngling worlds as a member of a large and well-organized team, his course of study had not been designed to prepare him for exploratory missions requiring actual contact with those worlds' natives.

We went on into the dimly lighted foyer of the Great Hall, and Randil hurried ahead to his place in the procession. I forgot all about him because in spite of myself the thrill was taking hold of me: the music, the ceremonial torches—those things do something to you whether you've been sworn for five minutes or fifty years. It wasn't a night to waste worrying about whether the Director knew his job.

Yet I did worry. Not about Randil, particularly; more, I suppose, about myself. A solo mission . . . was I crazy? To accept a solo mission so soon, a volunteer mission that was admittedly hazardous and perhaps hopeless? Whatever made me think that I could be resourceful enough to get by alone on a planet that hadn't even been surveyed? A planet torn by war, suspicion—what if I couldn't manage to stay alive long enough to learn anything of value?

And then, as the processional gave way to the opening strains of the Anthem, all those futile doubts suddenly melted. The ritual's power gripped me, and there was no room in me for anything but joy. From my place in the inner ring I could not see those who like myself were already sworn, yet in the telepathic litany our minds touched, and I sensed that we were all part of something sure and strong and splendid. I stared down at the Emblem I wore, watching the flicker of torchlight reflected in its myriad facets of gleaming metal, and the sparkles blurred as if seen through tears. How could I have forgotten? The rite is more than a beautiful ceremony, more even than an expression of your consecration to the Service cause. It is a bulwark that stays with you and safeguards you for as long as you live! Much is demanded of you, but much is given, too. For once accepted into its fellowship, you know that you have what it takes to meet whatever you're confronted with; and you also know that there are others who trust you and who will back you all the way. You are not alone on any planet with that behind you.

Those who created the Service's traditions were wise; they knew that anybody whose job it was to explore unknown regions would have need of something besides training. Your training is designed to prepare you to go anywhere in the universe and cope with whatever strange and terrifying experiences you may be thrown into. But preparation isn't enough. On top of it you need something solid to cling to, an emotional anchor: something symbolic. I don't mean just a concrete thing, like the Emblem. The Emblem symbolizes the Oath, but our rituals concern deeper matters of which the Oath itself is only a symbol.

People outside the Service sometimes misunderstand the Oath. On the surface it looks as though having once sworn to hold our responsibility to Younglings above all other considerations, we're forced to act against our will or even against conscience. But it's not like that at all. The Oath doesn't bind us to anything we wouldn't otherwise do, only to what we *would* do if we had time to think through all the ramifications every time we were hit with a crisis. When we're stranded on some alien planet, we've got more than enough decisions to make without having to keep worrying about relative values! So it's a real help to have our main decision out of the way.

Of course, there's more to Service ritual than that. It's an expression of—well, an attitude, I guess, an attitude not only toward our responsibilities but toward the universe as a whole. If you're going to be an explorer, you have to trust the universe. You have to believe that the natural order of things has some sort of sense to it, some real if incomprehensible logic, and that what's true isn't to be feared. Otherwise you would just come apart if you met something really weird in a far-off corner of the galaxy. For that matter, you would be unable to bear what faced you on the average Youngling world. Some of the things an agent sees . . .

Such things have got to be considered as part of a pattern, and although we of the Service don't understand the whole pattern, we've learned enough from having observed worlds in various stages of development to trust that it is there. The most moving parts of our rites are those that affirm that trust, and even here—here in this dreary Torisian prison—I can repeat them to myself, and they do sustain me. I shut my eyes, and the walls recede, and for a while I don't feel the cold anymore. And beneath my eyelids blazes the clean flame of a torch; and the glory of the Anthem rings in my mind as I relive the evening when I last heard it.

That's what I think of when I picture that night, rather than any forebodings about Randil. Yet looking back, I do recall one small incident that may have some significance. There's a point in the ritual at which the candidate's mind is probed by the Dean in a way different from an ordinary telepathic exchange, a deeper, wordless way. We use such a level of communication for various purposes, when circumstances are compelling; but within the rite it's employed as a form of testing. Well, when that point was reached with Randil, there was a strange sort of pause: The Dean's hands were motionless a shade too long, and I saw the Emblem that he held ready tremble and catch the light as it swung on its chain.

It's hindsight that makes me mention this, of course, for I scarcely noticed it at the time. Neither Randil's sincerity nor his courage could have been questioned; the doubt, if there was one, must have concerned something quite different. The moment passed; he rose and stood within the circle of torches for the Presentation. But I wonder if the Dean will remember when what's happened on Toris becomes known.

t w o

A little while ago I awoke in cold panic, thinking that I could not endure this prison one more hour. It was not the intermittent blasts on the corridor siren that woke me; I have long since schooled my mind to ignore that, for if I hadn't I would never have gotten any sleep at all. It was the isolation, I guess, the loneliness. I am cut off not only from my own people but from the Younglings, too. I just don't know if I can bear that forever.

I *can*, of course. Only I must not expect it to be easy. I've known from the start that my job on Toris would not be easy; it requires a certain amount of fortitude, after all, just to live with the knowledge that a nuclear bomb may drop on you at any moment. Yet you get used to it. Even Younglings get used to it. In a way, though, it is easier for them because they haven't come from a world where such a threat would be unthinkable.

The situation here on Toris has grown steadily worse since we arrived. It could hardly have been expected to do otherwise, since this world's nations are divided into two blocs, armed to the teeth against each other. I am in the hands of the Neo-Statists, who believe that I am an agent of the Libertarians. It is quite true that my sympathies are with the Libertarians, whose political system is much more to my liking; but I am not spying for them.

I regret to say that there is nothing extraordinary about the Neo-Statists. All dictatorships are basically alike. The theories by which they justify themselves may sound different, but really, if you have studied one, you can understand them all. All Youngling worlds have them; it is, unhappily, a fact of nature. A few of them have even established interplanetary empires, for some Younglings have starships; there are peoples that have colonized many solar systems yet are still a long way from maturity.

The Neo-Statists are typical, almost a textbook case. The only thing at all unique about them is that they acknowledge their likeness to the original Statists who were defeated in a major, though nonnuclear, war about fifty Torisian years ago; usually these groups go to great lengths making themselves out to be the opposite of anything that has once failed. This one is so strong that it no longer bothers about such details. The dictator has a very forceful personality. He also has a very forceful secret police organization. Everybody is terrified of it, and with reason—as I am now in a position to know!

But the most dangerous thing about the Neo-Statists isn't their secret police, or even their military prowess. It is their false view of human beings. They believe that people, individual people, are less important than the State. I know it wouldn't be practical for Younglings to have the sort of government we have in the Federation, where everyone is free—really free—to make personal decisions, because to many Younglings *freedom* means freedom to hurt somebody else. There have to be laws to protect the innocent people from the troublemakers. The kinds of laws the Neo-Statists have do just the opposite, though. They give the troublemakers all the power.

My interrogator is a good example. He has rather a high rank in the secret police, I believe; at any rate, his own men are scared to death of him. I should be flattered, I suppose, that I rate his personal attention. This afternoon he gave me a long lecture on politics. I am sure that he was pleased by my avid interest, for he undoubtedly thought that he was making progress toward reforming me. Actually, of course, I was filing it all away in my memory among typical Youngling misconceptions, and if I ever get a chance to report again, it may add a bit to the data we've been collecting on what makes the Critical Stage critical.

The thing that impressed me, I guess, was that he honestly believed what he said, or at least he thought he did. I've read through reams of the official propaganda his cohorts put out, and I'm afraid I've considered it just that: propaganda. Ballyhoo for Our Glorious Dictator, and that sort of thing. But to this man it's not a mere sales pitch but literal truth. He is, in his own eyes, a champion of truth, and it is his so-called scientific objectivity that makes him so cold-blooded. Unlike some of his assistants, he is not a sadist; when he tells me that he has no wish to inflict pain on me, he is incredibly sincere. It is all for my own good! I am not sure just why he thinks himself such an expert judge of other people's good, but then that's characteristic of Younglings.

"You Libertarians are fighting a lost cause," he told me seriously. "The modern world is too complex to allow people to have independent thoughts; the State must make the decisions for the good of all. It is a matter of historical necessity."

I was near exhaustion; they had been questioning me in relays for some hours, and naturally they see to it that you are not feeling your best during these sessions. Though I can protect myself against pain, it's not an effortless defense, and I have found it necessary to save it for the times when it's really needed. The relatively minor things must be endured. So my head was splitting, my muscles ached intolerably from the awkward position in which I was being forced to stand, and for a moment I forgot that he was a Youngling and as such was entitled to my compassion. Impatiently I burst out, "You know nothing of history. History will prove you wrong; people will go right on thinking. They will have thoughts wiser than yours when you are dead."

He thought this, of course, mere empty defiance. Yet it got to him; perhaps I slipped and let something through telepathically. For the first time it dawned on him that I truly wasn't afraid of him, and since in his view all relationships are based on fear, he began to suspect, secretly, that *he* was afraid of *me*. I could tell, even without picking up his thoughts, for the long harangue he began was aimed more at his own doubts than at mine.

"Anyone who thinks himself independently wise is insane," he wound up. "You are insane, Elana. If you were not, you would repent of your crimes and tell us what we need to know; you would want to tell us. Who but a sick person would endure needless pain? Who else would willfully separate herself from the State, when only as members of the State can citizens' existence have value and meaning?"

That was a perfectly natural question from his standpoint, and since he had provided his own answer, it was obvious that he didn't want one from me. Foolishly, I replied, "If that is the only meaning your existence has, I feel sorry for you! It's lucky that most people know better, because if they were all like you this human race would never get anywhere at all."

You should never allow yourself to be drawn into an argument with your interrogators; it is very dangerous, because they cannot afford to let you win. Their ideas are well-fixed; they are not interested in logic, and their only aim is to make you angry. Anger, fear, pain—scientists of Toris are beginning to learn the power of these things; they are starting to perceive the relationships between emotions and the mind. But they have barely scratched the surface, and, as is usual with Younglings, they misuse their limited knowledge. Just as they use nuclear energy for bombs before they put it to constructive uses, they use psychological conditioning techniques to break people down long before they utilize them for building people up.

The Academy uses conditioning, too—even conditioning involving stress—but its methods are designed to make a person stronger, not weaker. Since I therefore know a good deal more about such techniques than my interrogator does, I don't fall into his traps; the one that caught me was of my own making. I thought that I was safe in saying what I did, because I was more exasperated than angry and I spoke from factual knowledge rather than from a need to prove myself right. Unfortunately, I didn't stop to consider *his* need to be right. That is what happens to you when you forget about empathy.

I shall pay for my unthinking cruelty. He will redouble his efforts, for he has to break me now; if he doesn't, he will never be sure again himself. Oh, I can resist. There is no danger of a disclosure, since he hasn't the power to tap my subconscious mind. (If Torisian science were that advanced, I could not, of course, have allowed myself to be arrested.) But I'm probably in for some highly unpleasant episodes.

Well, I'll have only myself to blame. When you are on an observation mission, you are not supposed to assert yourself before Younglings; you are supposed to be completely passive. You are supposed to listen and not answer, even when there's no disclosure involved. But that's hard. My passive role has been my greatest trial on Toris, right from the very beginning.

I came to Toris nearly half a year ago, on the eve of the vernal equinox, and on that night I was left alone to face an ordeal that was none the less frightening for being planned. I had been landed in semidarkness; the chill of early spring dawn soaked into me as I stood trembling, knee-deep in stiff, wet grass. I couldn't watch the small spherical landing craft rise noiselessly upward, for the sky overhead was black and it had used no lights. A veil of cloud hung between me and the stars.

It was rolling, barren country; the ship had come down in a small hollow amid the deserted low hills that surrounded the city of Cerne. Hurrying to the top of a nearby crest, I looked down on the light-studded belt of a major highway. I had barely half an hour to reach it, I knew, and I would have to walk fast. The awkward, unfamiliar Torisian clothes hampered me, particularly the shoes, which felt heavy and tight. Before I got to the road, dizziness had struck me, and I was shuddering from more than cold. I clenched my teeth and forced myself to run. Keeping my sense of direction proved hard, for the hills seemed to be swinging in an endless circle, and I could scarcely tell whether the roaring I heard came from the highway traffic or from my own head. They miscalculated, I thought frantically, they didn't allow enough time . . . Then my foot struck pavement and lights flashed in my eyes, disappearing as a vehicle whooshed past. More lights were approaching. At a safe distance from their path I slid to my knees and gave way to nausea. I was aware that I was losing consciousness; but then, I had expected that.

My briefings had been thorough. During my time aboard the starship I was, in fact, required to cram harder than for any of my exams at the Academy. Every scrap of information gleaned from the Service's monitoring of Torisian radio and telecasts had to be absorbed. Hypnosis helped, especially for learning the language of the country in which I was to be placed; but the bulk of the material demanded more than mere memorization. Bits and pieces had to be related not only to each other but to what was known of Youngling cultures in general, and that meant extensive review of nearly every subject I had ever studied. When you know that your life may depend on your mastery of the details, you are not tempted to cut corners.

Throughout the trip I was confined to my quarters, not only because every waking moment had to be devoted to study but because under the rules of solo I wasn't supposed to know who else was on board. I was permitted to see only my tutors, Meleny and Varned. My cabin was comfortable, with full computer facilities for library reference as well as automated meal service; I did not mind staying in it. Meleny dropped in frequently, though she couldn't stay long for she was coordinating the landing plans and had a number of other agents to work with.

Poor Meleny, she wanted desperately to go down herself. She would be retiring from fieldwork soon and might never again be involved in a mission of this magnitude. But unfortunately she could not pass as Torisian; she would have been spotted as alien immediately since she was of a race quite unlike the native one. "You're lucky, Elana," she said to me. "As far as looks go, you might have been born on Toris. We won't even have to darken your hair. Why, I'll bet you'd pass a medical exam without any trouble at all—"

She broke off, with a gleam in her eye that might have been a warning to me had I known the problem uppermost in her mind. It was Meleny's job to devise cover roles for the various agents she was briefing, a task that was far from easy. She couldn't follow the usual rule that an agent's cover should make him unnoticeable, since we would be lucky if we could turn ourselves into Torisians at all, let alone average Torisians. So the only recourse was boldness, and some of Meleny's plans were very bold indeed.

My other tutor, Varned, came aboard when our starship went into its Torisian orbit. He had actually been down to the surface; he and two other agents had been dropped off by the ship that had found Toris. By the time we arrived, they had managed to obtain the essential facts for us, facts that couldn't be learned from telecasts, such as what official identity papers for various nations should look like. He must have taken terrible risks to get his hands on the ones he had brought back as samples.

Varned talked at length over the ship's video hookup, and he also met with us individually for the purpose of establishing rapport. He was to be responsible for collecting my reports; and since we might not always be able to meet face-to-face, we had to get acquainted beforehand. Telepathic communication, even when backed by urgent emotion, just isn't practical over any distance unless the people involved know each other well.

We communicated silently right from the start, for practice. *How do I get in touch with you?* I asked.

You don't. I get in touch with you.

But in an emergency—

You deal with it alone, Elana. I'm simply a channel for passing on information.

His problems would be much greater than mine, I realized. Aside from the obvious ones connected with the work itself, he would be considered a member of a minority race in many Torisian countries, and on a Youngling world that presents difficulties. Toris, like most Critical Stage planets, is not yet fully integrated.

Can we meet in public, Varned? I mean, won't we attract attention if we're seen together? Hostility, even?

It'll work out. You'll see.

How often will you contact me?

I can't tell you that. You'll have no advance notice; most of the time I won't even be in your city.

What about pickup, when I'm recalled to the ship?

We'll cross that bridge when we come to it, Elana.

That was all he would say on the subject. It seemed, almost, that I was being kept in the dark on purpose. Well, I was. The Director had mentioned "a desperate scheme to make our handicaps work for us," and this was part of it.

Our chief handicap was that we were facing the unknown. Those who were doing the planning couldn't overcome that, so they decided to capitalize on it. There was some pretty smart psychology involved. For one thing, they were quite frank in admitting that we weren't being given all the facts as to how we would be contacted, so we remained happily under the illusion that *somebody* knew, although actually, Varned and the others who were to do the contacting had little notion of what would prove practical.

The main part of the scheme, however, had to do with expediting the job. We were all volunteers; we had been trained in self-reliance, and our mission was to learn as much as we could in as short a time as possible. So the planners used daring tactics. Knowing that they couldn't give us security, they did the exact opposite: They sent us in alone without any knowledge of how we were to be rescued in order to force us to look from inside out instead of from outside in. We were to live among the Torisians *as* Torisians, totally cut off from the ship and from each other, not only for disguise purposes but because that was the fastest way to absorb the Torisian viewpoint. We were forbidden to communicate even if we should happen to meet, which wasn't likely because no more than two agents would be assigned to the same city. For safety's sake as well as for maximum coverage of the planet, it was necessary to spread the available people around.

Still another reason for isolating us was to make sure that our observations would be independent. Each agent's reports were supposed to be based on his or her own judgment, free of the influence of the others' opinions, so that when they were all put together everyone's ideas would count. That way, the Service would end up with lots of different impressions to compare instead of a composite one that could be wrong.

"What exactly am I supposed to look for?" I asked Meleny once. "What sort of information, I mean?"

"I don't know," she replied, "and if I did, I wouldn't tell you. Any detail may be important—vital—we have no guidelines. We'll simply gather all the data we can in the time allotted to us."

Our cover roles were all quite different, on the theory that not all the eggs should be put in one basket. I was in an agony of curiosity to know what mine would be, but when Meleny finally told me, I almost wished she hadn't.

"Elana," she began, "we've got a cover worked out for you, a good one, but establishing it won't be fun. It'll be something of an ordeal, in fact; do you mind?"

"Not at all," I assured her, knowing that the question was purely rhetorical.

"We're assigning you to Cerne," Meleny said. "Now, getting into the Neo-Statist cities isn't going to be easy. They keep close tabs on their citizens; there's no free travel, as there is in the Libertarian countries. The secret police are very efficient, and they're on the lookout for people with fake papers."

I was silent. Naturally, there would be agents placed in the cities controlled by the dictatorship as well as in the free ones, but I had hoped I wouldn't be one of them. I should have known better. Having no physical idiosyncrasies in Torisian eyes, I could stand closer inspection than some—even medical inspection, Meleny thought—so despite my relative inexperience, I was bound to be given a difficult post.

Calmly, she continued, "You can't hope to avoid questioning by the secret police indefinitely. So your best chance is to get it over with, under circumstances that will lead them to believe that you have nothing to hide."

She went on to explain. Cerne was the capital of a country that had recently been taken over by the dictator, and its citizens, who weren't used to police-state rule, lived in fear. A great many of them were anxious to escape, and for that reason all access to the city was well guarded. Anyone coming or going had to have not only identity papers but also a travel permit; and because she didn't know the exact form of such a permit, she was as yet unable to forge one.

"Suppose I don't even get into the place?" I protested. "Can I talk my way past those guards?"

"No. And you can't evade them, either; there are roadblocks, and the open country is patrolled."

"Then—"

Meleny met my eyes. "Suppose you were found by the side of the main highway leading into the city, and you were ill, so ill that you required immediate hospitalization? Suppose you weren't conscious when your rescuers took you past that roadblock?"

"It might get me through if I could make it convincing enough. But what if I flubbed it? And besides, would they ever let me out of the hospital?"

"I think so—if when you came to, you didn't know why you had no travel permit; if you didn't know where your home was or what jobs you had held. You'd be an amnesia case. It would be obvious to all concerned that you would have to build a whole new life for yourself."

The idea was intriguing. The authorities might easily fall for it; no spy would ever call attention to herself by trying anything so brazen! "The only thing is," I told Meleny, "I'm not sure I'm that good an actress."

"Well, you see," she admitted, "you won't have to act, at first."

The details, when I heard them, were decidedly less intriguing. Just before I left the ship, I would receive an injection that would bring on the illness, real illness. I would barely have time to reach the road.

"What we give you will be entirely harmless," Meleny assured me, "but it won't feel harmless. It won't look harmless, either; there'll be no possible suspicion that it could have been deliberately arranged. That highway is heavily traveled, and someone is bound to stop for you. By the time you reach the checkpoint, you'll be unconscious and to all appearances an emergency case, so you won't be held. You'll wake up in the hospital, and you'll have time to get your bearings before you're questioned, because the illness will take several days to run its course."

"What if Torisian doctors try to treat it?" I asked feebly. "I mean, they probably aren't too advanced medically, and—"

"Nothing they're likely to try will make any difference one way or the other," Meleny said. "Don't worry, there's not much chance of their killing you through lack of skill."

"Just what symptoms am I going to have?" I demanded.

She smiled sympathetically. "I'm not going to tell you. And that means you'll feel confused and frightened and very helpless—which is how it should be. Do you understand why, Elana?"

"To make my 'amnesia' look realistic?"

"That's part of it. But there are more basic reasons."

I hesitated. This was before I had been given the full explanation of the mission's strategy, so I didn't realize that it was considered an advantage for the break with my own background to be as complete as possible. "Does it have anything to do with making me cautious?" I ventured.

She nodded. "You're safer if you start out thoroughly convinced that you are *not* a superior, invincible being in comparison to the Younglings, because in reality you'll have less practical knowledge of how to get along in that society than the children in its kindergartens. You want your confidence to grow as you gain that knowledge, not peter out when you start running into situations that show up your ignorance."

I knew she was right. Trying experiences were

bound to come sooner or later, and I would be much more confident of myself if I faced a few at the beginning than if I wore out my nerves dreading the first one. All the same, I got the shakes every time I thought about it, right up to the time when I was in the landing craft on my way down to the surface.

A Youngling might wonder how I ever expected to last out the mission if I was that scared to begin with. It would seem, maybe, that an agent would have to be a naturally intrepid type, devoid of fear and, indeed, of all emotion. Well, of course you do have to be adventurous even to want a Service career, and you do undergo some rather challenging tests of courage before you are accepted. But it's the resolute kind of courage, not fearlessness. After all, agents are chosen for sensitivity and imagination, among other things; and sensitive, imaginative people aren't fearless. They are usually more apprehensive than average.

The Service doesn't consider that a problem; at the Academy we are taught to deal with our feelings, not to suppress them. We learn the distinction between healthy fear and panic, and above all we find that we can handle ourselves. The underlying basis of panic is terror not of the threat itself but of how you'll react to it. Once you've learned how, you're more fit to be an explorer than you would be if you were unafraid to begin with.

So the fact that I was terrified didn't faze me as I looked out from the landing craft on the swarm of lights that was Cerne, and knew that in a few minutes I would be alone down there, miserably sick and without means of calling for help if things went wrong. The brief, heartening ritual words had been said; I slipped off the Emblem and gave it reluctantly into Meleny's keeping, feeling even more naked from its absence than from the bareness of my legs or the strange and uncomfortable feel of the skirt in which I was dressed. Though I had a wild impulse to withdraw from the whole affair, I ignored it and stood firm while she gave me the injection.

"Elana," Meleny warned, "some rather scary things are going to happen to you. They're designed to help you, to lessen your danger—but you won't enjoy them. Just remember that we wouldn't have arranged anything you weren't equal to."

"I trust you," I told her, with a determined laugh.

Putting her arm around my shoulders, she hugged me warmly. "Trust yourself," she said. "We're relying on you; we think you're a pretty good risk."

And I knew that however the mission turned out, I was somehow going to have to live up to that.

Several nights later, another landing craft set Randil down on the uninhabited south bank of a wide, deep river some distance upstream from Cerne. It was very dark and very cold, and as he peered at the blackness of the swift current into which he would shortly be required to throw himself, for the first time he felt real, heart-shaking apprehension: apprehension not only about the grueling entry scheme devised for him but about the days and weeks ahead.

In his briefings, Varned had been frank. "This is an experiment," he had said. "As you know, it's not usual for any untried agent to be sent alone into a situation of this kind, much less one who has not been fully trained for fieldwork. We think you have what it takes to adapt, and we think your viewpoint will prove valuable not only because of your special study of the Critical Stage but because you won't be influenced by any prior contact with Younglings. But you'll face special dangers, Randil; I've got to be sure you're aware of that."

"I know the dangers," Randil had declared. "I knew when I volunteered."

"I'm not talking about the physical dangers that all of us will share. There are more subtle ones to which you, by virtue of your inexperience and lack of thorough preparation, will be particularly vulnerable, dangers arising from the emotional involvement this mission will entail. We are taking a calculated risk in subjecting you to them. I'm not going to give you specific warnings because in the first place, you wouldn't heed them, and in the second place, if you did, your ability to look through Torisian eyes might be spoiled. I'll say only this: We're using you, and you're going to get hurt—perhaps badly hurt. If you aren't willing to be used, now is your chance to say so."

Randil didn't reply. All of this, too, had been plainly stated before he had accepted the mission, and it did not frighten him. Secretly, in fact, he was pleased and flattered at having been singled out for what everyone seemed to consider an assignment of unprecedented difficulty. Since he had been sworn for only a few days, his willingness to expose himself to theoretically unavoidable but vague hurts was at a new height; he found the idea rather exhilarating.

Varned's smile was rueful. "You don't understand what I'm talking about, and I've got a feeling I'm going to hate myself for letting you go into this, knowing as I do that you're not ready to understand. Still, you're a volunteer, and you're a sincere one. So let's get on with it."

In Randil's case, getting on with it meant not only thorough study of Toris but also explicit briefing for the role he was to assume, much more explicit than if he had been a seasoned agent. That briefing had begun with instruction in the task of getting himself into Cerne, which he was to accomplish by swimming downstream, staying beneath the surface while within range of the guards' floodlights.

"You could probably do it without any apparatus," Meleny told him, "considering the training in breath control you've had; but to be on the safe side, we'll give you a compact breathing unit. You'll drop it on the bottom when you leave the water, of course, and it's set to disintegrate after a few hours. It's far too advanced a technology to let the Torisians find, so just remember to ditch it in a hurry if anything goes wrong."

Randil thought of that advice when, abandoned by the landing craft, he adjusted the mask, rechecked the pocket containing his forged identity card and other valuables, and strode resolutely to the river's edge. The bank was steep, and in the darkness he could not see well enough to keep his footing, especially without shoes; he clambered down, clutching at clumps of weeds, but lost his balance before reaching the bottom and slid the rest of the way into deep water that closed immediately over his head. He found himself swept along by a current much stronger than he had expected. He could only hope it would carry him safely into the city, for he had no choice but to trust himself to it; swimming proved an almost superfluous effort, and he couldn't exert himself unduly while minimizing his intake of air. Reconnaissance from the ship had revealed no rapids or submerged rocks, but the instruments by which such things could be detected in the dark were not always wholly reliable.

He surfaced occasionally, and each time the lights of Cerne showed brighter on the horizon. Eventually, when they were close, he knew that he dared not come up again until well past the guarded area at the city's limit. He could tell that area by the illumination of the water above him; when all was dark again, he ditched the breathing unit and rose, choking, to find himself in a narrow stretch bordered by the black, forbidding shapes of massive buildings.

This was the most dangerous phase of the plan. He had been warned that he would probably be caught when he emerged from the water or shortly thereafter, for there was a curfew in Cerne and police patrolled the streets; but he had rehearsed a story that it was thought would sound plausible. It wouldn't occur to anyone that he might have come from outside the city, since no Youngling could have swum underwater as far as the lights extended.

Randil made his way toward the shore. There were cement embankments, but he could see a bridge beside which slimy stone steps ascended from a deserted boat landing. Exhausted and thoroughly chilled, he dragged himself up them, to be met at the top by the blinding flash of a patrolman's spotlight.

"Hail the glory of the State, citizen," said the voice behind the light in a stern tone. Randil echoed the remark with a calculated trace of sullenness, knowing it to be the prescribed greeting in cities under Neo-

Statist control. "Your passport," the guard continued harshly. Pulling the soaked card from the inner pocket of his dripping jacket, Randil handed it over. The guard frowned, turning the light aside momentarily in order to examine the barely legible document. It was seemingly in order.

"What have you to say for yourself?" he demanded, and then without waiting for a reply went on, "You didn't fall in the river by accident, not at this hour, and from the look of your clothes I suppose it's the usual story. Out of work, ineligible for the army, and too stubborn to welcome the State's generosity in granting you transport to the collective farms. Why didn't you have the guts to finish the job?"

Randil drew a breath of surprise. He hadn't even had to offer his alibi; it had been anticipated! Although he had been told that suicide attempts were common in occupied Cerne, he had found this hard to believe. "I got to thinking," he said slowly. "The university's entrance exams are this morning, and I—I decided to wait a day and give them a try."

The patrolman laughed. "The university? You? Well, it's your right to take the examinations, though you decided a bit late; if I were to haul you in for violation of curfew, you'd miss them." He lowered the light once more. "I'll give you a break. It'll come to the same thing in the end, since you're not likely to pass those exams; and a man who'd rather do away with himself than work for the State isn't worth much on the farms."

Randil was left shaking, overcome with relief and fatigue. It was his first encounter with callousness, yet he realized that the guard had considered himself merciful. It was quite true that he would have missed the crucial university entrance examinations if he had been treated as a curfew violator rather than as a would-be suicide of no consequence; that had been the biggest gamble in the scheme to establish his cover.

By morning he was sufficiently dry and rested to walk into the central business district of the city, and using the local coins Varned had given him, he bought shoes and a clean shirt. There was neither money nor time left for breakfast, but the taking of daylong examinations on an empty stomach was the sort of trial to which he had been well inured. The University of Cerne fronted on River Street, the city's main boulevard. Randil followed the crowd through the gate to the lines forming at the registration windows.

It was the opening day of Spring Term, and the entrance examinations, Varned had learned, were open to anyone upon presentation of his or her passport. Students' records weren't checked because the dictatorship did not recognize any evaluations made by the former school authorities. Those who scored high enough on the exams were permitted to study until they either graduated or proved "politically unreliable"; everyone else who wasn't already working was promptly drafted for factory or farm labor.

For Randil it was easy, almost too easy; he feared he might be overlooking something that would trip him up. He had, to be sure, been assigned to Cerne primarily because Meleny believed that of the available agents he had the best chance of succeeding: Not only was he younger than the rest and thus less likely to stand out among other university applicants, but she thought that his detailed study of Critical Stage cultures would enable him to answer the questions in a fitting way. The examinations consisted mostly of logical and mathematical aptitude tests, and on those his biggest problem was being sure not to get a suspiciously high score. The linguistic sections proved more challenging; for although monitoring of broadcasts had given him a good command of the local language, he had had little chance to see its written form. However, having been exposed to the tongues of countless worlds at the Academy, he got his bearings very quickly. Actually, the science test was the hardest; on that he had to estimate the extent of Torisian knowledge, and he knew that where he misjudged, his vastly superior scientific education was a handicap rather than an aid. Fortunately, there was no history test; the Neo-Statists had not yet had time to rewrite Cernese history, and consequently they were ignoring it.

The examination papers were graded immediately, by computer. When the afternoon ended, Randil had been admitted to the university and was as free as anyone else in Cerne. He got money to pay the tuition and dormitory fees by selling, at several different pawnshops, the gold rings with which he had been provided. Then, after a much-needed meal, he went out into the fading daylight to take a real look at his new environment.

A Critical Stage society! he thought. It was unbelievable. It was incredible that he, who had not even expected to do fieldwork, should be on a Youngling world masquerading as a man of the culture level to which he had devoted his Academy thesis—and it was also very exciting. Why had everyone told him that it would be so hard? He was getting by all right; he didn't feel that he would find it difficult to identify with the Torisians.

At first Cerne impressed him as a sprawling mess of confusion that gave no indication that it was a product of the minds of rational beings; the place looked as if inanimate things had come alive, going on a wild spree of uninhibited growth that had littered the earth with their profusion, and as suddenly died. It wasn't that he had expected any signs of mature civilization or of the conveniences he was used to, but much of what he saw appeared unnecessarily ugly and inefficient when judged by the planet's own stage of advancement. The city was dirty, for one thing. The buildings were grimy, many of them black with age; trash littered the streets; the very air itself was polluted. There were no open green spaces, no sparkling towers, for the aboveground area was a hodgepodge of ill-assorted and poorly designed utilitarian structures. Even the river was lined with them; and its water was not blue, but brown.

Still, there was something about being in a city—any city—that gave an atmosphere of warmth and aliveness that couldn't be felt on a ship. And there was something about a pale sky and diffused sunlight, even the strange orange-yellow sunlight of Toris, that created the haunting illusion that reality existed only in this one spot and that it was more important than all the universe.

And then, of course, there were the people. Randil looked at the people and spoke with them, and though he kept telling himself that they were Younglings, this was somehow hard to believe. On the planet of Service Headquarters, dress and custom had also been unlike those of his home city. On that planet too, the psychic powers basic to his own people's culture hadn't been used. Moreover, the Torisians physically resembled his own race far more closely than did many of his Academy classmates. He had thought Younglings would seem different. They did not.

On the surface they were no different from anyone else, except perhaps in one respect. They were less happy. Their faces reflected varying degrees of apathy, fear, and resignation, all the way to grim despair. They glanced furtively around them, and on every street the police were all too evident. There were, he supposed, other police—the secret police—whom he was as yet unable to spot. Furthermore, there was much talk about war and bombing. That startled Randil; he had assumed that the Torisians would be unaware of their peril, for surely, if they recognized it, they would be able to do something constructive about the situation! It did not seem to work that way.

Upon reflection, he realized that it could not. Having studied the Critical Stage, he knew that the sense of danger was a necessary incentive even in civilizations that came through safely. But he hadn't considered before what such a sense would mean to people, real people, who had to live with the stress. He had not guessed what it would be like to live among them.

That first evening, he began to consider it. He began to see the people of Toris as ordinary men and women instead of the objects of anthropological research. And before the week was out, Randil knew that he could not stand passively by and let those people die.

Meleny's warning hadn't been exaggerated; the things that happened to me during my first days on Toris were very scary indeed. To begin with, the illness I went through was a violent one, with symptoms that most definitely could not have been faked. During its most acute phase I had convulsions, though I wasn't conscious at the time. I was conscious, later, of fever, delirium, and an overpowering weakness that left me scarcely able to lift my head from the pillow. I had never experienced such things before. I had never been sick at all; there is no sickness on Federation worlds. And I was denied the comfort of remembering that my full recovery had been pre-arranged.

For the scariest thing of all was that when I woke up in that hospital, I couldn't remember *anything*. I had real amnesia.

It was brought on partly by drugs and partly, I'm sure, by posthypnotic suggestion. I had studied under hypnosis a good deal aboard the starship, and it would have been easy for Meleny to give me more than language lessons. I realize now that she would have had to; my normal psychic defenses, if not inhibited, would probably have made short work of my drug-induced physical symptoms despite any conscious decision on my part to go ahead and be sick. But she apparently went beyond that and set up temporary memory blocks that reduced me to a state of complete bewilderment. Looking back, I can see that it was a very skillful job. The knowledge I really needed was always available to me: For instance, I knew, without knowing why, that I must not reveal my psychic powers or speak aloud in the language that it seemed most natural to think in. And though I suffered terrifying uncertainties, I knew, underneath, that some sort of firm ground existed. The deep essential things—things concerned not with the outward situation but with my personal way of handling it—hadn't been tampered with.

But while I was going through the amnesia, I didn't understand all that. I only knew that I was alone, helpless, and nearly overcome with fright.

It's hard to imagine if you haven't been through it—not remembering. It's hard to pin down, somehow, even if you have. But I'll try to record some of my feelings because those feelings had a bearing on my whole approach to the mission. Meleny knew what she was doing, and it wasn't only a matter of helping me through those first crucial days when an unconvincing act would have been disastrous.

Of the dreams I had while I was delirious, I can say little; they were incoherent, indescribable not only in Youngling terms but in my own. And they faded almost immediately when my head cleared and I became aware, for the first time, of my surroundings. My main impression was of whiteness—whiteness of the ceiling, the walls, the bed—a dearth of color exceeded only by the blankness of my own memory. Why, I thought dazedly, I don't know where I am. I don't know who I am! And as I realized that, panic swept over me, and nausea, and I turned away from the light and buried my face in my arms.

I'm not sure how long I lay that way, but eventually a voice came silently from somewhere within me—not an immediate, personal voice such as you "hear" in telepathic communication, but an echo from the past I couldn't recall. *You must learn where you are!* it told me. *Hiding won't help; you must open your eyes to the world in which you find yourself. It will be strange, confusing, alien— but you mustn't fear that. You must use the time given you.*

With great effort, feeling as if I were under at least three times the gravity I had been born to, I rolled over and forced my eyes open again. A girl stood by my bed, her white dress merging fuzzily into the glaring whiteness of the room. I blinked and focused on her face. She had dark hair, about the color of mine, but she wore it longer and it was tied tightly back with a ribbon, I could not judge her age; she seemed very young, but perhaps it was only that her manner lacked poise and assurance.

"Oh, you're awake!" She smiled at me, a shy but friendly smile. "How do you feel, Elana?" When I didn't answer, she went on hesitantly, "Elana—that is your name, isn't it? That's what your passport says."

"I—I don't know," I answered weakly. At the moment this was true. But in the depths of my mind the voice echoed again: *You are not permitted to know, for now. You must not let it frighten you; you can meet what comes simply by being who you are, without knowing. We would not have arranged anything you weren't equal to.*

I didn't have any idea who had said that to me, but somehow the thought was reassuring. All the same, I was frightened. Your sense of identity is just about the most vital thing you have; if it suddenly evaporates, there isn't anything left to rely on, because your ability to cope with what's outside depends on your certainty of what's inside—that is, of yourself as *somebody*. If you don't know anything about the person you are, you haven't much basis for believing that you can keep yourself under control.

"You don't know if it's your name?" The girl stared, puzzled. "What happened to you?"

"I don't know that, either," I admitted. "I've been sick, haven't I?"

"Yes, awfully sick," she told me gently. "Ever since you were brought in. But I'm sure you'll be all right now. The doctor said you probably would be if you came out of the coma—" She broke off, apparently realizing that it wasn't her place to discuss the gravity of my condition.

"Are you my nurse?" I asked her.

"No, I'm only an aide. I bring the meals, tidy up the rooms, and so forth." She added, almost apologetically, "My name is Kari."

I tried to sit up but was unsuccessful. It took all the energy I could muster just to form sentences in the unfamiliar language that I felt compelled to use. "Where am I, Kari?" I asked feebly.

"In the hospital."

"Yes, but where?"

"What city, you mean? Why, Cerne. Didn't you come from here? You were found outside the blockade, of course—"

Cerne. It meant nothing to me. "What world is this?" I whispered, and then I wished, desperately, that I had not, for I had a sudden sense of having violated some deep and sacred taboo.

"What *world?*"

"I—I'm sorry. I've been out of my head, I guess; I've had all kinds of crazy nightmares, and I haven't gotten them sorted out yet." I was close to tears, for I really hadn't. "Kari, I'm not sure what's real."

She bent down and, awkwardly, touched my hand. "Oh, don't worry—please don't! You'll remember soon. Look, I've got to go now, but I'll send in the doctor."

As she disappeared, fear rose in me again. I still did not know what world I was on, nor why it seemed wrong to ask; and since apparently it *was* wrong, I could not imagine how I was ever going to find out. Moreover, there were other things from which I was barred by the same mysterious inner prompting. I was horribly thirsty, and on the table across the room from me stood a tall, cool-looking pitcher of water; yet somehow I could not bring myself to obtain it through psychokinesis, sure though I was that the weakness that kept me flat on my back wouldn't affect my normal mental powers.

And the arrival of the doctor was not exactly a comfort. I did my best to answer his questions, but all the while I was eyeing him warily in an agony of suspicion that I could neither explain nor banish. Poor man, he was well-meaning, I'm sure, and he would have been astonished had he known what caused my terror of him. I did not know myself; I only knew, as he stood over me with hypodermic in hand, that I did not trust him and that he could not possibly tell what was wrong with me, much less how to cure it. Instinctively, I fought the approaching needle.

"Hey now, calm down!" the doctor said. "This won't hurt."

It was not a matter of its hurting. It was a matter of being absolutely helpless in the hands of undependable strangers. Glancing frantically around, I saw stark white shapes gathering near my bed: another doctor, perhaps, and two or three nurses and orderlies. Kari, who had seemed a friend, was nowhere in sight. With strength born of desperation I struggled to rise. As if from far away I heard the command, "Restrain her. I'm going to inject a sedative." Strong arms gripped mine, and I think I screamed.

Then as the drug took hold, my panic subsided, freeing me to think. *It's all right,* the inner voice told me, *they can't harm you . . . you must trust that this will turn out all right. . . .* My thoughts were drifting, spinning, and I could not grasp any memory firmly. But for an instant the artificial wall dissolved, and I knew a flash of incredible clarity. There was a warmth, a sense of sureness, and words formed in my mind: solemn, exultant words telling of a universe of joy and beauty and design. I did not recognize them. They were, I suppose, from Service ritual; but of that I recalled nothing.

The next morning, things were a bit brighter. When I awoke, I still couldn't remember my past life, but my present one didn't seem quite so dismaying. The pattern of sunlight on the wall opposite my bed seemed almost cheerful.

Kari was busy at the table, arranging long-stemmed blooms in a pottery bowl. "I brought you some flowers," she said, noticing that my eyes were open. "Yellow ones, because your room was so bare, and"—her voice dropped—"and besides, it's Springtide."

"Thank you," I said, overwhelmed. Frowning, I added, "Springtide?"

Giving me a startled look, she exclaimed, "You really don't remember! Not anything! Unless—" She faltered and shrank apprehensively from my gaze.

"What is it?" I asked in alarm. "What's scared you?"

She stepped forward, her expression changing to one of relief and sympathetic concern. "Forgive me," she begged. "It was horrible of me, but for a minute, when you frowned like that, I—I thought you might be one of *them.*"

Not having the slightest idea what she was talking about, I did not attempt to answer. Kari stooped down and, in a low voice, continued, "It's forbidden to celebrate Springtide now. It's forbidden to speak of it, even; the first week of spring is supposed to mean a new calendar, and nothing more. But they can't stop people from thinking about it, can they?"

"No," I said positively. "No, they can't."

"I remember when I was a little girl," Kari went on, "after Devotions all our relatives used to come for the family dinner, and we'd have gift baskets, and yellow flowers in every room. And Granddad would complain that times weren't what they used to be; but Uncle Derk would laugh and say that as long as we kept Springtide, the human race wasn't in much danger." She paused and then added matter-of-factly, "Uncle Derk's dead now. They shot him during the Occupation."

"That's awful!" I burst out.

"Life *is* awful, I guess," Kari said resignedly. "The whole world is, and it's silly to pretend it won't always be." There was an awkward silence. Then, blushing, she hurried on, "How thoughtless I am, telling you my good memories when you can't remember at all. You must hate me."

"Of course I don't," I assured her. "And I want you to tell me more."

"More about what?"

"About anything—anything that might help me remember."

"All right," she agreed. "Only for a few minutes, though, because I've got to go after the lunch trays pretty soon."

"Start by explaining who *they* are," I suggested resolutely, although I wasn't at all sure I wanted to know.

She told me briefly how Cerne had been occupied by the dictator's army and how at present, though most of the troops were gone, a Neo-Statist puppet government was keeping the city under rigid control. I had many questions, for I had no conscious knowledge, then, of anything I had learned aboard the starship, or even of the fact that there was a starship. I did not think of the people among whom I found myself as "Younglings"; I had no cause to assume any difference between their situation and my own. That situation being a frightful one, the more I heard of it the worse I felt. Kari's own apprehension came through to me telepathically as she talked, and it told me far more than her guarded words.

From somewhere outside came the wail of a noon whistle, low-pitched and mournful. Kari straightened my bedclothes and turned to go. "In a way I envy you," she said slowly. "I keep thinking of what you said yesterday about having dreamed this wasn't the only world, and—well, maybe you're better off without sorting the dreams from the real things. Because they aren't nice things to remember. The world is decaying, people say; but then of course the Bomb will probably wipe out civilization before very long. Sometimes I wish I could have amnesia, too."

"The Bomb?" I asked, horrified.

She offered no explanation; it was to her simply a fact of life, like pain. "I shouldn't have reminded you," she said, sighing, and then she fled from the room. As she went, my eyes fell on the bowl of flowers she had left me—yellow flowers, for Springtide—and I noticed that the ribbon that bound back her hair, which on the previous day had been black, was now a vibrant, defiant yellow.

Bomb? I repeated to myself. Before long? Maybe I was better off dreaming, at that.

No, insisted that inexplicable inner voice that was always with me. *You must use the time given you; you must learn all you can. There's nothing to be afraid of.*

But there is . . . there *is,* I protested. Memory or no memory, I still had common sense, and it was pretty obvious that there was nothing safe about the place I was in. Nothing safe, nothing comforting . . .

The sun had gone under. I lay back against the pillows, staring out through streaked windowpanes at the still-bare branches of a tall, gaunt tree silhouetted against a white sky. *Who am I?* I thought despairingly. *Who am I, that I should find myself in this sort of a world? Armies . . . bombs . . . what kind of a nightmare have I fallen into?* And for that, there was no answer.

There is a theme that recurs in the folklore of all worlds, a myth of death and rebirth. (We studied such things at the Academy, for they are basic to the understanding of Youngling cultures.) This particular theme, which is widespread among primitive peoples, is often acted out symbolically in rites of passage like tribal initiation ceremonies. The idea is that if a person is suddenly going to become somebody different—for example, an adult tribesman instead of a child—he must forget all about what he used to be, at least temporarily. He must "die" as far as that life's concerned and be "born" into a new one. And since that can't really happen, he can only do it by undergoing some overwhelming experience that makes him feel as if it had.

Well, what I went through was a little like that, I think. Younglings aren't stupid; their folklore usually has a lot of truth behind it. They interpret that truth in strange ways, maybe, but all the same it's there. This business of "dying" to your former life is simply a quick way of accomplishing something that under less dramatic circumstances would have to happen gradually. Whether it's mixed up with mythology or not doesn't matter. And whether you are subjected to it by a superstitious witch doctor or by a fully trained scientist like Meleny, the result is the same: You get a whole new slant on things.

I don't mean that I literally thought I was dying; sick though I was for a while, my symptoms weren't that bad. But to wake without memory is in some ways very much like being born. The thing is, you have no frame of reference. Everything is unstable and confusing because you have no positive facts to hold on to. It's an unbearable feeling, so you throw all your energy into getting yourself oriented.

You learn fast, of course, because your mind is better developed than a baby's and you've got an unconscious backlog of knowledge to draw on. Besides, you have nothing more pressing to distract you. By the time I had gotten my physical strength back, I knew all I needed to know in order to pass as a native-born Torisian. What's more, I knew it in a different way than I would have if I had simply superimposed that knowledge on my normal pattern of thought. My Torisian identity was—well, more basic. I was living it instead of acting; I was committed to it, for I believed I *was* Torisian.

Most of my information came from Kari. I saw her only in the morning, however, for her job at the hospital was a part-time one; afternoons she had classes at the university. The nurses were rushed and uncommunicative, and I begged to be put in a ward where there would be other patients to talk to. But the doctor refused; not having been able to diagnose my illness, he was still afraid that it might prove contagious. So between Kari's visits I had to be content with the small radio she brought me.

On the fifth day I had visitors. Kari announced them, her eyes dark with dismay. "Elana," she said shakily, "there are two men here to see you. I—I think"—her voice fell to a whisper—"I think they're SSP."

I swallowed. The SSP, the State Security Police whom I had already learned to fear . . .

"What do they want?" I quavered. "I haven't done anything, at least I don't think I have. But Kari, I don't really remember."

She was struggling for composure. "Of course you haven't," she soothed. "It's only that you didn't have a travel permit. They'll ask you why, I suppose. But what can they do if you don't know?"

"They'll believe me, won't they?"

"They'll have to. Besides, they're talking to the doctor now; he'll tell them, and—" She stopped short, the pallor of fright spreading across her face. "And I guess they'll ask *me.*"

Her terror at the prospect was obvious, and I was troubled at having gotten her involved. From all I had heard of the SSP, they were quite likely to suspect her simply for having shown me friendship. "I'm sorry," I said sincerely. "It's all my fault."

"Don't be silly," she said. "You couldn't help being sick."

The interview, as it turned out, was not too difficult. The men's questions were perfunctory, for the doctor had apparently convinced them that my memory was truly gone. He had also made it clear that since I'd been at death's door for several days, I could not possibly be faking. My passport appeared to be in order; and as I had neither money nor a travel permit, it was the consensus of opinion that both had been stolen by thieves who had left me to die beside the highway. Though a routine check had turned up no record of anyone by my name, that wasn't surprising because the files for the recently conquered Cerne were in turmoil. Luckily, my case wasn't considered worth a more thorough investigation.

Kari was questioned separately. She knew nothing about my background and they had no reason to doubt her; but after they had gone, she sat down in the chair beside my bed and burst into tears. "I c-can't help it," she sobbed. "I know I've got no right to act this way, when it's you that's in trouble. But I can't bear those men! Oh, Elana, they see into people's minds; they can punish a person for even thinking things—"

She didn't put all her fears into words; she didn't dare to. But she wanted desperately to tell me, so the rest came through telepathically. Kari was a Libertarian sympathizer in a country where Libertarian sympathies were deemed a criminal offense. No wonder she felt guilty in the presence of the dread secret police; she was agonizingly aware that her beliefs, should they detect them, would land her in a labor camp or worse. And what's more, she was blaming herself for not being brave enough to act on those beliefs as her Uncle Derk had.

Stricken, I reached for her hand and squeezed it. She had been kind to me, acting against, I now realized, her normal instinct to stay clear of involvement with anyone whose status was suspect. She had gone out of her way to talk to me, to spend every spare moment in my room, simply because she had known that I was lost and alone.

"I just can't live like this," she concluded hysterically. "I hate it! Not only what's happened here in Cerne. The whole world's bad now; everything people used to have faith in is gone. Or maybe it never really existed."

Kari, don't feel that way! I cried silently. *It isn't true! There's plenty to have faith in; there's a whole universe*—I cut off in midthought, stopped by the abrupt realization that I should not be communicating in that fashion. It was another of the warnings that I had come to accept as a natural restraint on my mental processes. But this time I suddenly wondered, Why? Why shouldn't I help Kari? What harm could it do?

And then I thought, What was it I wanted to tell her? I was just as scared as she was. She had taught me all I knew of the world; why did her judgment of it strike me as wrong, untrue? What did I see that she didn't?

A whole universe?

A universe of joy and beauty and design. A world in danger but not surely doomed; and a mission for which I had volunteered in full knowledge of the awesome difficulties involved.

The pieces fell into place; in the span of a drawn breath I knew everything. I knew who I was, where I had come from, and why I must conceal that knowledge even from Kari, who was my friend. And I knew that I had received a lesson in the Youngling viewpoint that could not have been given in any other way.

I would not have understood Kari if I hadn't been through what I had gone through; I would have thought her a hopeless coward. As it was, I had seen through her eyes. Why, I thought wonderingly, it was she who had no adequate frame of reference! To her, Toris was the universe, and that universe was falling apart.

Kari had stopped crying and was staring at me. In an urgent voice she demanded, "What did you just say?"

"Nothing," I said gently. "There's nothing I can say, Kari." It was the only possible reply; but as I spoke, it came to me for the first time how hard the passive role was going to be.

t h r e e

Poor Kari—she gave me friendship, and I have brought her only trouble, I'm afraid. I hope she hasn't guessed that I am here in this prison. Yet it's all too likely that she has, for we've been sharing an apartment since my release from the hospital, and when I didn't come home—well, when people disappear in Cerne, people that the Missing Persons Bureau won't do anything about, it's not exactly a mystery as to where they have ended up.

She must be sick with terror, not only for me but from the fear that I will be forced to betray her. Like other Torisians, she has a fatalistic concept of brainwashing. Once, some weeks back, we were awakened in the middle of the night by a loud pounding on the door of the apartment next to us. We lay still in our beds, not moving, not even whispering, but I sensed Kari's thoughts clearly enough. The couple who lived in that apartment had been recklessly outspoken, and we had known in our hearts that it was only a matter of time until their arrest. When the sirens receded—SSP men always use sirens, presumably to remind the whole neighborhood of their omnipotence—Kari's tears overflowed. She had liked the young wife; they had sometimes had lunch together, though Kari had always been careful to conceal her own political views.

"What's it like in—in that place?" Kari asked me, with anguish. Despite the fact that she still believed me the victim of amnesia, she had somehow come to rely on me as an infallible source of wisdom, or at least of comfort.

"I don't know, Kari," I said, although I did, because dictators' political prisons are pretty much the same anywhere you find them.

"Do you think those rumors are true?"

The rumors, which we had discussed before, concerned specific means of persuasion employed in the interrogation of prisoners. They were not all true, but in essence they summed up the situation, as both of us knew perfectly well. Kari was hoping I would deny it, but I didn't. I believed, as I still do, that in a crisis she'd prove stronger than she thought she would.

"It's not going to happen to us," I said reassuringly. "But Kari, if it ever did, we'd—well, we'd face up to it. Nothing is as awful as it seems on the surface."

"We couldn't face it," she protested. "Not torture."

"Don't worry. It won't happen," I repeated.

Now it is happening to me.

Of course it is not the same for me as it would be for Kari, since I don't really suffer. It is challenging, but not terrible, for I haven't been injured; the means my interrogator employs is electrical and does not damage my body. He has chosen this means for his own benefit rather than for mine; he thinks it's worse for me because it can be kept up longer. So far he hasn't caught on to the fact that I am immune.

Immune isn't exactly the right word. I've no inborn immunity to pain, far from it. Pain is, after all, extremely useful; from the biological standpoint it's a safeguard, a protection. I mean, if things like touching a hot stove didn't hurt, a small child might incur all sorts of serious injuries without bothering to avoid them. Eliminating pain wouldn't be desirable even if it were possible, which it's not. That's why the defense isn't as easily mastered as other psychic skills like telepathy, psychokinesis, or even the Shield. It must be acquired through training. Such training is one of the types agents receive, and we learn more from it than how to protect ourselves when necessary. We learn to understand Younglings better; it increases our empathy. For in the course of our ordinary lives we don't experience physical pain because our science has done away with practically all instances of it. Federation worlds are exceedingly safe. We rarely hurt ourselves; we don't get sick; if we ever do need medical treatment, we have perfect anesthetics—actually, the whole issue is abstract for us. But for Younglings it isn't. Younglings know how pain feels; and in order to comprehend that, agents need to know, too. In the initial training sessions we find out.

So my present hard-won "immunity" doesn't keep me from understanding Kari's fear.

I do not think they will ever arrest her; she has been very, very careful. There is no one who could denounce her except Randil or me. She has no connections in the Resistance, and of course she hasn't *done* anything. Her only "crime" is the private opinion she holds, and Kari has too little confidence in herself to express any of her opinions, let alone proscribed ones. In her college classes she is usually a quiet little mouse. And it's a role she's miserable in, the opposite of everything she feels inside, except that she doesn't really know her own feelings. They come through to Randil and me only because of our telepathic sensitivity.

I've tried to help. I've discussed things openly with Kari that she would never have dared to utter had I not forced the issue. At first she was aghast. "The walls have ears," she told me. They do, I suppose, in many places, particularly in this prison. But not in our apartment, not yet; Toris isn't quite that far along on the road to totalitarianism.

She trusted me. She trusted Randil; and by now she must be aware that he too is missing, for they've been dating frequently and she knows that he wouldn't stand her up voluntarily. Oh, if only she weren't such a pessimist! If only she could believe that some things truly aren't as awful as they seem!

Whatever happens, neither Randil nor I will involve Kari in this. We would never endanger her . . . except insofar as we may already have endangered her whole planet.

My initial weeks on Toris were difficult, but in a rather different way than I had expected. I had anticipated danger; I had been prepared to undergo some narrow escapes. I had not been prepared for the tedium and despair of a Youngling's day-by-day existence.

I didn't run into any danger. Nobody questioned my cover; the "amnesia" was an infallible and never-challenged excuse for my ignorance of everything from how to buy clothes to the names of popular film stars. And when it came to more serious issues, I soon found that few citizens of Cerne were any better informed than I was. What they knew, they got from watching the same telecasts I watched; and I had the advantage of being more aware than they of the subtle manner in which these government-produced programs were slanted.

But I could not learn anything of value to the mission by watching Torisian television, which was, after all, being continuously monitored from the starship. My task was to observe, to talk to people, and to read. Somehow it hadn't occurred to me that I would have very little time to devote to these pursuits while spending more than half my waking hours on such work as washing dishes in a hospital kitchen.

I had known, of course, that I would have to hold a job in order to support myself, possession of jewelry to pawn being inconsistent with the role I had assumed. I had known that it wouldn't be a glamorous job, since as an amnesiac I would have no training or experience to offer. Kari considered me fantastically lucky to get a kitchen aide's position, for jobs were hard to come by and able-bodied persons who failed to find employment were summarily assigned to government munitions plants or shipped off to the collective farms. She had happened to hear of the hospital opening before it was posted, and I was thus the first to apply for it. My qualifications consisted solely of my recent clean bill of health from the doctor; the hospital didn't have to go through the red tape of having me reexamined. As to temperamental qualifications, I had none. For the first time I began to appreciate the Director's concern over my possible lack of self-discipline.

Younglings grow up with the expectation that they will spend all day, most days, performing some less-than-fascinating sort of work. Federation citizens do not. On Federation worlds everything routine is automated; the work done by people is creative. I had never worked, except in the sense that study is work. I was fresh from the Academy, where I had become knowledgeable in the intricacies of countless civilizations and where my days had been filled with unending mental stimulation. Washing dishes was not an easy occupation to adapt to.

At the beginning it was a game; I was acting a part, and it was challenge enough simply to prove that I could do it successfully. That challenge wore out before long. Being on my feet all day in the steamy kitchen, forcing myself to go through dreary, monotonous physical motions that bore no relationship to my true task, was an agonizing waste of time and energy. I wished heartily that I need never see another dish, and having more to wash at home, after every meal, was an added irritation. I had grown up on a world where all dishes were recycled.

For a short while I was engrossed in getting acquainted with my coworkers and in absorbing their view of things, but socializing, too, proved painful. The average hospital dishwasher is not an expert on the affairs of her world, and although I had known this in theory, it was rather dismaying to learn how limited my conversational scope was going to be. Within the Federation everyone has an equal opportunity for education; on Youngling worlds that's not the case. Though my fellow kitchen aides were by no means stupid, they didn't have the background to enter into the kind of intellectual discussion I was used to. My attempts to start such discussions were not welcomed. People who had been friendly at first soon began to avoid me. It took me about three days to figure out what was wrong; then suddenly one evening when it dawned on me what I had been doing—how deficient I had been in the empathy that is an agent's prime responsibility—I burst into tears from remorse, fatigue, and sheer frustration.

Kari found me crying; I had been too absorbed in my own emotions to hear her enter the room. "Oh, Elana," she begged, "please don't! Don't worry so. You'll remember someday; I'm sure you will. I know how hard it must be."

"It's not that," I confessed, longing, not for the first time, to be free of the awful burden of deceiving my most intimate friend. "I—I've hurt someone, Kari. More than one person, in fact."

"You wouldn't hurt anyone," she declared in a tone of absolute conviction.

"I didn't mean to. It just happened. I'm not like the others at work, and—and I'm afraid I've been making them feel as if I thought I was better than they are."

She hesitated, at a loss for a comforting reply. "They'll forgive you," she said finally. "They won't expect a victim of amnesia to act like everybody else. I don't see how anyone could know you, Elana, and believe you'd pretend to be something you aren't."

That made me feel worse than ever, since it was Kari I had been least honest with; Kari, to whom I owed the most. She had been looking for a roommate, her former one having recently married; but she didn't have to choose me. Even without knowing my real problems, she had been aware that I had serious ones—not the least of which, in her eyes, was the presence of my name in the files of the secret police—and yet she had taken me in. Had she not done so, the loneliness of my position would have been unbearable, I think, even if I had managed to find a job without her help. Adapting yourself to an alien environment, an environment in which your likeness to other people is largely a sham, is no picnic.

On top of that difficulty, there were the disquieting issues of the dictatorship and the Bomb. Younglings, I decided, were amazing. They were far braver than they thought themselves to be. I could never have lived under the conditions prevailing in Cerne if it hadn't been for my training; I would have been utterly paralyzed, I'm sure. Yet the Torisians, without any training at all, seemed to live what were for them normal lives, even though they knew their world might blow up around them before the year was out, or even the current week. Yes, they knew! That was the thing that surprised me most of all. They all talked about it, and their newspapers were full of it. Not a day went by when it wasn't mentioned on their television. The wonder was not that some of them behaved irresponsibly but that the vast majority retained their equilibrium.

It was all in what you grew up to, I supposed.

Or maybe it wasn't. Maybe it was simply that people live with what they have to live with, whether they think they can face it or not. Kari thought she couldn't, but she did so just the same.

Since it was fruitless to wonder how or when Varned would contact me, I found it best to work under the assumption that I must live indefinitely without such contact. On the other hand, I knew that I must be ready for it at any moment. So every night before I slept I mentally "recorded" every scrap of information, every detail that had come to my attention during the day. None of those details seemed in any way significant. I had been warned that this would be so; I realized that significance, if it showed up at all, would be observable only after compilation of the reports from all agents on Toris. But it was discouraging not to know whether I was accomplishing anything.

The hours of dishwashing grew more and more trying. I learned to make small talk with my coworkers; I acquired an ability to converse without giving a false impression of feeling superior. People became friendly again and began inviting me to social affairs, affairs that I'd have liked to attend; but I couldn't allow them to cut into my precious free evenings. For the one activity that offered me hope of gaining deep insight into the planet's culture was reading, and I had access to the reading material I needed only during the brief period between quitting time and curfew.

The curfew was very strictly enforced; Kari and I had to literally run, sometimes, on our way home from the university library. Kari herself had to study in the library almost every night, and she accepted my apparently desperate search for a clue to my past as a legitimate excuse for my avid desire to spend as much time there as possible. I met her inside after work, never hinting that the reason I arrived early was that I generally skipped the free dinner to which I was entitled upon finishing my shift in the kitchen.

In the library I went from shelf to shelf, scanning volume after volume of the accumulated wisdom of Toris—history, literature, science, philosophy—anything I happened to pick up. Kari and the others who saw me thought I was skimming at random; they had no way of guessing that I, like any well-educated Federation citizen, could read as fast as I could turn the pages. There would have been no need for me to borrow books even if I had been allowed to—which I wasn't, not being enrolled as a student.

Occasionally, however, I wanted to look back over something I had previously gone through, especially if I had read it while still relatively unaccustomed to the written form of Cerne's language. There was one book in particular, one dealing with a political theory that I had found a bit more enlightened than most I had encountered on Toris. I knew just where I had seen it, and I thought I remembered the name of the author. When I couldn't locate the volume, I assumed it had been checked out, but I looked it up in the catalog to be sure.

It was not in the catalog, either. Nor was there anything else written by the same man.

On the way home I said to Kari, "Have you noticed that the bookshelves don't seem as crowded as they used to?"

"Everybody knows that," she said bitterly.

Puzzled, I asked, "Knows what?"

"That the government censors have been busy lately. It happens in every city that's occupied, only it takes a while; at first they're too busy eliminating people to bother about books. But naturally they wouldn't leave anything with a Libertarian slant around for very long." She added in a guarded whisper, "It's lucky you haven't been checking books out, because I've heard that they make note of the charge numbers."

I shouldn't have had to be told, of course; having studied Youngling dictatorships, I ought not to have let their barbarisms startle me. Murder and cruelty I had met before and had learned to take in stride. But the deliberate suppression of knowledge? In the newspapers, yes, for it hadn't taken me long to discover that those were mere propaganda vehicles. The purging of the library was in another class entirely, and what I "recorded" that night was, I'm afraid, nearly as pessimistic as the talk I had been hearing from the Torisians.

This pessimism of theirs troubled me increasingly, despite my conviction that it was immature. Pessimistic people are to be found in any society; but that the society itself should be discouraged, guilt-ridden, convinced that it was heading for disaster—was that natural? I soon found that there was nothing unique about Kari's hopelessness. The local citizens were divided into two main groups: those who believed the official story concerning the villainy of the Libertarians and the likelihood of their dropping the Bomb on Cerne without any provocation whatsoever, and those who knew better, but who were convinced that the Neo-Statists would fulfill their announced intent of making war on the Libertarians and that Cerne would be wiped out in retaliation. I met scarcely anyone who thought that the world might ultimately be saved, or even that it was worth saving.

Was it different in the Libertarian countries? I hoped so. For if it wasn't, perhaps this race's gloom was more than a painful phase; perhaps it was a true premonition.

To Kari, I said nothing of my despondency. She was depressed enough already. Not that she didn't have grounds for it; as time went on, it became obvious that there was evil and injustice everywhere on Toris, among the Libertarians as well as under the dictator's rule. The films shown in Cerne's newscasts—films of poverty, intolerance, and rioting within the free nations—were presented out of context and gave a falsely one-sided picture, but they were not fakes. It was enough to dishearten anyone who didn't know that such problems exist on every Youngling world.

Maybe, I thought, unrelieved despair was characteristic of all Critical Stage cultures, not only of those doomed to failure. If you must live under a threat you can't do anything about, you are not too likely to feel optimistic; personal experience was teaching me that! And individual Torisians couldn't do anything more about the Bomb than I could.

Talking about her fears seemed to help Kari, so I urged her to be frank. Talking about her suppressed hatred of the Neo-Statist regime helped even more. We became very close, and it was increasingly difficult to guard my comments in such a way as to preserve the pretense of amnesia. Even without that cover role, I would have been permitted to offer only such help as a true native of her world could give. Still, I tried to encourage her, as any friend might. Kari had high regard for my judgment; she considered me the ultimate authority on just about everything despite the mysterious gaps in my recollection of specific events, and it hurt to be barred from revealing my true feelings.

Never before had I known anyone who had as little confidence as Kari did. To be sure, my circle of friends had been limited; having grown up among Service people, I was less experienced with different personality types than some agents. Kari's insecurity puzzled me because it was so unwarranted. She was much more capable than she knew, though getting her to see this was an uphill struggle. I'm still not sure whether her want of self-trust arose from her lack of trust in anything outside herself, or vice versa; I suppose it was a vicious circle.

One time, I came close to reaching her. It was a dismal evening: We were tired; it was raining; the news had been even more sickening than usual, for the execution of another twenty-five "traitors against the people" had been reported with relish, and new successes in the current attack on a brave but hopelessly outmatched neighboring country had been announced. We got ready for bed in silence, but before switching off the light Kari turned to me, her eyes wet. "Do you believe in God, Elana?" she asked in a low voice.

I hesitated, perturbed. That was one subject on which I could not—would not—lie to her. She must have the truth—couched in ambiguous terms, perhaps, but still the unfabricated truth. "It depends on what you mean by God," I said slowly, with a fervent hope that she would not give me some narrow, Youngling-style definition that I must deny.

She didn't; her concern for my sensitivity about the past saved me. "Oh, I'm sorry," she whispered. "I suppose you've lost your memory of your religion, too."

To have let the subject drop would have been easy, but I owed Kari more. "Some things can never be lost," I told her. "There's a Power in the universe that all religions reach out toward. I can't tell you what name I used for it. The name doesn't matter; different people, different places, have different ones. I have not forgotten that it exists."

Kari looked somewhat surprised. "I used to go to Devotions," she confessed unhappily, "but then after the Occupation—well, it all seemed so senseless. The priest said that no matter how many people were massacred, we shouldn't lose faith; that even the bad part was leading somewhere. But I don't see how it could be."

"No one sees," I replied soberly. "Yet just the same it is. Thousands of years from now, looking back, people will know where it led; and they still won't see what's coming next. No matter how much knowledge they have—knowledge of the whole universe, maybe—they'll still have to trust without seeing."

"What makes you so sure?" she protested. "What makes you think the world will even be here thousands of years from now?"

"I'm not sure," I admitted. "But whether it is or not, there's a pattern that takes in more than this world. I don't understand it, and neither does anybody else. We can't expect to understand it when we don't have all the facts, but that's no reason for deciding that everything is senseless! If it were, we might as well blow up the whole planet right now and be done with it, because what would it matter?"

"Oh, Elana," she reproached, "of course it would matter."

"Yes. You see, you've no doubt that it would; so underneath you know as well as I do that things aren't senseless and they are leading somewhere."

"I never looked at it that way before," she said thoughtfully. "At Devotions they talk mostly about the Holy Prophet that the sacred writings say will someday be sent down out of the sky to give us all sorts of magical powers. And you just know *that* couldn't be true."

"A very wise man once told me," I said gently, "that there are different kinds of truth. You don't necessarily have to interpret things just the way someone else does in order to believe them. What's important is the basic idea, and the one behind the words used at Devotions may not be so far off. It's an expression of faith in a changing future, anyway. That makes it truer than the ideas some people have."

"Like the Neo-Statists," Kari mused. "They tell us we don't need anything more than what we'll have after they've got the world all organized. Once they've conquered the Libertarians, everything will be perfect and nothing will ever change. The State will go on forever, just like clockwork."

"It wouldn't, you know."

"I know, and I'm glad! I think almost anything would be better than that."

"Well, if you don't believe that the world is so bad that blowing it up wouldn't matter, and you don't believe that the State's going to make it perfect, what's left?"

Wonderingly, she answered, "I see what you mean. The people who go to Devotions may not know everything, but at least they agree that there's a third alternative."

I thought that perhaps this discussion would buoy her up, but its effect was short-lived. We went to Devotions; I found the service dignified, reverent, and laden with symbolic truth. But the congregation was small, for the dictatorship frowned upon religion and few citizens cared deeply enough to take an independent stand. No doubt the very ones most capable of doing so had been put off by the metaphors concerning the Holy Prophet, having failed to see through that imagery to the essential truth beneath it; Critical Stage cultures are notoriously literal-minded. The priest was a courageous man who was doing his best to uphold one pillar of surety in a crumbling world, but his doom was inevitable. The day we attended our third service the dictator's government came out with a particularly obnoxious proclamation branding members of minority races as second-class citizens. The priest spoke out openly against the proclamation, being unable, in good conscience, to do otherwise. When he left the sanctuary that evening, the police were waiting for him.

"Kari," I said steadily, "he'll get through it, one way or another. He's got something to draw on." But my own mood was too low for me to convince her.

There is evil and injustice on all Youngling worlds. There are problems. But problems don't get solved if nobody tries to solve them, and I wasn't at all sure that enough people on Toris were trying.

I went over and over it. I've been over it since then, hundreds of times, and I still can't find the answer. I know that I must not expect to find it alone. I know that I was placed here alone, to trace a thread in a pattern I cannot see, because that is the only way in which the right pattern can emerge; and it's quite likely that I shall never be sure that any answer is accessible. Meanwhile, all I can do is to handle the situation I've landed in, and I guess that's all anybody can do.

But it's an awfully hard truth to adjust to. I did not adjust quickly; for a time, in fact, it was an open question as to whether my underlying hope would boost Kari's or her lack of it would destroy mine. I don't know what would have happened if we hadn't gone to the carnival.

We were definitely not in a carnival mood, so when the advertisement arrived in the mail—addressed, surprisingly, to me personally—I threw it aside with scarcely a glance. But the next morning, a holiday, Kari picked up the brightly colored sheet that had fallen to the floor beside the breakfast table. "Look at this," she said ruefully. "Roller coasters, jugglers, fortune-tellers—do people actually enjoy all that nowadays?"

"Well, it's one thing that hasn't been banned, at any rate," I said.

"You don't feel like going, do you?"

"No," I admitted. And then, as she held up the unfolded page, I caught sight of the picture on the back of it: a gaudily robed fortune-teller, obviously of the scorned, but in some roles tolerated, minority race, whose deep, penetrating eyes jumped out at me from an astonishingly familiar face.

It was Varned.

Luckily, the paper hid my reaction from Kari, for the breath was knocked right out of me. How could I have been so negligent? Weary and discouraged though I was, how could I have failed to examine with care a thing that had come to me by name, a name few Torisians had even heard? To have missed my contact would have been unforgivable; and besides, I had nearly lost what might be my only chance to communicate with my own people for a long, long time. A chill spread through me, for I suddenly felt that I would die if I had to go one more week without communicating.

Varned had come in the nick of time. A fortune-teller! It was a perfect cover; the carnival would travel from city to city with no questions asked. Moreover, Varned would be a phenomenal success as a fortune-teller, considering that people usually think about what they want to be told, for he would have no difficulty in picking up telepathic projections of that type. Perhaps he was the juggler, too; psychokinesis would make him an incredibly good one. And as a carnival performer, he wouldn't be seriously hindered by his atypical racial coloring.

"I don't exactly feel like going," I continued, by great effort keeping my voice calm. "But maybe we ought to relax once in a while, Kari. Why don't we forget all about the dictator and the war and the Bomb, and just have fun for a change?"

"We can't," she said sadly. "We can't forget, and we can't *make* things fun."

"We could try," I persisted. "I'm beginning to get enthusiastic."

Kari is a suggestible person, and when I'm sure of

myself I can practically always get her to follow my lead. We went. My enthusiasm was no act: communication at last, I was thinking, and soon! I did not see how I had survived the past weeks without it. I didn't see how I could live through the long bus ride out to the fairgrounds.

As we passed through the gate onto the crowded midway, I probed tentatively, *Varned?* There was no response. Kari and I walked slowly past booth after booth, oblivious to the color and noise and gaiety of our surroundings, seeing nothing that interested us but pretending, each for the other's sake, that we were enjoying ourselves. All the while I was repeating, with growing tension, *Varned? Varned?*

As we stood before a confection vendor's cart buying candy that neither of us had any appetite for, Varned's answer hit me: a single word, forceful and very stern. *Wait.*

Wait? For what? Oh, Varned—

Come to my tent. Buy a ticket like anyone else. Don't attempt contact until you're inside.

I obeyed. Having waited so long already, I could endure a few minutes more. The fortune-teller's striped tent was already visible not far up the midway; I started toward it.

Kari was dubious. "Oh, Elana," she said when my intent became plain, "you don't think a fortune-teller would know about your past!"

"No," I said, "not really, though there are plenty of unexplained talents in the world. But it might be amusing to see what he has to say. Come on, let's do it."

She went along with me, as usual, and we stood in line behind a group of giggling schoolgirls. Excitement

and relief welled up in me until I thought I would
burst; it was all I could do to keep from reaching out to
Varned's mind, though I knew he must have given the
command to wait for good reason. Surely he was aware
of what I was feeling, and would not needlessly deny
me a single instant of the mental contact I craved. How
long would he be in the city? I wondered. Long enough
for us to meet several times? Never before in my life
had I realized what it means simply to exchange ideas
with someone who knows you for what you really are.

After a seemingly endless delay, my turn came; I
paid the admission fee and was ushered into the darkened tent. Heavy gold curtains were held aside for me.
Beyond them, Varned was seated before a small, flick-
ering lamp, dressed as in the advertisement in the traditional robes and turban of a Torisian seer. *Oh, Varned,*
I began, *I'm so glad you've come!*

"Show me your hand, young lady, and I will tell
you what your future holds," he said in an impassive
voice, motioning me to sit. Silently, he responded to me
with only a brief, cold command: *Report.*

*But can't we talk first? There's so much I want to know—
Report! We've no time to waste. Ignore what I say aloud.*

Chastened, I began to "read back," telepathically,
all the data I had "recorded" since my arrival in Cerne.
This process is considerably faster than speech; it did
not consume much more time than the average fortune-
teller's interview.

Throughout, Varned continued to speak, giving me
a typical spiel for the benefit of the listening attendant;
his ability to do so while simultaneously "recording"
my report in his own mind was evidence of very advanced mental control.

When I had finished, I begged, *Now will you tell me what's happening? Has anything important been discovered yet? I—I've got some problems, Varned; I need advice.*

Cruelly, he cut me off with a formal speech of dismissal.

"I can tell you nothing more, my dear. You must be content with what I have said."

But you've said nothing! Won't you give me just a few seconds more? Or are you going to contact me again, somewhere, before you leave Cerne?

He raised his eyes from my hand, meeting my anguish with quiet compassion. *I will if you request it; but if you do, you're disqualifying yourself for solo credit.*

There were overtones of warmth in his thought, warmth that he was trying to conceal, and with chagrin I realized why he had been so brusque with me. He was not permitted to give me any moral support whatsoever, for such support would be unavailable to me in a normal solo. I was not on Toris primarily for testing; I was at liberty to violate my test status and receive his sympathy and aid. The temptation, in that moment, was very great. But my pride was greater. I had been offered a job that would ordinarily be entrusted only to an agent who had already come through the trial of solo; the least I could do was to stick by the rules.

I've got only one request, then, I told him as I stood up. *The young woman in line after me—she's unsure of herself, afraid. Give her something, Varned! Give her some kind of encouragement; she deserves it.* Without waiting for a reply, I turned and pushed through the curtains into the hazy sunshine of the carnival midway.

Kari stared at me. "Did he help you?" she asked skeptically.

"Yes," I said. "He helped a lot. Go on in, Kari. He's no mere charlatan; he's wise and kind, and you can trust what he tells you."

Waiting for her, I felt happiness rise in me, and the music of the nearby carousel actually sounded joyous. Varned had indeed helped, I reflected. I had been right in what I had said to Kari about his wisdom. I'd have thought his refusal to communicate would have made me feel more lost and hopeless than ever, but it hadn't; it had lifted my spirits. If he had granted me communication, I would only have hungered for more. As it was, I had freely chosen to forgo that comfort, and so for the first time I knew, deep inside, that I did not really need it.

In a few minutes Kari came out, wearing an expression of puzzled wonder. "Elana," she said slowly, "he told me that I'm destined to do something terribly brave someday! I just sat there, thinking he couldn't possibly be more wrong about me, and it—it was almost as if he read my mind. He said that I was unhappy because I hated myself for being so afraid all the time. How do you suppose he knew?"

Randil came away from his interviews with Varned in a mood of impotent rage and rebellion. They had had several exchanges and had conversed telepathically amid the crowds of the huge carnival restaurant pavilion as well as in the fortune-teller's tent. He was receiving closer guidance than the other agents on Toris, since he had not been trained for fieldwork. He had confessed his misgivings honestly, but Varned, though he had heard him out, had not seemed to understand what Randil was protesting against. *I told you it would hurt,* he had said at the last. *You must stick it out, Randil. It's going to get worse before you're through, but you'll bear up. I've got no doubts on that score.*

This reassurance only added to Randil's irritation, implying as it did that his ability to bear up was open to question. His personal feelings were not the issue; he had adjusted well to the life of a Cernese university student, difficult though it was to participate in class discussions and write term papers without revealing that he knew more than the professors. He was still willing to face whatever ordeals might be in store for him, although having made friends among his fellow dorm residents and even dated several of them, he had begun to discover just how painful living among Younglings—and caring about them—could be. The isolation, the constant pretense, he found trying but scarcely intolerable. His frustration arose not from the problems of his cover role, but from the fact that Varned had flatly refused to admit that there could be any chance of saving Toris through intervention.

One thing more, Varned had said in parting, *I get the impression that you're identifying a little more closely with the Torisians than you need to. Their danger may not be as great as they think, you know; most worlds come safely through the Critical Stage. To feel empathy is good, but watch out that you don't become their champion. It's not well for a scientist to abandon impartial observation in order to champion a cause he doesn't fully understand.*

But he did understand, Randil reflected indignantly as he looked out at the garishly lit streets of Cerne through the window of the last bus back from the fairgrounds. Hadn't he studied everything ever written on the Critical Stage, perhaps more extensively than Varned himself? He understood very clearly that the Torisians were doomed unless they immediately turned their attention to the colonization of space, and it didn't seem as if such a shift in their attention would be too hard to bring about.

He thought back over the basic theory of the Critical Stage he had learned at the Academy. *There comes a point for every human race when for the first—and only—time in its history it has the ability to destroy itself completely, and that point coincides with the point at which it is ready to take its first steps beyond its home world. The level of technology that creates one possibility simultaneously creates the other. If the colonization of space is undertaken, it becomes all-absorbing, full-scale war is forgotten, and the danger is averted—permanently, for never again will the species be isolated on one small and vulnerable planet. All the mature peoples of the Federation have resolved their challenge in this way; global civilizations are destined to expand or face destruction.*

Yet the Torisians showed no interest at all in space. Randil had looked up everything he could find on the subject in the university library, and it was all wild speculation, none of it endorsed by reputable scientists and none of it backed either by the application of current technological knowledge or by any foundation in philosophy. In short, the concept of space travel wasn't taken seriously. Even the fiction about it was classed as pure fantasy.

To be sure, enthusiasm for astronautics couldn't have been expected to arise as early as on some worlds, for Toris lacked a natural moon. That was a handicap because it meant the first extra-orbital space voyage would have to be a relatively long one: to the nearest neighboring planet, Juta. But since plenty of Federation worlds had no moons either, the handicap was by no means insurmountable. Moreover, Juta was more suitable for colonization than the average planet; not often was a human race blessed with such a convenient outpost in its own solar system.

Unfortunately, nobody on Toris had any idea how important colonization was. Not only the average man in the street but even the farsighted people—the ones who were bothered by the filthiness of the river and the murk of the city air and who realized that if the Bomb didn't wipe out civilization, overpopulation and pollution would—failed to see that there was really only one long-range solution to the problem. They hadn't even identified the problem. Those who hadn't fallen for the Neo-Statists' assertions about "Libertarian imperialism" thought the threat of war an indication that technology had gotten out of step with sociology.

If only he could tell them, Randil thought. It wasn't right for the Service not to tell them! He remembered what he had studied and wished, defiantly, that he could slip it into the paper he was writing now at the university. *Human species progress only when challenged. If sociological advance were to make war impossible before a planet's technology was sufficiently developed, the people of that planet would never achieve the means to expand to other worlds. If they waited for overpopulation to confront them, it would be too late; they would either become the victims of mass starvation and chaos, or resort to ruthless, planned killing without the "excuse" of war, followed by an irreversible decadence. . . . But the fuse is necessarily short. The technology, once achieved, must be used for expansion; otherwise the tendency toward war outlives its purpose and results in inescapable disaster. . . .*

He could imagine what Varned would say if he did such a thing. Agents were, after all, under strict orders to avoid exerting even the subtlest and most indirect influence on Torisian affairs. And yet . . . why? Randil knew the accepted explanation; he knew all the platitudes about how harmful it was to interfere with the development of Younglings. He had been told at the Academy; he had absorbed the applicable portions of Service ritual; and Varned had just gone over it again during the heated argument that had precipitated his current rancor. But was that all there was to it? Were those really sufficient grounds for withholding knowledge from a human race that was manifestly about to destroy itself?

Perhaps the Service had other reasons, reasons concerned less with the welfare of the Torisians than with the nature of the data being sought.

With a start, Randil realized that he had missed his bus stop. He got off at the next one and walked back, forgetting the race to beat curfew in his sudden, shocked concern about what these reasons might be. He asked himself why the Service was giving such high priority to a mission that would yield no unique results if the Critical Stage on Toris were to be resolved as it had been on most worlds. He asked why that mission had been set up as it had—why, for instance, he was kept in the dark about many phases of the plans and why he was forbidden to communicate with Elana, whom he knew to be also in Cerne but whose cover role hadn't been disclosed to him.

Aboard the starship, Varned and Meleny had given

him an answer. Was it the only conceivable one? It was not, Randil decided; and the alternate answer that occurred to him he did not like at all.

Kari didn't have much of a social life; her shyness prevented her from mixing easily, and though she went out occasionally, she was not dating anyone in particular. So I was a bit surprised the day she told me, abruptly during our lunch hour, that she had been asked to a party that evening and would like me to come along. There was something peculiar in her whole attitude toward the affair—not just her normal reticence but a strange mixture of eagerness and fear. It was unlike Kari; usually she turned down invitations from people she wasn't sure she would be comfortable with.

"Please come with me, Elana," she said almost desperately. "I haven't a date, and I don't want to go by myself."

"Are you sure I'm invited, too?"

"Yes, I checked. I don't know anyone who'll be there very well," she added hastily. "I can't imagine why they asked me, unless—unless it's because of the thing that happened last week. I—I've heard talk about this crowd; it's said that their parties are more than just parties. I had to promise I wouldn't give out the address."

On the point of refusal, I stopped short. Kari had told me what had happened on campus some days before: There had been a discussion in one of her classes before the professor arrived, and stimulated by the newfound frankness with which she had been expressing herself to me, she had made an unguarded remark. She had been dreadfully upset afterward. Well, it hadn't been noticed by an informer, for if it had, she would have been reprimanded before this. But apparently, it had been noticed by someone else.

"The girl I talked to did have some questions about you," Kari was saying. "I told her about the amnesia— that's all, of course. It seemed to satisfy her. If her friends were doing anything dangerous, they'd be more careful, wouldn't they? Oh, Elana, I hope it wasn't wrong of me to mention—"

"Certainly not," I assured her. "I want to go; you knew I would." I really did. I oughtn't to; although this invitation was probably quite innocent, it could be an overture from the Resistance, and I could under no circumstances get mixed up in the Resistance. I could not take on responsibilities that my own work might prevent me from fulfilling. Yet it would be the making of Kari! The mere fact that she was willing to attend what she suspected to be an illegal gathering showed that I was at last getting somewhere in my efforts to increase her confidence.

But nothing, I realized, would be settled at the first party we went to. An underground group would have to be very sure of us before taking any steps toward recruiting us; we would undoubtedly be tested, and Kari would need help and encouragement. Surely, at the last minute I myself could contrive not to qualify.

It was a hot night, and there were several hours of daylight left when we started out. The pavement burned despite the heavy soles of the Torisian shoes I still wasn't used to. The address Kari had been given was in a run-down neighborhood on the opposite side of the campus; by the time we got there, we were weary and breathless. I wasn't much impressed by the grimy hallway of the aged apartment building in which we found ourselves.

Kari knocked tentatively. While we were waiting, she turned to me and said anxiously, "Elana, maybe we're crazy! I'm scared."

"Don't be. We're not committed to anything. Let's just see what happens."

The music blaring out of the apartment was scarcely an encouraging sign; though of a kind popular among Torisian youth, it was not to my taste nor, I knew, to Kari's, and it didn't strike me as anything that would appeal to the sort of student likely to be engaged in underground work. It could, of course, be a cover. I hoped so.

The door opened a crack and then, almost immediately, wider, revealing a young but tired-eyed woman who did not seem particularly pleased to see us. "Oh, it's you, Kari," she said brusquely, her voice flat with disappointment. "Come on in."

Afterward, I wondered why we were accepted so easily, and then realized that those at the party knew Kari wouldn't report them. They were witnesses to her indiscretion in class, after all; and they knew her normal caution. I believe they really wanted to help her. I believe they thought they could.

Once inside, we proceeded down a narrow flight of basement stairs. The dingy room into which we were ushered was windowless and sweltering. It didn't have much furniture, though cushions were strewn over the floor, and the walls were blotched with whorls of vari-colored paint. There were about a dozen people present, more than half male. Their appearance was, to say the least, startling. If this was a cover, it was a strange one, for their mode of dress was in itself prohibited. All but the hostess were clothed in the style of a bygone century, with grotesquely painted faces and short, closely cropped hair that would have been considered an insult to public decency had it been revealed on the street. Such fashions had been worn openly until the Neo-Statist takeover; since then, it was rumored, they continued to thrive within a clandestine youth movement. But there were other rumors about that movement, disturbing ones that didn't coincide with what I knew of the Resistance, or indeed of organized resistance efforts in any dictatorship. If we had stumbled into a genuine group of its followers, we might be in hot water. If only I could have done some investigating before letting Kari get involved!

Everyone was simply standing around doing nothing. They were not even drinking anything; there were no glasses in sight, let alone food. And there was very little talking. The void was filled by the loud, raucous music, which no one was paying any attention to, but which, I guessed, would be immediately missed were it to stop. There was an air of tension about the place—not excitement, not the natural tenseness of people embarking upon a dangerous job, but simply the unbearable emptiness of—waiting. It wasn't a happy feeling.

Kari looked at me, puzzled, and I began to think about how we might manage a graceful exit. But at that moment we were approached by a wildly clad young man whose intelligent eyes belied the defiant garishness of his facial paint. "You must be the girl with amnesia," he said to me.

"Yes," I admitted cautiously. "I don't remember anything before ten weeks ago."

"I should be so lucky," he muttered. But I could not read his emotions; they seemed well buried beneath a mask of apathy and indifference. "I don't suppose you feel that way," he said. "I suppose it scares you. Well, we'll fix you up. Maybe you will remember; the stuff does funny things sometimes. In any case you'll be better off for a while."

Sick dread rose in me at this confirmation of my darkest suspicions, dread not for myself but for Kari. She had been elated by these dissenters' invitation to her, and elated too by her own daring in accepting it. It was I who had been urging her on; if she had landed in a situation she wasn't equipped to handle, the responsibility was mine. Somehow I would have to get her away before whoever was bringing "the stuff" put in an appearance.

But it wasn't so simple. Kari had been taken in tow by two or three of the more animated people, and, flushed with excitement, she was following my well-meant advice. "I—I don't believe what they tell us about the State!" she was saying as I came up to them. "I don't believe we're just machines to serve the State, never doing anything for ourselves or for each other. That sort of life isn't worth living."

"Right you are," said the hostess, toying nervously with a limp strand of the long hair she quite obviously wished to be rid of. "The State's a drag."

"It's not for you, Kari," added the student I had been talking to. "We knew it wasn't by what you said before class last week."

"No," Kari agreed, spellbound. "It's not for me."

"What is for you, then?" I put in quickly.

"Freedom," she whispered.

"There's only one kind of freedom," he said intensely. "The kind inside you. The country of your mind is a fascinating realm to explore. No rules, no signposts. No stupid authorities telling you what you should do and what you shouldn't—"

"Yes, but can you come and go as you choose?" I asked. "Is your will in the driver's seat? You can't be free unless it is."

"You don't need will; you don't want it. You let your inner mind sweep you along. It's *you*. And it's the whole world. Everything's one—you'll see. We can't talk about it; it's got to be experienced, or else we're on two sides of a wall. When you've crossed over, you'll *know.*"

He didn't suspect that I was already more knowledgeable than he in such matters, and it was difficult to argue without letting on; yet I knew that to maintain the amnesia ruse, I would have to make my point while pretending to be on the same side of the wall as the average Youngling. In desperation I protested, "But outside, the world is still there. The dictator is still running things."

"Not for us. Let civilization go its way; it'll fall of its own weight in time."

"What'll replace it? What about human progress?"

The young man laughed. "There's no such thing."

"You mean history isn't going anywhere even if we don't have a nuclear war?" All Younglings were blind, I thought, and yet was this a normal attitude for the Critical Stage? Or was it peculiar to peoples who did not go anywhere? Was it a portent of disaster, tied in with the key I had come to find?

"It's never gone anywhere yet," the long-haired hostess answered cynically, "except from bad to worse."

Though I had known that many Torisians felt this way, it was still a shock to hear it stated so flatly. The idea of civilization itself being worthless was worse than the prevalent fear of its being wiped out by the Bomb. It was horrible. It was more horrible than all the horrors of their history that these people were without hope. No wonder they wore the garb of the past, if they did not believe in the future! No wonder they sacrificed will and thought in a drug-induced plunge into the inner realms of the mind. A universe without direction does not bear thinking about.

The door buzzer sounded again, and the hostess rushed for the stairs. A moment later she was back, transformed, and not only by relief, for her hair was as short as everyone else's, and the long, decorous tresses—a wig—dangled from her hand. With her was a quite ordinary-looking young man who threw off his cloak to reveal clothes even more bizarre than those of the rest. He too removed a wig; his head was almost smooth-shaven.

"It's all right," he told the group clustering around him. "No slipup, and I wasn't followed. We'll be ready in a couple of minutes." He and the hostess, arm in arm, retired into the kitchen.

"Kari," I said urgently, "let's leave. We don't want anything to do with this; it's too risky."

"No," she told me. "No, I want to stay." The others were making a circle, sitting cross-legged on the floor. Someone had turned up the music; it was deafening. Gradually people began to sway in rhythm. Whether they were deliberately copying some primitive tribal ritual or whether it was subconscious reversion, I don't know; perhaps it was only as an anthropologist that I noticed the resemblance.

Kari found a place in the circle. There was no room for me next to her, and I had to squeeze in elsewhere, with no chance to speak to her privately. The tension grew. Finally, the newcomer reappeared—his face, like that of the hostess, having been daubed with color— settled across from us, and raised a tall, none-too-clean goblet filled with a pale liquid. "One swallow," he cautioned. "One swallow, and pass it on." He drank and, giving it to the student beside him, added, "Happy landings."

One swallow would be enough; more than enough, or they wouldn't dispense it so informally. Kari did not know! Their talk had been full of deceptive half-truths, they opposed the dictatorship, as she did, and the fact that they opposed too many other things was not obvious. Their sincerity, on the other hand, was unquestionable. She would not listen to my warning. She would follow their lead, when the glass came round to her, and drink.

She was not ready to meet what she would encounter. None of them were, but Kari was less so than average. For her it would not even be a happy realm; her will was neither weak enough to give up without struggle nor strong enough to win. So it would be dark and menacing, and though I could attempt to guide her, I was by no means fully qualified.

The beat of the music was insistent, almost hypnotic. Such music is for people who do not want to think. Kari was easy prey to it; like the others, she had found thought a burden of late, for was she not as lost in the gloom of the Torisian outlook as they? The goblet, half empty, was placed in her hands. She held it gingerly, stared for a moment in fascination, then with a rush of unaccustomed abandon raised it to her lips.

No, Kari! No! I cried silently, my fear for her overriding my resolution never to use telepathy. Slowly, painfully, she lowered the glass. She didn't know, of course, what had been the deciding factor; she had not recognized my communication for what it was. She thought she was stopped by her own last-minute apprehension, as perhaps she would have been even had I not intervened.

"You're a fool," the student on Kari's left told her as she handed him the drink, untasted. "It's a chance, sure—but it's the only chance. The only way to get happy, to find out how things are. Because nothing in the whole lousy world means anything; all the answers are within you, if there are answers, and if there aren't, how can you lose?"

"Does it matter?" said his date irritably, snatching the glass from him. "If she's afraid, what's it to us? All the more for the rest of us." She sipped and, with reluctance, passed it on to me.

Oh, you children, I thought as I took it; you poor, deluded children! If I dropped the thing seemingly by accident, could I save any of them? No, I decided. They had all been there before, and they would go again. They were not children. They were Younglings, and I could not save them from being harmed by drugs any more than I could save their world from the Critical Stage, of which rash experimentation of this kind was perhaps typical. Another item to report, I reflected bitterly: It has been observed that many in the current generation are finding the situation unbearable. They turn inward, through drugs; is that cause or effect, if their planet is truly doomed?

"Come on, Kari," I said, relinquishing the goblet into the eager grasp of the intelligent-seeming young man with whom I had tried to argue. "Let's go."

She rose, not lifting her eyes, and followed me. No one in the circle even noticed; they were oblivious to everything but the progress of the glass. In a little while, I supposed, they would be unaware not only of their surroundings but of their personal identity, which was, after all, the only thing worth defending against the State. *The country of your mind is a fascinating realm to explore*, he had said. So it is, but not if it's entered that way; not if you think it will be easier to face than what is outside.

On the street, though the sun had barely set, the air seemed fresh and cool by comparison with the stuffy room. For a few minutes we walked in silence. Finally, Kari said in a low, flat voice, "I'd hoped that if I ever met any activists, I'd feel as if I might learn to be like them, but I guess I just don't fit."

"You wouldn't want to fit in with that bunch!" I exclaimed, realizing with surprise that she hadn't seen the difference between the people at the party and the true rebels we had been expecting. "Those weren't activists, Kari; they were about as passive as they could get."

"They were defying the State—resisting."

"Not resisting, retreating. Withdrawing into a world of their own."

"Maybe it's a better world."

"Did it look like one?"

"Not on the outside. Inside—well, from the things they said—"

"From the things they said, I judge that they've given up on the human race and are simply looking for some sort of anesthetic. It can't be had, Kari. The world is the way it is. There's no place to hide; we've got to live in it and bear up under the pressure."

"I always thought you approved of the underground," she said accusingly.

"I do, if by underground you mean the constructive one—the Resistance—that's working to restore democratic government. Surely you know that the Resistance wouldn't recruit any of those people! They couldn't be trusted for five minutes."

"But what if overthrowing the dictatorship is a lost cause?" Kari persisted. "What if the only freedom is in people's minds, like they told us?"

If there's anything harder to counter than a clever lie, it's a truth that's been honestly misinterpreted. "Freedom is in people's minds, all right," I said, "but those people were destroying theirs."

"How do you know?" she burst out. "Have you ever drunk any of that stuff, stuff that makes you *see?* I've wanted to, only I never thought I'd have the chance, and now—oh, I wish I weren't such a coward!"

"There's quite a difference between cowardice and common sense," I pointed out. "Drugs like that are dangerous, not to mention being illegal."

"Practically everything you and I talk about is illegal," she reminded me. "What you just now said about the Resistance was enough to get us arrested."

I frowned. It was true that I could scarcely argue against drugs on the grounds of their illegality after working so hard to encourage Kari in her antidictatorship sentiments. "I don't mean dangerous in the sense of the secret police catching us," I told her. "I mean really dangerous, harmful."

"Isn't that just propaganda?" she protested. "A few people go psychotic, maybe, but who's to say they weren't on the border anyway? I'm surprised at you, Elana; knowing you, I'd think you'd be insisting that if drugs can open our minds to a new experience, we shouldn't run away from it. And I wish I dared see what it's like."

"That's like saying you wished you dared swim the Equatorial Ocean," I said quietly. "Mind-changing drugs aren't anything to fool around with! I—I remember underneath, perhaps." I fell back on the old unchallengeable excuse, at a loss for any other authority to explain the strength of my conviction.

Kari was right on one score: If the drug was what I supposed, a primitive psychedelic, then there was indeed something to be experienced. There was far more than the students at that party had an inkling of, but aside from the fact that they were seeking it for the wrong reasons, they weren't anywhere near ready for it. Very few Younglings are, at any age; even among Federation citizens, expansion of consciousness is normally undertaken only by older people. It's a tremendous challenge—one of the biggest challenges open to us on our home worlds—but the last thing anyone needs is a drug that forces such an experience, because a person who hasn't the maturity to cope with it is all too likely to be permanently overwhelmed. There are more natural approaches, which someone who is truly ready will discover, just as in rare instances Younglings discover their psychic powers.

Within the Federation, to be sure, these purely mental methods are understood, and the Academy has means of testing readiness as well as ways—safe ways—of teaching its students to confront the various levels of consciousness. I am not uninitiated; while most such training is given at the postgraduate level, all agents get a brief introduction to it, which is considered necessary protection because of what they may encounter in certain Youngling cultures. So the drug wouldn't have hurt my mind, although it could have done me physical harm since it was undoubtedly some crude poison with unpredictable side effects.

It's a pity I couldn't get the point across to Kari. I've tried since then, but she doesn't see it; she still thinks that hidden mental depths can be reached only through chemistry. I can't help being reminded of the Andrecians, who believed in magic potions.

It was only a few evenings later that I turned a corner in the library stacks and came face-to-face with Randil.

We were both overcome with astonishment, but he recovered first; to my amazement, he attempted telepathic contact. *Elana!* he exclaimed. *I've been hunting everywhere for you! Why, I've been doing my reading in the daytime so that I could search evenings, when you wouldn't be working. I never thought of your coming here, when you're not a student.*

I managed to retain enough presence of mind to give no answer, but inwardly I was in turmoil. Randil, in Cerne! All along he must have been at the university; we might have run into each other any number of times, and if he had approached me before my encounter with Varned, I might not have been strong enough to withhold response. I was no longer subject to temptation, however. It wasn't just a matter of my unwillingness to cheat on solo rules, but of the fact that the whole strategy of the mission prohibited contact between agents. Randil knew that as well as I; what business did he have trying to communicate with me?

I had known, of course, that Randil was somewhere on Toris. He had told me of his assignment innocently; on graduation night he hadn't been aware that I was to receive solo credit from the mission. The majority of the agents, who had already been through their solos, were informed of each other's whereabouts despite the fact that communication between them was forbidden; so it was natural enough that he should know of my presence in the city. But that he should seek me out was a direct violation of orders.

Elana, what's the matter with you? he persisted. *I know you understand me! You're not in real trouble, are you? You haven't lost your telepathic powers?*

"I'm sorry," I said aloud. "I think you've mistaken me for someone else. Will you let me by, please?"

I walked quickly through the stacks toward the study area, Randil following. *I've got to talk to you, Elana,* he went on insistently. *Something has come up; something that demands action.*

At that moment I spotted Kari, waiting for me near the exit, and I made what was possibly the most tragic mistake of my entire life. I joined her, and, feigning embarrassment, I said in a low but clearly audible voice,

"Kari, this man thinks he knows me. I—I'm not sure what to say to him. Maybe he really does, and yet—"

She squeezed my hand sympathetically. "Don't worry, I'll explain." Turning to Randil, who was right on my heels, she said, "You'll have to forgive my friend. She's been sick, with amnesia, and she can't remember anything at all about her past. If you do know her, you could be a big help, but if you're just—well, it's awfully cruel in this case. So leave her alone, will you, please?"

Randil looked puzzled. "Amnesia?" he asked. "Since when?"

Kari mentioned the date. Randil's face cleared, and he said, "I apologize. I made an honest mistake." Silently he continued, *So that's your cover. And you're playing it by the book. Elana, didn't it ever occur to you that the book might be wrong? This world is in danger, serious danger, and something has got to be done about it. I need your help!*

I ignored him. Kari shifted her load of books from one arm to the other and said, "Come on, Elana. It's almost curfew; we've got to rush."

"Wait." Randil hurried after us. "Look, I'm sorry if I offended you; I wasn't trying to pick you up or anything." To Kari he added, "Can't I take some of those?"

"No, thanks. Elana carries half after we pass the desk."

"You live near each other, then?"

"We're roommates."

He looked at Kari closely, for the first time fixing his attention on her instead of on me. "I don't want this to sound like another phony gambit, but haven't I seen you in one of my classes?"

She smiled, blushing a little. "Yes, you have. The science survey lectures. I—I usually sit near the back."

I waited, surprised but relieved by the ease with which he had been diverted from his determination to communicate. It seems incredible, now, that I could have been so blind to his interest in her.

"Tomorrow," he told Kari, "I think I'll sit in back, too." I did not even see the inherent danger.

f o u r

I have just returned from another long session with my interrogator, a session at which my precomposed confession was again the issue. The thing is not a total fabrication; it does contain a few statements that happen to be true, though they are grossly distorted even in terms of what the Torisians know about me. For instance, the part admitting that I was deliberately made ill as a ploy to establish my cover is indisputable, but the conclusion that this was "a typical Libertarian atrocity in the field of biological experimentation" does not follow. Nor do the reasons given for my alleged actions bear any relationship to what might be a Libertarian's real ones. Even if I were the spy they think I am, that document couldn't possibly be taken seriously; it reads like something out of a comic melodrama.

Nevertheless, we go over and over it, for hours on

end. I don't know what my interrogator would do if I did sign it, because actually he doesn't care a bit about my signature, which he could easily forge. What he wants is to make me believe it. He is well aware that I will never endorse a false confession while knowing it to be false; his hope is that if I can be brought to the point where I can no longer differentiate my true motives from those ascribed to me, the information he is after will be forthcoming.

Crazy though it sounds for anybody to think that a prisoner could really be rendered incapable of telling truth from falsehood, such things do happen among Younglings. That's one of the grimmer realities that an agent must accept. Younglings are not trained in the control of their own minds, and so sometimes their minds can be bent by others. Men like my interrogator, unfortunately, have developed ways to take advantage of that fact. The ways are complicated; sooner or later, he believes, he will hit upon one that will crush me. He is going to get a surprise.

He does not rely on browbeating alone to influence me, nor even upon pain. No detail is overlooked. My hair has been clipped short, a sign of indecency and shame in Torisian eyes, although it doesn't affect me as such since there are no taboos against it in my own culture. To this, as to a number of stronger measures, my reaction has been much calmer than he expected. Quite often they can crack someone—especially a woman— more easily through indignities than through torture.

There has been only one incident so far where I nearly lost my composure in his presence. Ironically, it was accidental; it wasn't even something he had planned.

We had come to the end of an interview, an easier one than some because though I had undergone a longer-than-average physical ordeal, my psychic defense had protected me, and I had meanwhile been free of the need to listen and respond. (It's much more difficult to stand at attention, with the spotlights focused on my face and my interrogator's incessant questions hammering away at me—questions to which my answers must be carefully calculated and always, of course, consistent—than it is to sit back and pretend to be enduring extreme agony.) Anyway, as usual we had arrived at an impasse, and the guards were about to escort me back to my cell. The door to the corridor stood open, but the interrogator spoke, halting us.

"You are very foolish, Elana," he said to me, not for the first time. "Brave, yes—but others have been brave. Others have suffered. Their stoicism got them nowhere; heroes or cowards, they were all led to the same place in the end." With studied indifference, he added, "You realize, don't you, that even if you proved to be an exception, no one outside these walls would ever hear of it? The Libertarian nations would never know that you had held out."

"I'm sure they wouldn't," I agreed indifferently. I laughed a little too loudly, perhaps, for fatigue was making me jumpy and there was a certain ludicrousness in the idea that he could not possibly see what I had found amusing.

At that moment, from another room somewhere down the corridor, came an anguished moan, followed almost immediately by a shrill, piercing shriek.

The blood rushed from my face; my skin turned clammy, and I knew an instant of vertigo. It must have been noticeable, for I would have swayed had the guards not been gripping my arms. My interrogator looked at me very intently, wondering, I suppose, why I should be frightened by the cry of someone in pain no worse than what I had repeatedly withstood.

I was not frightened. I was overcome by sheer horror at my own complacency. Though it wasn't news to me that there is nothing unique about the treatment I'm receiving, I had not encountered such eloquent evidence before. I had scoffed at the stresses to which I was subjected, knowing myself a match for them; but the bravery I had been credited with was sham. I have not been truly suffering. There are others, I fear, who have.

I must forge ahead with the history of the mission, I suppose. From here on it will be a painful process, for the things that happened aren't pleasant to recall.

The meeting with Randil marked the end of my brief period of relative serenity. For several days I stayed away from the library, browsing through bookstores instead. Yet I knew in my heart that if he had found me once he would find me again, and that when he did, I would have a real problem on my hands. It had been evident that Randil had tried to communicate not from inability to endure his isolation but with some definite purpose in mind, and although he undoubtedly meant well, I feared that it would lead to no good.

I knew he would find me, yet I didn't guess how— or how soon. So when one morning on our way to the hospital Kari mentioned that she had a date for the evening, I felt nothing but pleasure. Kari didn't have enough dates, and I was glad that she had been asked out by someone new and interesting. "What's he like?" I asked casually.

"He's different from anybody I've ever known before," she declared enthusiastically. "It makes me feel important, somehow, to think he'd even notice me. You got the wrong impression of him, really you did."

"I? When did I meet him?"

"At the library the other night," she confessed.

"Randil!" I exclaimed, too startled to hide my dismay. "You gave him our address?"

"Well, of course; he's going to call for me." She looked at me strangely. "I didn't think you knew his name."

"He mentioned it," I whispered, stricken.

"Elana, you're not afraid of him, are you? He mistook you for someone else! He wasn't trying to pick you up; he's just not that kind of person. And he certainly isn't a shadow from your past. He's only been in Cerne since the beginning of the college term."

"I'm sorry, Kari," I said with forced composure. "It's just that when someone you don't remember claims to know you—"

"Poor Elana," she said softly. "I wish I could help."

I felt cheap enough already about the undeserved pity I elicited from her, and this latest development made matters even worse. I had added to her troubles again. She was obviously attracted to Randil, and she would be desolate, I thought, when he failed to call her again after their first date.

But that was one problem that didn't arise.

Incredibly, Randil dated Kari three or four times a week. If I was there when he brought her home, he begged me, silently, to communicate, an overture that I steadfastly resisted; sometimes on weekends I had to entertain him while Kari was getting ready, and I developed the ability to make polite conversation while shutting out his insistent telepathic appeals. But he didn't come around only to see me. He learned that I could time my arrival for moments before curfew, so that he had to leave before I got there in order to avoid arrest; he kept right on coming. He saw Kari on nights when he could easily have cornered me in the library. He met her on campus frequently, when he knew perfectly well that I was working.

Meanwhile, the world news went from bad to worse. It got so depressing that I hated to turn on the television, and reading the newspapers—which I was required to analyze thoroughly—was an even less palatable ordeal. I did not take them at face value, of course; still, the reports of international crises, while heavily slanted toward arousing ire against the Libertarians, contained elements of all-too-plausible truth. There were also certain radio broadcasts, strictly illegal, that were spoken of in whispers, and to them I gave more credence. Their tone was not hopeful.

And there were other sinister happenings. Life in Cerne grew less secure. People disappeared more often, and our nights were repeatedly disturbed by the spine-chilling blare of sirens. Kari's favorite professor, a kindly, white-haired gentleman of distinguished reputation, was replaced one day by a younger man who seemed inordinately interested in reviewing the past progress of the class. Apparently, it displeased him, for the professor was not seen again. Some of the less cautious students signed a petition of protest; they were not seen again, either.

Through all this, I expected Kari to become more fearful and withdrawn than ever, despite the fact that she had learned to express herself freely to me whenever we were sure that we could not be overheard. That didn't happen. Instead, she blossomed. It seemed not to bother her that bomb-shelter drills were held at ever more frequent intervals, that a general order was issued banning assembly of more than ten people without a police permit, that women—including ourselves— were suddenly required to register for the military draft. She was happy anyway, happier than I had ever seen her; she had decided that the world was not such a dreadful place after all. Kari, for the first time in her life, was in love.

People in love always say a good deal to their friends, I suppose, about how the person they care for is unlike any other human being in the entire world. Kari went on at rapturous lengths in that vein, and the ironic thing was that in her case what she believed about Randil happened to be true. He was indeed unlike other men. He was a Federation citizen and a sworn agent of the Anthropological Service, though he had come perilously close to forgetting that, and it broke my heart to see how he was breaking Kari's.

It was all very innocent. Randil never meant for Kari to be hurt, and he didn't set out to sweep her off her feet. He simply didn't realize how a shy, insecure girl who had never had anyone to love before would react to the attentions of an obviously intelligent man who truly valued her as a person. I'm now aware that he had no idea how deeply affected she was until he himself was too involved to turn away. And by that time it would have been cruel to break off with her; she would have been shattered anyway, as she will be at the inevitable end. It's good, perhaps, that she has had these extra weeks of happiness.

But it would have been better if I had stepped in sooner.

I blame myself. Communicating with Randil earlier would not have done nearly as much harm as his involvement with Kari has done, and I can't deny that my own selfish pride was a factor in my silence. One contact with Randil meant giving up my solo credit. As soon as I put it to myself in those terms, I knew I must disobey orders and make the contact, for Kari's sake and for Randil's. By then, it was too late to do any good.

We communicated for the first time one evening when he called for Kari; she was in the bedroom dressing, and I was carrying on my usual impersonal, inane dialogue with Randil, ignoring his silent pleas. And then suddenly I took the plunge and responded. *You've won,* I told him. *Kari is my best friend; I'm too fond of her to let this go on. I must say you chose an effective weapon against me, but it was a dirty one. It was a breach of the Oath, even: You put your personal interests ahead of a Youngling's.*

He stared at me, absolutely stunned, and the emotional pain of his reply nearly overloaded my long-unused telepathic faculties. *Elana, you don't think ...*

I had thought so, and it was mortifying to realize how I had misjudged him. *I'm sorry,* I faltered, struggling to regain my balance. *I seem to have gotten the wrong impression.*

You weren't wrong about the beginning, he admitted. *I*

*dated her just to learn your address. But only that once!
Afterward I kept on because she was lonely and unhappy and I
liked her; I simply wanted to give her some fun. I—I didn't
know what we were getting into.*

But you know now, I observed with sadness, seeing
that my warning was no longer of any use. I, of all people, should have been more perceptive, considering
that it had once happened to me. You don't believe it
can, with a Youngling; you don't look at Younglings in
that way. And then when it does happen, you don't
look at the person involved as a Youngling at all.

Elana, he confessed miserably, *I love her. I want to
marry her.*

You know that's impossible.

Is it?

*Randil, you're not serious! Younglings can never be taken
from their native worlds. Even if it weren't forbidden, it would
be bad for everybody concerned. Kari would be a misfit in the
Federation; she'd suffer terribly. And besides, an agent can't
marry outside the Service.*

I don't expect to take her away, he informed me.

*You're certainly not going to marry her and then desert
her!*

*What do you think I am? No, Elana, I—well, I'm becom-
ing a Torisian.*

I don't believe that I have ever received a greater
shock. Dazed, I protested, *But Randil, you're sworn.*

He met the challenge squarely. *I won't be breaking the
Oath,* he contended. *Policy, maybe, but not the Oath.*

That needs a lot of explaining, Randil, I declared.

*I know. It's what I've been trying to explain all these weeks
when you wouldn't listen. This isn't just a matter of me and
Kari. It started long before that.* Randil paused, and then,

desperately earnest, he continued, *Look, Elana, when we took the Oath, we swore to put the Younglings' best interests ahead of everything else, right?*

Of course, I agreed, knowing that I would have to hear him out before even attempting to argue.

We vowed to make any sacrifice, no matter what we might bring on ourselves?

Yes.

Then what if there's a conflict between policy and that basic principle?

Slowly I replied, *You don't have to ask me that, Randil. I answered it before a Court of Inquiry after the Andrecian mission, and the results of that hearing were common knowledge at the Academy.*

Smiling, he told me: *I haven't forgotten. We all admired your spirit. You were charged with violating a provision of the Oath, and the judges gave you a pretty bad time, but in the end you were exonerated on the grounds that you had acted in the best interests of the Andrecians. That's why I know you'll help me, once I can make you see what has to be done to save Toris. I know you've got the courage for it because you've gone against policy before.*

I made no comment, for he didn't know the whole story. The Court of Inquiry had been unexpectedly tough with me; as a test of my convictions, I had been led to believe that contrary to Father's original reassurances, I would be censured. But later I had understood that my judges' severity had been a calculated kindness. The fact was, my decision to break policy on Andrecia had not been quite as noble as Randil supposed, a personal consideration having played a part in it; so despite the comfort I had received from Father, there'd been lingering doubt in me as to the rightness of what I'd done. By forcing me to defend myself under pressure, the inquiry had dispelled that doubt, and my ultimate vindication had given me a peace of mind I might never have obtained from the judgment of a more lenient court.

With sober intensity Randil went on: *We won't be exonerated this time, Elana. We'll be defying every tradition in the book, and we'll go down in Service history as renegades. We'll have to relinquish our Federation citizenship and cast our lot with the Torisians—for good.*

In the name of the Oath? I asked incredulously.

In the name of the Oath. Are you with me, Elana?

I hesitated, wondering how best to deal with such an overwhelming proposal. Randil's sincerity was beyond question. Whatever his plan was, he believed that he could save Toris by it; I didn't want him to think I would be unwilling to pay the price. Yet that was exactly what he would think if, as seemed likely, I wound up having to point out that Service policy has a good deal of wisdom behind it.

I know you'll be sacrificing more than I will, he continued. *You're engaged to an agent, while the girl I love is here.*

A moment of frightening uncertainty hit me, and I dropped my eyes. *Would* I be willing? If by some remote chance there should be a way of saving this planet through unauthorized intervention, would I be capable of giving up so much? Evrek . . . the Service . . . every pleasure, every comfort of the world I had been born to . . . all the wonders of the universe? Would I, for instance, if it meant keeping that dishwashing job until I was old enough to retire from it?

I might, I decided, if such a sacrifice would accomplish anything; but how could it? There was a flaw in

Randil's reasoning. He spoke in terms of certain condemnation rather than of risk, yet if we took justifiable action we would not be condemned. Unjustified action, on the other hand, would carry its own penalty: not banishment, but the awesome burden of answerability for whatever damage that action caused. Randil apparently had no fear of causing damage; still, he believed that we could not hope for exoneration. Why? Didn't he trust the Service to deal fairly with us? Or was he simply rationalizing, telling himself that since he would have to stay on Toris anyway, he might as well get married?

In either case, his basic assertion was sound. Father himself had once told me that the Oath demands more of an agent than blind obedience, that its literal words are anchors, not shackles. And there are times when anchors must be abandoned. I sensed danger, terrible danger, in Randil's line of thought; but I could not in honesty judge it unless I was prepared to commit myself fully to whatever course would best serve the interests of Toris.

My heart pounding, I turned back to Randil. *I'm with you,* I pledged, *if you can prove to me that what you have in mind will truly help the Torisians.*

I can't promise that. We may fail. But if we do, so does their civilization; and when the bombing starts, I'd rather die here with Kari than be rescued.

You don't believe there's any chance of the war being averted without intervention?

Do you?

I—I don't know. If we knew, none of us would be here, would we?

We might, he answered grimly.

What do you mean?

Elana, don't you realize that if Toris gets through the Critical Stage, not one thing will be learned from this mission? That, from the Service's standpoint, all the risk and effort of it will be wasted unless a nuclear war takes place?

That's a pretty callous way of putting it, I objected. *Besides, something can be learned from every Youngling race.*

Maybe, but not the sort of key factor we were sent here to find. I've studied the Critical Stage; I wrote my thesis on it! The only thing lacking for a complete analysis is data from a planet that didn't make the grade.

Certainly. The Director told me that.

Did he also point out that the policymakers would hardly assign all the top agents they could recruit to a crash priority mission that they weren't hoping would accomplish its purpose?

I gasped. *Randil, if you're insinuating—*

I'm not insinuating, I'm accusing! We were told that no action of ours could save this world. And we fell for it. But what if this world has been written off? What if it's classed as expendable, a test case?

You actually believe that the Service would value data on the Critical Stage higher than the survival of a whole Youngling race? That—that a feasible action would be deliberately withheld?

The bitterness of his thought intensified its telepathic force; he seemed to be shouting. *Take a good look at it! Everything fits: the secrecy about the master plans; our isolation; the ban on contact—they knew that if a bunch of us got together we'd catch on.*

Oh, Randil, it isn't true! It couldn't be!

Look, Elana, he insisted, *Varned practically admitted it. Back on the starship he told me in so many words that I was being used! I didn't understand then—*

And you still don't!

You got the pitch about what's learned here enabling us to save other worlds, didn't you? Well, I don't want to save other worlds in some dim, hypothetical future; I want to save this one! I want to save Kari's world, and I'm going to try, and if you don't help, I'll try alone.

I'll help, I assured him. *I'll help, if it's as you say. But Randil, I'm not convinced yet. We've got to think this through.*

I've done nothing else!

We've got to be absolutely sure that there's no chance of our doing more harm than good.

The bedroom door opened, and Kari stood there, radiant as always at the mere sight of Randil. Our faces must have been a puzzle to her. "Why, you two look glum," she chided, with a light laugh. "And so quiet! I haven't heard you say a word for the last ten minutes."

"I—I'm tired this evening, Kari," I murmured. "I'll probably be asleep when you get home."

But privately, I knew that I would be unlikely to do any sleeping for a long, long time.

That night I went over my entire life, step by step, memory by memory, searching for touchstones by which to judge Randil's appalling accusation. I thought of my mother, whom I remembered but dimly, and of her Emblem brushing my forehead as she stooped to kiss me good-bye upon her departure for the mission from which she never returned; of my grandparents—retired field agents—and of the view of the Service's work they had given me, the concept of a sacred trust embedded in the fascinating adventure stories on which I had been raised; of my school years,

years when all my dreams had been focused on the proud day when I would be admitted, as a probationer, to the Academy. I thought of Father, upon whom from earliest childhood my deepest confidence and affection had been bestowed: of Father standing before the Andrecian campfire as he invested me and witnessed my Oath, and of his quiet strength in helping me through the painful awakenings that had come with my first attempts to live up to its demands. I thought of Evrek, of the love we shared, the plans we had, the future we had founded our hopes on. I looked back on my training: the challenges and the insights; the grim but always salutary trials of mental discipline; the instructors' seeming ruthlessness that without exception had proved a mere facade for warm and sympathetic wisdom in which I had found I could place absolute trust. I recalled the Director's unmistakable sorrow when he had warned me that I was going as a helpless observer to a world that I would be powerless to save. And of course, I thought through the whole complex of Service ritual, reliving my last evening at the Academy: the traditions, the symbols, the solemn, joyous words of consecration and of faith.

I reviewed these things and many more, in the dark by myself and later, feigning sleep, while Kari tiptoed in and undressed for bed and lay down smiling, warm with the memory of Randil's kiss and secure in the newfound refuge of his love. I reviewed them until dawn brightened the window, shedding pale light on the face of the clock that told me I must soon get up and pull myself together for another weary day of kitchen work. And in the end I came to three conclusions.

First of all I knew, as surely as I shall ever know anything, that it could not be the way Randil said.

If the Service could do what Randil claimed it was doing, everything I had ever had faith in was false and hollow. I couldn't believe that. One recollection alone was sufficient grounds for disbelief: the thought of what Father had said to me the first time I had observed the suffering of Younglings, and had demanded to know why we were taking no steps to alleviate it. "I believe that the weight of the evidence is on the side of the policy as it stands," he had declared, "but then if I didn't, I wouldn't be here." Father was highly enough regarded in the Service to be counted among the policy-makers. He would not be there if there were any possibility of a whole human race being allowed to die simply to provide test data.

Randil hadn't grown up with the Service as I had; his association with it extended no further back than his admission to the Academy, and he had never before set foot on a Youngling world. He had not been prepared for direct contact with Younglings during his training. Without such preparation, which would have alerted him to the dangers of being thrown off balance, he hadn't the perspective for a solo job; his cynicism was closer to the outlook of a Critical Stage culture than to that of a Federation anthropologist. He had carried empathy a little too far. The people of this planet were the first Younglings he had ever known, and he had identified with them to the point where his Torisian cover role was overshadowing his own background. Falling in love with Kari had been the last straw; he was well on the way toward losing his objectivity as an observer. Somehow, I had to make him see that.

Second, it was possible that Randil was wrong about the Service's motives and yet right about there being a way for us to keep nuclear war from occurring, some way that no one else had thought of. Should that prove true, I would have to go along with him. I had committed myself, and though "defying every tradition in the book" wasn't an appealing prospect, his estimation of me had been accurate enough. If we had a real chance of saving Toris, no personal renunciation would carry any weight with me; underneath I knew that I would do whatever needed doing.

But there was a third possibility, a possibility still more dismaying. Randil might be wrong on both counts, and he might refuse to admit it. He had said, after all, that he would go ahead with his plan with or without my help, and if in my judgment that plan could be harmful to Toris—well, I would be in a very difficult position. I was alone; I had no means of contacting my superiors. The Oath is specific in regard to your responsibility in such a case. It binds you to prevent the harm by any means open to you, if necessary, even by force. Force is contrary to the Federation's principles, but where Younglings are endangered by a renegade agent, it is considered the lesser of two evils.

The morning was a dark one. I could not stick it out in the kitchen for more than a couple of hours; telling my supervisor that I felt ill—which was not far from the truth—I escaped and headed for the campus. Since I knew Randil's class schedule, I was waiting for him when he came out of the lecture hall. We had to have a long, private discussion, and it could be held only while Kari was busy with her nurse's aide job. I hated to think what could happen if someone who knew her saw us together, but it was a risk that couldn't be avoided.

We sat on a bench in a secluded garden between two stone buildings. Clouds blanketed the sky, threatening rain, but none fell. From above them came the rumble of aircraft, carrying out one of the large-scale military exercises that had been all too common of late.

Randil was relieved that I had taken the initiative in meeting him; he had, after all, run quite a risk by confiding in me. "Did you think it through?" he asked eagerly.

"I thought. You're mistaken, Randil. The Service would not stand by and observe a nuclear war that could be prevented; I'd stake my life on it."

"And the lives of all the people on this planet?"

"Yes," I declared with conviction; then, as clearly as I could, I told him why.

He wasn't impressed. "Forgive me if I sound skeptical," he said slowly. "I know your family is Service from way back, and I know that gives you a different slant than mine; but Elana, isn't it possible that it could be a prejudiced slant? I'm not saying that your father would personally condone this setup—"

"I hope you're not!" I exploded.

"Let me finish. I'm sure he wouldn't; I know what kind of man he is. But he's away on an expedition right now. Policy is made by the Council, in which he has only one vote. You can't assume that his values are shared by all the others."

"Yes, I can, because he knows the others and he knows what kind of people *they* are. But more than that, we all know. We're sworn. We've been through investiture, and we're aware of what it entails. Randil, you've said a lot about upholding the spirit of the Oath. Do you think you have a monopoly on that attitude? Don't you realize that the Council is equally bound by it, that no member could support a policy that would let Toris be written off?"

"The Council's composed of old people. Some of them haven't been in the field for decades."

"What has that got to do with it?"

"They have a stake in the results of the mission. There are scholars who've been waiting all their lives for a discovery like this; abstract theory means more to them than what happens to a particular race of Younglings. I admit that they must once have had what it takes to go through investiture, but—well, they've forgotten."

"Oh, Randil. Are *you* going to forget when you're old?"

I couldn't budge him. Randil can be very stubborn, and that morning I began to realize it. Eventually, knowing that I had only a little while left in which to cover a great deal of ground, I tried a different tack. "Just why do you think that there is any feasible means of intervention?" I asked. "What could the Service do if it wanted to? What can we do, assuming that we've got to act alone?"

"But Elana," he burst out, "it's so obvious! That's how I know that the decision not to implement it was deliberate."

"I'm afraid it's not obvious to me."

He began to explain, and as I listened I felt sicker and sicker. There were only three things obvious about Randil's plan: that it indeed involved violation of basic policies set forth in the Oath; that it also entailed an unjustifiable risk of backfiring; and that whatever the consequences to us both, I could not possibly support it.

Randil was stunned by Elana's opposition to the action he suggested. To him it was very clear-cut. He knew, to be sure, that all interference in the affairs of Younglings was potentially harmful; but these people had the power—and, he feared, the inclination—to destroy themselves. Only during the Critical Stage was that possible, and the Service had never encountered a Critical Stage culture before. Surely agents who found themselves in such a culture were morally justified in establishing a new precedent. It would be—well, *murder* if they didn't, just as much as if they were to burn all life off the face of Toris! He therefore felt no qualms about intervening.

The Service, he believed, would not forgive any such independent move. The Service's primary mission was to gather knowledge, and in this case it was plainly buying that knowledge through the sacrifice of a race that would have died anyway if left alone. Perhaps that wasn't murder to everyone, but in Randil's estimation it was. He had thought Elana would see it the same way. Knowing of her infraction of the Oath on Andrecia, he hadn't thought that she would be one to balk at defying orders; that was why he had tried to enlist her help.

Yet she demurred. She seemed unconvinced that action would be of any use. Why? Wasn't it known positively that the Torisians would be out of danger once they committed themselves irrevocably to the colonization of space? And wasn't it evident that they could be led to do so if Federation agents were to assume positions of influence? There would be no disclosure involved; he and Elana would simply earn the reputation of "brilliant scientists" by revealing a small portion of the advanced knowledge that was theirs, as he had already begun to do in what he wrote for his university classes. In a little while they would become respected authorities to whom people would listen, and—backed by the telepathic influence they could exert—even become media celebrities who could easily sway world opinion. Perhaps Toris hadn't even a little while to spare, but the chance was certainly worth taking.

"What possible harm could we do?" he demanded.

"That's the whole point," Elana said. "We don't know what harm we could do, but it might be considerable. What are we here for, if not to gain insight into a process that's so far a mystery to us? We can't even begin to foresee the consequences—"

"Could they be worse than the consequences of doing nothing?"

"Maybe. And in any case, we'd invalidate all the data that is being collected. Any tampering at all would make whatever is observed about key factors in the Critical Stage completely meaningless because our actions would be affecting those factors."

He turned on her angrily. "I know that would be the official objection, but I didn't expect it from you."

"I wouldn't care how much data we invalidated if we could be sure we were helping matters," she retorted. "We can't, though, because the data is the only thing that would tell us."

Her argument didn't hold water, Randil decided.

The information being sought was concerned solely with *why* some civilizations didn't pursue space technology when ready to do so; the fact that those who did attempt it were saved was indisputable. Nothing could totally destroy a human race that had colonized worlds beyond its own: not localized warfare, not epidemics, not starvation, not pollution or depletion of its mother planet—nothing! Not even a natural disaster such as a catastrophic meteor strike. And as for interplanetary warfare, never in the annals of the Service's experience had that been reported. Peoples who were occupied with a bigger and more exciting challenge had no need to let off steam in such a primitive fashion.

Of course, fully independent colonies took many decades to establish. That was why the exploration of space and utilization of its energy and mineral resources had to be undertaken long before a people could comprehend the necessity for it. That was the place of global conflict in the scheme of things: It was the stimulus, the spur. When the need for an incentive was past, such conflict disappeared; what could be wrong with eliminating that need artificially?

"It would be easier to speak out if we were in a Libertarian country," he told Elana. "We'd be freer, and we'd get more publicity. I'd thought that one of us could try to escape over the border."

"One of us? You mean me, don't you? After all, there's Kari."

Randil avoided her eyes. He had indeed assumed that it would be logical for her to go and for him to stay, but originally it had been merely because he was already established at the university. He had evolved the whole plan before he had even met Kari; his decision to act had been made the night Varned had left, in the heat of his anger at the dawning suspicion that the mission's strategy had been formed in the best interests of Federation science rather than of Toris. If Elana wasn't going to participate, the question of whether he himself should escape from Cerne was academic, for if he were caught crossing the border, there would be no one left to do what must be done. But supposing he were faced with a choice? Would he carry out the plan if it meant leaving Kari behind?

At first, renouncing his Service career had been a real sacrifice, and making up his mind to it had cost him much pain. Randil had been raised in an orbiting city circling a small planet far from the center of the galaxy; his family hadn't been wealthy by Federation standards, and his dream of seeing more of the universe had seemed fantastic. He had applied to the Academy simply as a defiant gesture. His acceptance, which had astonished him, had opened the gates of longings he had scarcely been aware of; once fully awakened, his hunger to study the cultures of many worlds had become an urgent passion. The unsurpassed opportunities for scholarly research at Service Headquarters meant much to him, and the idea of staying on Toris forever—in circumstances even less satisfying than those to which he had been born—was anything but inviting.

But something else had awakened in Randil during his Academy years; his consecration at investiture had been genuine, as his entrance tests had no doubt predicted it would be. He had taken the Oath in dead seriousness, and it was infuriating to think that others of more cosmopolitan backgrounds might not look at it quite so idealistically. Since defiant gestures still came naturally to him, the idea of voluntary martyrdom to the cause of saving a world held a certain attraction over and above his wholehearted desire to defend the Torisians.

And then he had started dating Kari, and things had gotten much more complicated.

He had not wanted to fall in love with Kari. It had never occurred to him that he might; he had dated plenty of women at the Academy who were far more beautiful than she as well as better suited to him in every way, and he'd had no interest in a permanent relationship with any one of them. That he should have grown to care so deeply for any woman, let alone a Youngling woman, was the biggest surprise of his life.

His mind told him that nothing could come of it, that it would be unfair to her to let anything come of it. His heart told him otherwise. When he was with her, he actually convinced himself that he might someday be free to marry her. When he kissed her, he was sure of it; only the fact that he was sworn kept him from acting on that assumption.

They often walked across the campus on their way home from the library, when the grass was damp and fragrant and the archaic streetlights shed pallid circles on the bricks beneath their feet, and the stars were only specks in the sky, deceptively faint and distant-seeming. Kari would look at him with a kind of wistfulness, expecting something he wanted desperately to give and yet must withhold without explanation, and he would find himself envying the men of Toris despite their narrow horizons and their despair and the all too real threat that hung over them.

So, gradually, the sacrifice had become no sacrifice at all, and Randil no longer knew whether he was capable of doing the sort of thing that had once seemed so magnificently heroic. Elana probably believed that he had set himself against his heritage for Kari's sake, and in a sense it was true, for Kari had become a symbol of all that was individual and appealing in her race, all that made Toris more than a cold entry in the Service's files of examples-to-be-studied. Which had come first? he wondered. Did he love her because he had needed a symbol?

It didn't matter anymore. Love couldn't be explained; it could only be felt, and what he had come to feel for Kari was too powerful to be analyzed away. Nor could his determination to help Toris be altered. Randil was committed, one way or another, and nothing Elana said or did was going to change that.

The most frightening aspect of what Randil had in mind was that it was workable; that is, the practical side of it was. He proposed that he and I should set out to shape public opinion, and we could do it. Any agent could; that's the prime reason for all the screening, all the testing, all the emphasis on dedication and self-sacrifice that accompanies investiture. A trained agent, armed with knowledge of mass psychology as well as of scientific discoveries centuries ahead of the local civilization's, could become a very eminent person indeed in a Youngling society. With telepathically enhanced charisma, we could become world leaders, even dictators, if we wanted to; so the Service takes extreme care to select people who will not want to.

Had Randil been susceptible to the temptations of power, he would never have gotten into the Academy. He wasn't; his aim was wholly unselfish. Nevertheless, it was in direct opposition to one of the most basic provisions of the Oath, second only to the ban on disclosure. We were sworn never to exert even the slightest influence on the development of a Youngling culture. Yet he planned to seek worldwide renown for his "farsighted" vision of this world's future! He was correct enough in thinking he could accomplish this within a comparatively short time; if he worked at it, he would have no difficulty getting himself acclaimed as a genius. People would listen to him, all right, and if he came out strongly in favor of a major push into space . . .

There were all sorts of alarming ramifications. The Neo-Statists were not interested in space; they were interested in conquering the Libertarians, a fact that Randil didn't fully appreciate. But so far it hadn't occurred to them that there might be a connection between the two. If a famous scientist were inadvertently to reveal the military potential of a space program, they would undoubtedly establish such a program at once, and other nations would follow suit.

Sometimes a space race works out very well. Quite often, in fact, it is a vital factor in motivating a species to develop space-based technology. But we had no guarantee that it would work for Toris. On how many of those devastated worlds had a powerful dictatorship *won* the race?

"Randil," I protested, "don't you see that we'd be playing with fire? If we started to meddle, we'd be manipulating the very forces we've come to learn about! Do you really believe we're so wise and noble that it's up to us to save the Torisians from themselves, that the odds would be better for them under our management than under nature's?"

"Nature is prodigal. In every species more young are born than survive to maturity, and by the same token a certain percentage of human races fail to survive. A percentage of Federation children would die, too, if we didn't use our knowledge of medicine to save them."

"Maybe so, but a doctor doesn't experiment on a patient who's likely to recover anyway!"

"He doesn't sit back and watch a patient die for lack of treatment, either. Elana, haven't you been watching the newscasts lately? Don't you know the situation is liable to explode any time now?"

I got nowhere with him, either on that first day or in any of our subsequent discussions. My refusal to join his effort really surprised Randil, I think. It's hard to convince someone that you're sincere when you happen to be on the side of the established policy.

The warning I gave him didn't help any. I knew it wouldn't; I knew he would think me either cowardly or self-righteous, or both; yet I felt honor bound to go through with it. *Randil,* I began one evening in the silence of the library, *you realize, don't you, that if you do anything overt, anything that another agent finds out about and considers harmful, you'll be stopped? Stopped by force, if necessary? The Service won't let you endanger this world.*

I know there's that risk, he affirmed. *You've never objected to risking your life among Younglings; is risking it by turning renegade so different?* He stared at me, suddenly grasping the full import of my statement. *Or by "the Service" do you mean yourself?*

I'm sworn, Randil, I answered wretchedly, knowing I

must make my position plain. I couldn't allow Randil to presume an alliance between us that I might later be forced to betray.

After that, Randil went ahead without my cooperation, though he had by no means given up the hope of eventually winning me over. He wrote not only the astonishingly mature term papers he had begun earlier, but also articles for submission under a pen name to both scholarly and popular magazines. They were printed. Naturally, Randil could turn out work far surpassing anything a Torisian student—or even a faculty member—could produce, once he dropped his cover to the extent of revealing his actual abilities. His articles attracted much attention, for they rang true. They ought to have! He made them very vivid through the simple expedient of "imagining" many colorful details about the potential benefits of space travel, as well as about the nature of the universe.

Before long he began to speak in public as well as to write, mainly at campus functions. He could not identify himself as the author of the published articles for fear of being found out by Varned or agents in other cities, so he was more circumspect in what he said; still, he made no attempt to hide his brilliance. The professors shook their heads in wonder. At the end of the term he was reclassified as a special student, with a fellowship and a teaching assistantship. To my dismay, Randil took over the Introductory Astronomy classes, and lecture attendance tripled. He taught quite a lot that was beyond the scope of the textbook.

Kari was ecstatic. He let her in on the secret of his writing career, giving fear of the government censors as the reason for his use of a pseudonym and cautioning her that she must mention it to no one but me. "I told you he was smarter than any man I've ever known before," she said excitedly the first time one of Randil's articles appeared in a major magazine. "Just read this, Elana! Isn't it wonderful?"

I read the article with cold shock. It might have been lifted from his own thesis on the Critical Stage, except that he had livened it up a bit. It was persuasive, all too persuasive. That it constituted unjustifiable intervention could not be doubted. But was it harmful enough to demand action on my part? No, I decided. I hadn't sufficient grounds for resorting to drastic measures . . . had I? In torment, I realized that I might never be capable of making a truly objective decision. Underneath, I knew that as long as Randil's actions were confined to what the Torisians would dismiss as theorizing, I would do nothing beyond trying to bring him to his senses.

For a while I had hopes that the government would indeed restrain him in some way, but the censors proved happy to encourage public interest in a subject that had no Libertarian overtones. Though the SSP could have learned his identity, I don't think they bothered, for Randil was very careful to steer clear of politics. When he wrote about the coming age of peaceful space exploration, he did not say that it would be a Neo-Statist age; however, since according to official dogma all glories of future ages would be brought about by the then victorious and worldwide State, it wasn't hard to put that interpretation on his "vision." No doubt the dictator's propagandists thought that he was doing them a service by taking people's minds off the grim problems of the present.

That he might truly be doing so was not inconceivable, and it was a possibility to which I devoted a good deal of worry. A dictatorship is an immature form of government; both Randil and I knew that, and we knew that if Toris got through its Critical Stage, individual liberties would eventually be restored throughout the world. But Randil seemed to be assuming that this fact meant the Neo-Statists' aims weren't really dangerous. He was acting as if the launching of a few spaceships would in itself lead to off-world colonies and thus solve all the problems at once. "If it were that easy," I argued, "Federation anthropologists would have had it figured out long ago. What more data would we need?" I failed to make any impression.

Kari's love and admiration for Randil expanded into near-worship; yet much of what he wrote was beyond her comprehension and she was too thoughtful a person to accept it uncritically, particularly since my efforts to draw her out had borne fruit. One evening when the three of us were sitting around the dinner table in our apartment, Kari and I having hoarded enough ration stamps to invite him for a home-cooked meal, she brought up one of his recent articles. "I just don't see how you can make a statement like this," she told him, holding out the page. "It sounds like something the Neo-Statists would say."

Randil read it aloud: "'War prior to a civilization's readiness for space travel is necessary to human survival, while war carried over into the era of potential space colonization is a serious threat to survival.' That's simple truth," he maintained. "You know I didn't mean it as an excuse for attacking the Libertarians."

I writhed inwardly. Kari knew, but I doubted

whether the general public did; it was that sort of thing—a complex idea taken out of the context of the Federation's perspective—that got his work past the censors. Randil didn't realize the extent to which Younglings can misinterpret concepts they aren't ready for.

"But you make it seem as if you approve of war!" Kari persisted. "I don't think anything so terrible as war could ever have a—a purpose."

"Everything is purposeful," I said gently. "Even the terrible things. But we don't understand them while they're happening. People die in wars, for instance, thinking it's for a very worthwhile cause, and then later it seems futile, as if nothing got accomplished after all. Yet it did, even if it wasn't what those people thought they were accomplishing."

"Humanity couldn't have made any progress without the incentives wars provided," Randil contended.

"Are you saying war isn't bad?" Kari demanded indignantly.

"No, of course not," I declared. "We're saying that the bad is as much a part of natural law as the good."

"If people had never fought one another, this world would have been overpopulated long before we'd matured enough to spread beyond it," added Randil.

Kari frowned. It wasn't often she disagreed with him, adoring him as she did; but we were getting into waters too deep for her, and we were of necessity oversimplifying. "I'm not sure we ought to spread beyond it," she said unhappily, "in spite of all the reasons you've been writing about. Shouldn't we learn to live in peace on this planet before we go looking for others to spoil?"

"That's a fatal idea!" Randil exclaimed. "We're ready to expand, and if we don't reach for space, we'll be in trouble. If a bottle is filled too full and corked too tightly, it's likely to explode."

I noticed that *we* came easily to Randil even when he was excited; he didn't have to watch his words as closely as I did, for much of the time he thought like a Torisian. "Randil is right," I told Kari. "There's only one way to avert war now, and that's to throw all our strength into something more constructive. We wouldn't spoil other planets in this solar system by settling there; they don't have life on them, after all—" I broke off, realizing that I had just let slip a fact not known on Toris. Anyway, I could hardly explain that the only potential harm connected with colonization—the occupation of *inhabited* worlds—is something from which most starfaring species refrain.

"How about conservation of this planet?" Kari persisted. "Isn't learning to control our population and save our resources the most important project of all?"

"That's necessary," I agreed, "but it's only a stopgap. As long as we're confined to a single planet where resources are finite, there will be people who fight over them. And even without fighting, they'd eventually be used up. Then it would be too late to build space colonies; we wouldn't have the means to establish them, and we'd be trapped forever on a world we've outgrown."

"More people would die from mass starvation and disease than would die now in a war," Randil added. That's true; there have been cases like that, worlds that lost their technology—even primitive space technology—because they waited too long to attempt colonization. The traces we find of extinct civilizations sometimes include orbiting debris. And who can say such an end, though far slower than a war of annihilation, is not as tragic?

Kari protested, "If population growth stopped completely, nobody would have to starve."

"But it couldn't," I told her, "because the biological imperative toward growth is stronger than human laws. And even if it could, that would lead to stagnation. No civilization can remain at a standstill; it must always be changing, moving on. Besides, you've seen what happens when the State tries to control things."

Shuddering, Kari admitted, "It would end up like the Neo-Statists' clockwork world. But if we expanded to other planets, wouldn't people just take their aggressive impulses along with them? Wouldn't we have worse wars than before?"

"Our so-called aggressive nature is simply the hardy spirit that had to be built into our species from the beginning," Randil said. "It's what drove past explorers, and what will make space exploration possible."

"There won't be any more large-scale wars once our need for risk is being met in a more constructive way," I explained.

"What do you mean, need for risk?" Kari asked. "People need security, not the opposite! I've been studying about that in my psychology class."

I hesitated. Torisian psychology, I knew, had a rather primitive conception of human needs; yet Kari of all people oughtn't to cling to the prevalent "security" notion. "Real security comes from proving yourself," I began. "The need for risk, for danger, is as deeply built into people as the need for love."

"Not in me, it isn't."

"No? You're human, Kari, and the need to take risks is what sets human beings apart from the animals, what makes it possible for us to advance. Without it, we'd still be living in caves."

"Frustration of that need is responsible for a lot of neuroses," Randil told her, "and on the social level it's a basic cause of warfare. We'll outgrow wars once we're facing the challenges beyond our home world, just as other races must have."

Kari laughed ruefully. "You're always so sure that we aren't the only inhabitants of the universe," she said. "What makes you believe the others are better than we? Couldn't it be wishful thinking, Randil?"

I came to his rescue, fearing that he might stumble into some too revealing remark. "Not better, just more mature," I said. "If they exist, it's logical that some must be further advanced than we are. Randil's point is that getting rid of war isn't a utopian dream; it's a natural part of evolution."

"What it boils down to," he affirmed, "is that war was necessary and unavoidable in the past; it forced us to develop the technology that can take us into space. Now that we've got that technology, though, to use it for war would be a perversion."

"We're at a turning point," I added. "There's great danger, but there's also hope, Kari. There's more hope than you may think, because if you look at it this way, you see that the fact that we couldn't stop war in the past doesn't necessarily have any bearing on the present."

"That's all very well for you to say, Elana," Kari protested. "You don't have any memories of the

Occupation. You didn't have to watch people get shot, hundreds of people, all dying for nothing—"

"No, not for nothing," I said with conviction. "For the future, a sort of future they couldn't begin to see."

"But suppose the world doesn't have one?"

Randil and I sensed each other's feelings, and our eyes met in anguish. "That's something none of us can see," I answered finally. "We're facing real peril, horribly real. A nuclear war could mean extinction of the human race! But so long as there is a future, everything that happens leads up to it; good comes out of the bad."

"Then should we just sit back and stop caring?" she objected. "Let the bad things happen without even trying to prevent them?"

"No! It doesn't work that way."

"Doesn't it?" said Randil dryly, silently adding, *You're the one who thinks we should do just that.*

I ignored him. Kari looked from one to the other of us, puzzled. "It's a paradox," I admitted. "Events themselves can't be labeled 'evil,' but people's actions can. Their motives can. To hate, for example—to fight and kill out of hatred—that's evil. Not to care is evil. If nobody cared, there'd be no channel for good left."

Randil declared pointedly, "I care. I care too much to be passive while this world gets closer and closer to the brink of all-out war."

"So do we all," Kari agreed. "But Randil, what choice do we have?"

"Some of us," he asserted, "have more choice than others." There was silence, for I didn't rise to the bait, and after a few minutes he moved his chair closer to Kari's and took her in his arms. "Don't worry over it, sweetheart," he said softly, smoothing her hair. "I get carried away. It's all terribly confusing, and I—I have ideas I can't explain. I shouldn't have said so much; I didn't mean to upset you—"

"We can't help being upset," I interrupted. "None of us can: you, or me, or Randil, or anyone who's bright enough to notice what's going on in the world. As for choices, we all have to make our own."

"How can individual people have any influence on what happens?" Kari questioned. "The Bomb exists, and sooner or later somebody is going to use it. What can we do?"

"You can't do anything, darling," Randil said, in an ill-advised attempt to be reassuring.

But you can? I challenged him. *You're so much higher than Kari that you're qualified to arrange her world's salvation?* Aloud I said, "Such things can't be foreseen. But if a choice about doing something is ever offered you, Kari, you'll know."

As the weeks passed, Randil went on writing, and I went on debating with him whenever I got a chance. We communicated silently in the library; when he picked Kari up or brought her home; and even through the closed doors of the hospital kitchen, while he was ostensibly waiting at the employees' entrance for a lunch date with her. Moreover, we sometimes met after I got off work for longer, vocal discussions, agonizingly aware that it was only a matter of time till Kari would find us out, yet willing to chance it because we each still believed that it was possible to convert the other.

To me, it became more and more evident that

Randil's sense of perspective was slipping away from him. Perhaps, I thought, my opposition was merely placing him on the defensive. He had become so strong an advocate of the Torisians, looked so thoroughly through their eyes, that he felt—as they did—that doom was almost certain. He also shared their belief that the world could be transformed overnight. What he had learned at the Academy about human evolution remained abstract theory to him; he could recite it, but he couldn't apply it. And what was worse, he misinterpreted the Torisian political situation. The conflict between the Neo-Statists and the Libertarians, being immature, struck him as meaningless; he had studied so many successfully resolved Critical Stages that he seemed to think the nations were squabbling over nothing.

"Look, Elana," he said to me during what proved to be our last clandestine meeting, "we know that the immediate causes of Youngling wars aren't the real causes. We know that Cold Wars in Critical Stage cultures are a natural and universal means of stimulating peoples' technology to the point where they can colonize space."

"Of course, but this Cold War could turn hot."

"Certainly it could. It's going to, if we don't step in. It'll happen by accident, though; the issues themselves aren't worth fighting over."

"Liberty is worth fighting for!" I protested. "Not with nuclear weapons, naturally; but the fact that a nuclear war wouldn't solve anything doesn't mean that Neo-Statist ideas aren't wrong and dangerous."

"Nobody really believes in the Neo-Statist regime," he asserted. "Nobody could! The only thing that gives it any momentum is the Torisians' underlying need to be challenged. If they could get pushed into space some other way, the dictatorship would just fold up."

"Randil, I don't think it's quite that simple."

We were sitting in a sidewalk café near the university's main gate, and the chill breeze off the river made me tremble despite the warmth of the hot drink I was sipping. Autumn was setting in, and dusk would soon be on us. Randil leaned forward, his face somber as he asked in an accusing tone, "You don't suppose any of the people on either side *want* war, do you?"

"Most of them don't," I replied. "But unfortunately they don't have anything to say about it. The Neo-Statist rulers don't give their people a voice in the matter, and the Libertarians must be ready to defend themselves. If they weren't, pretty soon those rulers would take over the whole world."

"I can't believe that even the dictator wants war," Randil maintained stubbornly.

"He doesn't want a war he can't win. If he thought he'd come out ahead, I'm afraid he'd be only too eager to make the first move."

"Not if his mind was on conquering space."

"But it wouldn't be," I said. "You're mixing up individual aims with the progress of a civilization as a whole, Randil. You're taking Critical Stage theory and trying to apply it to each and every person on this planet. Well, it just doesn't work like that. The dictator is what he is, and his aim is personal power. You've heard him speak on television, haven't you? How can you doubt what he's after?"

Randil frowned. "You're awfully cynical all of a sudden," he declared.

"No. I'm realistic. I've dealt with Younglings! On

Andrecia I was captured by two different sets of them, some less advanced than the Torisians and some more so. In the beginning I didn't believe they could deliberately hurt anyone, but I learned otherwise. They were ready to do anything they thought they could gain from."

He shook his head. "I see how that would color your thinking. Yet you know as well as any other agent that Younglings aren't evil; they're simply immature."

"That's true," I agreed, "they do bad things because of their immaturity—but they do them, all the same. You've got to remember, Randil, that Younglings haven't the benefit of your hindsight. They're motivated by immediate goals."

"So once I can get them to make space their goal—"

I sighed. "If they knew it would save them from extinction, they'd give it top priority," I admitted wearily, "but they don't know, and they aren't going to believe you when you tell them. If they were capable of looking that far ahead, they wouldn't have needed a Cold War in the first place. The theory of the Critical Stage would be groundless."

"I know one thing they'd believe," Randil muttered. "A practical demonstration."

"What do you mean by that?" I asked, with inward foreboding.

"Elana," he said slowly, "I wish there were a way for me to do more than tell them. I'm beginning to think you're right about one thing: The sort of influence I can exert won't do the trick. We're running out of time. I—well, I wish I could speed things up by providing them with a usable spaceship."

It was such an insane idea that at first I thought he

was joking. When I saw that he wasn't, I was too shaken to attack the major fallacies in it; I got off onto the lesser but more apparent ones.

"You can't teach them to build a spaceship," I said. "You're an anthropologist, not an engineer."

"I don't mean build one. I mean give them one of ours. Not a starship, of course; just a landing craft that would give them a head start on colonizing their own solar system."

Horrified, I exclaimed, "You're speaking of disclosure!"

"It wouldn't be disclosure, Elana."

"What else could you call it, if you were to hand over an unmistakably alien ship?"

"I'd tell them I was Jutan."

"That you were *what?*"

"Jutan. You know, the planet Juta, fifth from their sun."

"There isn't any intelligent life on Juta."

"They don't know that. They've been writing wild tales about life on Juta for years."

"But Randil, two humanoid races in one solar system? It's too incredible."

"They don't know that, either."

He had a point. Juta has a thick atmosphere that Torisian telescopes cannot penetrate. And the biologists of this world have no notion of the principles governing life in the universe; it would be all one to them if Jutans were humanoid, reptilian, or bright green dwarfs with two tails.

It is not disclosure unless Younglings learn that there's an interstellar civilization with which they can't hope to compete.

But they *would* learn. They would get to Juta within a few weeks and find no life there, so before long they'd be drawing the obvious conclusions. Initially, to be sure, they might think the unknown people from the stars their equals; yet in time their scientists couldn't fail to recognize a Federation landing craft as the product of a technology vastly superior to that of Toris. They would know simply from the fact that its principles of operation would remain totally incomprehensible to them.

I don't know why I wasted time arguing these points with Randil, since there was no way for either of us to get hold of a landing craft anyway; we were dependent—fortunately, I felt—on pickup initiated by Varned or by someone else in contact with the starship. So I shouldn't have let practical considerations sidetrack me. That there were serious flaws in Randil's conception of the Critical Stage I could see from his mere suggestion of such a scheme, and I should have spent our precious remaining minutes pointing them out.

Unfortunately, though, I was not only sidetracked but deeply disturbed; by the time the bells in the campus clock tower chimed the hour, telling us that Kari's late lab session was over and that Randil had only a few moments before she would be looking for him, I was seething with indignation as well. Hadn't I enough difficulties on Toris without having to cope with the misconceived notions of a fellow agent?

"It's impossible," he acknowledged regretfully as he got up to go. "But I think a ship could save them, and I'm afraid they have too little time left to develop their own. If I could get my hands on one, nothing could stop me from turning it over."

"And just who do you think you are?" I demanded bitterly. "The Holy Prophet? Is that the role in which you've cast yourself? You'd fit it nicely; it's said in their sacred writings, you know, that the Prophet is to appear out of the sky and give them advanced powers."

Randil recoiled from me, stricken. "Elana, don't!" he said vehemently. "I've been to Devotions with Kari, and I've heard the Prophecy; it's taken seriously. It's their religion, not mere legend—what you're saying is blasphemy."

"I agree," I said. "That was my point. You want to arrange the destiny of a whole world, personally sway its people in the direction you think they should go— well, that's more than blasphemy, Randil. It comes awfully close to setting yourself up as God."

He was furious, of course—he refused to communicate after that evening—and I can't say I blame him. It was an unforgivable thing for me to say; the element of truth in it made it all the more cruel. I don't usually lash out at people that way. But I was incensed, too, and what's more, I was desperate. I knew underneath that Randil's line of thought would ultimately lead to tragedy of some sort and that when it did, the fault would be partly mine. Yet I couldn't admit it. I couldn't bring myself to act. When Varned came again, I thought, I would shift the whole burden into his capable hands. I knew that if he failed to convince Randil, he would have him immediately recalled, but I also knew I could trust the Service's handling of the affair. Randil would be judged by his motives. He would be taught a few lessons, no doubt, but he would not be punished.

I expected Varned soon. The carnival might not return until summer, but he would contact us before that, for our next reports couldn't be allowed to wait much longer. I was right; a large advertisement appeared in the newspaper one day, bearing Varned's picture. His fame had grown as a fortune-teller and also as a magician; he was to give several performances in a local theater, and its box office was setting up appointments for private consultations as well. Jubilant with relief, I got tickets in advance for myself and for Kari. Varned had helped her before, and this time, I hoped, he would somehow manage to prepare her for the grief she must face at Randil's departure.

Then, on the evening when the show was to open, the government announced that all members of minority races were "enemies of the State" and would henceforth be sent to concentration camps.

I had seen it coming. Public reaction against the dictatorship was growing, and the campaign to deflect this resentment onto the Libertarians hadn't been too successful. The citizens of Cerne were basically Libertarian in outlook; having had a free press until the Occupation, they were aware of certain truths that no amount of propaganda could distort. They did not automatically hate everybody on the other side of the world. It was inevitable that the Neo-Statist officials would look for a more immediate outlet for the city's smoldering discontent.

There had been race riots, seemingly spontaneous but in fact skillfully engineered. The people were in a mood to riot, and it was merely a matter of applied psychology to get them fighting against each other instead of against the police state that was the true object of their wrath. Then, after everyone was sick of the fighting, it was a still simpler matter to fix the blame. Though few approved of concentration camps, I'm very much afraid that there were those who believed that as long as the SSP was busy rounding up minority groups it would spend less time ferreting out the secret "guilt" of political dissenters.

Varned must have seen it coming also, but he could scarcely have known what he was walking into when he timed his visit to Cerne. I realized that he must have arrived in the city shortly before the proclamation was issued and that he might already have been arrested. If he hadn't been, his only chance of escape would be to use the route by which Randil had entered: the river. He could not keep his appointments or show himself in public, so there was little chance of our making contact, either at this time or ever again. If anyone was to call a halt to Randil's activism, it would have to be me. Yet I had done all I could by way of persuasion; Randil would no longer even listen.

There was still an avenue open to me. Because Randil and I had been communicating, we were technically a team. In every team one member is designated as the Senior Agent, whom the others, while in the field, are bound by the Oath to obey. Since no appointment had been made in this case, I had both the right and the duty to assume that position. I had been sworn longer than Randil. The seniority was unquestionably mine; the fact that in the normal course of events I would need at least ten years' experience to qualify for a place as Senior did not matter.

But it was a step I shrank from, a last resort that I would turn to only in a true emergency. For the Senior bears the responsibility. If he or she fails to order that which the Oath clearly demands, he is no less forsworn than if he actively breaks it; and if a team member brings harm to Younglings, the Senior is equally answerable. I knew that once I accepted such responsibility—once I gave Randil a direct order to abandon his attempts at intervention—I would be obliged, by fair means or foul, to enforce it.

f i v e

It is the little things that get you down, even more
than the major ones you are geared to withstand —
a fact that my interrogator is well aware of. When
I returned to my cell this evening and found that the
guards had covered the window, I almost lost control
for a while. I suppose their spy camera showed how
often I stood on the bunk to look out. And they have
other subtle cruelties. I was horribly sick again last
night, and it was not, I'm afraid, by accident. I have no
doubt that my food is sometimes drugged, yet I know
better than to let myself fall victim to their scheme for
weakening me through my own choice. If they wanted
to starve me, they could do it much more easily by
direct means; their aim is to destroy my confidence by
making me afraid to eat anything at all. No, thanks! It
may be foolproof as far as their laboratory animals are
concerned, but it won't work on a person who can see
through it.

Holding out is a matter of how you look at things, really. There's a lot more to it than psychic powers; some of the techniques that help me most could be used just as well by Younglings, if only they knew how. But they don't, and it's awfully sad. When I was first brought here, I was left for some hours in an anteroom where there were other prisoners waiting to be questioned. They were, I suppose, underground resistance workers, although there may have been innocent citizens among them and perhaps a few actual Libertarian agents. And they were for the most part woefully ill-prepared for what they were about to encounter.

Oh, they were brave. They were willing to endure pain and knew, in a vague sort of way, that they would probably have to. But they were unbelievably ignorant of the types of pressure likely to be applied. I suspect that many of them had avoided such knowledge—which I'm sure must be available, even in Libertarian countries—and if they had refused to face the mere information, they certainly hadn't much chance when confronted by the actuality. Half the battle was lost right there. The other half was lost through the fact that these people had no notion that there is any means of defense.

"No one can resist brainwashing," one of them said to me. (He undoubtedly thought that I, being young and seemingly innocent, was in need of that sort of comfort.) "It's no disgrace to break, because when it happens you won't have anything to say about it. The mind can be controlled by scientific conditioning just as surely as a computer can be programmed." My interrogator himself couldn't have put it better! And so the poor man was defeated from the beginning, because underneath he already believed the basic idea they would try to push him into accepting: that he was a mere cog in a machine called "society" and that his mind was subject to control by outside influences. He was as sure as they were that there is no power in the individual mind. If a person isn't aware of his own inner freedom, how can he stick by a commitment to political freedom? The two go together, after all.

The man I speak of was called for interrogation shortly after our conversation, and I broke the rules; I tried to contact him telepathically, for I could not bear the grim hopelessness of his defiance, a defiance more like that of a cornered animal than of a free human being. He did not know how to respond to me. I suppose he'll crack eventually, not from lack of courage or stamina, but simply from the weight of his misconceptions.

I don't mean to imply, of course, that anyone can hold out against anything. It's not nearly so simple, because there is always the question of what you're holding out for. If the pressure is extreme, you can't buck it unless you've got an awfully valid reason. I have such a reason. I'm not holding out for the sake of pride, or even of the Oath, but simply because the Neo-Statists are ready to use the Bomb, and right now I'm all that's stopping them.

Randil felt only despair when he learned of Varned's impending arrival, for he had counted on not being contacted by anyone from the starship before he had won Elana over to his side. He did not, of course, intend to tell Varned of his activities.

Originally he had assumed that she wouldn't tell either, and that since his articles had been published under a pseudonym he would therefore be safe. By now he knew better. Elana was adamant; there no longer seemed to be any possibility of converting her, and she appeared quite sincere in her belief that his intervention was not serving the best interests of Toris. Despondently, he admitted to himself that without her cooperation there was little chance for his plan to succeed. Once other agents were alerted, he would have to flee the city, and it would then be almost impossible to sway public opinion without attracting the attention of the secret police, not to mention the Service, which would be much harder to elude.

Since it was essential for him to see Varned before Elana did, he made the first appointment available for a "fortune-telling" consultation, as well as a date with Kari for later the same evening. He knew it might be the last date he would have with her. As he realized that, he also realized that the choice he had feared had been made without conscious deliberation. The alternative to flight hadn't even entered his mind. If he were to speak freely to Varned and agree to attempt no further action, would he be allowed to stay in Cerne? Maybe, but he could not do that. His love for Kari was inextricably entwined with his determination to save her world from war. He might fail; he probably would fail; but it would be self-defeating to gain a little more time with her by abandoning his sole hope of preventing her death in a nuclear holocaust.

When he presented himself at the theater, Varned greeted him warmly, and Randil, fortified by the self-discipline in which his Service training had schooled him, began an impassive telepathic report that gave no hint of his true feelings. He was halfway through it when a costumed magician's assistant, shaken with fright, interrupted them. "Master," the man quavered, "forgive the intrusion, but there's been news—"

It was chilling news, an edict proclaiming the imminent arrest of all whose racial coloring resembled Varned's. Not only were the innocent to be interned for an indefinite period, but "known criminals," it seemed, were to be shot without trial.

Varned took it calmly. "I will finish this interview," he said. "Leave us."

"But Master—"

"Leave us! Cancel the rest of my appointments and tonight's performance." Gently and with a reassuring smile, he added, "Don't worry about me, my friend. I don't fear the police."

The assistant retreated, giving Varned a look of worshipful awe, and Randil perceived that not only was he devoted to his "master" but that very probably he credited him with truly supernatural powers. Perhaps he thought the magician could vanish, as indeed he could once he reached the river. It wouldn't be easy to swim past the guards unaided by a breathing unit, but Randil had no doubt that it could be managed; he had considered trying it himself. Inwardly, he confessed that he had felt joy when he'd heard that Varned must go instead. It meant reprieve! Varned would not see Elana, nor would he be able to return to Cerne in the future.

You got into the city from the east by water, Varned communicated swiftly. *Will you be able to get out on the west side, the downstream side, without breathing apparatus?*

Randil, aghast, was afraid he had given his thoughts away until he took in the urgency behind Varned's question. *Me?* he responded. *Yes, I think so, but why? You're the one who's got to escape. And you've got to hurry; they know you're performing here tonight, and they'll come for you.*

They've already come for me, Randil. All the exits to this building are blocked. Grimly he responded to Randil's unexpressed shock. *I'm more clairvoyant than most people; I've just scanned. Besides, in my case it was to be expected. My race is simply a convenient excuse. I wouldn't be surprised to know they'd purposely withheld the announcement until they had me trapped.*

What are you going to do, then? Randil asked in dismay. His personal relief didn't extend to a desire to have Varned fall into real danger; it hadn't occurred to him that that might happen.

The only thing that can be done, Varned informed him. *Randil, you've inherited a rough job. I've got a report that's too valuable to be lost, a collection of the latest data from half a dozen agents. Your being here means we can get it to the starship.*

But surely you won't be in any concentration camp for long; the Service will find some way to rescue you.

Levelly, Varned declared, *I'll never reach a concentration camp. They'll have me before a firing squad before the night's out. "Known criminals will be shot," remember?*

Randil stared at him, horrified. *You're not a criminal! Not even by their standards.*

I'm a potential danger to them, though. This cover role has been excellent in some ways, but it's forced me to reveal too much of myself; I'm too good at winning people's trust. You saw the way my assistant looked at me. That man would die for me, literally, and so would others; I've acquired a following. The dictatorship can't afford to keep me alive as a rallying point.

You—you're just going to let them shoot you? What about the Shield?

Face facts, Randil! Varned reproved him. *Using the Shield would mean disclosure.* Less sharply he continued, *These things happen. You know that. If there's a way out, I'll find it, but we've got to proceed under the assumption that there isn't. Now, stop railing against what can't be helped and "record" my report.*

Reluctantly, Randil obeyed. The concentration demanded left him no chance to dwell on the remorse he felt over having been glad, at first, about the edict; there was little time to spare, and the mind-to-mind transfer was performed at a speed much greater than that to which he was accustomed. At the end he remained seated, his head resting in his clasped hands, not wanting to meet Varned's eyes. Enraged though he had been at the older man's unbending adherence to policy, he had never wished him any harm. He had underrated Varned's sincerity, perhaps. No one could speak matter-of-factly of firing squads who didn't honestly believe that his cause was a worthy one.

Randil was torn in two. He could not imagine himself failing to pass on the information for which Varned had gambled his life; yet if he accepted pickup, what would happen to the plan? Didn't the welfare of Toris come first? It was that to which he was sworn. Personal loyalty to other agents, however brave they might be, was a secondary consideration. And how could he leave Kari for any reason other than to save her?

Randil, take this! Varned commanded, extending his

hand. In its palm lay a ring, an intricately carved gold ring with a huge amber stone. He had, Randil remembered, worn it at their former interviews as well as during this one, presumably as part of his fortune-teller's costume. *Hurry! Hide it before someone comes. It's your link to the starship, your signaling device.*

To request pickup? Randil was surprised, for the ring looked too small to contain a communicator; in any case, he had assumed the time and place of pickup to be prearranged. The Service wouldn't risk letting any type of communicator fall into Torisian hands.

Varned explained: *There are unmanned landing craft in orbit, enough so that there's always one within range. Swim out, go into the hills where you won't be disturbed, and call a ship down under automatic control. You do it psychokinetically, by closing the gap between two tiny wires embedded in the stone.* At the wordless level of telepathy, he imparted specific instructions.

Exultantly, Randil closed his fingers over the ring, with difficulty suppressing the emotions swelling inside him. They were so overwhelming that he felt Varned must surely sense them. This unlooked-for granting of his deepest wish left him dizzy with wonder. It was incredible; a ring that to a Youngling would be no more unique than the rest of the jewelry agents had pawned, and yet through two microscopic wires — wires that could be manipulated only through psychokinesis — it had the power to summon a landing craft! An *unmanned* landing craft! The impossible scheme had become a reality.

There was the tramp of heavy boots in the hallway; the door burst open, revealing men in the sinister black uniforms of the SSP. His back to them, Varned addressed Randil formally. "Only a shadow of the future can be foreseen," he said aloud. "If I have shown you dark things, remember that darkness is the precursor of all light. It can serve unexpected ends, sometimes."

A speech characteristic of a fortune-teller's cryptic prophecies, Randil thought dazedly, but still quite true. Hadn't Varned, unknowingly, been foretelling the result of his own arrest? Fate was watching out for Toris after all; that it should work at Varned's expense was simply the way life was. Varned wasn't afraid. If he didn't mind sacrificing his life merely to collect data, he would unquestionably be even more willing to do so in order that this world might be saved. The irony of it was that he would never understand. He was so blinded by Service tradition that he wouldn't believe a Federation ship could help the Torisians any more than Elana did; but then, Elana herself had told Kari that terrible things could be purposeful, purposeful even when the people involved weren't aware of the real ends served, and Varned's words proved that he agreed.

Read the report into the recorder you'll find in the ship, Varned ordered silently. *Then send it back into orbit, with the ring inside.*

Randil didn't respond, for he had no intention of returning the landing craft to orbit. He had a much more urgent use for that ship.

Putting it to such use would, he knew, mean giving up Kari, just when he was free to stay with her and to go on with the original plan. If he posed as a Jutan, he would have to disappear before Juta was found to be uninhabited; he would never see her again.

But she would be safe. Her world would be safe. The ship would save Toris once and for all.

The police grasped Varned's arms, and, unresisting, he went with them. From beyond the door his thought was clear and strong: *Good luck, Randil.*

Good luck to you, Randil answered fervidly. *Yet if it comes to the worst, Varned, I swear I won't let it happen in vain.*

Varned's execution was announced on the evening newscast, which I watched alone in the apartment, Kari being out with Randil at the time. I was thankful that she was not present, for I could control neither my horror nor my grief. And she too would have been stricken, for the report included pictures of the "criminals" who had been shot; she would have recognized Varned as the amazingly perceptive fortune-teller who had once given her hope.

She would not, of course, have realized what it had meant for Varned to face a firing squad. She would not have known that he had posssesed the power to save himself, which he had consciously set aside. We of the Federation are protected by the Shield: a semiautomatic psychic defense that is as effective against a bullet as against any other physical injury. An agent is forbidden to use the Shield under circumstances that would result in disclosure.

I had been aware of the likelihood of his arrest, but I had not guessed that they would kill him without so much as a trumped-up charge. My tears didn't subside quickly. After a while I remembered that the people aboard the starship, who were monitoring all telecasts, would have gathered for the formal rite of tribute and farewell; I whispered its ritual phrases softly to myself, aching to reach out telepathically toward someone who could feel for Varned as I felt. But the distance was too great, even under the stress of sorrow. There was no contact, nor would there be in the foreseeable future, except with Randil.

The impact of that suddenly hit me—it was now beyond question that I would have to deal with the problem of Randil alone.

Eventually, someone would take Varned's place. I would be given the opportunity to report. But there was no telling how long it would take for another agent to establish cover that would permit free access to various cities as well as a means of communication with the starship. Varned, I knew, must have had such a means; otherwise all the data we had collected would have been lost with him. Such a chance would not have been taken, for it had been known from the beginning that his position was at best precarious.

Meanwhile, Randil's efforts might upset the delicate balance of the Critical Stage. I was on my own; I could no longer put off a decision about curbing them. And as it turned out, I didn't get any chance to delay.

I was lying on my bed when Kari and Randil got back; I heard them come in and started to turn up the volume of the radio, for the living room walls were thin and I did not want to eavesdrop. To my surprise, however, Randil's thought reached me almost immediately, though on previous occasions he had waited until he had bid Kari goodnight and was outside in the hallway. *Elana?*

I'm here.

Elana, I was with Varned tonight when they took him. He

recounted what had happened and then, frankly, told me what he planned to do with the landing craft he had been empowered to summon.

Numb with dismay, I protested, *Randil, no! You mustn't!*

We've argued this all out before. I know you don't agree.

You don't understand why! We were interrupted before we'd finished discussing it; but Randil, it would do serious damage—

I don't expect you to approve, he broke in. *Still, I owe you advance notice. You'll find out anyway when it's announced, and besides, I—I want you to give some sort of explanation to Kari. I can't see her again, you know. Not after I convince the authorities that I'm Jutan.*

His calm statement floored me. I hadn't thought he had it in him; I had suspected that his desire for Kari and for action to help Toris went hand in hand. I had been wrong. Whatever Randil's underlying motives might be, they weren't selfish ones. That he should give up not only the Service, Federation citizenship, and the freedom of the universe, but also his hope of marriage—well, his belief in the rightness of what he proposed had to be pretty sincere. It was heartbreaking. It made what I had to do all the harder, yet I knew I couldn't hesitate. There was no more time for argument; I must take firm steps.

Ruthlessly suppressing my compassion for him, I declared, *I won't allow this, Randil.*

What do you mean, you won't allow it? It's not your decision.

Yes, it is. I assert my authority as Senior. We've communicated, which makes us a team; I order you to carry out Varned's instructions. What's more, I order you to go back to the starship in that landing craft instead of returning to Cerne.

He was too astonished to be angry. *You're not serious!*

I wish I didn't have to be. Legally, though, I'm Senior Agent whether I want the job or not.

Maybe so, Randil conceded, *but that doesn't mean I'll take your orders.*

Under the Oath you're obliged to.

I'm obliged to do what I think is right, he insisted. *I'm already forsworn in the technical sense. Do you suppose I'll give any more weight to the pledge of obedience than to the others I've violated?*

No, I admitted, *I don't. That's not the point, Randil.*

Then what is? Are you playing it safe in case you're ever called to account? I've been mistaken about you, Elana; I wouldn't have thought you so eager to protect yourself.

I'm not protecting myself. I'm protecting this planet. Do I have to spell it out for you? You say you have to do what you think is right; well, I do, too. I wouldn't claim authority I didn't intend to use, and you know perfectly well that a Senior is bound to enforce orders that affect the welfare of Younglings.

Enforce them? You can't keep me from turning that ship over to the Torisians!

Miserably I answered, *I can if I have to. Don't make me, Randil, please don't!*

Don't make you what? Nothing you could do would stop me, short of— He broke off, incredulous. *Elana, are you threatening me?*

Not threatening, warning. That's why I went through the formality of giving you a direct and legal order.

He didn't respond at first, but finally he told me: *I take back what I said; I wasn't mistaken about you. You've got backbone enough if you mean what I think you mean, and you must really believe that helping the Torisians into space could*

cause harm. But I don't. I believe that it's the lesser of two evils.
I guess we both have to follow our own consciences, so good-bye,
Elana.

Wait, Randil! I cried. *You've never let me explain the*
harm —

I heard him speak softly to Kari, and then there
was a long silence during which he shut me out completely. After that the hall door closed, and, moments
later, curfew sounded. Kari burst into the bedroom,
flustered, her eyes big with fear. "He'll be arrested!"
she moaned. "Oh, Elana, we—we forgot to watch the
time. It hasn't happened before; we've been so careful.
But tonight he held me without saying a word, and his
mind was—well, off somewhere, until all at once he began kissing me as if he never expected to see me again."

"Kari," I said steadily, "don't be afraid for Randil.
No matter what happens, he wouldn't want you to be
afraid. He isn't, himself, you know."

"Do you see it, too?" she asked. "I guess you would,
just from talking to him. He's different from other people: strong, sure of himself, as if he knew some wonderful secret that makes all the horrible things easier to
bear. But you're like that, yourself! It's funny, you and
Randil are quite a bit alike in lots of ways."

"Maybe we are," I agreed. "Maybe we have a good
deal in common. And yet his closest bond is with you.
He loves you, Kari. Never forget that he loves you, and
that through his love you share all the strength and
surety that is his. If he should ever be in trouble, you
would owe it to him to live up to that."

It was the only warning I could devise, though I
was aware that the three of us were about to face a
more harrowing trial than she had yet pictured. She

didn't dream that Randil was involved in anything more serious than curfew-breaking, aside from the secret Libertarian sympathies we all shared. That the future of her whole planet had come to rest in his hands and in mine was something she could never be allowed to know; and though I would have given much to spare her pain, the planet's safety had to come first.

Randil's attempts to sway the Torisians toward space travel had been bad enough; unwise, I believed, but not positively damaging. For him to give them a Federation ship was something else entirely. When he had talked of it before, I hadn't been too worried, for I had assumed he would never get the opportunity to take such a step. I had not gotten around to presenting the main arguments against it; we had discussed nothing beyond the possibility of eventual disclosure. Although that in itself was enough to throw their evolution out of kilter, it was not the most immediate danger.

In his study of Critical Stage cultures, Randil had taken a broad view based on hindsight; he had read histories of Federation races that subsequently spread beyond their mother worlds. He had, apparently, failed to grasp the time span involved in the initial breakout. Merely traveling into space didn't put an end to their wars, obvious though it is that those wars weren't apocalyptic ones—and we even know that some devastated worlds had space programs. There is often a long period when it's touch-and-go as to whether a spacefaring civilization will move beyond occasional excursions into orbit. Had he forgotten entirely that some species die from resource depletion without ever progressing to colonization? Or did he assume that because a ship of ours—unlike the earliest ships that could be built on Toris—would be fast and reliable enough to support a permanent base on Juta, a major colonization effort was sure to follow?

There were no grounds for such an assumption! After all, the key to triggering that effort was exactly what we had come to find. And there was a still deadlier peril.

A ship of advanced design would have tremendous impact on the Torisians whether or not they ever guessed its true origin. It was likely enough that they would turn their attention to space, and by Randil's reasoning, they should therefore pass out of the Critical Stage wherein, according to the Federation's experience, lie the only threats to a technological species' survival. But they would bypass a great deal. The landing craft could reach the orbit of Juta in seventeen days. At that rate it wouldn't take them very long to explore their solar system or even, if they did so choose, to colonize it, for they could duplicate the ship without fully understanding the scientific principles that had led to such a spacecraft's invention. And what then? They were not ready for the stars. What could be gleaned from study of the landing craft was as far from the stardrive as their first steam engine had been from that spaceship itself; there was no chance of premature contact with other races. The danger was that they would have no reachable goal left to strive for.

He was giving them a fascinating toy. But what would happen when they got tired of playing with it? Like overprivileged children in machine-oriented societies who have been given factory-made model planes instead of materials to build their own, might not the

Torisians, who should be learning to build, learn instead to smash and destroy?

Randil maintained that peoples who have colonized space never turn to full-scale war. And that's true, in the natural sequence of things. They have no need to. The exploration and settlement of their own solar systems with primitive rockets is challenge enough. He had read that developing such a capability is crucial, yet he had missed the biggest implication. The Torisians would not have developed anything; they would simply have crossed space in a borrowed ship. The venture would not even have involved much risk.

The people of Toris wouldn't be safe from a war of annihilation if they conquered space that way. They would be less safe than at present, deprived of the challenge for which the Cold War was preparing them! They would take their wars into space with them; there would be interplanetary combat, a thing that has not occurred in any solar system that has ever been studied. No matter how much they wanted peace, they would be drawn into war whenever their need for risk was not being fulfilled otherwise; the need for a Cause, a Cause that involves peril and hardship and drama that can stir the imagination of society, an exciting Cause in which every person can share. Even we of the Federation have such a need; were we not beginning to look toward other galaxies—galaxies where we may encounter forms of intelligent life totally different from the humanoid ones we've so far found—we too would face extinction, if not from a revival of war, then from decadence.

Normally, the colonization of space is a slow, gradual process. It does far more than provide resources and room for expansion; it absorbs a people's creative skills, its energy, its courage—all its finest qualities, which if perverted can become its worst ones. How could Randil not see? The Torisians needed to make the effort not in spite of the fact that it would be difficult, but because of that fact. If it was easy, it would lose its power to save them; they would remain in the Critical Stage forever, until they destroyed themselves.

Without question, Randil was about to plunge Toris out of the frying pan and into the fire, a fire that would be the hottest and most uncontrollable that had ever engulfed a human race because it would result from artificial disruption of evolutionary laws. By handing that ship to the Torisians, he would be setting in motion forces that would kill them just as surely as if he had planted a time bomb in the heart of their sun.

I could not let that happen.

The responsibility was mine. It had been mine all along, even before I had acknowledged it by assuming the authority of Senior Agent. I had known that Randil was treading on dangerous ground, yet I had taken no action; I had been unable to face the prospect of what action would mean: for him, for Kari, and for myself. But if in sure knowledge of his present intent I let him carry it through, what happened to the people of this world would be as much my fault as his—more, even, since I knew the consequences and he did not. I was sworn. There was only one course compatible with my Oath to hold the welfare of Toris above all other considerations.

I had given him fair warning. I had told him that I could stop him, and there was a simple means of doing so. It took all night for me to muster the courage. But in the morning, after an agonizingly cheerful conversation with Kari on our way to the hospital, I took leave of her at the kitchen entrance as usual, watched her disappear into the elevator, and turned resolutely back into the street. I walked six blocks in blind, sick misery. Then, steeling myself to the enormity of the betrayal, I strode into SSP headquarters and denounced Randil to the secret police.

The secret police give a warm reception to informers. It was not hard to concoct a story calculated to arouse suspicion against Randil. It wasn't at all difficult to implant the suggestion that his passport should be checked, nor did it take much imagination to guess what would happen when they discovered it to be a forgery. Randil would get no opportunity to do any more meddling.

And as for me, I would have to go home and live with Kari.

He would not suffer if he was tortured; like me, he had been trained in psychic defense. But Kari didn't know that. She would know, in time, of his arrest. She was aware of what arrest by the SSP usually means.

Imprisonment would be a grueling ordeal for Randil despite his defensive powers, not only in itself but because of his sincere though erroneous belief that the intervention from which he was barred could save Toris. He would be equal to that ordeal. He would be equal to the situation Varned had faced, if it came to that; and I could not deny that it might. If it did, I would find it no more a torment to live with Kari than with myself.

"You are a good citizen," the officer behind the desk declared condescendingly. "Your patriotism will not go unrewarded."

I kept my face impassive, but inwardly I was seething. If they offered me money, I thought, I would be utterly incapable of faking the appropriate satisfaction.

The man spoke into his telephone, then turned back to me. "There will be a few more questions," he said. "If you will come this way, please."

For the first time it occurred to me that the police might recheck my own passport. The idea didn't disturb me; I almost hoped they would.

I was told to wait in a small, rather luxurious office. I sat stiffly in a leather-upholstered chair; there was a painting on the wall opposite, upon which I fixed my attention, but I cannot say what it looked like. The hour I spent there was one of the worst of my life, not excepting the interrogations I have since undergone.

Another officer entered, to whom I was required to repeat my story. At the end of it he frowned. "You were right to come to us with your suspicions of this man," he said slowly. "Your vigilance is appreciated. In this particular case, however, there are certain complications. It would be best if you did not speak of the incident."

"As you wish, sir," I assented, wondering what his motive could be. Usually the dictatorship was only too happy to proclaim the apprehension of a suspected "people's enemy."

"It so happens," he went on, "that we already know about the man of whom you speak. It's quite true that he is not what he has pretended to be."

I recoiled with shock. What could they know?

How? They might conceivably have traced the authorship of his articles, but that seemed unlikely since his work had never been censored or disapproved.

The officer continued smugly, "He is actually an undercover agent who has done the People's State a great service. I'm sure you understand that I am not at liberty to give you the details; but you need have no fear of his being a traitor. Rather, through him our cause against the Libertarian imperialists has been immeasurably advanced."

Aghast, I realized that such a statement could mean just one thing. I was too late! The overnight delay, the hours I had spent in anguished indecision, had been seized by Randil as his one and only chance. He had anticipated what I would do, and had already turned the ship over to the local authorities.

Though my effort to hide my reaction wasn't successful, it was misinterpreted. "Have no fear," the officer repeated. "There will be no reprisals against you; had the man been what he seemed, you would have received the credit for uncovering his crimes. But take care never to speak of him to anyone." As an afterthought he added, "You will not see him again. He has been taken into custody for his own protection, since it would be most unfortunate if he were to fall into the hands of the Libertarians."

My alarm grew. If they held him until they reached Juta, he would never be able to come up with a credible story; disclosure would be not only inevitable but immediate. "Why do you tell me this?" I asked boldly, knowing that I must get all the information I could. "If I were so inclined, I could let the Libertarians know whom to look for."

He laughed. "Do you think I'm unaware of your background? You are an amnesiac, and you've been under surveillance ever since you arrived in this city. You have no contacts among Libertarian sympathizers, and as you obviously did not come here to sell what you knew, it's unlikely that you would put a price on your silence. But I'm taking no risk. The man is beyond reach, as is the secret weapon of which he has knowledge. As for the Libertarians, their days are numbered. We will obliterate them! We've said so before and they scoffed, but by this time next week they'll believe us, if there are any left alive."

Dizziness struck me, and I was afraid I would be sick right there in front of him. Secret weapon? They had the ship, and they were keeping it secret; they would first use it not to explore space but against the Libertarians! Even I had not seen that—I, who had tried so hard to convince Randil that they were bent on conquest. I had been so intent on the long-range perils that I had overlooked the obvious short-range one.

A Service landing craft is swift, silent, and readily maneuverable. It can cross continents in mere minutes; it can ascend and descend vertically, with incredible speed and with no visible means of propulsion. It is shielded not only against damage but against detection, and cannot be tracked by any radar network on Toris. How many cities could it wipe out on a single mission? There was no precedent, the Federation never having used one for any such purpose; but the number might well be limited only by the number of nuclear bombs the Neo-Statists could cram in.

"You are free to go," the officer was saying to me. "Hail the glory of the State, citizen."

"Hail the glory of the State," I replied mechanically. Had the words been in my own language instead of a Youngling one, I would have choked on them. I turned and left the building with no plans, no purpose, only an aimless, wretched sense of despair. *By this time next week.* Would the Libertarians retaliate? Probably, yet that wouldn't deter a dictator with a vastly superior striking force. The power to retaliate creates a balance that can stave off disaster, but our presence had upset that balance, and there was no way it could be restored. The civilization of Toris was doomed.

For a moment I was so incensed against Randil that I very nearly stopped hating myself for having denounced him, but my rage softened as I pictured the agony he must be experiencing. I couldn't feel that he deserved it; Randil's judgment was tragically poor, but he had honestly tried to bring peace to Toris. The knowledge that he had instead brought more war was a heavier punishment than should be wished on anyone.

And then I realized that he didn't know. They would not have told him. If they had believed his story—as they must have—that he had come in peace from the planet Juta, they would not reveal their plans in his presence. For he would have said that his purpose was to unite both worlds in pursuit of a common goal, and they would play along with that, using him to teach them about the ship while deceiving him as to their true intent. He would not guess it. His identification with the Torisians worked both ways: Not only did he feel himself one of them, but he assumed they thought as he did. Evil was an abstraction to Randil; he was blind to its power over the minds of Younglings.

I crossed the street, so absorbed in my bitterness that a car almost grazed me, and then walked along the cement esplanade beside the river. The noonday sun shone on the water and on the boats that plied up- and downstream. On the opposite shore I could see a tree-lined park where a few children, too young for school, dabbled in the shallows under the watchful eye of an old woman. Those children would never grow up, I thought hopelessly. The fatalism of people like Kari had been only too accurate. But it might not have been, if we had never come to Toris. How could the Service dare to visit Youngling worlds if all its wisdom, all its dedication, all the safeguards of its Oath still weren't enough to keep two well-meaning but fallible agents from loosing the nightmare of a nuclear holocaust?

Leaning against the iron railing that bordered the river, I looked down at the brownish waves lapping against the embankment. *Oh, Randil, Randil!* I cried silently, throwing every bit of my energy and emotion into the most desperate telepathic appeal I had ever attempted. But it was no use. Wherever they had him, it was too far. And he did not know! He was out there somewhere, downriver, probably, showing them how to work the controls of that ship; whereas if he knew, he would surely have destroyed it.

I drew in my breath, startled by the thought. The ship could be destroyed. It could be vaporized from the starship, by remote control, which would already have been done if the Service knew it to be in the possession of Younglings; Randil must have disabled the signaling mechanism by which its location could be pinpointed. But there was another method. A landing craft is equipped with a built-in destruct device, and every agent is taught to operate it, for there are times when its use is the only possible means of preventing a disclosure. You do not need to be inside the ship to set off the explosion; it can be done psychokinetically, from a short distance away.

My responsibility suddenly became clear. Randil did not know the situation. I could not contact him, and, because of my solo status, Varned and Meleny had kept me from knowing what other agents were on Toris. I had no alternative but to get within range of that landing craft somehow and destroy it myself. The damage caused by Randil's misjudgment and my own weak-willed procrastination could not be undone in any other way.

The idea sickened me; it went against my most deep-seated instincts, and I could scarcely force myself to think it through. I would not be dangerously close to the ship when it blew up, but others would. There were undoubtedly guards, technicians, scientists studying its design—perhaps even Randil himself. Destruction of the landing craft could not fail to result in the deaths of innocent people.

To Younglings, accustomed as they are to lightly tossing away people's lives—in worthy causes and some not so worthy—that fact might not seem so appalling. And in a sense I saw it more objectively than they. I had studied Youngling wars, both those of Toris and those of countless other worlds, and I understood that though innocent people do die, it is unavoidable and natural. I had told Kari that the people killed in the Occupation had not died in vain, and I had meant it. But those people had not died through any act of mine.

We of the Federation do not kill. We are not casual

about human life. The Service eschews violence, and
agents are at all times unarmed. We gamble our own
lives, yes, and sacrifice them if necessary; but we do not
intentionally take those of others. I did not see how I,
personally, could ever go through with such a thing.

Yet if there should be nuclear war, those men
would die anyway. For me to kill them would be
wrong, but not to do so would be a greater wrong. The
fate of a whole planet against the premature death of a
few of its people—what other choice had I? When the
question was put that way, the demands of the Oath
were unquestionable. To pledge that you will value the
best interests of a world above everything else means
that if you must, to save that world, you will sacrifice
whatever it is that one loses by committing an act as
terrible as premeditated killing.

I knew that I would lose something. I knew that I
would not be quite the same person after it was over.
But, staring into the murky depths of the river, I also
knew that I was going to plunge into it that night and
swim downstream, as Randil undoubtedly had, to find
the ship.

The remaining daylight hours were inter-
minable. I didn't go back to the hospital, and
though I knew Kari would be frantic when I didn't
show up at the apartment either, there was just nothing
I could tell her that would not be worse than my failure
to appear. Randil, of course, had made no more dates
with her; it would be a day or two before she became
aware of the fact that he was also missing. By that time
either I would be back to help her face what she must,

or I would have disappeared permanently—and in the latter case Kari might not have long to worry about anything.

I was aware that my chances were slight. There was no way out of Cerne save by the river, and I did not know the river patrol system as Randil did. Meleny had doubted whether even he could manage it without breathing apparatus; although knowing that he had obviously done so when leaving the city was encouraging, it was no true assurance that I would be equally successful. And supposing that I did get past the guards safely, what then? Would I be able to reach the ship?

The one hope was that Randil had not gone too far from the river before summoning the landing craft. There was a fairly good possibility that he hadn't. He had not wanted to conceal it, so he would have had no reason to go off into the hills as Varned would have. And since the military authorities who had taken charge were aiming at secrecy, they would be more likely to camouflage the ship than to attempt to move it prematurely and in broad daylight. Wherever it was, though, it was undoubtedly well guarded. My ability to approach within psychokinetic range would depend on the available cover, the presence of floodlights, and all sorts of unpredictable variables.

And then, of course, there was the very questionable issue of whether I could ever swim upstream, back into the city. That was a minor consideration, to be sure, but for Kari's sake I hoped it would be possible even if I failed to destroy the ship; and if I didn't fail, it would be my job to resume my observation duties. The risks of the return would be still greater than those of the trip out, however.

I did not allow myself to think of the truly central problem, the moment when I would actually come to the point of setting off an explosion in which unsuspecting people would die before my eyes.

It would have been useful to take the River Street bus to the city limits, where I could have gotten a look at the guard setup at the bridge that marked the outer bounds of legal traffic; but I did not dare. I had been told that I was under surveillance, and while it probably hadn't been close surveillance so far, I might well be followed for the next few days. My failure to go back to work after my interview with the police would be dismissed as simple laziness, but any trip to Cerne's outskirts could arouse suspicion.

So I did my best to act like a typical kitchen worker guiltily snatching a rare and unexpected opportunity to loaf. I crossed the river by ferry in order to reach the park, which was the only place in the downtown area where I would have free access to the water. There I stretched out on the grass, letting the sun warm me, and forced myself to perform the mental exercises through which I had been taught to relax under stress. I would need rest, I knew, if I was to get through the coming night's ordeal, for the previous night had been sleepless.

I would also need food to keep my strength up, though despite having skipped both breakfast and lunch I had little appetite after my hours of self-imposed relaxation. I entered a nearly empty café across from the park and determinedly downed a nourishing but tasteless meal. For a while I was afraid that it was not going to stay down, but fortunately it did.

There was still some time to wait before it would be

dark enough to try the swim. Next door was a tawdry cinema; I went in and sat through two showings of a film that I cannot even remember the name of. It had few patrons, none of whom seemed to be watching me, but I kept track to be sure that everyone who had arrived soon after me left before I did. When I came out again, I went directly to the narrow strip of beach. It was deserted; since curfew had not yet sounded, no patrolmen were on duty. Hesitation would merely increase the risk. I took off my shoes, tying their laces around my belt so that I need not abandon them, and waded into the current.

The water was dirty and ill-smelling, and much colder than I had expected. It felt horrible. As quickly and as quietly as possible I got out into the deep channel and plunged under. I had no idea of the distance I would have to swim, and I knew that I must find out how well I could hold my breath before approaching the patrolled area.

Breathing exercises are a useful form of discipline, an aid in learning to bring automatic processes—both physical and mental—under voluntary control; they have sometimes been used as such even by Younglings. I had developed a fair amount of skill early in my training, but as a means to an end, not in anticipation of putting it to practical use. And part of the trick lies in slowing your bodily functions so that you won't need so much air; you cannot do that and swim at the same time. The current, to be sure, was with me; I could never have fought it. Just the same, I found that although I could stay down far longer than any Torisian could have, it might not be long enough to get me past that guarded bridge.

I did not have time to worry, for all too soon it was upon me. It was a drawbridge, and from some distance away, the last time I had dared surface, I had seen that it stood open. I dove deeper and kept going until I was scarcely conscious, ignoring the ache of my lungs. But it was no use. I could not go without breathing any longer, not while expending the energy to swim. Yet the water above me was illuminated by floodlights; if I came up for air, I would surely be seen, and escapees were invariably shot without ceremony.

Then, with sudden elation, I realized how stupid I had been. It would not matter! Of course the guards would see me, and of course they would shoot; but against those shots it would be permissible to use the Shield. They would never know that their bullets hadn't injured me; on the contrary, when I went down again, they would assume that I was dead. Randil, perhaps, had resorted to just such a ploy, though he couldn't have done so while entering the city for fear they would make the connection when he was caught getting out of the water.

Use of the Shield requires no effort; the thing that demands self-control is *not* using it. I simply relaxed, let myself feel the natural fear of being shot at that would activate my psychic protection, and rose to the surface. Drawing deep, steady breaths, I waited. It didn't take long. The beam of a powerful spotlight fell across my body, supplementing the floods, and shots were fired from both banks. One was a direct—although harmless—hit. I dove, my lungs well filled, and all was quiet.

After that it was easy. I swam a long way past the floodlit sector of the river before needing to breathe again, and from there on I stayed above water. Over my shoulder I could see the glow of Cerne brightening the sky. Ahead was blackness; but far to the right, on the north bank, sparkled a brilliant cluster of lights.

When I was opposite it, I clambered ashore, untied my shoes from my belt, and slipped into them. Being waterlogged, they were heavier than ever and squished uncomfortably as I walked. As I approached the lights, I could see that they were focused on a tall sheet-metal fence, obviously hastily constructed, beyond which I could not hope to penetrate. But rising above the barricade was a huge, shapeless mass covered with a tent-like canopy. It was about the right size for one of the spherical landing craft I was familiar with; there could be little doubt that I had found what I was looking for.

At the sight of it, I knew that relieved though I was, there was a part of me that was inwardly sorry.

The countryside surrounding Cerne is largely bare of trees, but scattered thickets bordered the river; I was able to get close enough to the fence to do what must be done without exposing myself. Guards patrolled its circumference, and there were a good many of them at the gate. As I watched, a car pulled up to join those already parked nearby. Five or six men got out; they were not all in uniform, and some, I guessed, might be distinguished scientists eager to grasp the unbelievable opportunity they had been offered to examine the product of a technology surpassing their own. And they would die! I thought in anguish. Why couldn't they have come ten minutes later?

Some Torisian scientists, even the tools of the dictatorship, had a deep and sincere interest in the universe beyond their planet. Through such people alone could the vital space program be initiated. Was the damage irreversible? In warding off an immediate nuclear attack, might I not be killing one of the men destined to play a key role in bringing Toris's Critical Stage to a close?

I couldn't know. The Service would never know. From this point on, if a nuclear war did occur, we could never be sure that our actions hadn't caused it.

I sank to my knees, exhausted and shivering, my soggy clothes clinging to my skin. The bushes that concealed me offered no protection from the raw wind. *Randil?* I called silently. It was quite possible that Randil was inside the enclosure, and if he was, I must warn him. He might be able to send the ship back into orbit. If not, perhaps on some pretext he could get everyone out, or at least save himself; but failing that, he must be given the chance to take the initiative. The sacrifice of an agent's life is always fully voluntary, except in the rare case where only an imposed decision can prevent serious harm to a Youngling world.

Randil? I repeated. *Randil, are you there?* I got no answer; still I knew he might "hear" and yet withhold response. So I went on to summarize the situation, not omitting a frank statement of how I had come by my knowledge. *Randil,* I concluded resolutely, *if you can't get that landing craft away from here, we've got to vaporize it. You see, don't you? Will you do it, or shall I?*

He was not in there. I couldn't believe that he would choose to evade such a choice, for whatever his failings, Randil was no coward. Probably, they had given him comfortable accommodations elsewhere; believing him an envoy from another planet, they would treat him with respect, though they wouldn't let him out of their sight.

I couldn't delay any longer. My nerve wasn't increasing, and besides, still another car might arrive soon. Shutting out all distractions, I closed my eyes and visualized the ship, attempting to initiate a process for which I had been specifically trained. But my mind was not ready; I got nowhere.

Psychokinesis, like all psychic powers, is enhanced by emotion; to accomplish it over this distance, a very strong emotional impetus would be required. I felt plenty of emotion, all right. The trouble was that my feelings were conflicting ones. Psychic control depends upon absolute sureness. It's impossible to use your powers in a way that you believe wrong unless you happen to be a psychopath with no conscience at all.

Realizing that, I felt a flash of comfort. To throw all the force of my mind to destruction would be painful, but I need not fear it, for I could not carry the thing through unless I honestly thought it to be the lesser evil confronting me. The really unethical course would be to hide from the issue, refuse to face it squarely; if I did that, I would be abdicating my responsibility not only as an agent but as a human being.

I faced it. I imagined that ship rising from the riverbank, speeding out over oceans and landmasses, descending noiselessly upon city after city of the nations that had rejected the dictator's rule. I imagined the fiery cloud pillars; the irreclaimable land; the millions who would die in the blasts and the rest who would die slowly, in pain, and without hope of any future for humanity . . . and the emotion was magnified in me, and the sureness came.

The psychokinetic force to be exerted was slight: simply a matter of throwing one small switch hidden beneath a protective panel on the landing craft's control board. The complications arose not only from the distance involved but from the fact that I couldn't see what I was doing. My talent for clairvoyance is small, and I knew I could not expect it to be of much use at this range. I had been taught the position of the switch, however. I could picture it clearly. I had, in practice sessions, handled a dummy switch successfully under comparable conditions.

So when after repeated tries the ship did not vaporize, I knew there was something wrong.

Was I too far away? No, I had been still farther during some of the training sessions, and my emotions were much stronger than they had been then. I *had* to destroy that ship—I had to! If I didn't, it would destroy Toris: if not immediately, then surely through prolongation of the Critical Stage, as I had known before even hearing of its imminent use for delivering nuclear bombs. There was no doubt left in me at all. Nor was there any debilitating doubt of my own mental power; I had received too rigorous a course of psychic conditioning for that.

The switch itself was not operative. There could be no other explanation for my failure.

None of the men guarding the ship could have tampered with that switch; it was well hidden, and they would not have known what it was for. Despairingly, I realized that Randil had again anticipated me. He had guessed that I or some other agent would eventually do just what I had done; without knowing the urgency, he had taken no chances on someone's considering the potential for disclosure too great. He had disconnected the destruct switch at the same time as he had disabled the device that would have allowed the landing craft to be located by the starship. Perhaps he would have done so anyway, simply as a precaution in case the Torisians ever found it and decided to experiment.

I was defeated; I could not repair the circuits without getting inside the ship, and that I could never manage. There were just too many guards.

As for my next move, I had learned that to swim upstream would be impossible, considering the strength of the current, even if I were not so tired. Moreover, I could not use the trick of surfacing again. The guards would be suspicious, having failed to recover my body, and if I were seen a second time, they would use boats. Even if I evaded them, they would be watching the riverbanks within the city; people entering illegally were assumed to be spies and were therefore investigated more thoroughly than mere escapees. It didn't much matter whether I went back, I supposed, the outlook for the future being what it was. Still, I would have liked to comfort Kari . . .

I sprawled on the ground there in the dark thicket, heedless of the cold and of the muddiness of my wet clothing, and I sobbed. I really don't know how long I sobbed. To have nerved myself to the thing and then to fail with such flat finality—it was a crushing letdown. And what would become of me? I could not go on with my original job. I could hide in the hills, probably, and survive; I might get far enough from Cerne to survive a retaliatory nuclear attack. If the fallout level didn't get too high, I might live for a long time. It was conceivable that I would be rescued, since other agents would eventually try to find me. In the event that Cerne itself escaped attack, they might help me reenter—for they had undoubtedly learned to forge travel permits by now—so that I could observe the last throes of a planet's dying civilization.

That too, I thought bitterly, was an opportunity the Service had not previously been given.

The night passed. Finally, when stars began to fade in the east, I became aware that I must go somewhere. The undergrowth was too sparse to hide me in daylight; otherwise I would have had hopes of waiting around for Randil's return. If I could ever make contact with him, convince him of the peril, then certainly he would find a way to reconnect the destruct device; but it was unrealistic to think that I could wait without being seized.

Was there any hope at all, I wondered, of Randil's catching on? Would the men in authority give themselves away? The possibility was slim, yet in theory it existed. The possibility that the starship would locate its missing landing craft existed, too. Given time . . . if only there were more time! If only there were some way to stall off the attack!

Then suddenly it occurred to me that there might be.

The idea hit me abruptly, breathtakingly, and I began trembling less with cold than with excitement and also, I must admit, with fright. In that moment I knew what I had to do. It was the only feasible stalling action; still, it was a wild, fantastic gamble, and what was more, the better it worked the worse off I would be. I would need all my resources of wit and self-discipline, not to mention fortitude. But with the stakes so high, wouldn't the tiniest chance of success be worth trying for?

Leaving the cover of the thicket, I started toward the fenced enclosure. The dim light of predawn was sufficient for me to be seen, though colors weren't yet discernible, and I could only hope that the sentries hadn't been ordered to shoot without warning. It would mean sure disclosure to use the Shield at close range; resolutely, I made the mental adjustment to drop it and walked forward unprotected. The men grouped at the gate trained their guns on me but did not fire. I went right up to them, and, calmly, I asked for Randil by name.

Sheer audacity can work wonders sometimes. They were so stunned that for a minute I thought they might actually let me in, eliminating the necessity for my elaborate alternate scheme. But they recovered before I had managed even a glimpse inside the gate, so I resigned myself to the still bolder tactics that I had planned. I had no illusions about what I was getting into. Yet the hoax had its comic aspects; had my opponents been less formidable, I would have been amused by the thought that I could deceive them best by telling them the literal truth.

"If Randil isn't here," I told the officer of the guard, "I'll wait for him in the ship. He's expecting me."

They all stared, appalled, because naturally no one without top-secret clearance was supposed to know that there was any ship. Within seconds they had converged on me. The secret police are not noted for chivalry. I must have been a sorry sight in my soaked and mud-splattered kitchen aide's uniform, but I was a worse one after I had been subjected to the thoroughgoing search that is their standard procedure. When it was over, one of the younger and less hardened men tossed me a drab raincoat, which was at least voluminous and dry.

Meanwhile, since regular telephones hadn't been installed yet, the officer had been busy on his car phone; nobody in the SSP ever makes a decision without orders from above. He approached me, scowling. "I know who you are," he declared. "You visited headquarters yesterday; you put on a good show of denouncing a man whose true identity you must already have known. Why?"

"You tell me," I suggested insolently.

"All right. You came after information. You were somehow able to interpret statements that you could not have interpreted if you were what we originally thought. You're no amnesiac; you are an enemy of the People's State! And you are undoubtedly in league with others."

"I needed no information about this ship," I announced in as scornful a tone as I could affect. "Right now I know more about it than you will ever learn. I'm aware, for instance, that there is an explosive device in it, a bomb that can be set off soon or that will, in any case, prevent it from ever reaching its first target—"

He gripped my arm with brutal force. "You are lying! There could have been no sabotage."

"Suit yourself," I said, inwardly satisfied. My assertion being true, I had backed it telepathically, and I knew he was hooked. "In any case, you are not likely to find the device. If you were, I wouldn't have told you; but as the matter stands, it seemed only fair to warn you, considering that as chief of security here you'll bear the blame."

That struck home; from his emotions I sensed that

his laugh was merely an attempt to save face in the presence of his subordinates. "If it exists, we'll find it," he assured me, "because you will show us where it is. You are stupid, like all Libertarian conspirators; by your arrogance you've condemned yourself."

"Nothing I've said can prevent the bomb from exploding," I maintained, "and as for myself, I was already condemned. I'm obviously not going to succeed in eliminating the Jutan and your top scientists along with the ship, and since I've blown my cover by trying, there'd be little point in playing innocent."

"You're a cool one," he admitted. "But you'll lose your coolness. You will tell us everything within your first day of interrogation."

"Don't think you can scare me with threats," I retorted, hoping that in my effort to sound fearless I wasn't overdoing the melodrama. "After all, if I'd accomplished what I came here to do, I'd have been dead half an hour ago."

"I am not threatening you with death," he said ominously.

I was well aware of what he was threatening, and I can't deny that I felt a surge of terror, wondering if I had overestimated my own stamina. My mouth went dry, for even a trace of self-doubt could be disastrous. There is no guarantee attached to psychic defenses, no matter how thorough your training; if you panic, you lose them.

They handcuffed me and shoved me into a car. As we drove back along the dirt road that paralleled the river, I watched the sun rise, spreading streamers of reddish gold over the multitoothed skyline of Cerne. The guards pressed close on either side of me in forbidding silence. At the checkpoint we paused only briefly, and long before reaching the city's central district we turned off onto a street that plunged underground for several blocks. Beneath the raincoat my skin turned to gooseflesh. I had passed through what was popularly spoken of as the Tunnel of No Return, for on emerging we halted, as I had known we would, before the grim brick facade of the SSP's newest and most dreaded prison.

s i x

Well, there it is. That's how I got here; I tried to crash the gate, they believe, and they arrested me. I knew they would; I knew there wasn't one chance in ten thousand of my getting inside—but they don't know that I knew it.

And that's my scheme, my frantic, last-ditch maneuver to forestall them. I came right out and admitted that I had been attempting to destroy the ship; I even boasted about it. I implied that the plot was a lot more complicated than it was, that it involved other people, their own people, and that it had at least partially succeeded. And they fell for my claims.

So now, since they won't find anyone else involved, they won't dare use that ship until they break me.

It's not that they wouldn't risk their own men on a mission that might be booby-trapped, but simply that the ship is so important to them that they can't take any chances with it at all. In their view it's their one-and-only providential opportunity to conquer the world in one decisive blow, and they're willing to wait a little while to make absolutely sure that they aren't jeopardizing that opportunity. They do not expect to wait long. Everybody breaks if enough pressure is applied; that is a basic tenet of their faith.

There are two kinds of brainwashing, that designed to convert the victim and that meant merely to extract information, and while they naturally prefer to accomplish both at the same time, in my case conversion is secondary. They want the information, and they want it now—or rather, they wanted it some days ago—so they don't really care whether or not I repent of my sins and embrace their political system. Oh, they go through all the standard indoctrination speeches; that's automatic with them, they could not turn it off if they tried, and perhaps they think it'll throw me off guard. But mainly they are trying to get a confession. A full confession, of course, not merely my signature on the text they have written out for me. They've got to have the details about the bomb. That's to my advantage, because it means they have to keep me in shape to remember the details and communicate them.

They've assigned their top man to me: Commander Feric. He has never had a failure. He is neither uncivilized nor sadistic, but rather a professional man who is sincerely interested in his work. He considers it highly valuable work, not at all degrading. To be sure, he doesn't resort to having me beaten up or anything that crude. People who respond to that sort of handling never get anywhere near Commander Feric's office; he simply doesn't bother with them.

By now, Commander Feric has learned a little about

what he's up against, and he is, I believe, impressed. Though I told him he couldn't hurt me, he didn't think I meant it literally! And he still doesn't think so; he can't, for he has no notion that there are such things as psychic defenses. He must be very puzzled indeed. But he is a long way from giving up, particularly now that his personal self-image is involved. I feel sorry for him, in a way, because he has built his whole life around the philosophy that force always wins, and when in the end I disprove it, he will be cast adrift.

It's not strictly true, of course, that he can't hurt me, since there are certain conditions under which I would have to let him. Those conditions haven't arisen yet, both because he dares not risk my life and because after I do talk, which he's still convinced I will, the government wants a public trial for propaganda purposes. I wouldn't be surprised if they were planning to televise it. It's too bad we'll never reach that stage; it would be a nice way of informing the starship where I am.

From the beginning, Commander Feric and I have been more or less frank with each other. By the time we met, I had already been subjected to the usual sort of grilling by less prominent interrogators, and it was an accepted fact that I was neither naive, stupid, nor easily intimidated. "Let's not beat around the bush," he said at our first interview. "It's my job to secure your cooperation, and I'll get it, one way or another, as we both know. What's already established may as well be acknowledged. You're an admitted saboteur, and we're aware that you are not with the Resistance but are instead a Libertarian agent—"

"I am not a Libertarian agent," I interrupted. After all, I wasn't, and unless I consistently denied it the

Libertarians would be blamed for the nonexistent sabotage plot. Probably, they would be anyway, but the slightest trace of evidence, such as my taped concession of the point, might lead to retaliations that could trigger war.

"Why do you lie to me?" he demanded. "It can't help you, since you'll be executed in either case—and we have proof. Your passport is a blatant forgery. There is no record of either you or your parents in the city you claim as your birthplace. I must say, it was a clumsy job; your people's intelligence agencies are usually more adroit."

I said nothing. They had been bound to find out about the passport, and from their standpoint only lack of efficiency had prevented it from being unmasked sooner. Those men who interviewed me in the hospital and failed to follow through are now, I suppose, in a labor camp; among Younglings, there must always be a scapegoat.

"You yourself, however," my interrogator went on, "are far from dull-witted. Anybody able to fool the entire staff of a major hospital with a fake illness and fake amnesia is very bright indeed. I'll grant that, and I shall not waste my time telling you that you are nobody and nothing; you would not be taken in. Let me use a less orthodox approach: You are important. You are so important that we will spare no trouble, no resource, in getting what we want from you. And you are bright enough to know what that will entail."

That was where I made my little speech about how the human mind can't be forced, more out of pride and bravado, I suppose, than for any legitimate reason. Commander Feric simply laughed. "I've acknowledged your intelligence," he said, "so the least you can do is to credit me with as much. Young though you seem, you're obviously no amateur. You've shown neither surprise nor shock at anything that's happened to you, and that means you've had training. It's not possible that you're unaware of the fact that we *will* force you, and that the only question concerns how long it will take."

"Longer than you have to devote to it, anyway," I murmured.

He glared at me, for the first time slightly nonplussed. "I could threaten to punish you for your insolence," he said thoughtfully, "but it would be an empty threat since there are no punishments worse than those you'll receive anyway. You know that, I suppose. Oh, well, I'll not stand on formalities. Perhaps it will be more entertaining for us both if I let you say what you please."

It was, which was why I kept up with it. I didn't have to make any replies at all; I could have just sat there, and he could have made no meaningful threat then, either. But, knowing that I was in for a good many grueling hours of questioning, I decided to make a game of it: I decided to tell the closest to the absolute truth that I could without actually giving away any secrets, even to the extent of being completely frank about my methods of defense. The Commander thought that I was simply whistling in the dark, but he found it difficult to keep the discussion moving in the direction that he was used to.

Finally, after getting nowhere with the "soft" approach, in which he insinuated that anyone as bright as I would do well to sell out her friends and perhaps receive not only a pardon but a lucrative position as an agent of his own organization, he got down to business. "Look, Elana," he told me. "I like you. I admire your spirit. Don't force me to turn you into a vegetable! You are resigned to death, I'm sure, but you still have your pride. I can break that pride, if I have to, but how much better it will be for you to die with it intact—" He broke off, watching my face. "All right. It would not be intact if you confessed voluntarily. But you'll confess eventually—you know it, and I know it—and all I'm saying is, don't wait too long. Don't wait till we've destroyed your mind. The freedom of that mind is evidently of importance to you, the very thing you're holding out for."

"If you destroyed my mind," I reminded him, "you would not get much information from it."

"You know all the answers. You know, then, that we won't use the slow, sure method, the method that would bring you around to our way of thinking. A hundred days or so of treatment, the appropriate drugs, and you would no longer have the same set of values. You would beg for the chance to help us in any way you could; it would no longer seem a self-betrayal." He sighed and, pressing a buzzer on his desk, continued, "It would be far less painful, in the long run. But unfortunately we must proceed more quickly than that."

Guards appeared; I was strapped firmly into my chair, which was equipped to pick up my heartbeat, respiration rate, and the like, displaying them on a scope before my interrogator. During this preparation he talked on in a vein designed, obviously, to unnerve me. "Pain has been used to compel obedience since the beginning of history," he said conversationally. "There were, however, undesirable side effects. There were limits to intensity and duration; the subject, if brave enough, sometimes expired before being persuaded to cooperate. Perhaps that's what you are counting on. If so, you will be disappointed, for recently we have developed a method that does not have such disadvantages."

"Yes, I know," I commented, and at my smile it was he who was unnerved. I forced myself to relax while the guards attached electrodes to various points on my body, reminding myself that the shiver of fear spreading through me was necessary and good.

Commander Feric met my eyes. "This machine may look simple," he went on, "but don't let its appearance fool you. It is capable of producing the most severe pain the human body can feel, since it stimulates the nerves directly. Yet it inflicts no injury. Tomorrow, the next day, as many days as this takes—each morning we start afresh. We could keep it up indefinitely without weakening your body in any way." He paused and added significantly, "The mind, of course, is less durable."

Which just goes to show how little Younglings know about things.

That first time he used the machine on me, I was a bit apprehensive, not having actually met such a thing under field conditions before. I could not shield myself from the electric current, for if I did his instruments wouldn't register properly; I would have to deal with the pain itself. Still, I had no real doubt of my ability to do so. During the course of an Academy education we're prepared for any eventuality, prepared in the same way as we're trained to use the rest of our psychic powers: through experience.

That's not as terrible as it sounds. The experience isn't fun, but it isn't awfully bad, either; not nearly so bad as it would seem if I were to describe it. It is given in a way that is absolutely harmless, and you have plenty of moral support—telepathic support, even, in the early stages while that's needed. What's more, by the time you come to it, you have learned that the experiences provided for you invariably turn out well, so you are not really afraid.

And it does turn out well. It gives you a tremendous lift because you learn things you never suspected about the powers of your mind. You are not asked to be stoic; you're taught that you don't need to be, that you don't need to suffer at all. You can feel pain and not *mind*. The feeling is indescribable, like the difference between knowing how to use psychokinesis and not knowing. But once you have it, you never lose it. Before I took the training, I heard all sorts of scare stories that made me wonder whether it would be worth going through. It wasn't till afterward that I realized the comments had all come from people who hadn't yet undergone it rather than those who had.

There's a difference, of course, between being safe in the hands of sympathetic instructors and being at the mercy of an interrogator who is out to break you. But actually that difference works to your advantage. The biggest problem in the training is that after the early stages you tend not to be frightened enough, and your instructors work hard to overcome that, because a certain amount of fear is good for you; it's what enables your mind to perform effectively. Fear and panic, however, are two different things. If you panic, you lose control and suffer. I was on the edge a couple of times during that first interrogation session; it was not an episode I would care to repeat.

Needless to say, Commander Feric thinks I am absolutely phenomenal. I've had to act some; otherwise he would be convinced that his machine wasn't working. He did call in technicians to check it, that first day, and he also called in a psychiatrist to verify that I was not in a hypnotic trance. Now I scream (convincingly, I hope) when we reach the high points. I can tell when they come, for I do feel and discriminate; it's simply that I'm emotionally detached from the physical sensations. They just don't bother me. The Commander has never before met anyone whom it does not bother. He knows in his heart that it would bother *him,* so he finds the whole business most upsetting.

I have met the psychiatrist, Dr. Sturn, on several other occasions. It is his aim to analyze me in order to find out my hidden terrors. This game, too, I play voluntarily (they could hardly force me, any more than they can force me to do anything else) because I'm sure that I am learning more from it than he is. I have drawn the line at describing my childhood for him, since I don't know quite enough about Toris to invent a good one. But other than that, I answer his questions honestly, and he is very confused.

Take the ink blot test. Well, what one of those blots looked like to me was a certain reptilian creature from the tenth planet of the star Zentha, and I was trying to think of a better answer, because naturally I couldn't say *that*—when suddenly I thought, Why not? So I said it, and Dr. Sturn turned purple. Commander Feric laughed; I don't believe there's much love lost between those two. "I told you, Sturn," he said somewhat triumphantly, "that you would not get typical responses."

Not all of the tests are so amusing, for my captors are searching for ways to horrify me, and they know what is likely to horrify the average person. Some of what I've been exposed to has been distasteful, but hardly shocking in the sense that they mean to shock me, because that kind of shock depends on the ways you have been made to feel guilty as a child; besides which, it's largely culture-dependent, and an agent who has studied the customs of many worlds has a certain objectivity in such matters. A lot of it is just plain ridiculous. For instance, most Torisians have strong taboos regarding particular words in their language. I don't mean merely that such words are considered rude by polite society—which they un-questionably are—but people get highly emotional over them. Well, when these words started to show up on the word-association tests Dr. Sturn gave me, I didn't recognize them, because I had encountered them neither in the broadcasts we had monitored nor in my reading. So my outward reaction was just what he expected: I froze and said nothing; but he frowned and shook his head over my pulse and respiration rates, which weren't showing any change at all. When I finally caught on to what sort of words they were, I burst out laughing at the idea that he thought he could gain any power over me through such a silly trifle.

I'm making resistance sound too easy, perhaps. Matching wits with them may be a game, and handling the pain an exciting challenge, but in between come hunger and cold and loneliness. I am not allowed much sleep; what little I do get is restful only because my mind is able to shut out distractions. And there are various other discomforts that I shall not dwell on, not all of which can be dismissed so easily.

And of course, there are the drugs. The slow-acting ones I throw off—Meleny herself, after all, had to hypnotize me to keep my subconscious defenses from throwing off the illness she wanted me to have—but it's a strain, and I don't ever feel well. Besides, I have to fake the effects to some extent, and that means letting myself feel those effects long enough to determine what sort of stuff I've been given. It varies from day to day, but I've learned that whenever I begin to feel more tense or anxious or depressed than usual, it's a safe bet that the drugs have something to do with it.

But none of these ordeals endanger my secrets. If I have to endure them, I can. My only real fear is that the Neo-Statists will get tired of waiting and will chance using the ship.

They are not to that point yet, though. They think I'm part of a major operation, the uncovering of which has top priority. "One thing is sure," Commander Feric said on the phone this morning, "whatever organization is behind her, it's a big one; and they certainly trained her thoroughly."

And with that, I had to agree!

I have just survived a truly harrowing experience. Commander Feric tried a new technique on me, something calculated to unhinge me completely. The results weren't quite what he was expecting. During the course of it, though, I didn't know what was going to happen, and I must confess that he had me pretty scared.

He has finally conceded that he isn't going to get anywhere with his pain machine. "Don't delude yourself," he told me. "If I gave you enough, at maximum intensity, uninterrupted—well, it would take some time, no doubt, but despite your abnormally high threshold, you'd eventually go to pieces. Unfortunately, you would then be unreachable, incapable of remembering your own name, much less those of your fellow conspirators. So we must approach this from a different angle."

The angle that he went on to discuss did not sound encouraging. "I've never used this method before," he admitted. "It is highly experimental, and as you're already aware, I don't want to destroy your mind. Dr. Sturn believes that the risk is within acceptable limits, but we must remember that the doctor is more interested in compiling test results than in redeeming enemies of the State. He assures me that in a matter of hours he can safely accomplish what would require many weeks of conventional treatment. If so, he may revolutionize this department; but if he's wrong, he'll be held accountable. I warned him. All the same, he is willing to proceed, and since time is of the essence, I have decided to take the chance."

I wondered how much of that was sheer fabrication aimed at undermining my nerve. Commander Feric's frankness can be very disarming, which is the secret of his success in his profession. He rarely contradicts himself with telepathic overtones; for when he says something, he really believes it, at least while he's talking.

"We do not have the necessary facilities in this

building," he informed me. "You will therefore be taken
elsewhere, but you'll be back soon—with a more pli-
able personality, I trust."

I was handcuffed, blindfolded, and driven some distance from the prison. The Commander did not accom-
pany us. In spite of myself, I got more and more apprehensive during the long ride. By the time I was led into
an elevator and out—many floors below—into a room
with a faint hospital-like smell, I was weak with terror;
and when at last the blindfold was removed, revealing a
laboratory filled with all manner of horrendous-looking
apparatus, my knees nearly gave way under me.

The guards were dismissed; they were scarcely
needed, since at least ten white-coated technicians
were present. Dr. Sturn came toward me. "Don't be
frightened, my dear," he said smoothly. "This will not
be painful. I'm afraid it may be rather unpleasant for
you, but you will feel no pain. You will not feel anything at all."

His emphasis on that last remark seemed excessive,
as if he was attaching extraordinary and sinister significance to it, but as yet I couldn't decipher that significance. I looked around at one of the most intricate
computer installations I had seen on Toris, complete
with tape drives, banks of dials, and a primitive array
of flashing lights, but overshadowed by the room's central feature: a huge, incongruous tank of water that
looked deep enough to harbor sharks. *Take it easy,* I told
myself. *Pretend this is just another training exercise.*

At the thought, I relaxed a little, seeing a true comparison with the sort of "games" at which the Academy
excels. The theory behind them is that since on alien
planets you may be plunged into alarming and totally

unpredictable situations, you need plenty of practice in meeting simulated ones. I'm sure the instructors must spend a lot of time dreaming up diabolical ways to try you out. They, too, tell you "don't be frightened" while skillfully steering your feelings in the opposite direction. You're aware, of course, that they won't let you come to harm; but they have ways of counteracting that, ways that work beneath the level of your reason. For instance, they don't really need all the paraphernalia they surround you with—incomprehensible machines, disorienting gravitational fields, and so forth— any more than my interrogator needs the elaborate setup he uses; those are all stage props. Well, Dr. Sturn was obviously playing by similar rules, and I would be all right if I approached this experience in the same manner: simply by taking it as it came.

I was conducted to a small examining room, where two coldly efficient nurses performed an exhaustive physical, taped various sensors to my body, and then ordered me to put on a thin, close-fitting rubber suit that encased me completely. I followed their instructions placidly, curiosity gradually overcoming my fright. Back in the main laboratory, Dr. Sturn again approached me. "I've been told by the Commander that I must explain what's going to be done to you and offer you the option of confessing voluntarily," he said. "I would prefer not to. I consider you an excellent subject for this experiment; I'm anxious to see how you'll react to it, and your reaction would be more valid from the scientific standpoint if you had no foreknowledge of what to expect. But I, for one, have learned that Commander Feric is not a man to be trifled with."

"I won't tell him," I said, "if you want to skip the preliminaries."

"You will tell him anything he asks when he next sees you." He appraised me judiciously. "You're skeptical. You think I'm planning to put you through some barbaric horror that I believe will break your spirit, and you feel superior, for unlike the esteemed Commander you're aware that some people, including yourself, can hold out against that sort of thing. Well, I am a scientist; I do not concern myself with primitive notions like 'spirit' or 'will.' The treatment I shall administer is not a form of persuasion and it's not designed to elicit your conscious cooperation. It pertains solely to the functioning of your brain."

I had a moment of pure panic, fearing that he might be a genius who had discovered a means of direct access to the subconscious mind far ahead of his time, though I knew Torisian science was nowhere near advanced enough. But I got hold of myself. Such a fear was ridiculous, for anybody who considered spirit and will "primitive notions" was no genius.

"The brain cannot function without inputs," Dr. Sturn continued. "Think of all the inputs it normally receives: from your eyes, your ears, your senses of smell, taste, and touch. Those inputs can be cut off. Sensory deprivation, it's called, if you want the technical name; in practical terms it means that you'll be placed in a tank where you can't see, hear, smell, taste, or touch anything. It doesn't sound too distressing, and at first it won't seem so; some of your feelings may even be enjoyable. Later—well, later you will experience uncontrollable terror, and then hallucinations, and when you're taken out you'll be temporarily detached from reality and will comply with whatever we suggest to you." He added reassuringly, "Don't worry about your safety. You'll suffer some hours of panic in its most extreme form, but we will, of course, keep track of you by means of our instruments to make sure that you do not die."

I didn't comment. They blindfolded me again, this time with tightly fitted goggles that shut out all light, and plugged my ears and nostrils. A breathing apparatus was put into my mouth in such a way as to ensure that I could move neither my lips nor my tongue, after which I felt the rubber face mask being pulled over my head. Then I was carried to the tank and lowered into it; but I could feel nothing, neither warmth nor cold, for the water was kept at the exact temperature of my blood. My limbs had been weighted so that I would float motionless, beneath the surface, in perfect equilibrium. I couldn't have thrashed around if I had wanted to, for in addition to the air hose there were restraining lines.

Slowly, deliberately, I began to think the situation through. I had heard of sensory deprivation, and I knew that what Dr. Sturn had said about it was absolutely true as far as it went: The brain cannot endure a total lack of inputs for very long. He didn't realize, however, that the senses are not the only source of input to the brain. When you are deprived of sensory inputs, your mind concentrates that much more on the extrasensory ones. It isn't harmful if you know how to deal with them. A Youngling who hasn't the use of any psychic skills would be in a bad spot—would panic and, in comparatively few hours, come completely unglued mentally. But for me, it need not be so.

Except for one small detail. There was no one near enough to communicate with.

I could "speak" telepathically to Younglings, but they would not respond; without knowing that I was addressing them, they wouldn't be able to interpret my thoughts. There was no one close by with whom I had previously established rapport, not even the ambivalent emotional rapport that existed between me and the Commander. There wasn't anyone at all, for that matter, whom I could contact without disclosure.

I had one other resource to draw on: clairvoyance. I wasn't good at it. I'd had scarcely any practice. Yet under these circumstances, if it was the only way to preserve my sanity, perhaps I might "see" clairvoyantly, provided I stayed free of panic. After all, my emotions were going to become pretty extreme, and strong emotion always enhances psychic power. . . .

Enhances it! All at once I was struck by an exciting implication: There was a chance that this ordeal would work to my advantage. Things turn out in strange ways sometimes. It was possible that Commander Feric, in his zeal to break me, had engineered the triumph of my scheme.

Could sensory deprivation enhance my telepathic powers to the extent of enabling me to contact Randil?

Randil was somewhere in the city. Normally, we would have to be in the same vicinity to communicate, though not necessarily in the same building. Under emotional stress we could make contact over a greater distance; but I had tried to do so, on that first agonized day when I had denounced him and many times since from my prison cell. He had been beyond range. Yet the inner desperation I had felt then, although great, had been nothing compared to what I would be feeling in a few hours. Moreover, for the first time in my life, my mind would be wholly free of outside distractions. Those two factors combined might make my thought intense enough to reach Randil, and the total absence of other input would undoubtedly increase my sensitivity to his response. Surely, it would be justifiable to gamble on that.

It would mean taking a calculated risk, a terrifying risk. I would have to avoid any attempt to "see," letting myself experience what Dr. Sturn intended me to experience, until I was perilously close to the breaking point; for only under the spur of uttermost necessity would my powers be sufficiently magnified. If I then failed to get a response from Randil, it might be too late to fall back on my undeveloped clairvoyance. The line between insurmountable terror and panic is very thin, and once I crossed it, I would be helpless. It would end as the doctor had described, and the result would be not only the failure of my stalling action, but disclosure.

Disclosure would destroy the Torisians. Yet the ship would destroy them sooner, and the only person who could do anything about the ship was Randil. Unhesitatingly, I committed myself to the risk.

I can't say how many hours I was in the tank, and I find the sensations of those hours difficult to put into words. At first, as Dr. Sturn had predicted, it did not seem so terrible; and for me, that stage lasted longer than it would have for a Youngling because of my training in relaxation and self-control. There were some pleasurable feelings: Mere movement of my fingers, for instance, took on significance it had never had before; it was positively delightful.

The time came, however, when I was sick and tired of absolute blackness, aloneness, *nothingness;* I would have given anything I had ever possessed for one sound, one touch, to assure me that I was still attached to the world. It was like being off in the middle of space, between galaxies, outside my ship and with no suns or planets anywhere around. Then the terror began to come. It wasn't like terror I had experienced in the past, terror connected with some outer threat that could be dealt with or endured. Rather, it was pure terror arising from the depths of my mind: a warning that my brain's needs were not being met.

But it was not uncontrollable terror. I still had free will, and though it was hard not to turn to clairvoyance—harder still not to make a premature and perhaps abortive attempt to reach Randil—I stuck by my decision. I knew that there was another stage to be gone through.

The mind protects itself. If its usual inputs aren't forthcoming, it finds a substitute. In my case, I wasn't unduly upset by the process because of my prior instruction in confronting different levels of consciousness; when I began to have altered perceptions of my body and to see vivid brilliantly colored images, I knew them for what they were and was not disturbed by them. Also because of the instruction, I slipped easily into a deeper psychedelic experience without the intervening period of panic most Younglings would have faced, and I retained full awareness of what was happening to me. But with that awareness I felt rational, well-justified fear.

An artificially induced and unguided psychedelic experience is, of course, extremely dangerous. It was less dangerous for me than for an untrained person because I had been taught how to snap out of it; but my instruction had been based on the supposition that there would be a real world there to make contact with. In the sensory deprivation tank no such contact was possible. I could not snap out of it. Without external aid, I could only sink further until my own will was dissolved and I succumbed to the sheer panic that would make me subject to the will of my captors, for I was neither mature enough nor strong enough to maintain the integrity of my personality in complete isolation from the outside world. I had known this turning point would come; it had been part of the risk I had accepted. But when I felt it upon me, the terror took hold, and it was worse than anything I had imagined. I was lost in that black, empty void. I was disintegrating . . .

I could save myself only by contacting Randil; the time had arrived, and there wasn't a second to lose. I poured all the intensity of the terror into one despairing appeal: *Randil, help me! Help me!*

I received no response. My personal identity was melting, but I knew that I was not dying in the physical sense. It would have been better if I had been, for only that could prevent disclosure; but it does not work that way. You cannot will yourself to die even when your will is strong, much less when it is being dispelled. *Please, Randil,* I implored. *Oh, please help me!*

Elana? Elana, are you in trouble? I was asleep—

That one message from outside, the first I had received in what my distorted time-sense perceived as weeks or years rather than hours, pulled me back from the abyss. *Oh, Randil, keep sending,* I begged. *Don't leave me!*

I won't, he agreed quickly, knowing from my emotions that I was closer to panic than any agent ought to be. *But where are you? How did you find me?*

I don't know where I am, or where you are either. We're quite far apart, I think. Swiftly I told him what I was being subjected to, more concerned with his next response than with explaining matters.

He realized at once that I was dependent on our link and did not waste time on questions. *Don't worry, I'll stick with you,* he promised. *Look, Elana, can you "record"?*

I think so, as long as I'm receiving.

All right. I'm going to give you Varned's report. I'll never get it back to the starship, but you might, and it shouldn't be lost.

It was ideal therapy; Varned's report, supplemented by Randil's own collection of information, constituted enough data to give my brain all the input it could absorb. By the time I had "recorded" it, I had regained my grip on myself and was ready to get on with the vital communication for which I had risked so much.

What I don't understand, Randil declared, *is how you got into such a fix. In the first place, why are they trying to brainwash you, and in the second place, why couldn't you save yourself through clairvoyance?*

To answer the second question first, I didn't try. I needed to reach you, Randil, and I knew I'd have to be at the end of my rope to do it. I went on, then, to tell him the whole story.

And a thing happened that had never, never occurred to me through all the days of steadfast stalling. He didn't believe me! He flatly refused to believe that the dictatorship would use our landing craft to deliver nuclear bombs.

From the start, my hopes had been pinned on holding out long enough to somehow get word to Randil. It had never entered my mind that he wouldn't take steps to get rid of the ship once he was fully informed. Even if he disagreed with me about the disastrous long-range consequences of its being in Torisian hands, I had thought that he could scarcely fail to see that he must at all costs forestall the immediate war of annihilation that his intervention was about to set off.

Yet he maintained, *Even if you were right about their plans, it's too late. I couldn't send the landing craft back into orbit if I wanted to; they've got it hidden underground now.*

I guessed they would. That's why it's got to be destroyed.

Stubbornly, Randil protested, *I'm sure you've done what you thought right, Elana, but there are thirty or forty people near the ship. More, probably, since they've got the underground installation finished; every top scientist in the country is in there. It would be murder!*

Do you suppose I didn't consider that? I demanded. I thought back over the past days: the anguished hours by the river; the desperate, repeated attempts to perform the psychokinetic detonation, a task that demanded not the mere pressure of a finger on a trigger but the willing of it with my whole mind; the endless interrogations, with Commander Feric's insidious voice telling me over and over again that if I could only come to believe in the enormity of my crime, I would find peace . . . *Who are you, Randil, to tell me what it would be?* I raged. *Do you suppose it would have hurt less for me? Do you think I tried to kill forty people because I wanted to?*

I don't know what to think, he admitted. *I'm pretty sure I couldn't kill anybody for any reason; I don't see how any agent could.*

Yet you could stand by and let less scrupulous men kill millions. You're putting an awfully high price on your own purity, Randil.

Two wrongs don't cancel each other out.

No, but there's a matter of degree to take into account! That's how it's been on every world, from primitive tribes right on up: People have had to commit certain wrongs to prevent bigger ones. Otherwise the bigger ones would have won out every time.

His response was delayed so long that I began to fear that our mental tie had been broken. Then I felt sudden pressure on the lines attached to my unbearably sensitized arms and legs, and I knew that they were raising me from the tank. *Randil!* I cried in renewed fear.

I don't know how to answer you, he told me. *The only thing I'm sure of is that nobody, not even the Neo-Statist rulers, could wipe out whole cities in cold blood. The Torisian people want peace! If war comes, it'll be by accident, simply because both sides distrust each other.*

That's naive! Randil, I order you— It was no use. I emerged from the tank, the contact irretrievably lost, to face a barrage of sensory impressions that was almost more than I could cope with. My goggles and earplugs were removed, and the pain of seeing and hearing again was excruciating until I was given dark glasses and earmuffs that reduced the stimuli of normal sight and sound to a level I could accept. Technicians helped me to a chair in which I collapsed, burying my face in my arms on the table before me. I could hear Dr. Sturn saying, "Frankly, I don't understand this. She was in the tank twice as long as anyone else has been, yet she displayed none of the physiological signs of panic. She came close once, some time ago, but she's been stable so long now that I removed her for fear she'd lapse into a coma."

Commander Feric's voice replied harshly, "You will regret it, Sturn, if you've damaged her memory."

I raised my head. "Don't worry, it's intact," I said, my own voice sounding unbelievably loud to me. "Not that it'll do you any good."

Their shock, magnified by my still-heightened tele-pathic sensitivity, flooded my mind; they had supposed me unable to say anything except in response to direct questioning. Finally, the Commander, with his eye on Dr. Sturn, declared with bitter sarcasm, "I trust you will forgive me, Elana, for any inconvenience you may have suffered in the hands of this bungler."

"I forgive you," I told him sincerely. "As a matter of fact, you couldn't have done me a greater favor if you'd tried."

So here I am back in my old cell, and I have no choice but to go on with the game, hopeless though it now seems. Perhaps Randil will meet someone like Commander Feric. Perhaps something will force open his eyes to what the men in power here are capable of. A mind-bending technique like sensory deprivation, for in-stance; *I* got through, but to know that Younglings in-flict such a thing on each other—well, it makes you sick. And yet . . . I think that if these people keep on with it, someday they will try it on the wrong person, or rather, the right one: the one who will learn what we of the

Federation know from experience about the enhancement of psychic powers. And that will be a real breakthrough for the Torisians. Would it be worth the suffering of all the other victims? Of course not, when there are better ways of achieving the same end. But it does show that good *can* come from evil.

⚛ Randil, in the luxurious but well-guarded suite provided for him at the residence of Cerne's military governor, was deeply despondent after his telepathic exchange with Elana. His disillusionment with the Service was complete, his hope of saving Toris shaken, and on top of all that, he was sickened by the to-be-expected but still abhorrent cruelty of the Younglings for whom he had sacrificed so much.

He looked out on the city, its lights dimming in the grayness of dawn, and thought bitterly that he had indeed been naive, although not in the sense Elana had meant when she had accused him of it. He didn't believe for a moment that there were any plans afoot to send his ship on a bombing mission. But to picture her at the mercy of the SSP . . .

He shouldn't be surprised, he told himself, not after what they had done to Varned. Yet underneath he was. Varned, at least, had not been tortured; and while Randil had known all along that torture was standard practice among the Torisians, as among most other Younglings, it was less of an abstraction when it happened to someone he knew.

Elana, to be sure, could cope. She had had the appropriate training, and she had chosen imprisonment voluntarily, with her eyes wide open. Chagrined, he re-

alized that he had misjudged her, just as he had misjudged Varned. Both of them had in their own way
lived up to the Oath with absolute seriousness. How
tragic, he thought, that they had both been misled by a
policy that was so ruthless beneath its apparent ideal-
ism!

For he now saw with horror that it was even more
ruthless than he had supposed. He had known when he
dismantled the ship's automatic signaling mechanism
and destruct device that the Service would take a dim
view of a Federation landing craft being in the possession of Younglings, but, not realizing how closely that
craft would be guarded, he had assumed it would simply be called back to orbit or perhaps destroyed while
empty. That someone might vaporize it even at the cost
of Youngling life had not occurred to him before. The
new awareness hurt; Randil did not see how any
Federation citizen, let alone a sworn agent, could consider the taking of life to be the lesser of two evils. In
his heart, though, he had to admit that Service policy
would demand just such an interpretation. That the
Oath itself might demand it was something he could
not bring himself to accept. And that Elana—*Elana,* of
all people—should be willing to go that far, well, that
was the worst shock of all.

He could forgive her for denouncing him to the police; he knew she had honestly believed that his action
would be ultimately harmful to the Torisians. But he
found her determination to destroy the ship more difficult to condone. He could not understand her conviction that she would be capable of destroying it, much
less her belief that he himself could do so.

At any rate, Randil thought, he had learned why no

attempt had yet been made to embark for Juta. That had puzzled him, since the authorities had obtained all the information they needed, and inexplicably, they seemed less and less eager for his advice. Lately, they had almost seemed to be concealing something from him. No wonder; they surely wouldn't want a Jutan to suspect that his gift to them had been sabotaged!

Elana's explanations from the sensory deprivation tank had been scarcely coherent, and for that he couldn't blame her. Sensory deprivation, he knew, did strange things to people's minds. Undoubtedly, it had given her a distorted concept of her captors' plans. She had taken a fearful risk in letting herself slip so close to the brink of insanity—and how unnecessary! Her whole gambit was unnecessary and pointless, for she was certainly wrong in her contention that the Neo-Statists would cold-bloodedly bomb other nations. No one could be so depraved as to start a nuclear war on purpose, without any provocation at all.

The men with whom he had been working did not seem depraved. They had been very friendly. To be sure, they had made him a virtual prisoner, which had been a surprise. They had explained, however, that it was a necessary precaution for his own safety, and in this he thought them sincere. Naturally, they couldn't risk letting anything happen to a man whom they believed to be the envoy of the planet Juta.

A still bigger surprise had been the authorities' insistence on keeping the ship secret, yet the explanation offered for that had also seemed reasonable. The people might panic, he had been told, if they learned that Juta was inhabited. They would fear an invasion. Randil had been astonished, never having looked at his story that way, but on reflection he had conceded that it could happen. The Torisians, after all, believed themselves the only intelligent race in the universe, and to find out otherwise would be upsetting when they had no way of knowing that not even an aggressive young interstellar empire would invade a planet with a civilization as highly developed as theirs. Perhaps it was just as well that he hadn't brought the ship into the city after getting aboard, as he had originally planned.

He had been unable to do so because it had been observed during its unpiloted descent to the riverbank; he'd had barely time to disable the signaling and destruct devices before troops had reached it. He had welcomed their arrival, for he had made no attempt at concealment and hadn't anticipated that they themselves would do so. There had been no trouble in convincing them that he had come from outer space. In the first place, the ship itself constituted proof: Its alien origin was indisputable, and he had taken several officers on a trial run into orbit, safe from detection by the starship because of the landing craft's shields, which gave off too much radiation for use near the ground but which effectively guarded against discovery outside the atmosphere. He had gone far enough out for Toris to be seen as a globe, and his passengers had been, to say the least, impressed.

Later, when they had checked his background, they had recognized his published articles—which he had proved that he had submitted under a pen name— as further corroboration of his claim to be the emissary of another world, for the unique quality of those articles was by no means lost on the scientists of Cerne. To the government, he had told the truth, although not the whole truth. He had confessed his illegal entry to the city via the river, explaining that he had wished to observe the Cernese people before handing the ship over to them, and he had been believed. No one had any cause not to believe him; besides, he had offered conclusive evidence of his alien birth by submitting to X-rays that revealed subtle differences between his anatomy and that of a Torisian. Few agents could, like Elana, pass medical scrutiny without being classed as freaks.

Randil's discussion with his "hosts" had required wit and patience. He had been questioned for hours by men who hadn't the faintest notion of the structure of the universe, one of whom had actually asked him to clarify the distinction between a planet and a star! They had demanded detailed information about the ship, seeming quite astonished that he could explain no more than the instructions for piloting it, which struck them as fantastically simple in comparison to the process of controlling the primitive aircraft with which they were familiar. In vain he had pointed out that he was not an engineer, and that they would hardly expect one of their own young pilots to create a complete set of blueprints for a jet plane. Eventually, however, he had gotten a chance to talk to some scientists—intelligent, perceptive people whose curiosity about the universe was genuine—and they, at least, were able to understand why he could tell them little concerning the ship's design, which was more than could be said of the military men.

Naturally, everyone had been most eager to hear about the civilization of Juta, but on that subject Randil had been steadfastly silent. He had simply stated that the Jutans offered friendship, but that as a condition of any exchange of knowledge, a delegation from Toris must make the trip to Juta alone, without any aid beyond the gift of the spacecraft. He himself, he had added, would stay behind on Toris to demonstrate Juta's good faith. That had been the most plausible story he could think of, and to his amazement it was accepted readily. The only hitch was that he had been placed under guard, when he had expected to drop out of sight once he had taught the Torisians to manage the ship themselves. He had expected to return to the starship, in fact, and had hidden Varned's ring in a rock cache by the riverbank—it being of traditional and elaborate Torisian design and therefore a suspiciously inappropriate possession for either a Jutan or an impoverished Cernese university student—so that when the time came, he would be able to summon another landing craft. It would be better to go back voluntarily than to wait for the Service to track him down, for to remain where Torisians might find him would be to run an unwarranted risk of disclosure.

Randil agreed with Elana that an actual disclosure would be damaging; indeed, when he considered the situation with painful honesty, he couldn't deny that she might also be justified in seeing a potential danger in his having enabled the people of Toris to conquer space too easily. He thought it a lesser danger than the current international situation, however. Yet in maintaining that his action must be nullified, she had implied that the ship shouldn't be allowed to remain in Torisian hands even for such use as he had intended! That was an appalling implication; how could any agent kill innocent people to forestall such a remote and nebulous peril? Interplanetary war, decades or even centuries in the future? They had no real knowledge that it would occur. It never had before. It was true that no Younglings had ever entered space with the Federation's assistance before; still, the reasoning Elana had presented while explaining why she had denounced him was all very theoretical. Would she have tried to destroy the ship on those grounds alone?

There was no telling; under normal circumstances she would have left the decision to the starship commander, since, with the risk of prolonging the Critical Stage a long-range one, there would have been no need for her to assume sole responsibility. That need had arisen from her conviction that the ship would be used to deliver nuclear bombs, which if based on fact would be a terrifying and all-too-potent argument. It was a mistaken conviction, he was sure. Yet on that basis, she was delaying the ship's use. Her ploy was not only pointless but dangerous, Randil believed, for every day of postponement increased the chances that the starship would somehow locate the missing landing craft and take drastic action. He must therefore see to it that the ship got into space, where its shields would protect it, as soon as possible.

Moreover, he felt a responsibility to Elana, who with the best of intentions was undergoing a very difficult ordeal. With sudden sympathy he realized that she had indeed suffered from her decision as well as from the treatment she was receiving; she was too sensitive not to have. What would he have done in her place, he wondered, if it were truly a choice between an act of murder and imminent war?

Randil turned from the window and reached for

the telephone. Captive though he was, his position did carry some weight. The one constructive step he could take, he decided, was to contact the SSP under the pretense of having heard rumors of a plot against the ship, and to convince them that Elana was entirely innocent of any sabotage.

The situation has changed. I am in trouble now; deeper trouble than ever before. I'm not sure that I can bear the thing I *must* bear. I should try to get some sleep, I suppose, but if I discipline myself to put what has happened into words first, it may help me to find an answer.

Yesterday afternoon I was interrogated again, and at the beginning Commander Feric seemed in a surprisingly affable mood. "So," he said, "even to sensory deprivation, you're immune. You're an amazing young woman, Elana." He smiled, not at all unpleasantly. "Dr. Sturn thinks you are insane, literally insane," he informed me. "Only a psychotic would fail to show a reaction to any of the things done to her."

I started guiltily, realizing with chagrin that I had slipped out of my role by overcontrolling myself. After all, Younglings have no conscious control over physiological reactions like pulse rate; even I hadn't, before I was taught. Yet at this very moment my heartbeat and so forth were being monitored by the chair into which I was strapped, and I was valiantly suppressing all evidence of emotion.

"Dr. Sturn is a fool!" the Commander burst out. "He looks at test results, tapes, graphs—did you know we have complete records of every moment you have spent in this room? — but he does not often converse with you. He monitors your cell, watching you sit for hours, motionless, staring at nothing, and he calls it catatonic withdrawal. I know better. I've listened to the things you say, and I know that something significant is going on in that mind of yours. It's too good a mind to waste! I want to help you, Elana, I really do, but Dr. Sturn has a lot of influence with the commandant."

It was standard interrogation procedure: the unexpected display of sympathy, the seeming desire to side with the victim against a less understanding colleague. I was not taken in. But in this case I thought that the facts had been honestly stated; Dr. Sturn could hardly have known how else to interpret my rigidly controlled responses, much less my frequent private "recording" sessions.

"In any case," Commander Feric went on, "I have some good news for you. It's been decided that you aren't to be killed."

"That's not news," I said with a dry laugh.

"Oh, I don't mean it the way you think," he added hastily. "Naturally, we can't kill you before you've confessed, and I've known all along that you were intelligent enough to realize that. I'm also aware that you're not holding out merely for that reason; that's why I haven't insulted you with offers of leniency in exchange for your cooperation."

Either his memory was short, or he thought mine was; he had made precisely such an offer on the first day. But the point was scarcely worth arguing.

"What I'm saying," he continued, "is that you will not be executed for your crimes. There will be a trial for the sake of public appearance, and you will, of course, be found guilty. But I can promise you that you won't be sentenced to death. You see, I rather admire you, Elana, and because of this admiration, I have convinced the commandant that such a punishment, however greatly deserved, is uncalled for."

He paused to let that sink in. I was not fooled; it is a very old trick: the sudden, unanticipated reprieve, the relief that lowers the victim's defenses—and then the punch line.

"For once, Dr. Sturn was on my side," Commander Feric remarked casually. "If you are insane, you obviously need treatment, not punishment. But if you are not, think what it will mean to the advancement of psychiatry! Here is a person who is apparently immune to the fear of death, to pain, to isolation; who displays no shock at forced confrontation with the taboos of the society in which she was raised; who does not even react normally to drugs or to sensory deprivation. Since such immunity would violate every principle known to the science of human behavior, the only explanation is that the limits of endurance are greater than we had supposed. Dr. Sturn and his associates would, I think, be happy to devote years to the exploration of those limits."

My heart jumped, and, remembering my previous error, I let it show. Seeing the Commander's smile as he watched the monitor scope, I made it show even more than my true feelings warranted. The prospect just presented to me, while chilling, was not really dangerous. Weeks or years, it would still be a matter of fortitude; techniques that could penetrate my defenses far enough to deprive me of conscious choice won't be known to Torisian science for at least another couple of centuries.

"You don't have years," I pointed out. "So whatever

Dr. Sturn's latest theory may be, it doesn't solve your problem."

"Certainly not," he agreed. "We're not discussing my problem. We are discussing what is going to happen to you after you confess."

"Then it's a pretty pointless discussion, unless you're trying to strike a bargain after all."

The interrogator's voice hardened. "There can be no bargains! We both know that I will never get a voluntary confession from you and that I have no more time to waste trying. Your future has been settled, and I am merely giving you the facts: I shall obtain the information I need by force, within the next three days, and after I am through with you, I shall give Dr. Sturn a free hand."

"Force? When you've just admitted that for all practical purposes I'm immune to force?"

Commander Feric stood up and as he approached me, looked straight into my eyes. "You're a realist," he said. "You're also both imaginative and remarkably well informed. Surely you know that I haven't yet exhausted all the possibilities."

So at last we were coming to it, as I had feared we would sooner or later. My immunity to physical force extended much further than he knew; he could not injure me unless I allowed it, for I had my psychic Shield. But I could not use the Shield. If I did, I would no longer be able to conceal my alien origin.

"Shall I describe those possibilities?" he asked. "Or would a demonstration be better, perhaps? In this prison we have many spies who are less important than you, and who have therefore been handled less gingerly. Some of them could be sent for. . . ."

He glanced back at the scope on which my heartbeat was displayed, and I sensed the triumph in him—triumph that, surprisingly, showed no signs of fading, though I succeeded in calming myself as he talked on. "But I doubt that it will be necessary to bother with that," he said decisively. "I simply ask you to bear in mind what I've just explained: You are not going to die when this is over, and if anything is done to you of a permanent nature, you will live with its effects for a very long time."

Keeping my voice steady, I declared, "You are making empty threats. You've already said that in my case a public trial is considered necessary, a trial at which I'll be seen by people who are not well informed and whom you don't wish to enlighten. Since I'm already sentenced, there's no other reason to have any trial."

The Commander shook his head. "Evidently, you have less imagination than I credited you with," he said wearily. "I won't need to disfigure you; there are ways more subtle than that. Suppose, for instance, that you were to appear at your trial wearing dark glasses. Now, that might mean a number of things. It might conceal the effects of certain drugs, drugs that the public knows well enough must sometimes be used. It might indicate that your eyes were unusually sensitive to bright lights, or simply that you had a desire for privacy that we had mercifully permitted you to indulge. On the other hand, Elana, it might conceal blindness."

His eyes were not on my face but on the scope that monitored my reactions, and I knew that he was pleased by what he saw. I had given up all attempts to regulate them, and I doubt that I would have even been capable of it. "I would allow you a day or two to consider," he said softly, "but as you know, our time is short."

"There's nothing to consider," I whispered. I do not suppose I sounded too convincing.

Unfastening my bonds, Commander Feric grasped my arm and escorted me over to the window. I looked down on a tree-lined avenue, where pale autumn sunlight shone on a torrent of yellow leaves. The sky was very wide and very blue. "Beautiful, isn't it?" he observed. "You haven't seen much beauty lately, for your cell is now bare and windowless. Perhaps you think it will always be so. But not necessarily; in a hospital, or even in another prison, you might be given a window with a view. At least a view of the stars, which I believe you used to enjoy watching. And you might eventually be allowed books. It would be a pity if you were unable to appreciate such advantages."

I didn't answer. Suppose I was rescued someday? Even Federation science couldn't always restore lost sight. Or suppose the whole thing was all for nothing, suppose they called my bluff and used the ship anyway?

"You are making a very big sacrifice for the sake of a day or two more of silence," he said. "Are you by any chance thinking that, since the value to me is less in the act itself than in the moments leading up to it, I will not carry the thing through? I assure you that's not the case. If we start this, we will finish it unless *you* give the word to stop. And then, tomorrow, we will try something a little different that will make today's heroics useless."

For a long moment we stood there, and then without waiting to be compelled I turned my back on the sunlit scene and returned to the chair. Commander Feric pressed the buzzer on his desk; two guards appeared at the door, followed by a white-clad orderly. I was strapped in again, and this time my head was secured, too, after which my eyes were taped open.

"There are a number of ways in which this can be done," the Commander told me, "some extremely painful, others less so. I'm not going to subject you to pain because we already know your reaction to that, and it is not the issue here. There will simply be a brilliant white flash, which will be the last thing your eyes respond to." I swallowed. Done that way, with light against which no barrier could be erected, not even the Shield could save me; I would at least be spared the ordeal of deliberately dropping it.

He rose again and came toward me, and the sympathy in his face at that moment was, I think, quite sincere. As I've said, he is not a sadist but merely a man who believes that anything leading toward his ultimate goal can be justified. And that is what we all believe; I do, too. People who justify immoral acts that way have set their sights too low, for the difference between us is in the ultimate goals we choose.

The four men put on dark, heavy goggles. "There will be a countdown of five minutes, called at thirty-second intervals," the Commander said. "Of course you realize that from my point of view, those minutes are the crucial ones. Use them wisely; don't let false pride interfere with your common sense."

They were the longest minutes that I have ever spent. Determinedly, I fixed my mind on phrases from Service ritual, remembering something one of my instructors once said: "If you ever find yourself faced with something really bad, something inescapable against which you have no defense, your only recourse is to accept it. Once you're absolutely sure that there's no way out, don't resist. Just relax and let it happen. That will seem hard, but believe me, it will be less painful than shrinking from the thing. You'll get something from it—you won't feel that you can; you won't understand; but in the end you will gain, if not from the experience itself, then simply from your bravery."

The flash, when it came, was so bright that I felt rather than saw it, and afterward there was only a red blur, fading into blackness. I remained perfectly still for a moment, numb with shock; then, unaccountably, I burst into hysterical, uncontrollable sobbing. All the pent-up tension of the past days came pouring out of me, leaving me limp, hollow, scarcely able to recall how it had felt to be in command of my feelings. Thinking back, I realize that that moment too was crucial and was a part of his design. Some people, once they break down like that, can't ever get control again.

I heard the order to unstrap me given and felt myself released, and as I dropped my head into my lap the Commander's voice asked solicitously, "Are you sorry, Elana? Would you like to go back and replay the last thirty seconds of countdown?"

Still crying, for I just couldn't get a grip on myself, I choked out, "No!"

"You are lying," he asserted. "You did not think I would go through with it; you gambled and lost."

"It's you who lost your gamble!" I lashed out fiercely. "Now you've nothing left to threaten me with."

"You think I can't put you through anything worse.

But you'll learn. Tomorrow will be much worse, and you will realize then how foolish you were not to give in sooner."

"I don't care what you do tomorrow."

"Not now, perhaps. Later, though, you'll feel differently." He put his arm around my shoulders in an almost fatherly way while, gradually, my sobs subsided. "So you have emotions after all," he commented. "Strange as it may seem to you, Elana, I mean it when I say that I admire you. I admire courage, and I've discovered that you have genuine courage. For the first time since your arrest, you were truly afraid."

There didn't seem to be much use in denying that, so I kept silent. Commander Feric went on, "That was what I had to find out. Before, you see, you were fearless, and I could not be sure how you would react to fear."

"Now you know," I said bitterly. "It won't help you much to prove the same point over again."

"No," he agreed.

"Then all your talk about tomorrow is meaningless."

My face was buried in my hands; he pulled them away from it and removed the tape from my eyelids, making me lift my head. "Elana, Elana," he said with a sigh, "when will you understand that I'm trying to help you? That I've never wanted you to be hurt?" After a short pause he went on, "Tell me, do you see anything—shapes, perhaps?"

That question didn't rate an answer, and I ignored it. I closed my useless eyes and concentrated on listening, idly wondering how long it would be before my other senses—and my latent extrasensory skills, such as clairvoyance—would be sharpened.

"You will see the shapes soon," the Commander said quietly. "I misled you; the effect of the flash is not permanent. You will be blind for only a few hours."

I sat motionless, not daring to speak or even to think. This might be merely a refinement of cruelty designed to raise my hopes so that they might be further dashed as those hours passed. Or else . . . With resignation, I declared, "I understand now. Tomorrow you will use a different method, one more—more physical."

He laughed. "You underrate my judgment. Oh, I'll not deny that in an ordinary case what you suggest might have occurred to me. It is a technique that sometimes works where others fail; few people can stand up to the same threat a second time. But I'm convinced that you can, just as I was convinced beforehand that you could withstand it today."

"Beforehand? Why did you waste your valuable time, then?"

"Only for your sake, Elana. Only to give you one last chance before subjecting you to what will be, for both of us, a less palatable form of pressure."

"If you're trying to scare me again," I said shakily, "you're succeeding! But why bother, when you just agreed that it'll do you no good to re-prove the point?"

Commander Feric walked away from me, his footsteps sounding oddly loud because I could not see him. "Since you know so much psychology, Elana," he said, "think about this: People are vulnerable to different things. Most are motivated by fear, so we start with that. Occasionally, we find someone who, like yourself, cannot be attacked successfully in that way; and then, of course, we are forced to change our tactics."

"Other tactics take time," I reminded him.

"Not always," he replied slowly. "Sometimes a day or two is sufficient, as it is bound to be in your case. You see, I know you better than you think I do. Like any other human being, you have a point of vulnerability, and I believe I've learned what it is."

He couldn't have, I thought. He couldn't possibly have guessed that I wasn't Torisian.

"Tomorrow," he went on, "we will use an entirely different procedure. You will be placed in a situation where your immunities will be of no use. If you were the usual hardened professional, you could probably cope with that situation; but you are not a typical agent, and for you, Elana, it will be intolerable."

Hearing statements like that from a disembodied voice, when I could not see anything around me, was doubly terrifying, as he had undoubtedly known it would be. Moreover, my physical blindness was heightening my telepathic sensitivity, and from his emotions I knew that he was now absolutely sure of himself.

"Come now," he was saying, "you're well versed in these matters; can't you guess what I'm talking about?"

I should have. I can't see how I could have been so unsuspecting, for I thought I had no illusions left about Younglings.

If he had wanted me to guess, I might have picked up his thought. But he did not; he no doubt felt that a night of agonized wondering would be more nerve-racking than the awful truth, which indeed it would have been, had I not been too drained of emotion to worry about anything at all. I was not taken back to my cell; instead, I was led to a room containing a soft bed, with blankets, and allowed an unbelievable twelve hours of uninterrupted sleep. The drugs I received must have been of a soothing variety, for I awoke feeling rested and refreshed. It was morning, and my sight had returned, and the sheer relief and joy of it almost made me forget that the day ahead was unlikely to be easy.

Furthermore, I was given an adequate breakfast, more food than I had seen at one meal in a long, long time. The guards came for me before I had finished it; thinking to fortify myself against the next hungry day, I unobtrusively slipped the remaining piece of bread into the pocket of my prison uniform.

At the intersection of corridors we turned not toward the interrogation room but toward my own cell, and I realized that I would be given plenty of time to worry after all. As I went through the familiar door I nearly stumbled over the corner of the bunk—the second bunk, the one that had hitherto been folded up against the wall. "You will no longer be isolated," the guard told me impassively. "From now on you will have a cellmate."

Astonished, I stared at the girl who was sprawled on the bunk, facedown, crying hysterically. I could not believe it. I was still too stupid to understand. They could not possibly think her my accomplice; if they did, they would have seized her long before this. And as for charging her with anything else, why, she had given them no cause even to suspect her opinions.

For it was Kari.

s e v e n

had thought that between the Academy's instruction and my education on Andrecia, I had been made aware of all the ways in which I could be hurt—aware and forearmed. I was wrong. There are always new horrors to face. If there weren't, who would need courage?

When I found Kari in my cell this morning, I did not immediately take in the situation. I tried to tell her that, being innocent, she had nothing serious to worry about. We were given an hour of waiting during which Kari continued to sob violently, so overcome by the realization that her worst fear had come true that she was unable to grasp my assurance—veiled, since the cell was bugged—that I had not betrayed her, voluntarily or otherwise. Then we were taken, together, to Commander Feric. He ignored Kari, turning away from her as the guards strapped her into the chair, and addressed me instead. "You can't complain to me, Elana," he said sadly, "that you were not warned."

It wasn't till then that I realized, with sickening despair, just why it was that they had arrested her.

The Commander is not as ignorant as I once thought him to be. He had judged me pretty accurately, as a matter of fact. I had boasted that his methods could not touch me; it was I who was naive. There was nothing very sophisticated or very startling in his new tactics. It doesn't take a knowledge of psychic defenses to know that a person who is insensitive with regard to her own pain may prove less so when it comes to the question of someone else's, especially when that someone is a close friend.

"You are," Commander Feric said to me thoughtfully, "the closest thing to a truly compassionate human being that I have ever encountered. You have more concern for others than for your personal welfare; that is the key to your motivation, the reason you've withstood every form of attack. And with that I will break you! It is not a strength, as you no doubt imagine, but your greatest weakness."

He brought in a panel of uniformed police to hurl the usual charges at Kari—espionage, attempted sabotage, and so forth—but although they bullied her unmercifully, alternating between screaming rage and icy sarcasm, none of them showed any evidence of actually believing these accusations. It was a theatrical performance, a carefully planned melodrama staged solely for my benefit. We went through some four or five hours of it, hours designed to wear down not Kari's nerve but mine. Kari herself, of course, did not know that. She was terror-stricken, hysterical, and finally simply stunned, though at least she retained enough presence of mind to deny everything. Near the end she fainted, and they had to give an injection to revive her.

Through it all I sat silent, alert to every detail of the proceedings and grimly aware that I had been given that extraordinary dose of rest and food precisely so that I would be. The Commander did not want me in a dazed condition any more than he had wanted me to be blind. For I knew, of course, what was coming next; they would not stop with mere questioning.

When the assistant interrogators were dismissed and the guards approached Kari with what was to me a familiar set of apparatus, I thought I was going to faint, too. Mercifully, she did not yet understand the purpose of the electrodes that were attached to her. The preparation was done slowly, with great deliberation, and Commander Feric's eyes were on me all the time. Finally, he leaned toward me and said, "All right, Elana. If this is the way it's going to be, you shall have the privilege of explaining to your friend what is about to happen to her—and why."

I could have refused. I could have faked an emotional collapse and pretended to be another helpless victim, so that Kari would be more likely to think that the things he would undoubtedly tell her about me were lies. That would have been the easiest way, for me. But Kari would have no support at all unless I gave it to her. The situation had to be faced squarely.

I stood up, feeling light-headed but in full command of myself, and went over to her. You have more to draw on than you think, I guess; you *can* do what you *have* to do. "Kari," I said frankly, "this is the thing you've heard rumors about. It will hurt. It will be very frightening, but it can't be avoided and it won't injure you in any way. I've been through it, and I know."

The Commander said harshly, "That is scarcely an adequate explanation, Elana. This girl has just heard herself denounced as a spy and saboteur, charges that she knows to be untrue. She is now about to be tortured into confession of a crime she did not commit. You have not told her how she got into such a fix, or that it is in your power to get her out of it."

Kari looked up at me incredulously, beginning to take this in. I wanted to tell her what was at stake, but I knew I must not say anything that would suggest she was a Libertarian sympathizer; quite possibly the police hadn't suspected that, and so far she had had more sense than to give herself away. So there could be no self-justification on my part. "I can't get either of us out of it, Kari," I said steadily.

"That is a barefaced lie," Commander Feric informed her. "This young woman who you think is your friend has in fact committed all the crimes of which you stand accused. Once she confesses to them, you will be free. It's true enough that she has been through the experience that you are about to undergo, and has proved remarkably resistant to it. We have reason to think you will be less so, and that in the end she will not allow you to suffer in her place."

"No," Kari whispered, "I don't believe you!"

"You don't? Ask her, then. Ask her where she came from before she so conveniently developed a case of amnesia that allowed her to build a cover for herself around your generosity! Really now, haven't you ever noticed anything strange about her? An air of mystery, so to speak, that doesn't quite fit the story she told you?"

Kari's face showed me that this advice had struck home, and indeed I picked up her doubt through telepathy; though her lips didn't move, she was crying desperately, *Oh, Elana, it can't be the way he says . . . can it?*

I couldn't answer her, for she wouldn't have recognized it as communication; the best I could hope for was that she would sense enough of my emotion to trust me. Aloud I said, "I don't expect you to understand, Kari. All I can tell you is that what we're mixed up in involves a lot of people besides you and me, so we've no choice but to be brave."

"A noble appeal," the interrogator said dryly, "but while you are being brave, Kari, remember that one word from her will stop this." He took the control dial into his hand and moved the switch.

Actually, what he gave Kari at that point was not very bad. I know; I felt her sensations telepathically. That sometimes happens when a person you know well and care about is in pain. The pain we experienced was only a mild foretaste of what I knew would come later; in fact Kari had probably had worse in the dentist's chair more than once. But her terror magnified it, and she had absolutely no knowledge of how to cope. So it was pretty awful for both of us.

She was screaming to me silently, and I was trying to shut out her agony by repeating the words of the Oath over and over in my mind: Above all other considerations . . . above *all* other considerations . . . And then suddenly I realized that my approach was all wrong. I should be helping her! I couldn't do it by giving in to them, not when that would mean plunging her whole planet into nuclear war. But I could help her to bear the pain; I could use my telepathic powers for that, surely, and somehow I must. Whatever courage I could muster, I must share.

Commander Feric released the switch and said to me coldly, "Enough, Elana?"

Ignoring him, I knelt on the floor beside Kari's chair and looked straight into her eyes, putting all the telepathic force I could gather behind my spoken words. The first step was to prove to her that defense was possible. "Kari, take my hand," I said. "Hold it tight, like this." I gripped her cold fingers firmly. "Now we will both feel it," I told her. "It's electrical, you see, and the current will pass from your body to mine."

She stared, awestruck. "Is that true?" she asked the interrogator. "Will she feel what I feel if we hold hands?"

He frowned. He must have had mixed feelings; though he knew pain didn't faze me, it would obviously be to his advantage for me to be made acutely aware of what was being done to Kari, and yet my voluntary acceptance of that awareness was not a hopeful sign. "Yes," he said slowly, "it's true. Possibly she is trying to assuage her feeling of guilt in that manner. I should warn you, though, that it is a dishonest attempt. She is insensitive to pain, inhumanly so; she will not suffer as you suffer."

"That's right, Kari," I admitted. "It won't be as bad for me because I've learned not to panic. But physically I'll experience just what you do, and neither of us will be harmed by it."

Could the telepathy work the other way? I wondered. Could I give the skill instead of receiving the anguish? Theoretically, yes, for that's the way it's taught at the Academy; you get telepathic assistance while you're learning. But you must be calm and resolute, and you must know what to expect. Kari was in no condition to be receptive. When the pain began again, I tried desperately to pass along my power over it, but I just couldn't reach her.

It did not go on long. Commander Feric wasn't trying to break Kari; his aim was simply to terrify her, in the hope that once we were alone together she would prevail upon me to yield. "Tomorrow," he promised grimly, "we will go further. We will go as far as we need to go. And let me remind you, Elana," he added as a parting shot, "that since this girl is known to be innocent, there is no advantage to us in filing formal charges that would lead to a public trial." Fortunately, Kari was too naive to understand the implication.

But *I* understand. And I cannot bear it! For the first time, I'm up against something I don't think I can bear. There's no doubt as to the right course; not only under the Oath, but any way I view the situation, Kari's life is no more worth the price than my own. But suppose I lose control of myself? Suppose I crack up? I will, I'm afraid, if he goes far enough—and he knows it. He has known it all along.

The Commander's remark about hardened professional agents makes sense to me now. I've been trained to meet horrors, but it's true that I'm not "hardened" in the way that he meant; the Service chooses people not for insensitivity but for empathy and compassion. If that is weakness, as he claims, then I prefer it to strength. Yet when a whole world's future may depend on a strength you don't have . . .

It would be different if Kari herself were strong. If it were a fellow agent, for instance—even someone I loved—I could endure whatever might happen. Because that would put it on a very different basis. A fellow agent could handle the pain, and besides, an agent would be willing. It's not innocence that matters, but consent. After all, innocent people often have to suffer in order to save things; that is the way of every world.

Yet the capacity for consent is in everyone—Kari, too! She is braver than she knows. If I simply said to her, "Look, Kari, it's either this or nuclear war tomorrow," what would she say? Wouldn't she be willing? Wouldn't anyone? Countless Younglings have been, over issues far less clear-cut.

Kari would be willing, at least she would want to be. But she wouldn't be capable of it. She couldn't maintain her courage when the going got really rough; she just hasn't the resources. That's what I can't bear: the fact that she is defenseless, like a little child. Yet she is not a child, and the potential is there, not only for consent but for the psychic powers too, as it is in other Younglings. That potential can be awakened sometimes! Only under very special conditions, to be sure, but still . . .

It is possible to create those conditions. If I were wise enough and skilled enough, I might know how. Father, Meleny, any of the senior people would be able to reach Kari, reach her and enable her to release the latent powers of her mind. Could I possibly do it? Should I try? I tried this afternoon and failed, but I didn't go at it in the right way. It takes preparation. It can't be done directly; there has to be a subterfuge of some kind, a foundation. I've studied the theory. I've even had some experience: On Andrecia we taught a Youngling to use psychokinesis, and the principles are just the same.

She is asleep now. They gave her a sedative, for they do not want to wear her down too soon. I haven't been able to tell her anything because of the cell's being bugged; I explained that quite openly, for Commander Feric is already aware that I know the surveillance camera is in here. I'm sure he's smart enough to realize that I won't confess to her. All the same, we will be carefully monitored tonight in the hope that I may let slip some small detail that could be of use to them, so I shall be severely limited in what I can say aloud. We have few hours left till morning, and I've as yet no idea of a workable scheme.

Yet somehow, some way, I must protect Kari; I must get through to her and teach her what she needs to know. That is the only solution there can be.

The hours have passed, and I have resorted to a rather deceitful stratagem. I don't know if I've done the right thing, but at least I've made an attempt—the only possible attempt—to fortify Kari. We have a while longer to wait before we're sent for, and I am going to "record" what I did, because if it doesn't work out I may not be in any shape to think about it later.

Last night I racked my brains for an endless time before coming to any conclusion. I was determined to activate Kari's latent defenses, but how? Why not hypnotize her? I thought suddenly. It would be easy for me to put her into a trance so deep that she would not feel any pain at all. Easy—but dangerous, too dangerous. I don't have enough skill; it takes a real expert, like Meleny, to do it so that things that ought not to be upset aren't tampered with. I might never get Kari all the way out of it, particularly if they separated us later. Besides, my sort of a job would be detectable. They would simply call Dr. Sturn, and he would bring her out of it fast.

No, Kari must learn to use her defenses consciously. Yet how could she? It had taken me days to learn! And they hadn't been easy days; you have to accept that, and trust you'll get through the rough part, which you're able to do only because you know that everybody else has gotten through. Younglings haven't any basis for that kind of trust. They can't ever learn psychic skills by the same methods we use; the initial failures shake their faith too much.

But there is a shortcut. It doesn't give full mastery, but once in a while it can enable a Youngling to use such powers in some particular circumstance such as arose on Andrecia. The key to it there was that our protégé was never allowed to fail—or even to suspect that he might fail—because he was given something external to trust in.

There are three prerequisites. The first, strong emotion, Kari would have no trouble with; she was thoroughly terrified. The second, telepathic help, I could provide. It was the third and most essential, absolute belief, that would be the difficulty. Kari did not believe in anything—not in herself, not in the fallibility of force, and certainly not in "supernatural" powers. And what you don't believe in, you just can't do.

On Andrecia it was simple. The culture was a comparatively primitive one, and the people believed in magic. We gave a man a magic talisman, telling him that it would give him psychokinetic powers, and it *did*. It did, even though it was not really "magic" at all.

But Kari would not believe in a magic talisman. People from materialistic cultures like the one of Toris scoff at anything that doesn't fit their concept of "science."

It was just plain hopeless, then—or was it? Excitedly, I realized that I had stumbled upon the germ of an answer. Materialism is a narrow view, but the belief in magic is pretty narrow, too; it's not the narrowness that counts when you work through a subterfuge. You must provide something external through which the Youngling thinks his or her power will come. When calling it "magic" won't do, you call it something else. Something that fits what that Youngling does believe. It was not true that Kari didn't believe in anything. Everybody believes in something, even if it's only something concrete.

Kari, like all Torisians, had unshakable faith in the materialistic brand of science that dominated her world. So what would she expect could alter her mental processes? Why, science. Drugs! When she had a headache she reached for her bottle of tablets, and when she was nervous she took a tranquilizer. There were three different kinds of tranquilizers in her drawer of our bedside table back at the apartment. Whenever Kari had to study for an exam, she used pep pills, which I had been unable to persuade her to abandon. After all, I had just barely kept her from trying that psychedelic drug we were offered, and then not on principle but only on the grounds of specific perils.

Of course I didn't have any drugs that would miraculously release Kari's psychic defenses; I didn't have any drugs at all. But I hadn't had a real magic talisman on Andrecia, either. I had used a quite ordinary thing that had looked like a talisman, and in this case a similar ruse could be employed.

There remained one major hurdle: the spy camera and the inevitable hidden microphone. I would have to talk to Kari, at least till I could teach her to recognize telepathic communication, and I would have to do some things that would look highly suspicious if monitored. The camera and microphone would have to be disabled. Since they were out of reach, there was only one way of accomplishing that—psychokinesis. I hadn't considered it before because it wouldn't solve anything for long; the guards would send someone to fix them. But if I could manage it, it might give me the few minutes I would need.

The psychokinesis itself would be easy. I had the required emotional impetus, certainly, and to disconnect a couple of wires would be very elementary. The hard part was knowing which wires, where. The camera was in the ventilator; there just wasn't any other place it could be, since the walls and ceiling were otherwise smooth and solid. The microphone was probably with it, although conceivably a microphone could be within a wall. The thing was, I had never seen them, and what you can't picture exactly you can't touch mentally. So before I could do anything, I had to see them clairvoyantly.

Clairvoyance has never been my strong point.

Psychic abilities, like abilities of any other kind, vary from person to person, and nobody is talented in everything. If I had been blinded, I would have become more clairvoyant, eventually. Or if, in the sensory deprivation tank, I had concentrated on a need to "see" rather than to communicate, I might have developed the skill there. Though the urgency of my current need would be a similar stimulus, I knew that my only chance to master that skill quickly was to give myself completely over to it. I must shut all worry, all speculation out of my mind and concentrate on the task at hand, and I must shut out all sensory inputs, too. Kari, fortunately, was still sleeping; resolutely I lay down on my bunk, closed my eyes, and, ignoring the unrelenting glare of the lightbulb, I tried to imagine myself back in the tank.

Passage of time is hard to judge in this cell, for the bulb never flickers, no light seeps through the opaque shutters that have been installed over the window, and I am fed at irregular intervals; still, I've developed an uncanny sense of duration, somehow. So I believe that it took about an hour of preparation. I knew better than to try too soon and shake myself with failure; I waited until I had succeeded in emptying my mind of absolutely everything but a vague murk of nothingness, a murk that made me ache for something, anything, to break the monotony. I let myself feel the terrifying vacuity I had experienced in the tank. Then, determinedly, I reached out mentally toward the ventilator and "looked" behind it.

The camera was there, all right, and so was the microphone. There were wires leading to them—I could "see" them, though I can't say what color they were—

and psychokinetically I jerked them free. Then I tried scanning behind the walls of the cell in case there should be a second microphone; but although I detected nothing, I could not be entirely sure. If I had missed anything, we would be in hot water, but the risk had to be taken. I had no choice but to speak with caution and hope for the best.

I judged it to be near morning by that time, and I went quickly to Kari's bunk and sat on the edge of it, knowing that whatever my doubts, however shaky I felt inside, I must push all uncertainty from me. I must be totally confident, totally sure of myself, and unswervingly courageous; for I could not communicate those things unless I felt them. Mustering all my strength of will, I put my hand on Kari's shoulder and gently shook her awake.

"We can talk now," I said quietly. "The camera is disabled for the time being, and so is the microphone; at least the one I know about is. There might be another, so we're taking a chance, and I can't say anything that could be important to the SSP."

She sat up, her eyes wide with fright and bewilderment. "But how?" she asked dazedly. "How could you disable the camera?"

"Never mind! They'll probably come to fix it before long, so we've got to hurry." I grasped her hands, warming them between my own. "We're in serious trouble, Kari, but there's a way out if we trust each other."

Kari's voice was low but solemn. "I trust you, Elana," she said slowly. "I'm not sure how, but when you took my hand, in there, I—well, I just *knew* . . . I knew you *wanted* to help me."

Thank goodness, I thought. At least the telepathy would be easy to establish.

"So then of course I knew the things he was saying about you must be lies," Kari continued.

This was the first crucial point, and I knew that the success or failure of my plan would rest on my handling of it. Meeting Kari's gaze, I said honestly, "They weren't lies, Kari. Everything he said was true, though naturally he did not tell you the whole story."

"You did those things? Spying? *Sabotage?* And you—you could have confessed, and they'd have let me go?"

"They want more from me than a confession," I explained. "They want information, information that I can't give them because if I did they'd win. Win forever, I mean, all over the world. They'd start the war tomorrow, and they'd use the Bomb, and in the end there wouldn't be much world left."

She didn't doubt me; unbelievable as it must have sounded, from my telepathic reinforcement she recognized it as the truth. "You really are a Libertarian agent, aren't you?" she said, awed.

"No, though they think I am."

"Then who are you? You're not like other people, I've always felt you weren't! He was right about that. Was he right about the amnesia, too? Was it only a—a cover?"

"I did lose my memory, Kari," I said gently, "but I got it back, and I wasn't free to tell you. Why and where I came from, doesn't matter; I simply don't want the dictator to start a nuclear war."

"Neither do I," she whispered. "Anyway, you know how much I hate his government. But oh, Elana—"

I hesitated. It was only fair to warn her. "I do know, and we've got to discuss it," I told her, "but you must realize the chance we're taking if there should be another microphone, because you see, the authorities don't suspect that you oppose them. They think you're a loyal citizen of their regime."

"But why did they ever arrest me, then?" she demanded.

"For exactly the reason the interrogator gave you," I admitted grimly.

"Just so they could torture me, and make you watch?"

"Yes. The information I've got is vital to them, and they're pretty desperate. They've done all kinds of things to *me*, but they weren't getting anywhere."

With a kind of reverence she asked incredulously, "Are you really insensitive to pain, Elana?"

"Not exactly. I'm protected against it, that's all." I drew a deep breath, for we had come to the second crucial point, the heart of the whole scheme. In this I must mislead her, and I must do it with absolute conviction, since any trace of doubt in my own mind would be communicated to hers. What I was about to tell her was not a categorical falsehood; if she fell for it, it would become true. If she didn't, or if that extra microphone was present, our situation was worse than hopeless.

From the pocket in which, providentially, I had hidden the remains of my bread from yesterday's breakfast, I drew forth two tiny pellets, pellets rolled from soft crumbs. They didn't look at all like bread to anyone who had been given no reason to suspect their origin. "Kari," I said levelly, "there's a means of protection, and I'm going to share it with you. You won't have to suffer at all. But you must go on trusting me; you must do exactly as I tell you and not ask questions."

She nodded, ready to grasp at the smallest straw of hope offered to her. "All right, then," I said. "Quickly, in case they come to repair the camera! Swallow this."

I gave her one of the pellets, eating the other myself with the greatest display of melodrama possible. She stared for a moment and then, trustingly, popped the thing into her mouth. "What—what will it do?" she asked in a small voice.

"Nothing harmful. It may seem strange and a little scary." I paused, deciding on the quickest way to put across this bit of shameless deception. "You remember, Kari, when we went to that party where they offered us drugs, mind-changing drugs—"

Her eyes grew dark with terror. "But Elana, those are dangerous! You said so yourself."

"Yes. But some are less dangerous than others, and a lot better than being tortured in any case." I smiled encouragingly. "This isn't like the bad ones. You won't start seeing things or lose your ability to reason or anything like that. What will happen is that you'll find your mind working in different ways than it has before. For instance, you'll be able to communicate with me even when we're not speaking aloud. We've both taken it, you see, and we'll have—well, telepathy."

"Telepathy? We'll read each other's *minds?*" She was skeptical, but not too skeptical. Why should she doubt me? As far as she knew, I could have no possible motive for making up a story like that! Besides, Kari was in an even more suggestible state than usual, and not by accident; the stresses of interrogation are carefully calculated to produce that state. Commander Feric, by his rigorous handling of her, had once again unwittingly helped me.

"We will when we both want to, just like conversation." Turning my back on her, I added soundlessly, *It's had time to take effect by now. This is the first thing you'll notice, but there's something else more important.*

"What's that?" Kari replied.

You'll be protected from pain; you won't suffer.

"I won't feel it?"

Yes, you'll feel it, but you won't care. The bad thing about pain is what goes on in your mind, not your body! Now your mind will react differently.

"But if my body hurts—" she protested.

If you were unconscious, it wouldn't hurt no matter what was done to you. So you see it's your mind that decides what being "hurt" is. Your emotions. The drug alters those emotions.

"I don't see," Kari said shakily, "how I can possibly be conscious and not care."

No, not yet, but you will later. Do you see how you can read my mind?

"I don't see that either," Kari admitted hopelessly. "Maybe I can't; maybe it won't work with me."

But it does work. I haven't said anything out loud for the last two or three minutes.

She was astonished. She hadn't known she was doing it. It wasn't all that hard, to be sure; I could have taught her to recognize telepathic communication merely by speaking to her in a foreign language and then pointing out that she had understood my strange words. I had tied it in with the "drug" simply to offer

dramatic proof of my assertions. And it was an effective ploy. Kari believed in that "drug" unequivocally
and was, I judged, ready to go on to a more advanced
lesson.

Which meant taking the most crucial step of all.
For me, it would be very demanding, very difficult; but
I knew that it was necessary and that if I flinched from
it my only chance to help Kari would be irredeemably
lost.

Now, this is the scary part, I told her. *I've got to show you
that what I've been saying about the pain is true, so you won't
be afraid later, with the machine.*

Show me? she wavered.

Gripping Kari's arm, I drew it around behind her.
I'm going to hurt you a little, I warned. *Just relax, and trust
me. There'll be a moment right at the beginning when your
mind will start to react in the old way, from habit, but that will
pass.*

She stiffened. Quickly I reached out to her mentally in the deep, wordless way that I had seldom had
the opportunity to practice. The skill I must teach her
could not be expressed in words; Younglings have no
words for it, any more than they have for the technique
of psychokinesis. She was receptive this time, but her
tenseness was still a barrier.

Trust me, Kari! I insisted. *Relax; let yourself go limp. I
know this is frightening, but remember, fear is all you'll suffer
from. Fear, not pain! The pain can't bother you because the
drug won't let it.*

Are you sure, Elana?

*They've used the machine on me lots of times. I don't mind
it; even the interrogator admits that I don't.*

Kari's eyes were closed and she was rigid, but she

didn't draw away. *The pain won't bother you,* I repeated, *but you'll expect it to, so it'll seem bad at first. Only for a minute, though. After that—well, I can't describe it, but you'll see. It's a joyous thing, Kari. Not terrible at all!* I felt a flash of conviction in her, and, taking advantage of it, I pulled her arm upward, twisting it sharply.

It was pure agony for an instant, and through our telepathic link I felt it as strongly as she. Resisting the impulse to relent, I threw those anguished feelings right back at her, mastering them, passing the skill from my mind to hers. And she responded! She grasped the concept, though she couldn't put it into words any more than I could, since in her language those words just didn't exist. Her terror faded; she relaxed at last; and, incredibly, she smiled.

Elana, it is joyous! It's not like anything I ever imagined; I feel so—so free.

Free . . . to her it must seem that way, I thought. Poor Kari, who had lived with fear so long, never guessing her own power; how sad that for her this couldn't last any longer than the bread crumbs held out! Perhaps it was worth what they were doing to her, just for a taste of such freedom.

I released her arm, returning her smile with warmth. *You see, you don't need to worry. The drug won't let you suffer.*

How soon will it wear off?

Not till late tonight, and then I'll give you more. I hoped they would not try an unprecedented marathon session; if they did, I would have to slip it to her somehow. I refused to consider the more frightful possibility, that Commander Feric might not stop with the use of the machine.

Elana? Kari asked suddenly. *Suppose there is another microphone in here; suppose they heard you mention the drug?*

Then we're in a bad spot, I replied honestly.

But you! They'll take it away from you, too!

Yes, I admitted, hoping that I could avoid telling an outright lie—that without it I too would suffer.

You shouldn't have taken the chance. Not if your secret is something they'd start a war over.

I squeezed Kari's hand. I had not misjudged her; she was by no means a coward, she only thought she was. She still thought so, in spite of the implications of what she had just said. *I won't give them any information, Kari, whatever happens,* I assured her. *You wouldn't, either. With the drug it's easier, that's all.*

Why haven't they searched you before this, and found it?

That's one of the questions you mustn't ask.

She thought, I suppose, that it had somehow been smuggled in to me; like the police she assumed that I must be part of a highly organized spy network, and it was an impression that I had to foster. She wouldn't demand to know such secrets, for she wouldn't trust herself with them.

That was the root of Kari's problem; she didn't trust herself. And I hadn't really solved it. What if something went wrong? What if the guards had overheard, or what if the Commander did something against which my makeshift measures couldn't protect her? Kari would break; whether they killed her or not, as a person she would be destroyed. She could not possibly hold out, not when she had nothing to hold out for.

It is easier when you do have a secret than when you don't.

I knew, then, what I must do. There was one more thing I could give Kari, one other kind of support I could offer. It would be dangerous, and in some ways cruel. If I was overestimating her strength, it would be very cruel indeed. Yet in a pinch, if she was what I believed she was, it could make the difference between helplessness and free choice.

It wasn't enough for her to trust me; she must have proof of my trust in her. She must be told something worth concealing, something in which she had a personal stake. *Kari,* I began, *there's one thing you ought to know.*

Don't tell me anything! I might give it away.

You won't. It's about Randil.

She turned pale. "Randil?" she gasped.

Don't say his name aloud! You must never give his name, Kari, or even admit that you know him.

Randil is mixed up in this, too? He's connected to your past after all? Oh, Elana, I've been so worried! I haven't been able to get in touch with him since the night he broke curfew, and they wouldn't have held him so long for that. Fighting back tears, she pleaded, *He's not in this place, is he?*

No. They're aware that he's involved, but he has them fooled; they haven't guessed that he's on our side.

If they do guess, will they arrest him? Torture him?

Yes! I replied implacably. *He knows the whole secret; everything I know.*

Does he have the drug?

No, and I won't be able to get it to him. So you see —

She clung to me, cold with a deeper terror than any she had previously shown. I hated myself; yet this half-truth could save her. It might be the only thing that could save her, and if so, Randil himself would be the first to say that it should be risked. *You mustn't be afraid,* I told her. *There is no way they can suspect him except through us.*

Then we can't tell them anything no matter what they do to me! Elana, promise me you won't!

I promise, I agreed, realizing with wonder that Kari, through the power of her love, was giving full and genuine consent after all. She will be all right now, whatever we have to face; at any rate I've convinced her that she will, projecting what solace I've been able to salvage from the remnants of my own once unshatterable faith.

We have lasted through a harrowing day. To escape what is ahead of us, we now have one frail chance. There has been a new development.

This morning, when we entered the interrogation room, we were hit with a real jolt: Randil was there, seated next to Commander Feric. Kari almost collapsed, but she had been bearing up amazingly well until that point and she was alert to my telepathic command. *Don't recognize him! Treat him as a stranger! He's not here as a prisoner; he's still pretending to side with them.*

But if Kari was appalled by Randil's presence, he was absolutely floored by hers. I have never seen an agent come so close to losing control. He had not, of course, known of her arrest, and he hadn't an inkling as to the reason for it. I told him, quickly and silently, realizing that I could do it more gently than Commander Feric would. Randil's emotions very nearly swamped us both, but the discipline of his training paid off and he showed no outward sign. There is no weakness in Randil, only naïveté.

He had come to help me, to try to get me released, and his idea of how to go about it was to convince the authorities that the ship couldn't possibly be endangered by anything I might be mixed up in. This well-meant attempt was the worst danger I had encountered, and it had to be squelched. Moreover, I was horribly afraid that his presence might jeopardize my scheme to protect Kari. They were pretending not to recognize each other, but did Commander Feric know of their connection? I had been under surveillance, and Randil's visits to our apartment might have been noted. The Commander could inflict a great deal of pain by telling her that I had denounced Randil, especially since in doing so, to avoid involving Kari, I had mentioned my own "dates" with him rather than hers. These facts could be presented in a very bad light; they might put too great a strain on her trust in me, whatever silent explanation I gave.

Yet in spite of everything, I was thankful for his appearance, which meant that there might be a chance for Toris after all. I was helpless; the best I could do was to stall for time. But Randil had access to the ship! He would destroy it, surely, if he could be forced to rethink those unrealistic assumptions of his.

My first impulse, when he grasped the significance of Kari's being strapped into the chair, was to reassure him: to explain that she wasn't really going to suffer. And then, just on the brink of it, I stopped. It was the cruelest decision I have ever made. I condemned Randil to an ordeal even worse, in view of his love for Kari, than what I had believed I myself couldn't bear; I did it coldly and deliberately. I *had* to. When I had communicated with him before, I had failed to convince him that the ship would be used for evil. I still couldn't convince him because he just couldn't comprehend the depths to which Younglings can sink. He needed proof, and the proof could be given only through shock treatment.

At the beginning, naturally, Randil tried to stop the proceedings. "This is insane," he told the interrogator. "Clearly, the second woman is innocent, no matter what this agent of your enemies may be concealing."

"I'm aware that she is innocent. Regrettably, she is the only tool we have, for the agent's sole weakness is her sensitivity to the suffering of others, and this girl was unfortunate enough to have been her roommate."

With relief I noted that he spoke of Kari as if she could be of no possible consequence to anyone but me. Apparently, if Randil's dates with her had been observed, they had not been recorded in my file, for he had been under no suspicion at the time. It was I whom the police had been watching, not him; they had been unaware that he was writing the articles and had thus assumed him to be an ordinary student until he had given them the ship. Afterward, therefore, they had had no way of connecting him with the man seen earlier, and though I had told them that he knew me, they would naturally suppose that if he also knew my roommate he would say so.

"It's monstrous!" Randil insisted. "You Torisians are barbarians; on Juta we do not torture innocent people. We don't torture people at all, as far as that goes."

Kari stared at him, flabbergasted. *Don't be surprised*

by anything Randil may say, I told her. *Much of it will sound strange, but it's all part of a complicated plot. They believe that he's Jutan—from the planet Juta, I mean.*

Randil? But he couldn't be!

Of course not. But as long as they think he is, he's safe. They assume that the Jutans are siding with them against the Libertarians.

Are there really Jutans, like in science fiction?

No, but that's another thing you must never tell.

"I will not be a party to this," Randil declared grimly.

"You were not asked to be a party to it," Commander Feric reminded him. "It was you who requested to be present at the examination of the agent, after all; and I must say I still don't see how you learned about her, for we never intended to trouble you with such affairs."

"I did not know what sort of examination you were planning. I thought I might assist you in clearing up the matter so that your use of the ship would be delayed no further, because personally I do not believe this nebulous sabotage plot is in any way dangerous. My advice is to forget it and to release both women at once."

Randil, no! I urged desperately. *If they stop believing in the plot, this is all for nothing; Kari will have suffered for nothing.*

Incredulously he burst out, *You won't really let them torture her! Elana, you can't! Not just to keep up this senseless pretense.*

It's not senseless. They'll have their nuclear bombs loaded in that ship within hours of the time I confess I'm bluffing.

They couldn't. I won't believe it!

Would you have believed they could use Kari to get my confession?

Commander Feric said, "I'm afraid you have insufficient knowledge of our ways to judge them; you must bear with us. The plot is a potential danger not only to the ship but to the relations between your planet and ours, and this agent is the key to it. She will break very shortly now, and you will then have the opportunity to question her at length, as is your right. We would not want Juta to get the impression that we of Toris are incapable of dealing with crimes against the State." Turning to me, he inquired, "Well, Elana? Have you decided to be sensible? I warn you that I'm not going to use the restraint I did yesterday, and you will spare your friend much pain if you give in now."

I answered neither him nor Randil, who was imploring, *Elana, please! Can't you pretend to confess, make up some harmless story?* Hardening my heart to him, I withheld response. To make up a story would be impossible; Randil had no conception of the details that would be demanded of me, or of the way in which those details would be checked. Commander Feric would first of all insist that I name my fellow conspirators.

I had, of course, warned Kari that she must put on a good act for the interrogator. *He's accepted the idea that I don't mind pain,* I had told her, *but if you show that you don't, he'll be suspicious, especially since you minded it yesterday. So you've got to pretend to be really terrified. And you've got to scream and carry on and beg me to make him stop.*

She did it beautifully. She's got far more acting talent than I have. Since they did not monitor her heartbeat or other physiological reactions, being less interested in her condition than in mine, neither Commander Feric nor Randil had any suspicion that she was faking.

And it was good for her. It's a funny thing, but if you try to act scared, any real fear you start out with stops bothering you; it becomes part of the game. It's like trying to cry; you just don't want to anymore, somehow. Kari actually was scared at the beginning, despite her conviction that she would be protected from pain. But when she threw her energy into acting more frightened than she felt, the fright faded away, simply because she was no longer afraid of being afraid.

We were not allowed to hold hands, but we communicated silently, and I knew what she was feeling. She didn't suffer; she didn't even come close to the edge, for between her trust in the "drug" and my continued telepathic help she was completely free of panic. It was a strange new experience for Kari: She felt in control of the situation. She could analyze her sensations, describe them to me, and yet keep an inward calm that she had never dreamed was possible.

The pain was intense; Commander Feric pulled no punches this time. He gave her the entire range. How he could listen to those realistic-sounding screams and remain impassive, I don't know; he had been, I suppose, desensitized through long experience. I picked up no emotional overtones, for to him it was all in the day's work. He got no enjoyment from tormenting people; in fact he rather looked down on the guards, one of whom was a brute and a sadist who obviously did, and whose emotions I took care to shut out after my first telepathic taste of them. The Commander no doubt considered this man an efficient tool, just as he considered all people tools of the State. He had his mind so well compartmentalized that he saw no conflict between such callousness and his sincere though erroneous social ideals.

For Randil it was excruciating. At Kari's first scream he froze, and for a moment I thought my shock treatment might prove too drastic. I shall never forget the look he gave me when he finally perceived that I wasn't going to yield. Though there was violent rage in him, he was powerless to make any move, for he remained aware that his sole chance of helping her depended on keeping the Commander's trust. But since his arguments had failed, he didn't know where to turn.

There's a course open to you, Randil, if you'll take an honest look at what's happening, I ventured, in an attempt to steer him onto the right track. I dared not communicate with him further, both because I was afraid I would succumb to compassion and give away the truth, and because I knew I must devote my whole mind to supporting Kari. They themselves had no telepathic contact; neither guessed that the other would be able to converse, and they were unconsciously avoiding emotional exchanges through their pretense not to know each other.

Seeing the anguish Randil was undergoing, Kari cried miserably to me, *Oh, Elana, if only there were some way to tell him!*

It took all my courage to remain merciless. *It's awful for him,* I admitted, *but he's got to bear it. You understand, don't you? He would save you if it were merely a matter of taking it on himself, but if he were to drop his role now, the Bomb could be used tomorrow.*

I know. But it's so useless for him to think I'm being hurt.

Not entirely useless, I trust. Randil didn't deserve what he went through; it was an unjustly harsh though necessary education. He mastered himself and took it in stride. I'm not sure what was going on in his mind; I can only hope. There is just the one hope left to us now.

For the time came when the Commander realized that I wasn't ready to crack. "I must compliment you," he said to me at last, switching off the machine. "I really didn't think you had it in you."

That was a dubious compliment, I thought, but in his eyes an honest one. Commander Feric went on, "You leave me no choice. We've come to understand each other fairly well, Elana, and I believe you're aware that I have no liking for the step I must take next. I've done everything in my power to avoid it. What comes now rests on your head, and yours alone."

He stood up, motioning the guards to release Kari. "Yesterday," he told me, "you assured your friend that although she would suffer she would not be injured. And that, apparently, is the answer to your surprising composure. This machine, advantageous as it may be in the case of a prisoner for whom we have further use, is unsuited to a situation of this kind, and in our next session we shall therefore have to revert to cruder and more old-fashioned techniques."

Kari blanched, Randil almost broke the arm of the wooden chair he was gripping, and I was too busy communicating with first one and then the other to give much thought to my own sick horror.

Elana, what does he mean? Kari pleaded.

Don't worry. Take one step at a time. Whatever happens, you will not suffer any pain.

Randil didn't have to ask what was meant; he was naive, but not quite that naive. *These Torisians are perverted!* he exclaimed vehemently. *Maybe that's the answer we came to find. Elana, Younglings who can do such things are wiped out because they're not worth saving!*

Nobody ever jumps from naïveté to realism; there's a cynical stage in between. That's true of worlds, and I guess it's true of people, too. *Isn't she worth saving?* I asked, with a glance at Kari, who, not having grasped the full significance of the interrogator's threat, was beginning to show the effects of her inner triumph. *And aren't there others like her?*

Of course—but oh, Elana, then there are no rational answers at all.

You're thinking just like Kari does! The Torisians are not perverted; they're simply Younglings! There are people capable of evil among all Younglings, but you've got to make allowances for them because they don't really know what they're doing.

Make allowances, when it's the innocent people who pay the price?

The price is always paid by the innocent. It always has been. It will be now, if our ship is used as the dictator intends.

He still couldn't let himself accept such an intent. *What sort of universe would it be,* he protested, *where a few evildoers could destroy all that's good in a world?*

Don't blame the universe! It was us, Randil. We gave them the power. There was a balance; the chances were against their risking this war, until we gave them power they could misuse.

We exchanged no more thoughts for a long time. Then, as the Commander moved to dismiss us, Randil entreated, *Elana, you can't hold out forever! If you're right about their plans, they'll bomb the Libertarians anyway once they guess your game. So save Kari at least; don't let her die this way, when in the end it won't solve anything.*

No, Randil. Only you can save her.

How?

By destroying the ship, so that they no longer have any need to break me. Commander Feric means what he says. He doesn't want to do this, and he won't do it merely for revenge.

How do you know he won't?

Because we've come to understand each other, as he said, and I've learned that he is evil only insofar as he's committed to an evil goal for humanity. Believe it or not, he has a conscience. I'll be his first failure, and his faith in force will come crashing down on him, yet he'll accept that rather than carry through something he can't justify to himself.

Justify? Randil exploded. *How could he possibly—*

The same way I justify the deaths involved in blowing up the ship, Randil: by subordinating the means to the end. That's the only way anybody can judge anything, and when such a judgment is immoral, it's because the end itself is worth less than what must be destroyed to achieve it. Evil lies not in a given act, but in a person's sense of values.

Slowly, reluctantly, Randil admitted, *I can't argue with you there. If I thought that killing innocent people was the only means of preventing something worse, truly worse—*

You'd do it. So I ask you again to take a good honest look at what's happening here and decide what sort of values these men have and what's likely to happen when they judge the potential of our ship by those values.

He didn't reply. Finally, I continued, *As Senior, I order you to get rid of that ship. Whether you obey is up to you. If you decide not to, though, you must come back tomorrow when—when I'm questioned.*

No!

You owe it to Kari, Randil. I—I'm going to teach her to understand telepathic communication; I'll give her what comfort I can. But you can give her something more. She loves you, and you've got to stick with her.

Commander Feric ushered us to the door. "The next time we meet," he informed me, "it will not be here; this office is hardly an appropriate setting for what will occur. I am going to be very rough with you, Elana. We both know that there are limits as to how far I can go—limits that do not apply to Kari—but you will both benefit, I think, from a short demonstration carried out on *you*. I would not want either of you to have any question about what you're letting your friend in for."

Randil had been totally unprepared for Kari's arrest and torture. It was a very great shock. He was so jolted that it took a long time for him to regain his capacity for logical thought; as he slowly came to himself, alone in his suite, the first thing to strike him was wonder that he had managed to get through the day without losing his grip. How could he possibly have taken leave of Commander Feric calmly, exacting a promise that he would be called the next time Elana was interrogated? How could he have coolly telephoned one after another of the men he had worked with in his role as a "Jutan," urgently but dispassionately insisting that the ship could not have been harmed by sabotage and appealing for their aid in calling a halt to the SSP's investigation? It did not seem right that he had observed such horror with composure. Why, he hadn't even felt Kari's pain, not in a physical sense; and that was incredible, for considering their closeness he ought to have experienced it telepathically. Perhaps, he thought, the whole thing had been nothing more than a nightmare.

Yet he knew it was no nightmare, and as the initial numbness wore off, the agony of his thoughts was intensified. He had been warned often enough, back at the Academy, that the evils of Youngling worlds were real and that his first personal confrontation with them would be painful. Just how painful, his instructors could not have guessed; they hadn't foreseen that he would be facing an evil resulting from something he himself had done. But fortunately, they had conditioned him to retain his self-control under stress, and that conditioning alone had upheld him, for he had been in no state to control himself consciously.

Throwing himself across the bed, Randil at last gave way to feelings that he could no longer push from his mind. His attempts to secure the release of Kari and Elana had met with no success; he had come up against a blank wall. The phone calls had achieved nothing, and the guards at the door of his suite had politely but firmly declined to let him contact anybody in person. What Elana had told him was true: The only way to keep Commander Feric's threat from being carried out was to destroy the ship. So there was no choice! He had brought unspeakable pain to Kari, whom he loved, and at all costs he must save her from the still worse torment—and perhaps death—that was in store for her.

Weak with delayed reaction, he wondered if, having once lost his artificial self-possession, he would be able to muster enough poise to take the necessary steps. The recollection of the morning's ordeal was fast overpowering him. Kari . . . those harrowing screams . . . and in between, what must she have been thinking? She had not looked at him with hatred; but then, she would have had no suspicion that any act of his was responsible for her arrest. Elana would surely have told her that his apparent friendship with the authorities, as well as his claim to be Jutan, was a ruse. No, the only hatred in that room had been in *him*. He had hated the Commander during those excruciating hours; he had even hated Elana for her stubborn silence and her all-too-successful endeavor to blackmail him into obeying her orders. Randil had never experienced hate before. He had not thought himself capable of sinking to that level, and the discovery revolted him.

Nor had he believed himself capable of succumbing to an impulse to go against his conscience. He was unfit to be an agent, he thought despairingly, unfit not because his action had harmed Kari but because he couldn't bear that fact. There was no choice about vaporizing the ship, he had just told himself! He, who had been so sure of his own moral strength, was ready to commit murder in order to save her; he was willing to abandon his effort to help Toris simply because he was incapable of watching her die! If that wasn't breaking the Oath, what was? To go back on his decision to give the Torisians that landing craft would certainly be to place a personal consideration ahead of the planet's welfare.

He had never questioned his ability to live up to the Oath. He had violated the letter but not the spirit of it; in all his sober reflections on its demands, not once had it occurred to him that he could be put to a test that he would fail.

Elana, he knew, had not failed. She had really thought she was serving Toris's best interests, and she too had suffered with Kari; the interrogator's analysis of her had been all too perceptive. He had hit upon the one way in which she could be deeply hurt. Though Randil had raged against her in his heart, even at the time he had realized that his anger was unfair. Elana hadn't been blackmailing him. If she could have spared Kari, she would have done so; only her belief that the ship would be used for bombing had kept her from it.

Randil stood up and paced across the room, driven by a burst of renewed resolution. Was he less courageous than Elana? To destroy the ship would be easy now, and it would be justifiable too, for he would simply be following orders. But he did have a choice, after all. The choice was suffering for Kari, and consequently for himself, balanced against the probable extinction of a whole human race. His course was still clear: Since only space colonization could divert the Torisians from war, they must keep the spaceship he had given them.

Yet Elana had faced the same choice and had felt her course to be equally clear. She was sure that the ship would not divert the Torisians but would instead precipitate the very war he was trying to prevent. Out of Randil's new knowledge of his own fallibility emerged a terrifying—though for Kari's sake, welcome—idea: Was it possible that Elana could be *right?*

Over and over, she had told him that Younglings were less enlightened than he thought them to be. She had maintained that although they were not in themselves evil, they could do evil things. He had not believed it—that is, he hadn't believed that they could do them deliberately, by conscious intent rather than merely by following their primitive but well-established customs.

But that had been before he had received a demonstration.

Take an honest look at what's happening, she had advised him. *Decide what sort of values these men have.* All at once, in a breakthrough of anguished awareness, Randil understood what she had meant. He understood that men who could do what they were doing to Kari were not so peace-loving as he had supposed. Those particular men weren't, no matter how the rest of their people might feel. If even a few of those in command were capable of torture, mightn't they also be capable of starting a nuclear war by cold design?

And he had thought the Service hypocritical for insisting that intervention could do harm!

If he hadn't been shown, he would not have accepted the truth, Randil reflected bitterly. If it weren't for his desire to save Kari, he might never have been able to admit to himself how mistaken he had been. She had not suffered for nothing; at least his eyes had been opened before it was too late.

He stood by the window, once again looking out across the twinkling lights of the city he had come to think of as home. There was so much, so very much that he hadn't comprehended. He'd been a child to judge himself wiser than agents who had met grim reality on countless Youngling planets throughout the universe! From all the worlds he might have learned about in the years ahead, would he have come to understand that reality, to reconcile himself to it? Would he have come to see the Service's policy of compassionate but nondirective scrutiny as the only possible means of reconciliation?

He was already thinking of himself in the past

tense, Randil noticed, and so underneath he must have known for quite a while what he was going to do.

Elana wasn't aware that destruction of the ship would necessarily involve his death; if she were, she would hardly have issued a direct order to carry it through, for by unbroken Service tradition such orders were not given. Randil was glad she didn't know. He wouldn't want her to think it a factor in his resistance, for it was not. He would never have hesitated on that account, even before the question of saving Kari had arisen; and in his present frame of mind, resigning himself to death was not difficult. Not that he would choose to die if it could be avoided, but unfortunately it couldn't. He had been rushed when he had disabled the destruct device, since men were approaching the ship; moreover, it hadn't occurred to him that there might ever be a need to activate it again. He had therefore ripped loose the wires heedlessly, and to repair the proper circuits for psychokinetic detonation would be a complex job that he would have neither the time nor the skill to complete. With luck, he could jury-rig a workable connection, but that connection would have to be made by hand.

The evening was almost gone; there was no time to waste. Once more Randil phoned the officer responsible for liaison with him. "I would like to inspect the ship tonight," he said determinedly. "If there has been sabotage, I can surely assist you in locating it."

That was impossible, he was told, and it was also unnecessary. He must not concern himself. The ship had been repeatedly searched for signs of damage, and by morning there would be new information to go on. When his aid was needed, he would be informed.

Appalled, Randil called the officer's superior. He got no further. There was no chance of his being allowed to visit the ship before morning. Or perhaps ever again, he thought wretchedly. As he hung up, he recalled that in recent days there had invariably been excuses to prevent his being taken back to the well-concealed underground cavern that had been constructed some distance from Cerne. He hadn't paid much attention, not having particularly wanted to go once he had finished explaining the controls; but he had not been allowed near the ship for almost a week. Were they already refitting it for a mission of attack, in the expectation that Elana would crack before Kari was killed?

He was helpless, he realized—as helpless as Elana herself. He had started something that he was powerless to stop.

At that moment the phone rang, and Randil snatched it with relief, assuming that there had been a last-minute decision to conciliate him. There hadn't. The voice that spoke was that of Commander Feric.

"The final interrogation of the agent will take place tonight," he announced ominously. "If you wish to be present, I will send a car for you."

"No—" Randil's protest came out as a scarcely audible gasp.

"You've changed your mind? I think I can promise you better results this time. I know this agent thoroughly; she is incapable of facing what I shall confront her with. I have been lenient too long. But I must admit she's earned my respect, in a sense, and I hoped not to have to use extreme measures."

Randil pulled himself together, knowing that he must do so if he was to assume any trace of his responsibility. "Send your car," he said shortly.

He did not believe he could endure what he would witness, yet he must try. It was all he could do for Kari. He had brought this on her not in a noble cause, as he had naively imagined, but through his own stubborn misjudgment; he had doomed the person he most cared for—along with her entire civilization. There was no redemption for him. There was only one thing left, his love. He could, if he had the courage, communicate that love, provided that Elana had indeed awakened Kari's latent telepathic faculties. Through love, he could give Kari what she had always lacked: the sustaining knowledge that evil, even victorious evil, was not the most powerful force in the universe.

e i g h t

The room in which we are now waiting might be, I suppose, termed a dungeon, though it's far from dark since its walls are whitewashed and it is illuminated by a number of those dazzling lights of which our captors seem so fond. There are no furnishings except a large, solid table and some wooden benches that we're not allowed to sit on. We are standing at attention; this is a requirement aimed at taxing our endurance, and naturally there are several guards present to enforce it.

I am afraid. I am more afraid than I've ever thought it possible to be. All the answers have evaporated; all the solutions have proved futile. Kari is in a very terrible situation, and I know I'm not going to be strong enough to see this through.

She has been transformed, to be sure. She didn't panic yesterday at the Commander's threats; she walked back to our cell, in fact, with her head high and a confidence that approached elation. For the first time in her life, she had found out what it was to meet a frightening experience without being thrown by it, and her courage had burst forth like water from a once-frozen spring. The infamous pain machine had been to her the ultimate terror, and she had faced it, and she was unharmed! I had promised that she would not suffer pain under any circumstances. It hadn't entered her head that they would kill her, much less what that process might involve. In the morning, I knew, I would have to prepare her; and I did not see how I could find the fortitude.

But they did not wait until morning. Sometime, around midnight I think, our cell was entered by a hard-faced female guard who ordered us to strip, handing us the briefest of shapeless gray knit garments to cover our nakedness. Kari cringed, speechless, but she obeyed with more poise than I would have thought possible from her. I too recoiled in horror, not from the indignity of it—for I had undergone worse more than once during the course of my imprisonment—but from the loss of those precious bits of bread in my pocket. As I removed my prison uniform, I managed to snatch a few crumbs, rolling them into a pellet within my clenched fist; I knew that our clothes would very likely disappear with the guard, which indeed proved to be the case. "Ready yourselves," she told us harshly. "You are being taken downstairs soon."

Kari, unfamiliar with the prison jargon that I had heard from the guards, didn't catch the implication of that, and I did not enlighten her. The fact was that *downstairs* meant not the ground floor but the basement, and the interrogation rooms of the basement were of a notoriously different nature from Commander Feric's well-furnished office. Few prisoners who went *downstairs* ever returned.

Quickly I ripped the wires loose from the camera and microphone again, which presented no problem now that I had once "seen" them, though the guards would surely be mystified by such a freakish "accident" occurring twice. Then I opened my hand, holding the bread pellet out to Kari. "Don't be afraid," I said, with as reassuring a smile as I could force. "I was able to hide one while she wasn't watching."

Kari reached for it, and then, suddenly, she drew back. "But Elana," she protested, "where's yours?"

Too late, I saw my mistake. I should have claimed to have already swallowed it! My hasty attempt to cover up did no good; Kari wasn't fooled. "You're lying," she asserted bluntly. "There's only one, and you're giving it to me."

"Yes, of course," I admitted.

"But that's not right! You're the one with the important secret, so you've got to have it. The interrogator told us he'd try whatever he's planning on you first."

I had backed myself into a corner. If she were to learn that the "drug" was superfluous for me, she would lose her faith in it; it would be useless for her, too. What lay before us was undoubtedly pretty ghastly, and without the support of the placebo Kari would have no chance at all. We would be right back where we started: She would suffer horribly, and in the end I might crack up.

Yet there was still a way out. "We'll toss for it, if you insist," I said confidently, knowing that through psychokinesis I could control the throw to let her win.

"That's too risky. I don't know anything important, so it doesn't matter what happens to me, but if you broke down, they'd have what they need to start the war."

I had no choice but to use my ultimate weapon, the half-truth that I still dared not mention aloud. *You do know something important,* I reminded her. *You know that they can get what they want through Randil, so it would come to the same thing in the end.*

Kari paled. *Oh, Elana, then there's no hope at all. Not for any of us, not even for the world!*

I put my arm around her trembling shoulders. "Yes, there is," I said quietly. "Kari, as I've said before, situations like this aren't always as hopeless as they seem on the surface. It's possible to face up to them, and you've just proved it."

"I've proved it? How?"

"By recognizing that underneath, you'd prefer to go through something really horrible rather than take a chance on letting millions of people be harmed."

"Well, of course I would—"

"But you didn't know it till now, did you?"

She stared at me, surprised. "I guess I didn't."

"What people may have told you about torture isn't true," I continued levelly. "Nobody can be *forced* to tell anything. There's always a choice. The choice you make depends on what sort of person you are and what's at stake, but it's a free choice. We're not robots, and we can't be controlled. The interrogator thinks we can, but then, he thinks everybody ought to be controlled, so his judgment isn't very reliable."

"I—I guess I see," she murmured thoughtfully. "If we agree that he can control us, it's the same as agreeing to their whole system—to everything we hate about it!"

"That's right." I made her face me. "Kari, have you ever experienced pain? Bad pain, I mean, worse than what you were given the first day with the machine?"

"No," she whispered.

"Well, I have. I'm going to be honest about it: In some ways it's more terrible than anything you imagine beforehand. But in another way it's less so. Panic is the worst part; you can keep your head, provided you don't panic and start worrying about what's coming instead of what's happening. And as long as you keep your head, you still have that free choice! So you see, whichever of us has to face this without the drug isn't going to give away any secrets, no matter how bad things get."

Kari had come a long way since her arrest. Before, I doubt if she would have dared to follow such a line of reasoning through, but she had learned to know herself better. Unfortunately, this self-knowledge had come too late to do her much good, unless Randil had managed to destroy that ship. The chances of that, I realized, were slim. Even if he had destroyed it, I might not find out in time, and Commander Feric's conscience might not prove as strong as I had claimed; it might not count for as much as his desire to save face. I had no illusions. But at least she would not suffer.

"Let's toss," I said with forced brightness.

"All right," Kari agreed. "What shall we use for a coin?"

And there we were stumped. We had no coins, naturally, but neither did we have anything else, not so much as a button. The cell was bare.

The faded, ill-fitting garments in which we were clad were old and worn; a thread was raveling from the shoulder strap of Kari's. She broke it off, in two pieces, saying, "We'll draw straws. The longest wins." She clutched them in her fist, ends protruding, and held it out to me.

I gasped. Over this I had no psychokinetic control! Clairvoyance? I wasn't good enough; I could not do it on the spur of the moment, without mental preparation. Telepathy? All I learned that way was that she hadn't kept track herself.

"Hurry and draw," Kari urged. "The guards may come for us any moment."

Helplessly, I drew—and I won.

"There, it's settled," Kari declared, valiantly suppressing the tremor of her voice.

"No," I protested. "No, Kari, I can't accept it! You'd never have been arrested if it hadn't been for me; it's my responsibility."

She turned away, her eyes brimming with tears. "I suppose you're right," she faltered, "in thinking you'll do better than me, since you've got so much more courage than I have." Sensing her emotions, I could feel her newfound confidence begin to melt, and with sudden insight I realized that to spare my own sensitive feelings I was destroying the only real good I had ever brought to Kari.

For once in her life she had done a truly brave thing. For once, she had understood herself for the person she really was. It was better to let her suffer pain than to rob her of that.

"I haven't any more courage than you," I asserted quickly. "I only thought that since the whole mess was my fault . . . but that's past, and we're both in it now." I was defeated. I did the only thing I could do: I gave in gracefully and swallowed that irreplaceable bread pellet myself.

A few minutes later we were taken to this basement dungeon, and whether either of us will ever leave it is a question best left unasked. Commander Feric is not here at the moment, for he has given us two hours in which to "think things over." We have also been given explicit and graphic instructions on what to think about. We were shown various instruments, the use of which was thoroughly described, and we were forced to examine some quite dreadful photographs. I shall not record the details; they are unspeakable.

So far, Kari has been upheld by our ongoing telepathic contact. Back in our cell I overlooked the fact that because of my original ruse she would interpret her continuing ability to communicate with me as a sign that her first dose of the "drug" hadn't yet fully worn off. On our way down here, though, she asked apprehensively, *How much longer will we be able to "talk" this way?* I realized then that unless I devised an adequate explanation, she might lose even her command of the telepathy that is usable at will between an agent and a once-initiated Youngling.

We'll keep right on, I told her. *Your mind has learned the trick now, and mine is so sensitive from having taken the drug repeatedly that it'll compensate for yours not being reinforced.*

My mind has learned the trick? How could it, when it was simply being affected by the drug?

Mind-changing drugs don't alter your mind. They only release what's already there. That's the big danger of the bad ones: People have ended up in the hospital, you know, because they kept on feeling the effects long after they'd taken the stuff.

Could it work that way with this? Not only for the telepathy, but for—for the other, too?

I dared not give too positive an assurance, for however strong I made it there would be doubt in her, and the defense against pain is too elusive a skill to permit any doubt. I couldn't jeopardize her trust in me if I was to sustain her during the ordeals to come. Still, there was a bare chance.

Possibly, I hedged, *if you go into this acting as if it will—not letting yourself be afraid. You've nothing to lose by trying.*

Since she had great faith in my judgment, she made a gallant effort to take this advice. She still had no suspicion, at that point, of what was in store for her; she was envisioning pain, perhaps severe pain, but nothing beyond. I had decided against any attempt to prepare her. It was best, I decided, to take things as they came. A person who is about to die deserves a chance to come to terms with herself; but if the Commander intended to kill Kari, she would be given more than enough opportunity. One thing I could be sure of was that whatever he was planning would not be over quickly.

Now, of course, she is better informed; Commander Feric tried hard to crack her composure. I knew when he began how it would be: He would draw it out, concentrating his main effort on the anticipatory phase, because he is convinced that if I break at all, it'll be while there's a chance of saving Kari, and he doesn't doubt that in the end she'll plead with me to do so. *We're probably going to go through a lot of rigmarole designed to frighten us,* I had warned her as we entered the room. *The Commander is a real expert at it! Don't panic, and don't take all that's said too seriously.*

But it was impossible not to take the things we were shown seriously. Kari is, I believe, somewhat benumbed by shock. Between the overwhelming events of the past two days and her discovery of the courage she never dreamed was in her, she has become unable to assimilate the fact that what's threatening her is real. Her self-possession astounds her; sick as she is with dread and revulsion, her thoughts are coherent and she's steady on her feet. I've cautioned her that this time she must show no fear, feigned or otherwise, because I don't think Commander Feric will begin on her until she seems ready to beg me for mercy. He will start with me, in the hope that her newfound poise will be destroyed by what she observes.

So here we stand, and we are indeed thinking things over, and though we're agreed that we must not yield, I'm very much aware that when it comes right down to it, we may not have what it takes to do otherwise. And even if we do have, it will be a dark victory. I've turned my mind to "recording" so that I won't dwell on that darkness, for Kari must not sense my despair. She has found something wonderful, and she must keep it to the end. *There's a way through this,* I've assured her. *Not out of it, perhaps, but through.*

Elana, she mused, *do you remember the fortune-teller who told me I was destined to do something brave?*

Of course.

Could he really have had knowledge of the future?

Maybe not in the way you mean. But he knew a great deal

more than most people in this world. I decided, suddenly, to tell her the facts, for it was a time to face the grim truth rather than to avoid it. *He was involved in the same thing we are, Kari; he was my—my contact, and Randil's, too. Randil was with him when they arrested him.*

Oh . . . Her feelings surged through me: surprise mingled with grief.

They killed him, I admitted, *yet he wasn't afraid. That's what I wanted you to know: He was wiser than any of us, and he truly wasn't afraid.*

She didn't respond for a long time. Then abruptly she asked me, *Do—do you still believe what you once said about God?*

Yes, I declared positively.

After your memory came back, did you know anything more about where things are leading?

I can't explain all I know, I told her, not saying why. *And there's a lot that nobody has ever known. A pattern exists, though. Underneath there are answers; you'll see.* But I can't see, myself.

My spirit has forsaken me. I've said the ritual phrases over and over; still, they've left me cold, unmoved. All the certitude, all the trust, all the lovely words about darkness being part of the fabric of the way things are, with good winning in the end no matter how much individual people have to suffer—well, I still believe those things intellectually, but I don't *feel* them. They no longer help. I'm still willing to die for them if need be, but that doesn't prove much because I'm not at all sure that I want to be alive anyway. It's an awful thing to say, but I really don't care if I'm ever rescued or not. Because having once stopped feeling the good, I can't imagine ever feeling it again.

It's the same universe, you see, as it has been all along. There is no more evil in it—or less good—than there was before this happened. The only change is in me; my eyes have been opened to a view I hadn't imagined before. And it hurts, and it will always haunt me, and if I am rescued, then years from now on some other planet I'll wake in the night and picture Kari's face, and feel her anguish . . . and I don't know if I'll be able to do my job there, either.

Randil has not appeared. I fear that if by some miracle he has destroyed the ship, I won't be told until just after the decisive point—whether I confess, or whether I let Kari die—which will mean that either way the Commander's campaign to make me hate myself will succeed. On the other hand, if the morning's shock didn't change Randil's mind, the destruction of Toris itself can't be held off much longer. In that case what we're about to face may prove meaningless; yet we've still got to face it, and I only hope that for Kari's sake Randil will be brave enough to come.

It is over. I do not know if I will be able to live with myself, but what's happened has happened, and I shall record it because if I'm ever contacted by my own people the record will be of importance.

Long before dawn Commander Feric came back to our dungeon, and with him were still more guards, among them the sadistic one whose emotions I dared not sense. And it was that guard who laid hands on me and propelled me over to the table, upon which I was required to lie prone. I offered no resistance; when the

Commander asked if I realized that this was my last chance, I simply nodded, knowing that he did not expect me to do anything else. He knew I didn't fear the pain, and while he no doubt hoped to weaken me through physical shock, the thing was carried through mainly to impress us with the fact that he meant business. From that standpoint it was successful: Kari's stamina at last gave way, and during the proceedings she collapsed. They allowed her to sit down after that, but they made her keep her eyes open and watch. I tried to console her, but for a while I was much too preoccupied to manage any telepathy.

I won't relate the particulars of what was done to me; they aren't details that I care to remember. Not that I suffered seriously; the pain of burning flesh is no worse than that of electrical nerve stimulation, though it seems so because of your instinctive and uncontrollable aversion to any sort of bodily damage. My well-practiced defense overrode most of the physical sensations. The trouble was, it couldn't banish the horror of anticipating those sensations for Kari, besides which I had the problem of consciously dropping the Shield. That had to take precedence, for it is hard to keep up two complex psychic processes at the same time.

There will, of course, be scars. (They won't show when I'm fully clothed; since Commander Feric was still planning to let me appear in public, he saw to it that certain restraints were observed.) I do not really mind, for here it scarcely matters, and if I am ever rescued, Federation doctors will be able to erase them easily enough.

Eventually, I was lifted from the table and helped over to the bench facing my interrogator, while Kari,

paralyzed with terror but still unprotesting, was bound
in my place. And at that moment, the door opened to
admit Randil. The Commander, supposing him to be
interested only in questioning me after I confessed, had
not seen fit to let him in sooner, for he knew he didn't
approve of torture, and he was sure that I would give in
rather than let Kari be harmed.

My last trace of hope evaporated. Randil had done
nothing about the ship. It was still intact; if it were not,
he would have told me instantly.

"What you've just experienced was only a small
sample," Commander Feric was saying to me. "I know
you, Elana. I know you can't watch your friend die in
such a fashion; you simply can't stomach it."

And I knew it, too. Yet I also knew that neither
could I give the word that would send that invulnerable Federation ship out across the continents, loaded
with nuclear bombs. Perhaps, I thought, I would simply go crazy . . . perhaps I'd fold up and become absolutely unhinged! The pain of my burns began to
break through, and I realized, almost with surprise,
that despite my inborn healing powers there would be
days of continuous pain, the control of which would
surely sap my psychic energy.

I was dizzy; I wasn't even thinking lucidly. Randil
was pale but in command of himself, and I wanted to
reach out to him for aid. He was trying to communicate, I felt dimly, but I seemed unable to respond or
even to understand.

"Well, Elana?" the Commander demanded. "Are
you ready to cooperate?"

Then one clear thought reached me, sure, insistent—a thought not from Randil but from Kari. *No,*

Elana! she urged. *No, let them kill me; don't tell them anything!*

It shook me out of my stupor, and I threw all the strength and all the faith I could summon into my reply. *I won't. There's nothing to fear, Kari. Inside you're all right; they can't touch your real self. We'll help you. I'll stay with you telepathically, and so will Randil.*

Randil? But how—?

I can't explain it to you. Call it a miracle if you like. But if you speak silently to him, he will answer.

Watching their faces, I knew that the contact had been made, and that to Kari it was indeed a miracle, a heaven-sent miracle to sustain her in the moment of her greatest need. Randil could give her more than I could, and I saw that he was strong enough to do it.

But if this had to happen, it must not happen for nothing! The ship could still be destroyed if Randil could be convinced. If shock treatment hadn't done it, there was only one thing that might: a direct admission of the Neo-Statists' plans from Commander Feric. The Commander would not make such an admission in front of Randil; he had been told that the Jutans had intended their gift to be used for peaceful purposes. He would not—unless, perhaps, he could be made angry enough to forget himself. That wasn't inconceivable, for if I was close to losing control, so was he; there was nothing worse he could do to me, and his own reputation—maybe even his safety—was at stake. I sensed unprecedented desperation in him and knew that I could capitalize on it.

"I will never give you any information," I declared staunchly. "Could my sympathy for one innocent woman be greater than my concern for all the people who'll die if my mission fails? I won't confess just for her sake, and *you* will bear the blame! You'll look pretty ridiculous, won't you, when the infallible secret weapon of your glorious State blows up after all? You've been telling the commandant that it can't happen because you've found the key to breaking me. But you haven't found it, and you have very little time left. Whom will he want to break, I wonder, when it's too late for you to make any more promises? His superiors will demand a scapegoat, I should imagine—"

Commander Feric's face darkened. He knew only too well that what I said was entirely true. If the "secret weapon" should be lost after he had had me in custody for days, he would be the laughingstock of the SSP; but worse, the dictator would exact a heavy price.

"You are less of a realist than I thought," he told me in cold fury. "I have found the key. I have touched your most sensitive spot. What you're suffering now is minor, a mere prelude. *One* innocent woman? Don't you know that there are a hundred innocents on the streets of Cerne whom I could have in this room through a single order? Do you think I would count them? Do you think their lives are of any consequence whatsoever, balanced against the victory of the People's State over the decadent governments of the Libertarians? I tell you, Elana, nothing will be allowed to stand in the way of that victory! You are deluding yourself if you think you have no limits. Your friend has agreed to martyr herself, that is now plain; perhaps she's not as innocent as I've believed. But there are plenty who will not agree, and when one after the other is put to death before your eyes—"

I didn't hear the rest; I fainted. I really did faint.

The next thing I knew, guards were splashing water over my face, and Dr. Sturn was there, and there were needle marks on my wrist. They had bandaged my burns, not out of mercy but out of concern for keeping me conscious. *Kari?* I probed fearfully.

I'm all right. They haven't done anything yet. I think we're in a nightmare, Elana; I think maybe we're going to wake up and find that none of this is true!

Perhaps that is what happens, I thought, when people die. Perhaps Kari is the luckiest one of us all. But that wouldn't make sense, for if that were the way of it, what point would there be in trying to save any world?

Randil's thought came through to me, distinctly this time, with unflinching steadiness. *I tried, Elana. I tried to get back to the ship, but I couldn't. They won't let me near it anymore.*

That he would be unable to reach it had never occurred to me. It meant utter failure. The "shock treatment" had been useless, and for that matter, so had my whole ordeal, not to mention Kari's.

Miserably, I explained to Randil how I had deceived him. He had already guessed most of it—Kari, in their first exchange, had assured him that what he had witnessed earlier had been an act—and he didn't reproach me. *It woke me up,* he admitted. *How much does she know?*

Practically nothing, except that the information they want from me would enable them to start a nuclear war. I told her that both you and I were involved in a plot to prevent it. To her, that was sufficient; she—she consented, Randil. You see why I had to hold out?

I saw after yesterday, he conceded grimly, *and we've no*

choice now but to go on stalling till I can do something. I haven't found a way to manage it alone; but if you've got any ideas, I'll take your orders. You are Senior.

His acknowledgment roused my last and deepest resources. There had to be some means of getting into that ship, and as Senior Agent, I knew it was up to me to figure it out.

You receive inspiration, I guess, when your need is desperate enough. Anyhow, a ruse came into my mind. It was an outside chance, but as Randil had said, we had to do *something*. Hastily, I communicated it to him, pretending to be not quite fully revived in order to gain time.

But Elana, he protested, *if it works, you'll die! The circuits for psychokinetic detonation can't be fixed; the thing has to be set off manually.*

You mean you'll die yourself, no matter how you get in? Randil, if I'd realized, I wouldn't have put what I said yesterday in the form of an order.

I know that. I hope you know it wasn't what made me so hard to convince. It can't be helped; but why both of us?

Can you think of anything else?

No, he admitted.

Then try the ruse! Never mind me; try it now, while we can still save Kari by it.

I left him no alternative. To Commander Feric he said slowly, "I've no doubt that you can break this woman in time by the method you've suggested, but frankly, it's as distasteful to me as it is to her. The people of Juta would find it equally so, if it ever became known to them; and should any accident befall this ship, you would surely not want them to refuse you another—"

"Another?" Commander Feric got hold of himself, immediately alert to the idea of hedging his bet. He had assumed that the Jutans' psychology was just like his own, and that they would interpret any sabotage involving the ship as a sign of weakness in his government. The thought that a replacement might be offered had never entered his head. "Have you some other suggestion?" he asked Randil. "Naturally, we don't want to offend the Jutan people."

"Yes," Randil declared. "I think that if the woman were questioned within the ship, she might betray herself."

"Why should she?"

Randil hesitated. "You have said that I don't understand your ways, but it's also true that you don't understand ours. We of Juta have many abilities of which I haven't yet told you."

Commander Feric regarded him thoughtfully. "Have you a way to induce this woman to speak?"

"Not to speak, but nonetheless to give herself away. She has boasted that an explosive device has been placed in the ship, yet your search has revealed nothing. Moreover, the ship cannot be damaged by an ordinary bomb; it is, as I have explained, invulnerable to all forces known on Toris. Obviously, any sabotage that has occurred involves damage to the power source or to the controls. I'm more familiar with that control board than any of your men, and I also have a certain facility at—well, at getting the truth from people's minds. Give me a few minutes in the ship with this agent, and she'll involuntarily reveal to me whatever she knows of what's been done to it. Of course I won't be able to get a full confession or the names of her associates; but once she has rendered the plot ineffective, I believe you'll find her easier to work with."

The Commander frowned; feeling that he was about to refuse, I embarked upon the ultimate gamble. *Tell him the truth!* I ordered. *Tell him you suspect that I've deceived him!*

"It is always possible," Randil continued, "that she has been bluffing all along. If so, I will know it when I sense her reactions; I'm sure I will. I pledge that the ship will be replaced if I judge her wrongly."

That clinched it. Commander Feric took the bait. He already suspected that Jutans possessed somewhat mysterious powers, since Randil's knowledge of my arrest had never been adequately explained; moreover he knew, once it was pointed out to him, that I could very well be bluffing. All the pieces fit: Randil's original insistence that the ship had not been endangered; the testimony of the guards; the SSP's failure to turn up any evidence of an organized plot; and above all, his own knowledge that I was cool enough and clever enough to pull it off. And I let him know. I averted my face while Randil spoke, but with telepathic projections I gave away the truth, and the Commander grasped it eagerly. He might not have dared to stake his life on it, but Randil had offered him the perfect out.

He fell for our ruse; it worked beautifully. There was only one thing we hadn't anticipated. He took Kari with us.

Why, I'm not really sure. Perhaps he thought her presence would deter me from any rash moves. Perhaps he planned to kill her right there, on the spot, if Randil showed no signs of getting anywhere with me. At any rate, we were both given back our regular prison uniforms, and after the doctor pronounced me in astonishingly good shape for a person who had just suffered third-degree burns, we were escorted under heavy guard to a waiting car.

Randil and I were aghast. Death for ourselves, yes; we were, after all, sworn agents. But for Kari, when it was so unnecessary . . .

At least it will be quick, merciful, I reminded him. *Better than the other way.*

Yes, he agreed, but his thought faltered, and I wasn't entirely sure that Randil would be capable of setting off that destruct device with Kari at his side.

⚛ In the car, Randil experienced the worst inner upheaval he had known. Kari was close to him, cut off by a heavy wire mesh barrier that separated the back seat from the front, yet closer than ever before because their minds had touched. But for the moment his thoughts were too turbulent for him to communicate any further.

Kari's calm bearing and the quiet way in which she had resigned herself to her fate were more than he could understand. But then, he thought, there was a great deal he didn't understand about what had gone on in the prison. Knowing the agony Kari would be facing, knowing the fright she had always felt at the mere mention of the secret police and their rumored treatment of prisoners, he had expected her to be past caring when he had gone back, despairingly, to share her ordeal. He had expected to give love, to sustain her through love, but he had not thought that she would be able to respond. To his amazement, she had returned as much as she had received.

Vaguely, Randil recalled having heard an old and distinguished agent, a veteran of missions to innumerable worlds, say that the most terrible things can, on occasion, be at the same time the most wonderful. That had been beyond his grasp; it had seemed too much of a paradox. He was beginning to fathom it, however, for something very wonderful had happened between himself and Kari. Their first telepathic contact had been uplifting for them both; the rapture of shared thought had overshadowed even the horror of the circumstances. Kari had been afraid, but she had risen above her fear to the extent of exulting in their newfound mental intimacy. He had not needed to tell her that love was stronger than pain. She had already known. In a sense it had been as though she were giving *him* courage! They had accepted what must come, not in despair but in the knowledge that nothing could violate either their inner wholeness or their love for one another; and for a brief time the darkness of that prison had been truly illuminated.

And then he had been plunged back into the real world, the harsh world, and the illumination had faded, and there was no more acceptance in him. Miraculously, he had won the opportunity to destroy the ship after all. It had become possible to prevent the disaster he had brought upon this planet, and he knew he should give thanks not only with his mind but with his whole heart. Instead, he found himself raging against the ironic twist of fortune that had handed him a decision harder than any he had yet made.

Earlier, he had wanted to do the thing; he had

wanted to because he could save Kari by it. Now, abruptly, the situation was reversed. Now it would not save Kari; it would kill her. To be sure, it would be better for Kari to die quickly than to die by torture; but was there no other possibility? There might be! Suddenly, Randil saw, with a tremendous surge of excitement, that Kari need not die at all.

The city was behind them. The road leading out to the ship's secret cavern was dark and deserted, and dawn was still far off. The car in which they were traveling was a special one, designed for transporting prisoners; Elana and Kari were alone in its back seat. No guards were with them since, because of the metal grille as well as the absence of inside door handles, there was no conceivable way for them to get out. In the front seat with Randil there was no one but Commander Feric and the driver, neither of whom had any reason to suspect him.

He could overpower them. He could do it without any trouble at all! There would be no need to start a fight; he could simply stop the car by psychokinetic tampering with its engine—which would cause the driver to get out and look for the trouble—and then take the Commander's gun by the same means. He would never, of course, injure the men, but they wouldn't know that. So once he had the gun, he could disarm the driver and force Commander Feric out, too. After taking the driver's uniform and papers, he would just drive away, and there would be no pursuit in such lonely countryside. The scheme was foolproof.

But if he used it, Randil realized hopelessly, there would be no way to gain access to the landing craft. It would be fine if he could let Kari and Elana out somewhere a safe distance away and go on to do what must be done, but that wouldn't work. The sentries at the gate would stop him. If they recognized him, they would not let him into the ship, not if they were concealing armaments; it would be too suspicious for him to arrive alone. And if they were new guards who didn't recognize him, they still wouldn't let him in, for he would not have the proper clearance. Only a known official like Commander Feric would be admitted to a top-secret installation. Unescorted by the Commander, he hadn't a chance of getting inside.

Escape, then, would be total escape, and it was all too tempting. On foot, miles from anywhere, the Commander wouldn't be able to raise an alarm until they were well out of the country. The border patrol wouldn't question an SSP car driven by a man with SSP identification. Once beyond the territory controlled by the dictatorship, they would be free. He and Kari would have at least a little time together before the Service caught up with him; even if nuclear war came, they might well live through it if they kept away from cities. Perhaps, in that event, the Service would never find him at all.

Not that what happened to him was important. What mattered was that Kari would live. He loved Kari; it was up to him to protect her. How could he kill her by his own hand?

The choice was clear-cut: escape for Kari and Elana, or the destruction of the landing craft. There was no way he could achieve both. It was unfair, Randil thought bitterly, that he should be presented with such a choice! He had made an error in judgment, and he was willing to pay for it with his life; about that there was no question. He was not willing to have Kari pay for it with hers, not when an alternative existed. Once again he was facing a test that he was very much afraid that he would fail.

Kari was innocent. It wasn't right that she should be the one to pay. Elana, too, was innocent, but with Elana it was different; she was sworn. She wouldn't want to buy her life at the cost of nuclear war for Toris any more than he himself would.

All at once a disturbing idea struck Randil: Would Kari?

Though he didn't communicate the question consciously, Kari's sudden thought broke in on his turmoil. *They're going to kill me anyway, aren't they, Randil? When we get wherever it is we're going, and Elana doesn't talk?*

No! No, darling, I won't let them.

But Elana said—

Never mind what she said. I couldn't stop them from scaring you back there, but I'm not going to let you die.

Gently Kari persisted, *She said yesterday that if either of you gave in to save me, it could start a nuclear war, a war that could mean the end of the human race. You wouldn't take a chance on that; you know you wouldn't.*

He had known it once, Randil thought. He had sworn an oath to that effect, and he had flattered himself that he took that Oath more seriously than anybody else in the Service! What was the matter with him, that it could seem so dim and distant now?

I don't know much about what's happening, Randil, Kari declared, *but I do know that I'd rather not be saved if that war could get started on account of it.*

Oh, Kari, you shouldn't ever have had to consider such things!

What do you think I am, Randil—a baby? I wouldn't blame you; I've acted like one often enough. I didn't understand myself very well till yesterday. She hesitated. *It's been funny . . . I was awfully scared in there, and yet there was another feeling too, even before you came—a feeling I can't describe. It was as if I didn't really mind what they did to me, because it wasn't important compared with what I was doing by resisting. I was free inside, and they couldn't change that; but I could stop them from doing harm to the world, so I had more power than any of them.*

Randil twisted around in the seat, looking at Kari in wonder and self-reproach. She had answered the question he could not have brought himself to think through, and with belated perception he saw what he had been doing. He had been mistaken about more than the Critical Stage. His gravest and most basic error had been in his judgment of people, not only the dictator and his kind, but the very people he cared about. He had misjudged Varned; he had misjudged Elana; and, he realized painfully, he had misjudged Kari, for whom he cared most of all. He had done worse than misjudge her. He had placed himself above her, diminished her, as he had diminished her race by taking on a role of protector and guardian that was not his to assume. In supposing that she would value her life above the future of her world, he had been guilty of the same patronizing approach toward Younglings as in his determination to control the destiny of the Torisians.

He had been a presumptuous fool. That the girl he loved must die as a result of his presumption was unfair, certainly, but he did her an injustice if he thought her less capable of sacrifice than he.

He reached out toward Kari with his mind as he longed to reach physically. *Darling*, he urged, *keep that feeling! Hold to it. You don't ever have to be afraid again. There's much I can't explain, but I promise you two things. I am not going to let the dictator's men hurt you, and I am not going to let them start a nuclear war either.*

How can you have it both ways? she protested.

I can; let's not worry about how. Let's try to get back what we had there tonight, the good, shining thing . . .

I don't think it lasts, Randil. The love, yes — we'll always have love. But the exaltation, the radiance . . . I think there has to be some urgent need for that.

I know, he agreed, *yet for a little while I think it will come back to us.* Their minds met wordlessly then, and it did come back, and he did not tell her that there was only a little while remaining.

I retreated into an apathetic, despairing silence during the long drive out to the ship. Kari and Randil were completely absorbed in each other, and I did not intrude on their thoughts. My own thoughts were hard enough to handle. I should feel joy, I knew, at the unexpected chance to save Toris — joy and relief. Instead there was only guilt and sorrow and resignation.

Resignation, not fear. Though I was close to death, I had been close to death before, on Andrecia. There too I had gone past the point of any hope, and so the numbness I felt was no surprise to me anymore. It was not quite the same sort of numbness, however; for then I had wanted to live, desperately, and this time I could not honestly say that I cared.

The mission had been a total loss. Varned was dead; both Randil and I soon would be, and neither of us had learned anything worthwhile. Through our own incompetence, we had almost brought disaster upon a Youngling world. At my order, we were about to kill a good many innocent people — Kari among them — in an attempt to stave off that disaster. The attempt might not even work, since retaliations for the "sabotage" might bring on war in any case. Moreover, during those final hours in the prison we had met evil: raw, loathsome evil by which my supposedly invincible trust in the universe had been abruptly quenched. These things swirled around in my mind while the car sped forward into the night. And always, hovering in the background, was the pain of the burns, over which my control was slipping; I was fast losing my powers from sheer exhaustion and inner tumult.

Ahead, as we emerged from the dark tunnel of deserted hills, was the well-illuminated enclosure that topped the underground installation where the ship was being kept. The car stopped only briefly at the entrance, for the guards, recognizing Commander Feric, respectfully waved us on; we swerved sharply and backed into a parking space facing the open gate. More guards surrounded us immediately, opening the front door for the Commander. Randil got out too, with the driver, and the three of them stood talking while Kari and I remained trapped in the back seat. Though I could have opened our doors by psychokinetic pressure on the outer handles, there was no chance of escape, what with all the armed men posted outside; we would have had nowhere to run in any case.

Kari was maintaining an icy calm. *Elana?* she asked

suddenly. *What's this all about? Why did Randil get them to bring you here?*

I can't tell you, Kari.

He wouldn't tell, either. But it's something dangerous, isn't it?

It's something necessary.

Afterward, what will happen to us?

We won't end up back in the interrogation room; I can promise you that.

This ship you've all been talking about: Is it really sabotaged?

I hesitated, then admitted slowly, *Yes.*

Kari didn't reply; her thought was abruptly masked. But I think she understood.

Commander Feric approached the car, motioning the guards to take us out. They stood ready with handcuffs, and their guns were drawn. Randil stood a little aside; he didn't contact me, but in the cold glare of the arc lights I could see his face. He was suffering not for himself, I knew, but for the others, and of course, for Kari. If only we could have saved Kari, I thought. If only that one little thing had been granted us.

It was then, in a last desperate flash of awareness, that I noticed two small details that might mean that it had been.

The gate of the enclosure had not yet been shut; our car faced it. And in the driverless front seat, sealed off from us by the wire barrier, the ignition keys still hung!

There was a way out after all. Not for Randil, to be sure, but I couldn't achieve anything of value by dying with Randil; by saving Kari, on the other hand, I would be doing the only thing that could possibly help him. I had only a few seconds left in which to act. Throwing all my mental strength into psychokinesis, I released the brake, turned the key in the ignition, and jammed the accelerator down hard.

The car surged forward. The guards, incredulous at the sight of it starting off without a driver, reacted slowly; we were through the gate before they could even think of getting it closed. Some wild shots were fired, and Kari screamed. "Get down!" I shouted, pushing her to the floor while I myself crouched low, peering over the top of the front seat so that I could see the road ahead. Belatedly, I "pulled" the knob for the headlights, and just in time, for suddenly the whole area was plunged into blackness. I had no chance to wonder how or why, for my psychokinetic skill was being taxed to its utmost; it required the full focus of my mind to manage the steering wheel while maintaining simultaneous pressure on the accelerator. But I know what must have occurred: Randil, as he saw the car lurch into motion, must have spotted the main power switch through the window of the brightly lighted gatehouse and—also psychokinetically—thrown it.

That was why the shots that followed missed us, and why we weren't pursued; it bought vital moments during which the guards were thrown into confusion. And amid that confusion, Randil somehow got down into the cavern that concealed the ship itself. *Elana?* he beseeched me. *Elana, are you clear?*

We're clear. We're safe, Randil—Kari's safe!

We had just reached the top of the pass when it happened. There was no sound, but behind us the sky blazed white, white enough to illuminate the barren hills with a reflected radiance brighter than any that had ever before shone upon Toris. Almost at once it faded; by the time I had stopped the car and turned to look back, nothing could be seen but a large and sterile crater, made visible only by its waning bluish glow.

Kari raised her head. *Randil?* she cried silently.

As we knelt on the seat, staring out the rear window, I wept for them: Randil . . . the scientists and technicians assigned to that ship . . . the guards . . . and even Commander Feric, about whom I somehow felt guiltiest of all because I suspected that for him my sorrow was not wholly sincere. He was, after all, less innocent than the others; moreover, I couldn't suppress a shameful twinge of regret at the thought that he had never known of my triumph.

I clutched Kari's hand. "Randil was the only one who could do this," I told her. "Once that ship had taken off, nothing could have stopped it: not the Libertarians, not anything. But they would have retaliated. It would have been full-scale nuclear war. The world's civilization would have been wiped out for good."

The tears were streaming down her face, but her voice was steady. "He knew from the beginning, didn't he?" she said. "That was why he would never talk about us getting married."

"He knew underneath that he couldn't ever marry you," I admitted gently. "He didn't want to hurt you, but he loved you too much to stay away."

"I—I'm proud to think he loved me. Only I don't believe I was worthy of anyone so brave."

"Don't ever say that, Kari! Don't ever think it! You were as brave as he was tonight; if you had not been, he wouldn't have been able to carry the thing through. He didn't know until the last minute, you see, that we would be able to get the car away."

For the first time, the miraculous aspects of our escape struck her. As she glanced around, noting the lack of a driver in the front seat, I forestalled the obvious questions by saying, "There's still a lot I can't tell you, Kari. So please don't ask—" I broke off, choking with my own tears; then all at once the pain engulfed me, and I collapsed on the seat, with Kari's arm cradling my head.

And so it is over, and though Toris is now safe from our interference, I am never going to find what's happened easy to live with. It makes no difference that it was Randil who threw the switch instead of me. I would have done it; I tried to, and if I had it to do over, I would try again. What's more, I gave the order; I assumed the position of Senior Agent, and in the end Randil acknowledged it. The Senior always bears the responsibility, although that doesn't release the other team members.

It's all very well to say that Randil brought on the whole mess by breaking the Oath in the first place. But you can't look at it like that; if you did, you could justify any sort of wrong simply by tracing it back to an earlier one.

Yet the fact that killing those people was wrong doesn't mean that it wasn't necessary.

Once, our last morning on Andrecia, Father said to me: *Sometimes we must be willing to do what's wrong, and take the consequences.* And that's true. People differ in their ideas about morality—the Younglings have their beliefs, a whole variety of them, and we have ours—but by and large everybody agrees that if you deliberately do wrong, somewhere, somehow, you will suffer for it. Well, you do, and it can't be avoided. The hardest thing of all to learn is that it is not always a matter of wrong versus right; sometimes the only choice is between two wrongs.

Kari and I are in hiding now; we abandoned the car when dawn came, and climbed higher into the hills. The police will naturally assume that we died in the explosion along with Commander Feric, so there is little chance that they'll search for us. But since we can't get back into the city without papers, there's nothing to do but wait. Sooner or later someone from the starship may come, for agents will have been trying to locate the landing craft, and the radiation given off by its vaporization, being unlike anything known on Toris, will be investigated.

Staying alive is no problem. There's a stream where we've managed to get some fish, and though the hills are treeless, there are plenty of edible plants around. An agent's preparation includes training in wilderness survival; I could live here indefinitely if I had to.

But Kari couldn't, and my chief worry is what to do about her. I can scarcely take her with me to meet an agent, nor can I leave her alone here. Any contact I make will be telepathic, of course, but if I'm picked up, I'll have to get some kind of appropriate clothes as well as a fake passport and travel permit for her; otherwise she'll have no place to go. She hasn't given that much thought yet. She trusts me; she believes I'm part of a well-organized resistance network, and besides, her grief for Randil is still too overwhelming.

My burns are healing rapidly, and now that I'm rested, I'm able to keep the pain under control. Kari, who believes that the "drug" must surely have worn off by this time, gives me credit for extreme heroism, which is rather embarrassing considering the fact that I don't in the least deserve it. My suffering is mental, not physical, and I am not feeling very brave.

From the crest of a nearby ridge we can look down on the crater. It is clean, smooth—almost glossy—and when the sun hits it, the walls sparkle. Men have approached, at first warily and heavily suited, carrying radioactivity detectors, but later with more confidence and in increasing numbers. Kari, too, expressed some initial concern about fallout, but I assured her that despite the brilliance of the original flash there can be no harmful radiation of any kind. I wonder what the Torisians will make of such a phenomenon.

I am leaving Toris. I'm in a landing craft, as a matter of fact, on my way back to the starship; and I am "recording" because if I were not doing so, I would be crying, and I don't want to cry in front of the people who have rescued me.

Last night while I was lying sleepless, staring up at the stars, the contact came: from Meleny herself, her thoughts warm and reassuring, though faint because she hadn't dared to bring her landing craft too low. I was able to give her only the briefest summary, but I did exact her promise that the ship that picked me up would bring clothes, money, and a new set of papers for Kari. So earlier tonight I had to go and get them. I asked Kari to once more place unquestioned faith in me

THE FAR SIDE OF EVIL ▪ 313

and stay alone while I took care of an errand that I was not free to divulge. She didn't argue. I retreated far enough into the hills so that the ship would not be seen, guided the pilot down telepathically, and agreed to return to the same spot in exactly four hours for pickup. Then I went back to explain the plan I had worked out for her and to say my farewells.

It was worse than I had imagined it could be. I knew Kari's experience had transformed her, but I hadn't guessed what had been going on in her mind for the past few days; I hadn't realized she had acquired initiative as well as strength. So I didn't anticipate what would happen when I told her I was leaving Cerne.

"I knew, of course, that you'd have to go away," she said calmly. "After all, you must be part of something awfully big."

"Very big, Kari," I admitted.

"And Randil was part of the same thing."

"Yes."

"I want to be part of it, too," Kari declared.

I suppose my face revealed my shock; I'm sure I didn't let anything through telepathically. Finally, I mustered enough composure to say quietly, "I'm afraid that isn't possible."

"But why not?" she protested with vehemence. "I've always known about the Resistance. Uncle Derk was in it, I think; anyway they claimed he was. I know how secret it is. I know why it has to be, because I've seen what happens to people who get caught—"

I had underestimated her—I, who had once known better than she herself what she was like inside! Kari had borne up bravely with my support and Randil's, as I had judged she would; but she was basically a dependent person, and I hadn't considered the possibility that she would develop the daring to seek involvement on her own after I had gone. I had assumed that she would want nothing more to do with the secret police under any circumstances.

"I used to be afraid to even think about things like that," she continued, "but now—well, now I'm pretty sure I wouldn't betray anybody. I've proved it, you said so yourself. You *meant* it, didn't you?"

Horrified, I exclaimed, "Of course I meant it! But I'm not a member of the Resistance."

"What else could you be? You said that you weren't a Libertarian spy."

"And I'm not."

"Elana," she said reproachfully, "you've just handed me a forged passport, a travel permit, a new name, and a whole new identity! You didn't pull them out of thin air."

I have never felt at such a loss. Though I had known that Kari would presume I had obtained the documents through underground connections, I had thought she would follow my instructions without question, as she had in the past. I had given her detailed directions for reaching the highway, where she could get a bus for the city. That her new life in Cerne would involve difficulties and sacrifice was obvious; she could not return to the university, where she was known, and if she failed to find a job before her money ran out she would be assigned to factory or farm work. Furthermore, her grief would be with her for a long time to come, and she would be unable even to contact any of her former friends. These burdens were heavy enough; while I didn't doubt her willingness to accept them, I had failed to foresee that she, unaided, would choose to give up her chance of safety in favor of an active role in the underground.

"I don't expect you to sit down and tell me all the secrets," Kari persisted. "I know it doesn't work like that. All I want is for you to arrange a contact. Just give me one name, one password—whatever is usually given to new recruits. I hate the dictatorship! I've been a dreadful coward all my life, but from now on I'm not going to be! I want to do something, the way you and Randil did: even the—the sort of thing Randil did."

"Oh, Kari," I said helplessly, "I don't have any contacts in the Resistance. I don't know any passwords at all."

She turned away, and I knew that she was not convinced and that she would not forgive me. Worse, she would not forgive herself, because her estimation of herself was tied to what she thought *I* thought. During those few hours that by all ordinary standards should have been the worst of Kari's life, she had gained some self-respect; and I was all too probably squelching it.

If only I could tell her the truth! I hesitated, shrinking under Kari's agonized gaze. I was sworn, and yet . . .

There could be no harm in telling Kari. Even if she repeated it, no one would believe her; they would only think she had a vivid imagination. Why should both she and I suffer by my silence, when there was no harm?

No harm that could be foreseen. But you can't know what sort of a chain you start by what you do. Suppose all the agents on all the planets told their friends, who they were sure wouldn't be believed;

surely, sooner or later, the secret would get out on at least one world.

That's what the Oath is for. Situations like that. Not for things like keeping quiet under interrogation, which you would do anyway when it was obvious how horrible the results would be if you didn't.

Even Randil had not told Kari.

Silently, for I knew she would not accept the truth of spoken words, I began, *Please trust me, Kari—*

I've always done that; haven't I proven trustworthy myself?

You have! I trust you absolutely, yet I'm not free to explain things. I cannot tell you where Randil and I came from, but we were never in the Resistance, and we never knew anybody who was. If you truly want to join, you'll find a way; I'm sure there's a place for any person as well qualified as you.

Staring at me with dawning suspicion, she whispered, "Was what Randil told the interrogator *true?* He knew so much about the universe . . . was he a—a Jutan after all? Were you *both* Jutans?"

"No, Kari," I said sadly, "we didn't come from Juta, either."

The starship is still orbiting Toris, but all agents were recalled some time ago. I've been making my full report on the data I gathered about the Torisian culture, and the others are doing the same. A few, like Varned and Randil, didn't come back; but most of us are safe.

I have just finished "reading back" my personal story to the computer, interspersing some parts told from Randil's viewpoint where they logically belong in the sequence of events, for this is the most fitting memorial I can give him. To his parents, who know little of the Service, it may be of some comfort. It will be placed in Federation archives, and someday the Torisians, having come to maturity, may find it there and know that two strangers then dead for many centuries once lived among them, and suffered, and in lieu of mere observation took a hand in shaping their world's destiny.

For the mission is complete now. And the answer? The key to the Critical Stage, the thing that was supposed to make the whole miserable business worthwhile?

We didn't find the answer. We did something better: We saved Toris! Unwittingly, we saved its people after all—not merely from the consequences of our interference but from the Critical Stage itself.

What I told Kari about good coming out of evil was truer than I knew. It does happen: not only in little things, like her arrest; not only in big things, like the Cold War that has been a necessary stimulus to Torisian technology; but occasionally even in things like a never-hopeful mission that ends in tragedy. Sometimes it's a good that no one could have foreseen.

I wondered how the Torisians would react to the landing craft's destruction. I wondered what they would make of silent, instantaneous vaporization; a clean crater; no atomic radiation; and for the moment I forgot that Randil had convinced them that the ship was invulnerable to all forces known on Toris.

They have remained convinced. They've therefore come to the conclusion that they've been attacked by the Jutans—and their sense of priorities has undergone an abrupt change. There was an emergency summit conference two days ago in which the Neo-Statists agreed to pool their resources with the Libertarians in an all-out, crash priority effort. . . .

And yesterday morning we monitored the newscasts and watched the inevitable wrath enflame Toris and listened to the cries of "Follow the invaders! Vengeance on the aliens who betrayed our trust!" Though the Neo-Statists no doubt suspect that Randil's discovery of their plans for the ship—which was known to the guards present at my final interrogation—may have had something to do with Juta's sudden hostility, they will never be able to admit it; the story they gave out to the world bore little resemblance to the facts. So the Torisians have found their vital Cause, and within the next few years we expect to see them span their solar system under their own power.

They will be irrevocably committed to expansion into space. They will be past their Critical Stage; their internal conflicts will be abandoned, for all their energy will be poured into the ships that have their sights on the planet Juta, a destination too far from home to be viewed as a mere temporary base. They won't find any aliens when they get there, naturally, but it's the effort that counts, not the motivation; and by that time they will have found better reasons for making the effort. Their thirst for revenge will have burned out long before they're ready to reach the stars. And when they're mature enough to join us, they'll have the wisdom to know that we bore them no malice.

Toris still has problems, of course. The Neo-Statists are a big problem, for their rule is evil and they are very strong. But they will not be strong forever.

Dictatorships always fall in the end; that's an incontrovertible law of nature. There will be a price. Innocent people will die; there will be hatred and violence and suffering. That is a law of nature, too. But there are always people, ordinary people like Kari, who are willing to pay the price for freedom.

For freedom, and for progress—real progress, not just new inventions but the social and psychic development that turns Youngling peoples into mature ones. There will be fighting before the Neo-Statists collapse, probably more fighting after that; but there will be no nuclear annihilation. The history of countless worlds assures us that the Torisians will not destroy themselves now that they have something more important on their minds.

This starship will be on its way before long, I guess. A team of observers is staying, composed of agents who have cover roles that they can safely resume. But I myself am being sent back to Headquarters, and though it's ostensibly for nothing more than medical treatment to remove the burn scars, I have a pretty good idea that Evrek is going to be there when I arrive. His current assignment ought to be nearly finished, and a few hints have been dropped about there being a pleasant surprise in store for me. It may be that I'll be granted solo credit after all, on the grounds that I assumed full responsibility. If so, we'll be free to marry, for he has undoubtedly done his own solo by now, and I think we're both due for some time off—just about enough for a honeymoon! A long honeymoon; there are plenty of Federation planets we haven't seen.

We could travel for a hundred years, in fact, without seeing half of them. We would never have to visit any Youngling worlds at all. So why did we take the Oath? It's a crazy sort of life we've chosen: all the danger, all the grief, all the horrors that other Federation citizens don't even know about. What makes us want it, then? I'm truly not too sure, and yet—well, when I reboarded the starship, the first thing I did was to get my Emblem back from Meleny, and as I put it on I knew that the thing that seemed dead in me, there in the dungeon, had not really died; it had only been submerged for a while.

The Service's official report on this mission will state that any data gathered about the key to the Critical Stage has been invalidated by the part its agents played in providing the incentive for the Torisians' first step into space. Certainly in this case, the crisis was artificially resolved—or was it? The Federation, after all, knows very little more about the mysterious ways of destiny than do the Younglings; and there are times when I wonder whether the power that sent us to Toris was that of chance, or natural law, or of something beyond either that we shall never fully comprehend.

Afterword

The *Far Side of Evil* was first published in 1971, during the era of the Apollo moon landings. At that time, I believed Earth would soon be safely out of the Critical Stage. It didn't occur to me that a planetary civilization, having once developed a capability for space travel, might cut back its thrust into space as ours has done. And so in this edition I have altered some of the wording to make plain that it is the ongoing colonization of space, not merely the invention of spaceships, that is needed to ensure the survival of a "human" species (ours, or any other that may exist elsewhere).

People I've talked to have frequently been surprised to learn how seriously I myself take the ideas I expressed in this novel; they've assumed its premise was a mere plot device. In fact, the vital importance of expanding Earth's civilization into space has been my deepest conviction for nearly fifty years. My opinions on this subject are discussed at my Web site, www.sylviaengdahl.com, and I hope readers who want more information about them will look for it there.

I should explain that this story is meant to be taken more literally than *Enchantress from the Stars*, which was purposely based on mythology: not only the mythology of its fairy-tale portions but that of "space opera" science fiction in which interplanetary explorers are traditionally portrayed as invaders with ray guns. I don't believe a real spacefaring civilization would behave as the Empire in *Enchantress* does, any more than real medieval woodcutters went around killing dragons. It's obvious that even now—and certainly in the future when we have starships—our culture as a whole wouldn't approve of colonizing *inhabited* planets. In saying that colonization is essential to human survival, I certainly don't wish to imply that it involves stealing worlds that belong to indigenous populations.

For this and other reasons, I regret having connected *The Far Side of Evil* specifically to *Enchantress from the Stars*, which is often enjoyed by younger readers than those for whom *Far Side* is intended. Though about the same Service, it is, after all, completely separate from Elana's earlier adventure and could easily have had a different heroine. It might then have been no surprise to those acquainted with her that this is a darker story, set on a planet in no way like a fairy-tale world.

Readers of the 1971 edition have sometimes assumed that if the book were being written today, it would not have a "Cold War" setting. But its setting never reflected current affairs; the planet of the story is like Earth as it was in the fifties, not the seventies. I wrote an initial draft of part of it, without Elana's involvement, in 1956, a year before the launch of Sputnik—an event that to my great joy made it impossible for the world portrayed to be our own. So the fact that we no longer have two superpowers on the verge of nuclear war in no way dates the story. Apart from the obvious premise that dictatorship is a bad thing and totalitarian rulers are motivated by desire for power, it is not about world conflicts, or about politics in any sense. (I used the term *Libertarians* on the basis of the word's generic meaning before becoming aware of the U.S. party by that name.) Some readers thought I used space fiction as a vehicle for political commentary when in fact it was the other way around: I used political melodrama to dramatize my ideas about the evolutionary importance of space.

Nevertheless, the story as originally written was dated in another way. It assumed that what the Service terms the Critical Stage (the stage during which a species has the technology to destroy its world yet is still confined to a single planet) is a relatively brief period, limited to the era in which the planet does have two superpowers on the verge of nuclear war. It didn't acknowledge that the prolongation of it leads to other threats, such as terrorism involving weapons of mass destruction, biological warfare, environmental degradation, and ultimately depletion of the resources needed to get sufficient "lead time" on extraterrestrial colonies before it's too late.

Thus in addition to my intentional simplification of a complex theory for a teenage audience, some of my assertions turned out to be oversimplified in terms of what we now know after thirty years of neglecting the space program. Insofar as minor revisions can remedy this, I have made them. What's said in this edition is, in my opinion, true. But there is a good deal more that should be said about why a species able to travel beyond its home world fails to do so, and what its fate is likely to be if it continues to cling solely to that world.

I suspect that the Service knows these things, and that Elana herself might know them later in her life.

And I will continue to add thoughts about them to my Web site, where there's also a lot of information about my other novels. Please do visit it. I welcome E-mail (sle@sylviaengdahl.com), which I promise to answer personally.

Made in the USA
San Bernardino, CA
03 November 2015

25574711R00188

STARTING
WITH
SCIENCE

Strategies for Introducing Young Children to Inquiry

Stenhouse Publishers
Portland, Maine

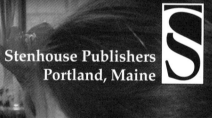

Stenhouse Publishers
www.stenhouse.com

Library of Congress Cataloging-in-Publication Data
Edson, Marcia Talhelm.
    Starting with science : strategies for introducing young children to inquiry / Marcia Talhelm Edson.
        pages cm
    Includes bibliographical references and index.
    ISBN 978-1-57110-807-4 (pbk. : alk. paper)—ISBN 978-1-57110-986-6 (ebook) 1. Science—Study and teaching (Preschool)—United States. 2. Science—Study and teaching (Elementary)—United States. I. Title.
    LB1140.5.S35E37 2013
    372.35—dc23

                                                                    2012050462

Cover design, interior design, and typesetting by Martha Drury

Manufactured in the United States of America
PRINTED ON 30% PCW
   RECYCLED PAPER

20 19 18 17 16 15 14   9 8 7 6 5 4 3 2

For Dan, Molly, and Peter

Contents

Acknowledgments   *vii*

Introduction   1

Chapter 1: **Understanding Inquiry-Based Science**   5

Chapter 2: **Strategies for Teaching in an
Inquiry-Focused Environment**   19

Chapter 3: **Science as a Context for Literacy:
Reading, Writing, and Speaking**   33

Chapter 4: **Assessing for Understanding**   61

Chapter 5: **Designing an Inquiry Unit**   75

Chapter 6: **Teachers Talk About Inquiry-Based
Science Teaching**   97

Chapter 7: **The Conversation Continues**   107

Appendixes 1–10   *111*

Bibliography   *139*

Index   *145*

Acknowledgments

Starting with Science may have my name on the cover, but the evolution of the ideas and the examples that drive home those ideas came from the insightful and curious children, students, teachers, and colleagues with whom I work. Their contributions to this book deserve recognition and my appreciation.

The children, families, student teachers, teachers, and staff of the Early Childhood Learning Lab—a demonstration preschool in the School of Education at Boston University—are first on my list of thank-yous. You'll see photographs of the children and read transcripts of their discussions. You'll read about the expertise of the teachers and student teachers, and you'll see glimpses of a remarkable classroom that invites children to investigate the world around them. The driving force behind this preschool is Jane Lannak, the vibrant, innovative, and wise preschool director, whose vision made inquiry the centerpiece of the school and whose photographs and suggestions enhanced this book. There are so many children, teachers, and student teachers from the Early Childhood Learning Lab to whom I owe my thanks. I especially want to thank those children I taught in the preschool, as well as my students in the Early Childhood program from whom I continue to learn so much.

I also want to credit the public school teachers, colleagues, and former students—now teachers—in their kindergarten, first-grade, and second-grade classrooms. They welcomed me to observe their teaching and discuss their approaches to inquiry-based science. Even though I can't thank you individually, I hope that you can recognize the impact your teaching had on my thinking and on the material presented in this book. One of the teachers I visited most, Christina Ryan, a former graduate student and now a master kindergarten teacher, was full of questions about how children think, how to design experiences that will tap into that thinking, and how to enable the children to do science. Her brilliance as a teacher has so much to do with inquiry, and I appreciate the strategies and materials she has shared for this book, and the many wonderful hours I spent observing her kindergartners as scientists.

Many thanks to the museum educators at Boston's Museum of Science, the Discovery Museum of Acton, and the Arnold Arboretum who generously gave me their time and access to resources that proved invaluable in my work.

My editor, Toby Gordon, deserves accolades for making this book happen. She kept it alive through her persistent nudges and wry humor. She was superb, always responsive, always on top of what needed to be done, and always ready to push me forward. I owe a huge thank-you to the rest of the talented staff at Stenhouse, especially Chris Downey and Nancy Sheridan, whose edits brought consistency and clarity to my writing.

And finally, thank you to my family—Dan, Molly, and Peter. They are my true inspiration.

Introduction

The story behind this book began many years ago when I was a young faculty member at Boston University, coteaching a methods course for early childhood majors. As my colleagues and I reviewed the structure and content of our early childhood courses, we recognized that unlike literacy and mathematics, our program's attention to science was limited to just a few sessions within a survey course on preschool curriculum. We talked about the possibility of developing a more robust science methods course that would delve into the nature of science, the appropriate science content for pre-K–second grade, and the pedagogy behind science instruction for these early years.

For some reason, the task of designing this course was given to me. My area of expertise was early literacy, not science, and although I had taught science as an elementary and preschool teacher, it was not a focal point of my classroom. I was much more interested in literacy. Knowing so little about science and the teaching of it, I wondered how I could possibly design an early childhood science methods course.

My program coordinator, Judy Schickedanz, and I met and talked about a vision for the course. The science would be a conceptual design, going deeply into the big ideas of a few topics and linking those content and teaching strategies to some sort of unit design. This was a start, but it didn't do much to quell my mounting apprehension and self-doubt.

That summer I immersed myself in all things science. I read textbooks and journals and found inspiration and knowledge in the work of David Hawkins, Eleanor Duckworth, and Wynne Harlen. I talked to experts who understood science and how to teach it: Seddon Beatty, a kindergarten teacher; Bob Kilburn, a university science educator; and Henry Robinson, a science museum educator. I plunged into children's nonfiction books and was captivated by the exquisite simplicity of science concepts as conveyed by Seymour Simon, Franklyn Branley, and Gail Gibbons. I started paying closer attention to things in my world that I had never really thought about: the slugs in our garden, the bubbles in my daughter's bath, and the way yeast responded to warm or cool water when I made bread. I also started paying close attention to my husband. Trained as a mechanical engineer, his approach to problem solving enthralled me; the observations he made and the questions he raised about how to deal with our leaky basement were so organized and logical—exactly the opposite of my plunge-in-and-do-it approach.

All of these influences nourished my expanding attraction to and understanding of science. I had unearthed a genuine curiosity about the world around me, and I was enjoying what I was learning. I was also learning about the practices of inquiry—observing, predicting, questioning, investigating, collaborating, testing theories, and collecting and sharing data. This was not the scientific method approach that I had learned in school. This approach to science didn't revolve around isolated answers and facts but was more about interacting with real things, wondering and coming up with theories, testing them out, finding connections, and asking more questions. I gradually came to realize that teaching inquiry-based science was really about inquiry and didn't require that I know all the answers. This kind of science resembled more of a joint venture between the children and the teacher that revolves around thoughtfully designed extended investigations in which children are doing the science—learning about big ideas by actively engaging with materials, observing, testing theories, looking for evidence, drawing, writing, talking, and working with peers to share data. The more I learned about inquiry, the more my apprehension about science subsided.

Coincidentally, I had the opportunity to return to teach in our lab school's preschool classroom for two semesters. During that time, my coteacher and I made inquiry-based science the centerpiece of our curriculum. We were starting from scratch, and there's no denying it was an exhausting experience. We faced several challenges: the day was too short, we needed more nonfiction books, our fish kept dying, we were trying to write an inquiry unit and teach it at the same time. As our efforts started to take shape, particularly around our inquiry into what would be a suitable pet for our classroom, we began to notice how inquiry connected with and affected the children. As experienced teachers, we had some notions of how it might impact our class, but we very much underestimated the intensity of engagement and curiosity and the intricacy of questions and thinking that we observed in the children's work.

What did the children learn from our foray into inquiry-based science? They learned science content, and they used the practices of science and in turn expanded their understanding of literacy and mathematics by applying those skills to their science work. What did I learn? I learned that science can and should be a pivotal element of early childhood education. I learned that teaching inquiry-based science made me a better teacher—more open to the world around me and to the children and adult students I teach. I learned that the impediments to mounting an inquiry-based science approach—self-doubt about science knowledge, lack of time and resources—are very real but can be resolved.

In this book about inquiry-based science, I do my best to explain what inquiry means in the context of early childhood and answer four questions:

1. What is inquiry-based science?
2. What roles do the children, the teacher, and the environment play in an inquiry-based science program?
3. What instructional strategies are effective in implementing inquiry-based science?
4. How can pre-K, kindergarten, and primary-grade teachers incorporate inquiry-based science in spite of limited science background, lack of time, and lack of resources?

I've tried to answer these questions with a balance of theory and practice. There are many examples of children's engagement with science and of the instructional practices that support this engagement. You will notice a strong bias that pervades the book—my belief that science should be at the center of every early childhood classroom. I have absolutely conquered my initial apprehension about teaching science. Inquiry has taught me that as a teacher I don't need to know all the answers, but I do need to know how to plan for inquiry: how to tap into the curiosity and wonder of young children and how to organize learning that supports children's acquisition of scientific knowledge as they engage in the practices of science. The thoughts and ideas that follow offer a framework that reflects these goals.

In the spirit of inquiry, I hope you will read this book with an attitude of curiosity and skepticism and find new ideas to enrich your science teaching, recognize practices you have already incorporated or want to incorporate into your teaching, and even bump up against ideas you disagree with and question. Inquiry-based science is not a neat, one-size-fits-all package, so be prepared to be a bit unsettled. Try to revive that "sense of wonder" that Rachel Carson underscores when she describes the way a child approaches the natural world. Activate your own sense of wonder so you can reflect on inquiry-based science as a teacher/researcher willing to learn and to question along with your children. When you include inquiry-based science in your classroom, you provide children with a knowledge base, a skill set for problem solving, and an attitude about learning that they will carry with them, not just to the next grade, but throughout their lives. Inquiry-based science should be much more than a Friday afternoon special; it should be the center of any early childhood classroom.

Chapter 1

Understanding Inquiry-Based Science

Three-year-old Joseph fills and refills the clear plastic tubing. He watches the water gush out the end, then plunges it back into the mouth of a plastic water bottle. David and Angela, who are four, consult on which blocks they can add to shore up their bridge. Five-year-olds Alex and Samaya take turns holding a flashlight and shadow puppets to find out how to make the biggest shadow. Marquis and Alice, both seven, show their class how they were able to lure ants to the tree on the playground and watch them carry food to a hole nearby.

Inquiry-based science taps directly into children's curiosity and interest in the natural world. It has structure and purpose and is grounded in the belief that children learn by exploring, by raising questions, and by actively constructing knowledge.

> *Inquiry is multifaceted activity that involves making observations; posing questions; examining books and other sources of information to see what is already known in light of experimental evidence; using tools to gather, analyze, and interpret data; proposing answers, explanations, and predictions; and communicating the results.* (National Resource Council 1996, 23)

Inquiry enables children to do what scientists do; they study the natural world through observing, questioning, and experimenting. They discuss and share their findings with each other, based on the evidence they have collected. In the context of a pre-K, kindergarten, first-grade, or second-grade class, inquiry-based science is a dynamic mixture of content, practices, and dispositions and occurs through extended units or investigations that address content or topics meaningful for young children.

The richness of inquiry-based science lies in the interrelation of the content and the practices of science. Children learn the *what* of science (the content) through the *how* of science (the practices). For example, in a kindergarten inquiry on insects, children look at, touch, and talk about real caterpillars and ladybugs. They use magnifying lenses to look more closely at body parts. They read information books about the life cycles of insects. They make predictions about how a chrysalis will change. They draw, write, and talk about these observations. They share and listen to the theories and questions of their classmates in small and large discussion groups, and they develop their understandings of the similarities and differences of insects. These children are engaged in the practices of science to learn about the characteristics, life cycles, and habitats of the insects they are studying—to develop a more comprehensive set of connections about the insect world.

Examining both the practices and the content of science will provide a clearer understanding of the kind of inquiry that is possible in pre-K, kindergarten, and the primary grades and the kind of teaching required to support this kind of science.

THE PRACTICES OF SCIENCE

The practices that follow are especially relevant for pre-K through second-grade science.

Observing

Observation is an essential piece of science, regardless of age or developmental ability. Simply put, this is the time children spend watching, touching, and exploring. For very young children, this includes time to just "mess about," followed by a more focused observation that connects to the learning goals established by the teacher. (See Figure 1.1.)

The observations the child makes when interacting with the rocks or water or ramps feed the ideas he or she constructs about the object or the

Figure 1.1 Observing is more than just looking.

situation. In pre-K and kindergarten, observations rely heavily on sensory experiences; by first and second grade, observations extend to include more exact measurement, categorization, and comparison. At every level, observation requires ongoing support from the teacher, who encourages thoughtful noticing through timely comments, probes, and questions.

Predicting

Working from observations—from real evidence—children propose their theory of what might happen next. It takes time for children to go from random guessing to developing ideas from evidence, but regular practice with investigations coupled with conversations and collaborations about those investigations will give them the experience they need to make logical predictions. Along with this regular practice, the teacher's timely questions and scaffolding provide the foundation for productive predictions.

Questioning

As children notice things in the world around them, they need the opportunity to raise questions about what they've noticed, what they are wondering about, and what they think should be tested. These questions lead to hypotheses or theories the children are developing. Some questions may seem more logical or useful than others, but it is the act of questioning that inquiry supports and requires. We want children to be questioners, but—as teachers—we sometimes feel uncomfortable, almost vulnerable, with the open-endedness of this aspect of inquiry. A preschool child asks, "Can we get a dog for our class pet?" A first grader asks, "How come our shadows look so big today?" We wonder what we would do if the questions don't make sense, if we don't know the answers, or if we don't ask the right question. That discomfort of not knowing can be paralyzing unless we understand that inquiry is more than providing the answer. It's also about learning how to find the answer. Whether I am teaching preschoolers or graduate students, questions come up that I can't answer. But I can say, "I'm not sure about that" because that's part of the inquiry process. Once we feel comfortable saying, "That's a great question, but I need to look that up," our confidence in teaching science will be stronger and our children will understand that the questions can sometimes be more important than the answers.

This is part of developing an ethos of questioning, an environment that welcomes and expects children's questions. Children need to be immersed in productive questions modeled by their teacher and need opportunities to raise their own questions that will be supported by their teacher's thoughtful scaffolding. (See Figure 1.2.)

Investigating

With the appropriate support and scaffolding, young children can actually design and execute simple investigations that come from their own questions and hypotheses. They have a proclivity for investigating, as evidenced by the common "What if?" questions we hear as they manipulate materials at the water table or in the block area, or as they observe the changes in their school garden or the way icicles form on the edge of the swings on the playground. Our job is to be open to these questions and to help the children organize their approach, to figure out what elements can be tested and how to design a systematic process for the investigation. This is a long-term developmental process that begins with teacher-directed investigations that focus the children on evidence (e.g., What would be a good pet for our classroom?). As children become more adept at observing, questioning, and hypothesizing, we can cede more responsibility to them

Figure 1.2 This teacher and the children share observations and questions about water.

to conceive and carry out a true scientific investigation, but in these early years of inquiry-based science, planning these investigations will most likely be a shared task that incorporates all the practices of science.

Collaborating

Learning how to work with others is fundamental to the social and emotional development of four- to eight-year-olds. Likewise, it is a basic underpinning of inquiry-based science. Inquiry requires a classroom culture in which children work together productively and respectfully to make observations, test their theories, and talk about what they've noticed. Successful collaboration requires intentional teaching of social and communicative skills such as listening, waiting for a turn to speak, and considering another point of view. This may not seem like science to the casual observer, but it is a foundational piece of the teacher's approach, especially for this age group. As children become more adept at the social-communicative piece of collaboration, their scientific input becomes grounded in evidence and richer in questioning.

Communicating

When young children do science, they have to talk. They describe what's happening, what they see, what they are going to do next, what they are wondering about, and what questions they have. They need a classroom atmosphere that promotes such talk and questioning. In addition to talk, the developmental uniqueness of the early childhood years also requires additional venues for children to record or express their ideas. Certainly, the continuum of representational skills is far reaching, from pre-K scribbles to second-grade paragraphs. Thoughtfully designed science notebooks can provide a context for these varying levels of graphic recording, including drawing, writing, and dictation. In addition, children, like scientists, make models to explain their ideas. Using a diverse array of materials—clay, blocks, even their own bodies—children construct models to create meaning. This is especially useful for English language learners and children with disabilities who might be more successful at showing rather than telling or writing. Young children need all of these communicative tools so they can be successful in explaining their scientific understandings.

Interpreting Information

Building on observations and predictions, children use their accumulated knowledge to make sense of a particular phenomenon and learn to interpret information. When kindergartners graph the temperature and the weather conditions each day, they accumulate data, but the interpretation of that data requires another step. When their teacher asks the children to compare the temperature graphs from March and April, the children have an opportunity to compare the similarities and differences in their data and develop theories about temperature variations during that time period.

Using Tools to Gather Information

When children have access to the tools of science—information books, magnifying lenses, balances, charts, computers—they are able to expand their understanding, answer their own questions, and ask more questions. (See Figure 1.3.)

Preschool and kindergarten teachers can gather and display fascinating information books about all sorts of science topics. Readability should be considered but should not limit the variety of books available to children. Even though the text of higher-level books may be too difficult for four- or

Figure 1.3 A magnifying lens helps reveal small details that the child might otherwise miss.

five-year-olds to comprehend, the diagrams, illustrations, and photographs may provide essential information. First and second graders can engage in independent research through specific links on classroom computers. And at every level, when teachers model how to use a magnifying lens, an index, or a weather chart, they initiate children into the use of the tools of science in a natural and meaningful context.

Looking at each of these practices separately creates somewhat of an artificial division, when in reality, they continuously overlap. Observing can require questioning and using the tools of science. Predicting can involve observing, questioning, and communicating. Investigating can include observing, questioning, collaborating, and using the tools of science. Interpreting can include observing, questioning, collaborating, and communicating. Our awareness of these possibilities will make us much more effective in scaffolding these inquiry skills. Children's competence in any of these skills will depend on their age, but perhaps more importantly, on their experience with real inquiry. While one might expect preschoolers to need a great deal of support with large-group discussions, second graders could be equally challenged if they have not had previous experience raising questions, connecting to evidence, and listening to others.

The National Research Council sums up this understanding of process skills in a simple but powerful sentence: "Learning science is something students do, not something that is done to them" (1996, 20). For some teachers this notion still presents a challenge. Devra is a kindergarten teacher who invited me to observe her teach a lesson from a unit on light and shadows. I watched while she expertly engaged the children in a reading and discussion of Clyde Robert Bulla's classic *What Makes a Shadow?* (1994). When she finished the book, she turned out the lights and told the children they were going to make shadows like the ones in the book. The children were noticeably excited as Devra showed them a flashlight and the overhead projector. She used a variety of shapes made of translucent and opaque materials to create the shadows. There was a lot of teacher talk: "This shadow is really light because the light can go right through the lid." "Look what happens when I put another triangle on top of the first shape." The children watched, answered some questions, but essentially did not do the science. When we discussed the lesson, Devra told me she needed to be in charge of the materials because she couldn't risk the chaos and silliness that might erupt if she let the children use them. Her point is well taken and underscores the importance of teaching children the skills as well as the content. Eventually, Devra came to understand that through thoughtful planning, organization, and teaching, her kindergartners could interact with materials, make observations, and talk about what they were doing without chaos and silliness.

When young children have the opportunity to observe, predict, question, design investigations, collaborate, interpret data, and use science tools, they are doing science; they are functioning as scientists. These are the science practices that enable children to learn and understand the content of science. And as in good inquiry-based science, we find ourselves faced with another essential question: What should the content of early childhood science be?

MEANINGFUL CONTENT

Recent research suggests that three- to eight-year-old children are far more competent in the realm of science understanding than previously known. They arrive in the classroom already possessing a variety of theories about the world. They are able to reason and consider evidence. Their understandings may be rudimentary or even false, but those understandings are evidence of a connection to and wonderment about the natural world. All children have a base of prior knowledge to work from as they consider the big ideas associated with life science, physical science, earth and space science, and technology and engineering. Their innate curiosity about animate and inanimate things, growth and change, and the characteristics of their environment fuels a deeper exploration of the connections and patterns that explain these big ideas.

What kind of science content is appropriate and worthy of study in pre-K, kindergarten, first-grade, and second-grade classrooms? National, state, and district standards provide a framework of science content goals and benchmarks for pre-K through second-grade classrooms. These are broad statements that frame the subject matter for either the K–4 span (National Science Education Standards) or the K–2 span (Benchmarks for Science Literacy). For example, in the Benchmarks for Science Literacy, the content standard for The Physical Setting, Processes That Shape the Earth states:

> *By the end of the 2nd grade, students should know that*
> * *Chunks of rocks come in many sizes and shapes, from boulders to grains of sand and even smaller.*
> * *Change is something that happens to many things. Animals and plants sometimes cause changes in their surroundings.* (American Association for the Advancement of Science 2009)

Guidance for preschool science content in the National Association for the Education of Young Children's *Developmentally Appropriate Practice* is even more general:

> *The curriculum includes concepts not only from life science/nature but also from physical science (e.g., rolling and sliding objects on ramps) and earth science (e.g., soil and rocks).* (Copple and Bredekamp 2009, 173)

State and district standards derived from these national guidelines may refer to actual topics of study, but they vary widely. The California science standards for first-grade physical science focus on properties of matter. The Vermont science standards present grades one and two together, and along with properties of matter, they include force and motion, heat and energy, and magnetism. In addition to units required by the district, teachers may also develop intriguing units that emerge from unique circumstances related to their classroom or school:

* A child's broken wrist led to a unit on the body.
* A school's close proximity to a river led to a unit on the river as a habitat.
* First graders' fascination with construction toys led to a simple machines inquiry.
* The death of a classroom pet led to an inquiry on classroom pets in pre-K.
* Road construction outside the school led to an inquiry on soil and rocks.

- A parent's job as a plumber led to a study of pipes and water flow.
- Pigeons around the school yard led to a second-grade unit on birds in the city.

All these variations in the content of early childhood science can be confusing for teachers. Chalufour and Worth (2006) suggest a set of criteria for determining kindergarten topics. They recommend considering topics from the life, physical, and earth and space sciences that children can actually explore over an extended period of time, that are meaningful to the actual group of children taking on the investigation, and that are built on key science understandings. In *Taking Science to School*, the Committee on Science Learning (2007) recommends the development of "progressions of learning," which take into account what knowledge and experiences children bring to school and what is unique about their circumstances, including culture, geography, and local interest. Central to these notions is the understanding that young children should study topics that are meaningful to them and that can be explored thoroughly, with concrete materials and a focus on building relationships and patterns.

Because we know so much more about how young children think, we need to look more closely at the topics that might be studied in the early childhood years. Typical units on the senses, sinking and floating, magnets, and the rain forest can be found in many preschool and kindergarten classrooms. Children like the activities in these units, but now that we know that young children can do more and understand more, we need to reconsider the worthiness of these topics. For instance, studying the rain forest in a kindergarten in Virginia would not make great sense, but if the kindergarten was in Costa Rica, children would have access to the rain forest, making this kind of inquiry more authentic.

Because it's easy to feel overwhelmed when thinking about what content is best for pre-K and the primary grades, consider these questions as a guide:

- Why is this topic especially worthwhile for *this* group of children?
- Is this a topic that children can explore in depth over several weeks?
- Can the children actively explore this topic through their senses, close observations, and scientific investigations?
- Can children engage in the practices of science (observation, prediction, interpretation, questioning, collaboration, and sharing information) in their study of this topic?

- Do I have access to resources (books, experts, materials, artifacts) to support an inquiry on this topic?
- Does this topic relate to the national and local standards?

These questions are not foolproof, but they offer a starting point. They speak to issues of relevance and developmental appropriateness.

INQUIRY: MORE THAN HANDS-ON ACTIVITIES

Inquiry-based science comprises all the essential elements of good early childhood teaching: active learning, collaborating with peers, talking, questioning, and using a variety of formats for representing learning including drawing, writing, constructing models, and conversation. Inquiry should be the kind of science that happens in every preschool and primary-grade classroom, but, even though the term is used to describe many science programs, in actuality the science that happens in a typical classroom is more limited and could be more accurately described as hands-on science. Both approaches employ interactive experiences with real materials, but they differ in the depth of the learning that occurs. A hands-on science unit consists of a series of activities that occur over a week or two; an inquiry-based unit would span several weeks or even months. Part of this has to do with the depth of content and part with the inquiry process itself.

In explaining the difference between the two approaches, an obvious starting point lies in the teacher's basic approach to designing a science unit or topic. The hands-on teacher typically starts with the activities, the interactive experiences that will help the children learn about the topic. Her first questions are, "What can I do to teach this topic? What activities will I plan for this unit?"

The inquiry-based teacher takes a different approach and asks, "What do I want the children to learn about this topic? What are the big ideas?" The answers to these questions become the concepts that are the framework of the unit. Once the teacher knows the concepts she wants to teach, she moves to the activities question that the hands-on teacher raised. Consider how the differences play out in these two preschool planning sessions:

In the hands-on class . . .

Teacher A: Let's figure out what we want to do with this unit on plants.

Teacher B: We can sprout seeds in latex gloves. They'll love that.

Teacher A: Right, and we'll want to do that upside-down bean planting activity, along with planting some beans and marigolds in pots they can decorate.

Teacher B: How about making seed mosaics? We can use the seeds we have left from last year.

In the inquiry-based class . . .

Teacher C: Let's think about what we want the children to understand about plants. It's such a big topic, but I'm thinking about three big ideas or questions to start. Where do plants come from? What is a seed? How do we use plants in our daily lives? So our basic concepts might be: 1. Plants grow from seeds, cuttings, and bulbs. 2. There are many different kinds of seeds, but each seed produces one kind of plant. 3. Plants need certain conditions in which to grow. 4. Plants have different parts that help them grow. 4. We use plants in our daily lives.

Teacher D: We also want to make a connection to the children's lives, so I would add something like, "We use plants for many different purposes in our lives (food, shelter, toys, music)."

Teacher C: We'll also want to find out what questions the children have, but let's start with those big ideas. Now how will we teach these concepts? Let's think about the first one, "Plants grow from seeds, cuttings, and bulbs." What activities will we plan to teach that concept?

Teacher D: We'll want to set up planting experiences with different kinds of seeds, narcissus bulbs, and cuttings from a geranium or grape ivy plant. The children can record their observations in a plant notebook.

Teacher C: We have a great collection of information books on plants and seeds, so we can set up a display of those. We might want to have a couple clipped open to good illustrations. Also, the Gail Gibbons book would be a good one to read during story time.

Teacher D: That's a great way to get started. And let's begin a KLEW chart, just the K part [*What I think I know about plants*].

This brief vignette illustrates a contrast in the planning and in the outcome. Both approaches offer interesting experiences, but the experiences in the inquiry approach are all linked to the big ideas of the topic, so that children will understand the connections between the concepts, rather than acquiring random facts about the topic.

The planning sessions highlight another unique aspect of inquiry-based science, which appears in Teacher C's comment, "We'll also want to find out what questions the children have." This is real inquiry, giving children a voice and a venue for exploring their questions. For many of us, this can be the most complicated part of an inquiry-based unit.

The concepts or big ideas make up the teacher's plan or framework, but this style of teaching allows for the plan to change depending on the theories and questions the children bring up in group discussions and as they engage with the planned activities. These questions and comments raised by the children may reveal understandings or misunderstandings that the teacher was not aware of when designing the unit.

At first, this type of flexible planning can be uncomfortable for teachers who are used to relying on a structured unit that has a defined beginning and end. The tipping point occurs when a teacher comes to understand that teaching science is more than delivering content—that inquiry requires opportunities for children to raise questions and attend to evidence. An inquiry-based approach should afford children enough time to engage in science as scientists: observing, predicting, raising and investigating questions, seeking evidence, collaborating, communicating what they've learned and what they understand about the topic, interpreting data, and using tools to gather information. These are the practices of science that are embedded in the various activities that comprise the unit, whatever the unit topic might be. (See Figure 1.4.)

PUTTING IT ALL TOGETHER

Early childhood teachers occupy a unique place in science education. They have an immediate advantage because of the curiosity and wonder young children bring to the classroom. Preschoolers want to know why some block structures are stable and some aren't. Kindergartners want to know about the ants on the playground. First graders want to know why their shadows are so long. This is what young children bring to us, the interest and curiosity about the world around them, and that's where inquiry-based science is rooted.

We know that even very young preschoolers bring information and basic reasoning skills to their study of weather or rocks or structures, but they lack the ability to relinquish their personal opinion when scientific

Hands–On Approach	Inquiry-Based Approach
Initial question • What activities can I design to teach this topic?	*Initial questions* • What are the big ideas, the concepts that children need to understand about this topic? • What questions do the children have about this topic?
Next step • Plan activities.	*Next steps* • Plan activities that teach the concepts. • Revise activities to connect to children's questions. • Make sure activities enable children to participate in the practices of science.
Length • Brief 1–2 week explorations	*Length* • Extensive, deep study that could last for several weeks
Teacher role • Sets up activities, facilitates interactions • May or may not assess learning	*Teacher role* • Determines concepts • Sets up activities, facilitates interactions • Encourages children's research • Continuously reflects on and evaluates children's understandings • Helps children identify patterns and make connections • Revises goals and plans to meet children's needs

Figure 1.4 Comparing the Hands-On Approach and Inquiry-Based Approach

evidence contradicts their findings. They also struggle with the ability to connect ideas and tie together relationships. So even though they are full of curiosity, questions, and wonder, developmentally they need thoughtfully planned experiences to expand their reasoning and understanding of the natural world. Inquiry-based science in the early years brings coherence to young children's haphazard attempts at understanding the big ideas of science.

Chapter 2

Strategies for Teaching in an Inquiry-Focused Environment

Teaching science through inquiry requires much more than choosing a good topic for investigation. Specific critical elements of instruction foster inquiry—each element contributing to the process of doing science. I am often amazed at the subtle but powerful techniques I observe in teachers who understand inquiry and how children think. Inquiry happens in their classrooms because these teachers are so skilled at attending to children's ideas, asking the right question at the right time, modeling the dispositions or attitudes of inquiry, and organizing a classroom that keeps inquiry alive.

WATCHING AND LISTENING

Listening, really listening, to young children does not come naturally, and it takes some time to learn to do this well. When we engage with children as they problem solve at the water table or make observations of their potato plant, we sometimes find it hard to quiet our immediate urge to ask or comment on what they are doing. I'm sure there were times that I unintentionally interrupted or, worse, even extinguished a child's thinking by asking, "Why did you . . . ?" Or, "What is . . . ?"

Experienced teachers who develop an atmosphere for inquiry operate differently. They approach, watch, listen, and then decide how to scaffold learning. "What will make a difference for this child? Is the time ripe for a comment, a question, or just a nod before moving on?" Student teachers who have the opportunity to witness this kind of thoughtful observing quickly catch on to the technique and the impact it has on supporting inquiry.

Ms. Walker's interaction with her first graders in the following vignette illustrates this cautious approach. Sitting near the window with Devin and Tamika, who were finishing a math sheet, Ms. Walker noticed them stop to watch Anya watering her narcissus bulb. As the teacher watched, Tamika moved her own bulb next to Devin's.

> **Tamika:** Aw, mine is so much littler. Look. What's wrong with it?
> **Devin** [*poking at the wet gravel*]: Too wet. Mine's got water on the bottom.
> **Anya** [*stops watering*]: I only let the water touch the roots.
> **Tamika:** But Anya, Terrell's is bigger than yours, and his water is way up.
> **Devin:** Maybe Terrell's is warmer. It's right next to the window.
> **Tamika:** So I'll move it by the window.
> **Anya:** But the water . . .
> **Ms. Walker** [*leaning in toward the children*]: It sounds like you have some ideas about how the bulbs are growing. I think the other children would like to hear about this. I'll bring your bulbs to our meeting this afternoon, and you can share your ideas and questions.

Because Ms. Walker took the time to watch and listen, she was able to recognize that the three first graders were engaged in several practices of inquiry—observing, questioning, predicting, investigating, and collaborating—in a spontaneous unplanned moment. She also recognized that they had uncovered a scientific question that deserved more discussion and testing, so she decided to take advantage of their discovery and the resulting questions and share them with the rest of the class. This sort of observing and noticing was now common practice for Ms. Walker, but it took some doing before it became routine.

Taking that extra time to listen, to really attend to what the children are talking about, requires a real commitment. It feels natural to just jump in and ask a direct question or make a comment, but when we do that, we take the chance of misreading the child's theory or idea. That can result in a missed learning opportunity. In Ms. Walker's class, the children were used to her background presence, which freed them up to talk more among themselves, rather than seeking her out for the answer.

First and second graders enjoy working in small groups to solve problems. Sharing information with friends is also basic to children in preschool and kindergarten. Young children also engage in what Vygotsky (1986) called "private speech." They talk to themselves as they work through a problem. Pre-K and kindergarten teachers who take the time to watch and listen can learn much from this private speech.

Jared's teacher often heard him talking to himself at the water table, in the sandbox, and one morning in the block area. Spanish was Jared's first language, and his teacher took note that he was beginning to use English as he played. Jared worked independently while he softly narrated the steps he was taking in the construction of his marble run. "This end stay—good. Big blocks here and here, hold tube. Now." He rolls the marble; it goes slowly down tube. "No good. Need long one." Like Ms. Walker, his teacher watched, listened, and did not intervene. She didn't say a word because she could see and hear that Jared had more ideas to try out. Another time and another set of circumstances might warrant more direct interaction, but taking the time to watch, listen, and gather information can lessen inappropriate questions and unnecessary interruptions.

QUESTIONING

Skillful teachers, who take the time to watch and listen, blend conversational prompts and what Harlen calls "productive questions" (Harlen 2001) to enhance the child's exploration and understanding. When we become more adept at watching and listening, we have more time to consider what kind of intervention will be most effective. Questions become timely and purposeful.

The quality of the question depends not only on the timing but also on the way the question is stated. If we imagine a questioning continuum, we would see the direct questions on one end and the open-ended questions on the other.

Direct questions

Open-ended questions

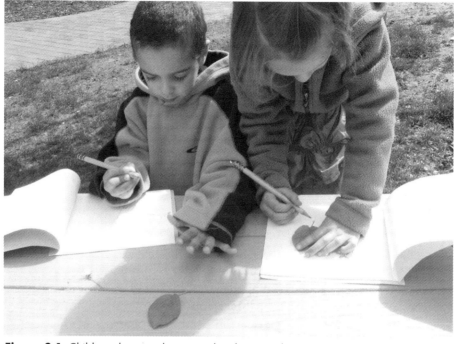

Figure 2.1 Children observing leaves on the playground

When I began my teaching career, most of my questions came from the left end of the continuum because I was focusing on factual recall, not inquiry. Now my questions are a mix of both, but most come from the right end because I'm looking for more than the correct answer. I'm supporting inquiry as described in the National Science Education Standards, which recommend "less emphasis on getting an answer" and "more emphasis on using evidence and strategies for developing or revising an explanation"(National Research Council 1996, 113). If I were teaching my first-grade unit on planting now, my questions would not be so focused on naming the parts of the plant and their function. Instead of questions like, "What does the stem do?" or, "What part of the tree protects it?" my questions would be more open-ended to promote the children's understanding of the connections and big ideas about plants: "What do you notice about the roots of your bean plant and the roots of our playground tree? What makes you say that the bark of the tree is like skin? How can you tell that the buds have changed? What is your evidence?" (See Figure 2.1.)

Like focused listening, developing questioning skills takes practice. It's a complex mix of timing and just the right wording. Certain questions are more effective for accessing certain kinds of information.

- Some questions will enhance exploration and take children deeper in their investigation:
  - What do you notice about . . . ?
  - Did you have a question you were wondering about?
  - Have you seen evidence of . . . ?
  - How are they the same?
  - How can you find out?
  - What makes you think that?
  - Can you think of a different plan?
  - What might happen if you . . . ?
  - What might you do next?
- Some questions will improve reasoning:
  - Can you think of some reasons why . . . ?
  - What did you find out when . . . ?
  - Why do you think that?
  - How does that connect to . . . ?
  - What have you learned?

In addition to thinking about effective questions, it also makes sense to consider conversational prompts that can be equally useful in supporting learning:

Tell me about this . . .
I'm curious about the way you . . .
Tell me why you think that.

Each of these prompts invites children to talk about what they are doing, to use their own words to explain their ideas or findings. Personalizing the prompt takes away the pressure for a right or wrong answer; the focus is on what *the child* thinks, what *the child* found. Like open-ended questions, these conversational prompts open the door to deeper, more descriptive responses.

When do you prompt rather than question? That's hard to say, but timely prompts can clarify without passing judgment. For example, when Anna showed me her scientific drawing of the kindergarten's bearded dragon lizard, I was struck by the precision and accuracy of her sketch: the exact number of toes, the way the claws connected to the toes and the toes to the feet. She had even included labels for the claws and the tail. But I was surprised to see how sloppy the coloration seemed. Anna had accurately chosen a light peach color for the reptile's body, but there was a swath of black crayon across the midsection that seemed totally out of place. As I ran my finger along her drawing, I pointed to the black section and said, "Tell me about this." The lizard was on the table in front of us, and Anna pointed to the bearded dragon's back as she explained, "See how this looks kinda gray. The rest is this pinkish color. See her scales. I made the scales underneath here." She points to the area on her drawing under the black. "I covered it with the black 'cause we don't have gray." In fact, I hadn't even noticed the scales she had drawn, and I hadn't noticed that the midsection of the lizard's back actually did look grayish. Anna's response to "Tell me about this" helped me see more and helped me understand her scientific drawing, which was, in fact, completely accurate.

The right question at the right time or the right prompt at the right time are basic instructional techniques for supporting inquiry. Questioning is one of the more obvious ways that teachers participate in the inquiry process. Another more understated strategy of teaching inquiry is the way we model the practices of science and the attitudes or feelings we project about science when we are with the children.

MODELING THE DISPOSITIONS AND PRACTICES OF SCIENCE

I've had many opportunities to observe and work with superb early childhood teachers. These master teachers project the skills and attitudes that we all strive for in our teaching. Their talents include skillful planning and teaching, but these teachers also exude a genuine delight in and curiosity about the natural world. They are just as excited as the children when the first butterfly emerges from a chrysalis or when the marble rolls down one ramp and up the next. During science meeting discussions, these teachers listen respectfully, ask for evidence, and comment on the qualities of an observational drawing. They are comfortable admitting when they don't know the answer. In fact, they use the opportunity to learn along with the children. During one morning meeting, after the class greeting, I observed a kindergarten teacher hold up one of the children's science notebooks and say to the class, "I have something very interesting to ask you about. I was reading Maria's science notebook. Look, she's drawn the hermit crabs' tank, and she wrote this question: 'Do crabs have teeth?' I thought to myself, what a great question. I'm curious about that, too. Do crabs have teeth? How do you think we could find out about that?" This teacher's eagerness to learn this new information was genuine. She didn't know the answer, but she was perfectly comfortable modeling enthusiasm and eagerness to join the children in learning.

Another important attitude of science that I observe in these master teachers is their ability to adjust and revise if their initial plans are not working out. You can only imagine the disappointment Mr. Enright felt at the end of his first grade's chick hatching unit, when not a single one of the twelve eggs hatched. The children and the teacher were very disheartened at the outcome, but Mr. Enright used the situation as an opportunity to problem solve, to raise questions and to develop hypotheses about what happened and what they might do differently. After the children discussed their theories and decided on the changes they would make, Mr. Enright procured another dozen fertilized eggs, and the class began the process a second time. Within the month, seven healthy chicks hatched. The success of the second attempt was thrilling for the class, but even more exciting was the opportunity to engage in hypothesizing, evidence gathering, and critical reflection. Their experience was also enriched by the way their teacher modeled an attitude of persistence and a disposition toward questioning and problem solving.

When we teach inquiry-based science, we not only influence the cognitive development of children by the plans we implement but also influence their affective development by the way we react to and talk about science. We project our values and feelings about the natural world through a combination of our body language and oral language. If we are dismissive or indifferent, we can diminish children's interest in and involvement with the natural world. On the other hand, if we are genuinely enthusiastic, we can inspire and motivate. (See Figure 2.2.)

The language we use in these encounters matters because it conveys specific information to the children. Consider how the following comments support the dispositions and attitudes of inquiry in an authentic way.

"I noticed something curious when I came into our room today."

"I am amazed. How did you get that marble to go around the corner?

"I was so excited when I looked in our aquarium this morning."

"I asked Jamil to show you his diagram of how his group moved the water from the tub to the water table because it really helped me understand how to do it."

"Of course you can bring in the worms to observe more closely, but how long should you keep them inside?"

Figure 2.2

When we model excitement, wonder, curiosity, respect for the environment, and open-mindedness, we are intentionally surrounding the children with the kinds of behaviors we want them to internalize.

ORGANIZING A CLASSROOM FOR INQUIRY

Early childhood classroom design is typically built around activity centers or areas, including art, blocks, dramatic play, literacy, library, math, and science. A science center might be outfitted with the materials and tools for doing science: something interesting to observe, magnifying lenses, rulers, a scale, science notebooks for recording data, and resource books. Although this is one way of presenting science in a classroom, we have to wonder what message this conveys to children. Can science only happen at that table? Do we limit our awareness of science opportunities by designating that table as the science center?

Rather than thinking about a specific area, it might make more sense to think about infusing science opportunities throughout the classroom, much like we experience science in the real world. In many of the classrooms I visit, not much happens in the science center, but I see countless examples of science occurring throughout the room and outside. In the meeting area, a child fills in the weather chart; in the house area, a child waters the plants on the bookcase; in the literacy center, children hold magnifying lenses up to the fish tank; at the sensory table, children test out clay boats they made at the art table; in the block area, children experiment with wooden and cardboard blocks for stability; at the chalkboard, a child notices the powdery dust in the tray; at the math table, children notice the details of an interesting selection of rocks they are weighing; in the library, children browse through a nonfiction book on simple machines; and on the playground, children prepare the soil to plant petunias. (See Figure 2.3.)

I often ask teachers to take an inventory of the opportunities for science that permeate their classrooms. They note the number and the variety of inquiry-based possibilities that stretch far beyond the science table. Teachers who are mindful and aware of inquiry tend to offer many opportunities outside the specified area. Their use of space and the materials of science is more expansive and enables children to connect with science beyond the science table and throughout the classroom.

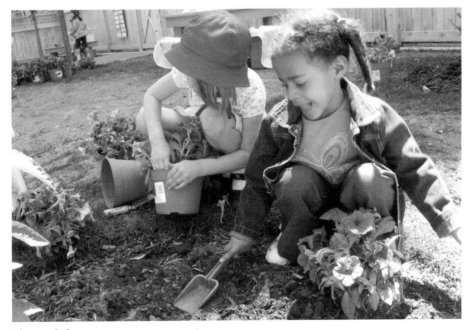

Figure 2.3

This perspective reflects the underlying principle of the Italian community preschools of Reggio Emilia, which look to the classroom environment as "the third teacher" (Gandini 1998, 46). Connecting this belief to science suggests that the classroom will be infused with elements of the natural world, displayed to ignite a child's curiosity. If we think about a science-rich classroom, much like a literacy-rich classroom, we would expect it to include interesting things to observe, elements of the natural world, and tools to support inquiry.

Every science-rich environment should include living things—perhaps a pet, fish in a tank, or an ant farm—as well as a variety of growing things, including seeds or bulbs the children have planted and small and large potted plants. When children help to care for the animals and plants, they are establishing a personal connection that contributes to their awareness of and respect for the natural world and to their understanding of the needs of organisms and their life cycles. (See Figure 2.4.)

Children need interesting things to look at, to touch, and to wonder about. Whether looking to display a cross section of a tree, a hornet's nest, or a snake skin, early childhood teachers are brilliant at locating fascinating items. The children and their families can also be a rich source of seasonal and unique artifacts to lend to the classroom for observation. Sending

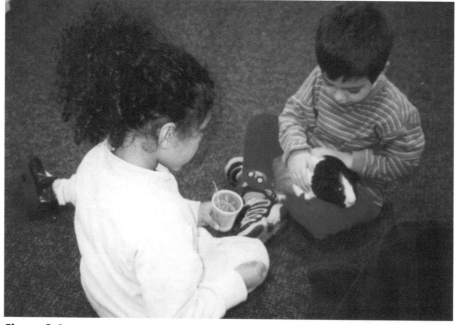

Figure 2.4

home a letter or an e-mail early in the year explaining your purpose may yield surprising results like a bin of worms, a fossil collection, or X-ray films.

Deciding how to display materials is another aspect of developing an environment for inquiry. Displays that are most engaging are simple, accessible, and easy to maintain. (See Figure 2.5.)

A tray displaying different kinds of palm fronds from the neighborhood, a vase of pussy willows, or a bird's nest all have potential for capturing the children's attention, but eventually they may need to be replaced or revitalized with additional materials. Consider adding a few items that may enhance the children's observation: perhaps a question to draw the children's attention to a certain aspect of the object or a nonfiction book open to a page that corresponds to it. A tray or container with magnifying lenses, observational drawing paper, and pencils might also be useful. Once interest wanes, remove the materials before they become dust catchers. If the objects are refreshed regularly, children will come to expect that, and they will be on the lookout for something new.

Tools for doing science will deepen the children's observations of these materials. Instead of keeping all the science tools (lenses, nonfiction books, science notebooks, scales, measuring tools) in the science center, distributing

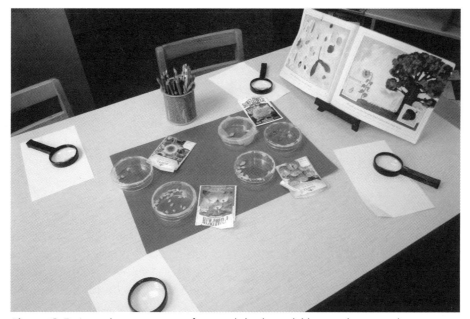

Figure 2.5 A simple arrangement of materials beckons children to observe and compare seeds, and perhaps record what they notice.

Science Around the Classroom

- A basket with Unifix cubes, rulers, notebooks, and pencils next to the paper-white bulbs growing on the windowsill

- An indoor/outdoor thermometer mounted at the children's eye level, along with two clipboards holding pencils and weather forms for recording the temperature and weather conditions

- A backpack for the playground outfitted with four clipboards with paper, colored pencils, binoculars, magnifying lenses, a bug box, ziplock bags for collecting, and assorted field guides

- Nonfiction books about pet care next to the pet's cage or tank

- A display of interesting natural materials with labels, or inviting questions

- Assorted plants that have varied leaf shapes (aloe, trailing ivy, oxalis), colors (coleus), scents (mint, lavender), flowers (geranium, peace lily)

---

these materials so they are close to the objects to be examined makes them accessible so the children can work independently and efficiently. Catching the children's interest in the pattern on the lizard's skin might not happen if they have to go across the room to find a magnifying lens. However, if two lenses and a notebook are kept next to the lizard's tank, then the possibility of doing science is heightened.

Creating a few small spaces that will serve two or three children, rather than one large space for five or six, will allow for more productive interactions. Distributing materials in small batches throughout the room will promote these small-group encounters, which will maximize children's conversations and ability to share ideas and raise questions.

Organize the science materials using the same principles you use to set up other areas of the room so that the children can replace materials independently and keep them in good order. Supplying oak-tag labels and outlines for containers and individual items and using small bins or segmented containers provides the children with a clear expectation of where each piece goes before they leave the area. (See Figure 2.6.)

When we think of classroom areas in which science opportunities can be integrated, the dramatic play area is one that is sometimes overlooked because it is usually outfitted to support themes like the home and family, the doctor's office, a school, a grocery store, or a restaurant. Why not include opportunities for children to construct knowledge about science content in a dramatic play area whose theme is science related? Designing

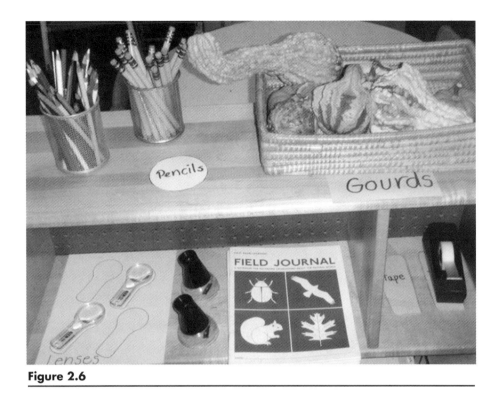

Figure 2.6

a dramatic play area that is part of the science inquiry unit topic could lead to all kinds of meaningful setups where children do science like scientists.

In our school, an inquiry unit on water included a "Water Lab" that replaced the house theme in the dramatic play area. When they entered the "Water Lab," the children donned lab coats, engaged in or set up water experiments, and collected data on their findings. Another time, the dramatic play area was restaged as an entomologist's laboratory for an insect unit. The laboratory included ladybugs and ants to observe, enlarged photos of insects with labeled body parts, clipboards with observation outlines, insect resource books, mounted samples of common insects, a calendar, nets for collecting samples, labels, pencils, notebooks, and lab coats. This dramatic play area was also expanded to include two areas for our pet inquiry unit. (See Appendix 3 for a thorough discussion of this unit.) We reorganized our space to include a small house area along with a pet store, which eventually became a veterinarian's office. In each of these areas, the children used the practices of science, the vocabulary of science, and the content of science as they played out the roles associated with that unit's big ideas of providing for pets' needs, acquiring pets, and caring for pets by taking them to the veterinarian. (See Figure 2.7.)

Figure 2.7 Veterinarians caring for a pet

At the end of an inquiry on simple machines, first graders designed a museum of simple machines with interactive displays. Labels written by the children explained how the machines made work easier; other stations had instruction cards (again written by the children) for building simple machines. A corner of the space was outfitted with pillows and a display of books on simple machines, along with a guest book for comments from the families and the kindergarten and first-grade classes the children invited to the museum.

Designing the physical environment for inquiry begins by considering possibilities—possibilities for observation, possibilities for wonder, and possibilities for connection to the natural world. Infusing science opportunities throughout the classroom contributes to a context for inquiry, a context in which children do science and enjoy science. But even the most interesting physical environment is still dependent on the subtle but powerful approaches that the teacher exhibits: careful observation and listening, finely tuned questions, and intentional modeling of the attitudes and skills of inquiry. This combination is the foundation that nourishes an inquiry-based approach to science in the early years.

Chapter 3

Science as a Context for Literacy

Reading, Writing, and Speaking

Much has been written about the interdependency of science and literacy, a great deal of it coming from the literacy world, which correctly sees science as a rich content source for developing readers and writers. If real inquiry is to occur, children have to talk, write, read, and be read to; so literacy is a basic underpinning of inquiry-based science. The integration of literacy and science can be especially beneficial for K–2 teachers in districts where required literacy and mathematics blocks dominate the daily schedule and teachers feel pressed for time to include science as a typical part of the school day.

Science offers some interesting opportunities for combined science and literacy teaching and learning. This chapter highlights three of these authentic contexts in which to develop science understandings and to prac-tice literacy skills:

- Science notebooks
- Nonfiction read-alouds
- Science meetings and discussion groups

SCIENCE NOTEBOOKS

Every scientist has a notebook to keep track of data, to make notes and drawings, to look back at early work. The inventive drawings, notes, and even cross-outs in Leonardo da Vinci's exquisite notebooks show ideas in the making. The meticulous sketches of the animals, insects, and fungi in Beatrix Potter's journals are evidence of close observation and attention to detail. Darwin, Curie, Audubon—these famous scientists used notebooks in the field and in the laboratory to record and organize information that was essential to their work. That same purpose is equally relevant for the not-so-famous scientists of preschool, kindergarten, and the primary grades.

What Is a Science Notebook for Young Children?

When we talk about science notebooks in a pre-K, kindergarten, or primary classroom, we are building on the same structure used in professional scientists' notebooks. These are working documents that enable children to record data and ideas and then use that data as evidence to develop theories, make judgments, raise questions, or share information with peers. These science notebooks are purposeful and descriptive. They may not appear as detailed or as professional as a scientist's notebook, but the contents of a child's science notebook echo the significance of writing and drawing about findings and wonderings.

The science notebook needs to be used in authentic ways, ways that make sense developmentally for young children. We might see children draw, write, or dictate their predictions, findings, and questions; sometimes they do this by themselves and sometimes with assistance. Pre-K entries tend to be mainly drawings or sketches with some writing, dictated text or labels that identify the key parts of the drawing. Jackson labeled his sketch of the crab-apple tree using the first letter of the words he needed, *c* for *crab apple* and *b* for *buds*. (See Figure 3.1.)

Helen chose to dictate part of her prediction about the amaryllis bulb she was observing, and write just *belb* (bulb) and *red* herself. (See Figure 3.2.)

Kindergarten notebooks showcase more of a mix of observational drawings and child-generated text, labels, and questions (see Figure 3.3), while first- and second-grade notebooks may have fewer drawings, more tables and graphs, and more extensive writing and interpretation or analysis. The opening entry in Anna's first-grade science notebook documents just what she does as a scientist. (See Figure 3.4.) Six-year-old Sam's entry is all text punctuated by the three question marks at the end:

Figure 3.1 Jackson used *B* to label the buds he observed on a crab-apple tree. He wrote a *C* to label all the crab apples.

Figure 3.2 Helen's entry is a combination of dictation and her writing.

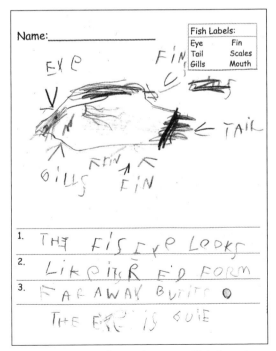

Figure 3.3 Note the combination of labels and text written by this kindergartner.

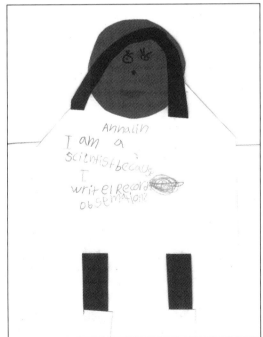

Figure 3.4 Anna writes, "I am a scientist because I write I record observations."

My pupa is hanging up. It looks like a yellow and green sock. There is a lot of frass the same color as the foodstuff. That was from the larva. Will there be any more frass now???

In each of these samples, children needed to access their phonetic knowledge to spell the words to create meaning. The print and drawings the children create in their science notebooks become their personal text to read and share with others.

Using the data collected in their notebooks, these children might also read or point out details from their entries to peers and teachers. As their notebooks expand, children can revisit data collected earlier in the year to reread, compare, and discuss with their classmates in the context of large- or small-group science meetings. Thus, the science notebook becomes the mechanism for reading, writing, and talking about science during the investigation and after the data has been recorded.

What Kind of Science Notebook Works Best?

Science notebooks for preschool, kindergarten, and the primary grades can take many forms: commercial notebooks sold through educational suppliers, three-ring binders with sectioned tabs, composition notebooks, and teacher-made notebooks with multiple pages and cover stapled together. When we start to consider the style of notebook that will meet our students' needs, there are some fundamental questions about the contents, layout, and ease of use that we need to ask.

Is there blank paper for drawing, lined paper for writing, and graph paper for measuring (if needed)? Does the layout include a space for the date of each entry and for page numbers? Are there designated pages for a table of contents and glossary? Is it the right size? The size and manageability of the notebook make a difference. Size is especially important for preschoolers, who require a compact notebook that they can easily carry, but even first graders need a notebook that is comfortable to write in and hold. Size also matters when we have to consider storage for twenty-plus notebooks that need to be accessible to the children. Is the science notebook compact enough to carry and store, while still providing adequate space for drawing and writing? Flexibility is another consideration. Does the notebook allow for the child's development (i.e., moving from drawing to writing or moving from collecting evidence to interpreting data)? Does the structure support an organized scrapbook approach (i.e., inserting found materials or nature samples, photographs, Venn diagrams, graphs, tables, resource pages, word banks)? Consider these points and the comparisons listed in Figure 3.5 as you think about the science notebook that will work best for you and your students.

Notebook Style	Advantages	Disadvantages
Three-ring binder	• Pages can be worked on separately and added later. • Additional pages can be added. • Pockets can be added for storing artifacts.	• Large size can be difficult to carry and work in outside the classroom. • Pages often rip away from rings.
Composition notebook	• Inexpensive • Size and durability (compact, easy to carry and store) • Teacher can designate sections for table of contents, topics, and glossary by inserting tabs.	• No blank pages for drawing • Binding makes it hard to insert artifacts or samples.
Teacher made for each topic	• Flexibility—can be made to meet teacher's exact needs • Size and durability (compact, easy to carry and store) • Pockets can be added for storing artifacts.	• Time consuming • Separate notebook for each topic limits children's ability to look back at previous entries from other investigations.
Commercially designed	• District funded, no cost to teacher • Size and durability (compact, easy to carry and store)	• Predetermined content, layout • Space allotment may not match children's needs (e.g., too much space for drawing, not enough for writing). • May not have space for table of contents, glossary, or index

Figure 3.5 Science Notebook Comparisons

Science Notebook Contents and Literacy Skills

The literacy experiences embedded in ways children use science notebooks are one of their many advantages. I know several teachers who overlap science and writer's workshop because writing in science notebooks gives their children the realistic context they need, not only for writing about a nonfiction topic, but also for incorporating the features of nonfiction texts such as a table of contents, labeled drawings, a glossary, and an index. We can also encourage children to read these entries or the dictation they have given, which is another opportunity to practice their emerging literacy skills. (See Figure 3.6.)

Observational Drawings

Observational or scientific drawings are probably the most common entry in a child's science notebook. Starting in preschool, children learn that these drawings have certain requirements; they are supposed to be pictures of what is real, not what is imagined. This takes some time and some teaching, but young children come to understand quite quickly that there is a difference between creative drawing and scientific drawing. Taking the time to look closely at an object or an organism and record what we see forces us to think about details that might otherwise be overlooked. This is one of the

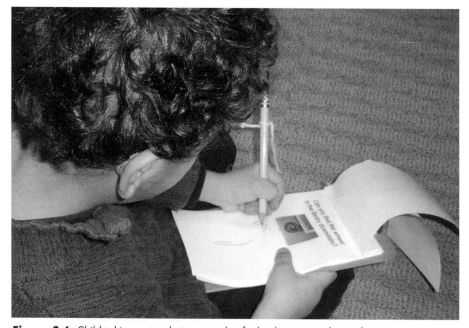

Figure 3.6 Child taking notes during a study of wheels in a simple machines unit

most important outcomes of the process of observational drawing. It gives children a chance to notice more, to become aware of the unexpected.

We know that young children's representational skills are emerging, so we don't expect that their observational drawings will be exact or even identifiable, but we do expect that they will gradually begin to demonstrate more accurate renderings. As children become more skilled, we begin to see a progression of developments: consistent use of true colors, recognition and replication of basic shapes of objects and organisms, attempts at drawing to scale, and techniques for showing motion and sequence. The developmental trajectory of this skill is a delight to observe. Children move from random color choices to accurate colors and gradually abandon fanciful eyelashes and smiles on organisms as they learn to record what they see, what is real. And even if these drawings appear more abstract than concrete, the labels and written or dictated descriptions that are included bring out the meaning. (See Figure 3.7.)

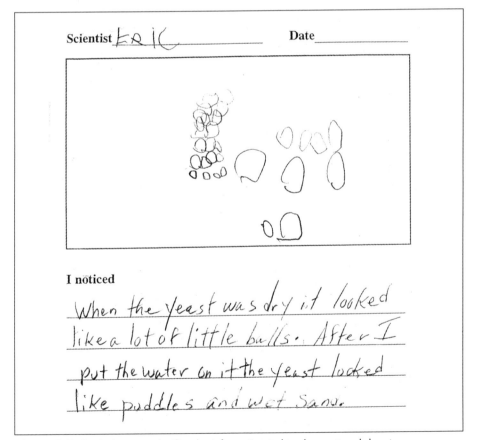

Figure 3.7 Eric's dictation clarifies the information in his observational drawing.

How can we scaffold such complex work for such young children? Not surprisingly, we need to do observational drawings ourselves, so that we can understand what is involved, intellectually and emotionally. When my first-grade colleagues and I were putting the final pieces together for our inquiry unit "What Grows Around Our School?" we decided to do observational drawings of the tree at the far end of the parking lot. We thought we could easily draw a tree, but the more we looked, the more we realized our image or idea of a tree was quite different from the one in front of us. It was a struggle for all of us to figure out how the branches connect to the trunk, how the trunk sits in the ground. Even the color of the bark proved problematic. Gwen had shaded in a brownish color on her tree, until Kate called her over to look more closely. The bark was actually more gray than brown, and there were some deep, almost black striations that she had missed completely. As we became comfortable with the task, we found ourselves talking more, describing what we saw and what we were doing to capture the details of the tree. This task confirmed what we had read about observational drawing—it helped us see more, wonder more, and capture and share what we saw.

How can we develop a supportive environment and teach this process to young children? First steps include making time for such an endeavor and providing the right materials. We need to give children time to look closely and time to record and talk about what they see. (See Figure 3.8.)

We need to make sure that we supply them with appropriate materials that make the drawing part easier, rather than more challenging. For example, markers can make the children's work more difficult because they can't be erased and the colors can't be blended. Drawing materials that enhance the details of scientific drawings include pencils, erasers, and colored pencils. Varying the kinds of paper in the science notebook can also make a difference. I've noticed that when children use small papers, like three-by-five-inch index

Figure 3.8

cards or six-inch-square sheets, they seem to jump into the experience more confidently. Written comments can be added when they glue the paper into their notebook.

Kindergarten teacher Christina Ryan has experimented with several types of notebook sheets that help her children organize and gather data. She set up a data-collection form to help children compare the behaviors they had observed in the class's two pet gerbils, Cocoa and Brownie, then interpret their findings in response to the question she posed at the bottom of the page, "What do you notice about your data?" (See Figure 3.9.) She also designed a page that would help children zoom in on specific things she wanted them to look more closely at. (See Appendix 2 for a blank form of this page.) The children had been talking about Philomena, their bearded dragon lizard, and her interesting feet, so Christina gave the children a template that directed them to look precisely at the lizard's feet. The notebook entry in Figure 3.10 shows how effective this format was. The child crossed out her first sketch and replaced it with a much more detailed drawing that accurately reflects Philomena's scaly skin and claws.

Figure 3.9 This child used data to conclude that Brownie did a lot of chewing!

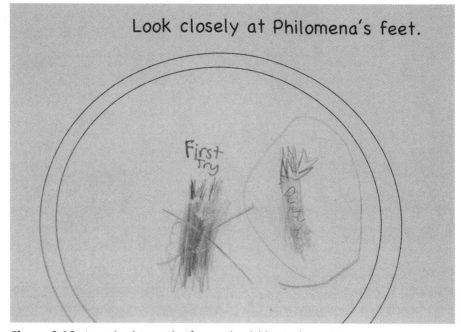

Figure 3.10 A notebook insert that focuses the children's observation

Something as simple as a worksheet that already has the outline of the cup or vessel that will be used over successive observations enables the children to focus on the actual observation and not on drawing the cup. (See Figure 3.11, which shows an example of a worksheet for observing snow melt.) You have probably introduced other templates and forms that would be useful for class notebooks.

Once these materials are in place, we can focus on the explicit teaching that needs to happen if children are going to be successful at observational drawing. Teaching children how to do scientific drawings is a continuous process, much like the scaffolding that happens in writing workshop. It requires quite a bit of modeling or demonstrating along with explaining or narrating what we are doing. In science, we model the steps we take to make the drawing, and, at the same time, we talk aloud about each step we go through.

When I introduced crickets to a first-grade class at morning meeting, we spent several minutes just looking at them—from all different angles— in their transparent cups. As we observed, the children talked about what they noticed: the way the legs were bent, the long thing sticking out of the back of the cricket's body, the markings on its back, the huge eyes, and the

Name _____   Date _____

1.   Put snow in cup.

2.   When the snow melts, guess how much water there will be.

3.   When the snow melted _____
     _____
     _____
     _____

Figure 3.11 Including the outline of the cup helps children focus on the process they are observing.

curvy antennae. After we had plenty of time to look closely, I set up my chart paper and began a mini-lesson on the scientific drawing of a cricket. What follows is a segment of that lesson:

Mrs. Edson: First I have to decide whether I want to draw the cricket from the top, the bottom, or the side. You can choose whichever view you like. [*I hold up the cup and look directly at the cricket.*] If I do the side view I can get a good view of his legs, which really interest me. Now let's see, what should I draw first?

Sean: Start with his antennae. They're easy.

Jessie: Maybe the head? Then you have something to put the antennae on.

Mrs. Edson: I see what you're saying Jessie. If I start with the body, then it will be easier to add on all the parts. What shape is the cricket's body?

Maria: It goes like this [*she moves her finger in a line, then circles back*]

Mrs. Edson: What kind of shape is that?

Maria: Sort of long and with curvy ends.

Mrs. Edson: Right, like a long oval. Let's all try what Maria did and sketch the cricket's body in the air. Now I'll try sketching it with a pencil. [*I draw an oval on the chart paper.*] That doesn't look right. [*I erase and make it again.*] Scientists use erasers a lot. They try really hard to make their drawings accurate or correct. [*I draw the body again.*] Look at your cricket, and see if I'm on the right track.

Alejandro: You still need a head. See it goes on the end of that body.

Mrs. Edson: Right, that's where it would go. Then I could add the antennae that Sean mentioned. But now it's your turn to start your scientific drawing of the cricket. Remember that you need to decide which view or perspective you will draw, and then think about the shape of each of the body parts and where they fit on the cricket's body. Take your time and draw what you see. [*I take down the chart paper and fold it up.*]

This brief transcript shows what a mini-lesson on observational drawing might look and sound like and how a combination of modeling, narrating, and seeking the children's ideas sets the stage for their own observational drawings. These drawings should be the children's work and should come from the children, but they do need some help getting started. That's why the sketch I make is rough. As I shape the form, I'm constantly narrating to help the children see how I problem-solve and make decisions about what to draw first and what comes next. Sometimes I'll leave my sketch up on the chart, but most times I remove it, because I don't want the children to look at my work. I want them to look at what they are observing.

The scaffolding continues as we help children find ways to represent what they see. Follow-up lessons might include suggestions for breaking down an object into specific parts and shapes, shading to show more depth, and using arrows to show movement. (See Figure 3.12.) Children often discover techniques on their own, which they can share to teach the rest of the class.

Figure 3.12 Note the tiny arrow indicating the way the bulb is growing.

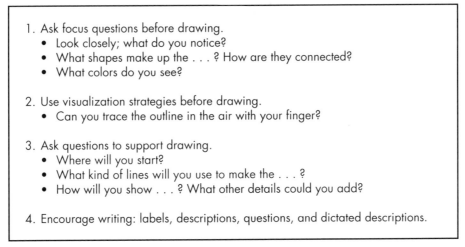

1. Ask focus questions before drawing.
   - Look closely; what do you notice?
   - What shapes make up the . . . ? How are they connected?
   - What colors do you see?

2. Use visualization strategies before drawing.
   - Can you trace the outline in the air with your finger?

3. Ask questions to support drawing.
   - Where will you start?
   - What kind of lines will you use to make the . . . ?
   - How will you show . . . ? What other details could you add?

4. Encourage writing: labels, descriptions, questions, and dictated descriptions.

Figure 3.13 Suggestions for Scaffolding Observational Drawings

As children become more adept at drawing, they can begin to look at the scale and proportions of the object and its parts. Naturalists use a pencil or their thumb as a measure to make an accurate comparison for their sketches (Canfield, 2011). When children are ready, we can model this technique to extend the accuracy of their work. Additional scaffolding suggestions are listed in Figure 3.13.

The last instructional suggestion in Figure 3.13 is a reminder that print is an essential component of observational drawings. As mentioned earlier, the written or dictated descriptions, labels, or questions the children provide bring clarity to the entry. The text the children see in their notebooks enriches both science and literacy development.

Moving from Pictures to Words

As children record an observation—as they list the steps to an experiment or compose a question to investigate—they gain experience in both explaining an idea and making sense of science. Accurate punctuation and spelling are not the primary goals when writing in science notebooks. But we can scaffold children's spelling of scientific terms when we supply a word bank—a page in the science notebook that lists science vocabulary— or employ a science word wall to help the children access the conventional spelling. I found first graders eager to access the scientific terms Mr. Tejada had stapled into the back of their science journals: *light, opaque, transparent, translucent, reflect, shadow, prediction, hypothesis, question.* Another first-grade teacher chose to set up a science word wall to support the children in their geology inquiry, while her kindergarten colleague used plastic frames to display a list of science vocabulary words the kindergartners might want to access during their inquiry unit.

We can tap into the children's entries as formative assessment data regarding children's growth in their literacy skills. One first-grade teacher I worked with showed me a series of comments her children wrote about a salmon they were observing. Adrian had written, "I noticed that it's eye is bouncy, it's fins are spiky, and it has dots everywhere and it has teeth." Adrian's teacher remarked that his entry was impressive for several reasons: his use of descriptive and accurate vocabulary; his attempts at punctuation, using commas and a period; and his almost accurate spelling. But she noticed that Adrian, like several other children in the class, didn't understand when to use *its* and *it's*, which prompted her to develop a mini-lesson to address this literacy skill—a skill she identified as lacking through the children's science notebook entries.

Science notebooks can also impact children who resist writing. Having the opportunity to draw rather than write allows these children to express what they know in a medium in which they feel competent. I saw evidence of this in a kindergarten classroom in which the children were making observational drawings of leaves they had collected on the playground. Nicola had just finished two detailed and precise drawings of elm leaves. Her teacher traced the veins and edges of the leaves that Nicola had replicated so exactly and said, "You were so careful in the way you drew the veins and these toothed edges. If you could label these, then everyone would know about these parts of the elm leaves." Her teacher moved on, and Nicola worked on adding the labels. When she was finished, she took her notebook to her teacher, pointed to the words she had written and said, "Look, toothed and vein. I did fancy writing." This was the first time Nicola had written anything other than her name or a friend's name. Her science work drew her into writing. Nicola, like other children who might be disinclined to write, moved gradually from drawing to dictation to more text-dominant entries that explained the science she was doing. Sometimes, children may move from writing to dictation just because they have more to say and don't want to take the time to write down their ideas. Adili's initial observational drawing shows the paper-white narcissus bulb, followed by the planted bulb in the pot. She also includes quite an accurate invented spelling label that indicates strong sound-letter correspondence and an understanding of word spacing. (See Figure 3.14.)

Two days later, Adili captured the growth of her paper-white bulb with another drawing in her science notebook, but this time she asked her

Figure 3.14 Adili labels her paper-white bulb and records the planted bulb.

This is this bulb. I noticed it started to be tall. 2/5/09 RB

Figure 3.15 Adili dictated her findings to her teacher.

teacher to write for her: "This is the bulb. I noticed it started to be tall." (See Figure 3.15.)

Adili watched as her teacher recorded her words, and then at her teacher's suggestion, Adili read the sentence back. This is another example of how a notebook entry can provide a meaningful literacy experience.

The writing prompts used in writing workshop can also be retooled to be used in science notebooks. The most common is the black-line master shown in Figure 3.16.

Writing prompts provide children with a structure that gives them practice reading the prompt and writing a complete sentence or statement. Additional prompts that refer to the practices of science can also be introduced.

Name_____ Date_____

I observed_____

I noticed_____

I'm wondering _____

Figure 3.16 Observational drawing template with writing prompt

- For predicting:
  "I predict that _____"
- For questioning:
  "My question is _____"
- For findings:
  "Today I found out that _____"

When we insert writing prompts into a science notebook entry, we do have to take into consideration their effects on the actual science that might happen. For some children, prompts can be just the ticket to start writing; for others, they can be limiting and tedious. Writing prompts can be beneficial in that they set up a common format from which to begin, and that can be especially helpful for English language learners and children with disabilities. Like any instructional tool in our teaching repertoire, we need to think about why and when it makes sense to use these prompts. We can consider writing prompts as a timely addition for our novice scientists, but ultimately our expectation should be that the children take charge of their science entries and write what they are thinking.

Comprehension and Meaning Making

While writing is a central piece of what children do with science notebooks, comprehension and meaning making are probably the most powerful literacy by-products of science notebook entries. Recording data forces children to observe more carefully. And the entries they make about those observations give children a chance to think about the meaning behind the observations or experiments, to make sense of what they are wondering about. Because so much of science has to do with raising questions and refining theories, the context of science notebooks gives children the chance to look over the data they've collected and, given a new observation or comparison of previous observations, make changes or revisions.

Much of this kind of work happens among children as they work in small groups on their notebook entries. The give-and-take, the collaborative conversation, happens when children sit side by side and comfortably show their notebooks to their friends and teachers. They might compare methods for how to show the edges of a rock or ask for suggestions on how to show the way water moves through tubing. These opportunities for discussion contribute to more accurate and more complex entries and give children a chance to use science vocabulary in a meaningful context.

While English language learners may have a more limited verbal role, sharing science notebooks and working collaboratively still gives them an

Figure 3.17

opportunity to engage with peers. They may have to depend on a mix of nonverbal signals, pointing to parts of their drawings and using one-word descriptions, but they can still be part of the conversation because it revolves around a common language they can access with their friends: their sketches in their science notebooks. (See Figure 3.17.)

There are so many possibilities for integrating literacy and science through the use of science notebooks. Some of the following suggestions may be familiar, and some may be new. We can sustain embedded literacy experiences by integrating some basic practices into our science/literacy instruction:

- Start with simple expectations for writing. Encourage children to label drawings, write, dictate, and read the text of their entries.
- Provide a date stamp and gradually move to writing the date using monthly abbreviations and then with numerals.
- Print out word lists of common scientific terms children may need in their entries. Make individual copies to paste into notebooks or display in plastic frames in science and literacy centers or set up a science word wall.

- Use writing prompts on worksheet pages to get children started; then gradually give children control of their entries.
- Include nonfiction text features in science notebooks: a blank table of contents, chapter/section headings, glossary, and index.
- Use individual science notebook entries to teach and to provoke discussion at large-group science meetings. Let the child present his or her work to the group, or use the entries as a way to teach science and literacy content information.

NONFICTION READ-ALOUDS

We are fortunate to be teaching science now, with the outstanding variety and quality of nonfiction trade books available for the early childhood years. It is no wonder children are so attracted to these science information books given the scope of topics, the attractive layouts, the fascinating photographs, and the interesting content. While fiction books still outnumber the nonfiction texts, field guides, and biographies found in pre-K through second-grade classrooms, the influx of this nonfiction genre is definitely making its mark. When we use these books with young children, we expose them to the nature of science, enhance their understanding of science content knowledge, and expand their understanding and use of higher-level vocabulary. Some of these effects occur when children browse through nonfiction resources, and some occur as a result of *well-planned* nonfiction read-alouds. *Well-planned* is highlighted because these books require an approach that is different from a typical fiction read-aloud. The content and layout require a different methodology. For instance, science nonfiction books, unlike fictional stories, are often read aloud in sections, rather than from cover to cover. Chapter heads are included, text is sometimes paraphrased, illustrations are highlighted, and special features like table of contents, index, and glossary are accessed.

It took some practice for me to become adept at reading nonfiction to children. When I prepared those early nonfiction read-alouds, I focused mainly on vocabulary, and I misjudged the amount of information presented in the book. When I stopped to think about how I used nonfiction books in my own life, I could see why my approach was so flawed. For instance, when I want to find out more about shade plants for my garden, I go the index, look for shade plants, go to that page, skim the information, and use the information. I would never think of reading a resource book on perennials from cover to cover. That realization brought me to a much different way of preparing nonfiction read-alouds. Rather than reading cover to cover and overwhelming the children, I began to select just the chapter or section that would inform their understanding. I became much more comfortable skipping over sections and putting more emphasis on analyzing the photographs, drawings, and diagrams. Consider these suggestions as you plan for successful nonfiction read-alouds:

- Read only selected portions of the text that support your goals. Feel free to skip sections, or return to those sections on another day.
- Model curiosity and wonder.
  - "I was amazed when I saw the photographs from the Hubble telescope in this book. I couldn't wait to show you."
  - "I wonder what the author means by . . ."
  - "That makes me want to ask . . ."
- Introduce a book by talking about specific information you want to learn about.
  - "This book is about the seashore, but we're only interested in tide pools, so that's the section we'll be reading."
  - "This book is all about air. We'll be using it throughout our inquiry, but today we're going to read just the opening chapter."
- Pause and reread sections that have important or challenging information.
  - "I'm going to read that sentence over again; that's a lot to think about."
  - "I want to remember that idea, so I'm going to read it again."
- Paraphrase rather than read word for word from the text if the information or writing is too challenging.
  - "A lot of what this author wrote about recycling is pretty complicated, so I'm not going to read every word to you."
  - "So it seems that the author wants us to remember three big ideas . . ."
- Explain what is going on in the illustrations, photographs, or charts.
  - "Can you see how the author shows the way the butterfly changes through this series of little drawings?"
- Use the table of contents, headings, glossary, and index authentically to look for information and to respond to questions the children raise.
  - "This heading says 'Levers.' That's what this section is all about."

- ○ "Let's check the index to find the page that chrysalis was mentioned on."
- ○ "Yesterday Bella asked what you call the big, puffy clouds we saw outside. I think this book on weather will help, but first we have to check the table of contents. This chapter says 'Types of clouds, page 12.' Now we can find out what those clouds are called."

In addition to science read-alouds, nonfiction texts on a variety of topics and spanning a range of reading levels should be included in the classroom library. Children should have access to field guides and sophisticated texts such as Walter Wick's *A Drop of Water* (1997) and David Macaulay's *Underground* (1983), as well as biographies such as Amy Ehrlich's *Rachel: The Story of Rachel Carson* (2008) and Robert Burleigh's *Into the Woods: John James Audubon Lives His Dream* (2003). The photographs and drawings in these books are so intriguing that children love to page through them. My preschoolers surprised me with their persistent interest in a dense zoology book on guinea pigs that I had borrowed from the Boston Museum of Science. The children were not interested in the text. It was the elegant line drawings and X-rays of the guinea pig's skeletal structure that drew them to the large and heavy volume. Browsing through field guides on insects, trees, or rocks can provoke informal conversations about prior experiences and questions about the topics.

Building a classroom culture that relies on nonfiction as an essential resource for understanding the natural world means thinking about how to connect young children with the genre:

- Provide an enticing variety of nonfiction—content-related resources including informational texts, biographies, field guides, charts, and websites. Don't feel constrained by the readability level, but make sure the content is accurate.
- Display nonfiction texts to promote access (e.g., a field guide next to the rock collection, fish information and care books next to the aquarium, architectural books in the block area, a local weather-report link on the computer).
- Make time to read nonfiction to the children, and schedule browsing time for them.
- Refine your nonfiction read-aloud style by explicitly modeling what a fluent reader does when reading for information: read only relevant sections of the book, pause and reread to reconsider an

idea, paraphrase or think aloud to clarify a point, make connections to prior experiences, explain illustrations and charts, ask questions, and summarize the big ideas.

- Use the features of nonfiction texts with the children during read-alouds or while browsing information books with them. Access the table of contents; point out headings; use the glossary, index, labeled drawings, cross sections, and charts; and talk about highlighted vocabulary words.
- Use nonfiction texts with the children to access information, procedures, and evidence.

SCIENCE DISCUSSIONS AND CONVERSATIONS

The National Science Research Council's recommendation on communication is aimed directly at the early childhood years:

From the very start of their science education, students should be asked to engage in the communication of science, especially regarding the investigations they are conducting and the observations they are making. (Committee on a Conceptual Framework for the New K–12 Science Education Standards 2012, 77)

The committee purposefully highlights communication as a practice of science for young children since this is how children process their observations, raise questions, and ultimately share what they understand. Just as we considered strategies for supporting their drawing and writing, so we need to consider strategies for supporting children's oral communication through informal conversations and through more organized science discussions. We've touched on the informal conversations that emerge during science observations or that are sparked by interesting materials in and outside the classroom, including nonfiction texts. But it's helpful to examine the role of talk more closely.

Developing science discussions that are productive and successful takes time. It takes time to teach children how to participate effectively, and it takes time to include discussions in what is already a full daily schedule. This commitment to science discussions not only yields richer science and cognitive development but also impacts children's literacy and social development. When we prepare them for successful science discussions, we begin with social constructs such as listening, turn taking, recognizing different perspectives, and respectful disagreement. Once children understand how to be both listeners and speakers, we can begin to develop the skills of science discourse.

All of this rests on our ability to create a classroom community in which children trust their teacher and feel comfortable with their peers. This is something teachers work on from the very first day of school. We demonstrate our interest and respect by sitting or squatting near the child to establish eye contact and giving him or her our full attention. This is a basic behavior we also want to scaffold for our large-group discussions, so the seating arrangement is a fundamental detail. Since our expectation is for each child to participate either as a listener or as a speaker, we need to organize the group in a circle so that the children can make eye contact with each other. Whether speaking, listening, watching, or waiting for a turn, each child in the circle is physically situated to be part of the meeting and can see herself or himself as a contributor.

And that brings us to the actual structure of the meeting. What does a science meeting and discussion look like? What kind of structure supports a productive and engaging meeting? Starting with a routine agenda is especially effective. Much like the daily schedule posted in our classrooms, a set agenda for a science meeting helps children anticipate what's coming next. For example:

> Here's our plan for today. Some children will have a chance to report on what happened when you experimented with your flashlights; then we'll have comments and questions, and at the very end we'll talk about what our next steps will be.

This teacher prepared the children for the meeting by making a clear statement about the purpose of the meeting and what would follow. Winokur and Worth suggest a stage-based similar model in which the role of the teacher moves from "setting the stage" to "moving further" to "bringing closure" (2006, 54).

Some teachers like to have a simple chart ready that lists the meeting agenda:

Science Meeting 9/15/11

1. Commenting on friends' scientific drawings

2. Final questions, thoughts from scientists

3. What we learned

At the beginning of the year the purpose of these science meetings is more about interactions then science findings. We teach how to take turns in a discussion, how to build on another child's idea, how to show work and explain it to the group, how to pay attention to the speaker, and how to ask questions. We do this through modeling and explicit teaching.

This is a transcript of a kindergarten science meeting held early in the year. This was one of several meetings in which the teacher's goal was to teach the class how to speak and how to listen.

Teacher [*using a whisper voice*]: I've noticed that some children speak very softly, like this when they are telling us something in meeting. Can you hear me very well?

Several children [*calling out*]: What? What did you say?

Teacher [*still using a whisper voice*]: So you can't hear me very well. What should I do so everyone can hear me?

Child 1: Talk loud.

Child 2: You have the clipboard in front. I can't hear.

Teacher [*using a normal voice*]: Okay, I'll sit up, look at you and use a stronger voice. How does this sound?

Child 2: Good.

Teacher: Now is there anything the audience can do so they can hear well? Who wants to come up and show us how the audience should act? [*She chooses two volunteers, who come up to the front of the circle, sit quietly in front of the teacher, and look directly at her.*] What are A and B doing?

Child 3: They're looking at you and not talking.

Teacher: That's just what scientists do at their meetings. If you are in the audience, you look at the speaker and listen, until it's time for you to raise your hand and talk. And if it's your turn to talk, you do just what I'm doing, sit up, look at the person you are talking to, and use a strong voice.

Practices that are more specific to science are taught much the same way, but more attention is given to the kind of questioning and prompts employed and to the use of scientific vocabulary in a meaningful way. (See Figure 3.18.)

Here is a partial transcript of another science meeting, but this time the purpose of the meeting was specific to science: to discuss the findings of the research group that had studied different pets and their needs. The teacher's goal for this meeting was to discuss what the two children had each learned about guinea pigs and hamsters.

Figure 3.18

Teacher: Today two students from the Pet Research group, Abigail and Sarah, are going to tell us what they learned about the animals they studied. You can ask questions or make comments about their findings. We'll take a few minutes at the end to talk about what we learned. Let's check the chart to see which animals Abigail studied [See Figure 3.19]. [*Teacher points to print, and children read along.*] Abigail . . . guinea pig and hamster. Abigail, what did you learn about the guinea pig?

Abigail: It needs a cage; it's furry and has toenails.

Teacher: You said the guinea pig needs a cage. Can you tell us more about that? Does it need anything else?

Abigail: You put stuff in the bottom of the cage, and it needs a water bottle and food.

Alejandro: A cat. I have a cat.

Teacher: That's right, you do, and Ishan will talk about cats tomorrow. [*Points to chart.*] Remember we're talking about guinea pigs now. Do you have a question for Abigail about a guinea pig?

Alejandro: Do guinea pigs run around?

Abigail: I think they like to sit a lot.

Caleb: No, my cousin has a guinea pig, and when he lets it out of the cage, it runs and hides in the yard.

Teacher: So Abigail thinks a guinea pig sits a lot and Caleb thinks it runs fast. I wonder how we could find out for sure.

Abigail: Maybe look in the guinea pig books we have?

William: Let's call Jim [*owner of the pet store*].

Teacher: Two great ideas for finding out the answer to Alejandro's question. I'll write that down so we don't forget.

Maddie: Can we take it out of the cage?

Abigail: Oh yeah, then we could hold it and feed it.

Figure 3.19 The Pet Research group's chart listing the animals they studied

Teacher: Tell me how you know we could hold a guinea pig.

Abigail: I saw a picture of a girl holding a black and white one.

Teacher: Caleb, does your cousin hold his guinea pig?

Caleb: I hold it and pet it a lot.

Teacher: So we have some evidence that you can hold guinea pigs. Abigail saw a photo in a book, and Caleb has held a guinea pig. We have time for one more question or comment for Abigail.

Kodai [*English language learner*]: What food?

Abigail: You buy guinea pig food, and they like carrots.

Teacher: So we need to find out if they run fast, but we know they are furry, live in a cage, and eat carrots, special food, and drink water. Now let's hear what Sarah and Abigail learned about hamsters.

You can probably identify many of the strategies this teacher used to scaffold the discussion. She began by stating her plan for the meeting. She kept the discussion focused on the topic, redirecting Alejandro when he wanted to talk about his cat. She restated the conflicting theories that Abigail and Caleb gave and asked for the children's ideas on where to find information. Her questions and prompts provoked the children to think more deeply: "Can you tell us more . . . ?" "I wonder how we could find out . . ." "Tell me how you know . . ." She used print in a practical way when she referred to the chart and when she wrote a reminder note to look into the ideas the children raised. She modeled curiosity and problem solving when she suggested looking deeper into the question of how fast guinea pigs move. She pushed for evidence and used the term in context, when Abigail said the children could hold a guinea pig.

There was an even give-and-take of comments and questions among the children which made for a true discussion. The children had a chance to learn from each other by talking about science. Their teacher used the meeting to teach science content and skills and as a formative assessment opportunity in which she could get a sense of what children understood and what misconceptions should be addressed.

Science meetings like this don't happen every day. Just as the children need to practice talking about science, so we need to practice our skills of facilitating a discussion that enables them to talk and think like scientists. We need to plan and have a purpose, but we also need to be flexible, to be able to respond to the spontaneous ideas and questions that the children bring to this experience. The unexpected has to be expected when you teach three- to eight-year-olds. We want to tap into the wonder and deep interest that oozes from this age group, and we can do so by providing a comfortable and supportive discussion environment in which their communication skills can flourish.

Here are some suggestions for facilitating constructive science meetings and discussions:

- Take time to build a comfortable community for discourse. Teach basic social skills that will enable children to speak, listen, ask questions, and be respectful of everyone's ideas.
- Develop a set routine for your meeting.
- Plan your meeting with a goal or purpose for communicating about the science topic, but be flexible and ready to adjust the discussion based on the input of the children.

- Model the skills you want the children to demonstrate: curiosity, interest, note taking, productive questioning, use of accurate science vocabulary, and attention to evidence.
- Use concrete materials to support discussion: science notebooks, artifacts, photographs of the children working.
- Integrate print in meaningful contexts: writing and reading charts, graphs, taking notes of children's comments.
- Encourage children's participation by inserting open-ended prompts and questions and by building connections in the discussion.

When we provide children with opportunities to read, write, draw, and talk about their science work, they become comfortable not only as scientists but also as readers, writers, and speakers. Our early childhood classrooms are the perfect setting for this kind of experience. Beginning in preschool, instructional tools like science notebooks, nonfiction read-alouds, and science discussions can be woven into our practice so that children can engage in an authentic blend of science and literacy experiences.

Chapter 4

Assessing for Understanding

Assessing and teaching are inseparable components of a quality inquiry-based science program. When we think about assessment of science, we think about the three components of inquiry and the goals behind each:

- *Content.* What are the concepts of the unit of study? What does the child understand about those concepts?
- *Practices.* How competent is the child at using the practices of science (observing, predicting, questioning, planning investigations, interpreting information, collaborating, communicating, and using scientific tools)?
- *Attitudes.* Are the children curious? Are they persistent? Are they respectful of the natural world?

While we are planning activities that will teach the science content and incorporate the practices of science, we are also planning ways to assess the children's knowledge of the material. What's especially important is that our assessments are ongoing, not just at the end of a unit.

61

This was not how I approached assessment in my early years of teaching. Then, when I planned, my focus was on my teaching, designing activities, and gathering materials. I didn't even think about assessment until everything else was in place. I mistakenly looked at curriculum planning and assessment as two very separate pieces. I got caught up in thinking about what the children would be doing and lost track of what they might be learning or not learning along the way. Most of my assessments in those early years were summative—evaluations at the end of the unit. These summative assessments were necessary, but I was ignorant of a more comprehensive assessment process, the formative assessments that should have been happening all along the way.

Formative assessments are ongoing; they give us information about the child's learning and our teaching throughout the course of the unit. Formative assessments tend to be embedded, authentic opportunities for children to demonstrate what they understand and how they do science. The evidence we gather from the children's conversations, from our observations of their interactions with materials, and from their science notebooks conveys data not only about the children's understanding but also about our instruction. This is the piece that was missing in my outcome-based assessment. I needed to plan for regular check-ins to find out whether the learning was happening or whether I needed to readjust my teaching plans. Now when I plan a unit, I look at my concepts and goals and then plan both the activities and the assessments that will occur throughout the unit. My limited view of assessment put me at risk of failing to notice misconceptions or questions that would require additional teaching or more experiences.

When I incorporated assessments into my ongoing plan, I became much more attuned to the learning that was—or wasn't—happening. For example, early in our life-cycle unit on insects, I overheard three of the children talking about the chrysalis they were looking at in our butterfly habitat. Their conversation went something like this:

> **Evan:** It's the chrysalis. Look.
> **Zoe:** Looks like a dead leaf all wrapped up.
> **Evan:** Where's the caterpillar?
> **Peter:** It's in the chrysalis.
> **Zoe:** Un-uh, the butterfly's in the chrysalis. It's waiting to come out.
> **Peter:** So where's that caterpillar?
> **Evan:** I think it died.
> **Peter:** Isn't it in the chrysalis, too?

What made me tune in to this very brief conversation? I stopped to listen because I had listed "Children's conversations" as an assessment source for each of the unit's concepts. What did I learn from the children's comments and questions? I learned that the children were comfortable discussing their observations and were using the scientific term *chrysalis*, but didn't really understand what was happening at that stage of metamorphosis. This isn't surprising, given the mysterious process of change that was occurring within the chrysalis. Still, at that point of the unit, we had done so much reading and talking that I thought everybody was pretty clear on what happened at each stage. What did I do with this assessment data? This conversation taught me I needed to back up a bit, and do some more teaching about the process of metamorphosis, especially this pupating stage. Had I not planned to check in through regular observations and listening to conversations, I would have moved forward oblivious to the confusions in the children's understanding.

PLANNING FOR ASSESSMENT

I've found a planning worksheet to be a helpful tool in planning for assessment; the simple one I use incorporates each element of an inquiry unit: the concepts, the activities, and the assessment opportunities. (See Figure 4.1.)

Once the concepts are in place, I can use this worksheet to plan activities and complimentary assessment strategies. A portion of Heidi Fessenden's Target Assessment Planner (Figure 4.2) illustrates another way to organize

Concepts	Activities	Assessment Opportunities

Figure 4.1 Inquiry Unit Planning Worksheet

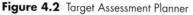

Geology, Grade 2, Fall Term	
Long-term content targets = **LT** Supporting targets = **ST**	Assessments OF Learning (summative) = **AOL** Assessment FOR Learning (formative) = **AFL**
LT: I can describe a mineral using what I learn from mineral tests. **ST:** I can describe the luster of a mineral. I can describe the transparency of a mineral. I can describe the hardness of a mineral. I can describe the streak color of a mineral. I can figure out a mystery mineral from its mineral tests.	**AOL:** final assessment (written/interview) final mystery mineral assignment **AFL:** mineral test activities mineral test worksheets science notebooks
LT: I can observe and describe properties of rocks and minerals. This means I can talk about their size, shape, color, and texture. **ST:** I can describe the inside and the outside of a rock. **ST:** I can compare and contrast rocks. This means I can say how they are the same and how they are different. **ST:** I can explain what a mineral is.	**AOL:** final assessment (written/interview) **AFL:** observational drawing words added to sketches for each property vocabulary in games / discussions when observing rocks (i.e., coming up with vocabulary for each property—get points for each word you come up with "breaking rocks" descriptors (inside versus outside): "The inside is ___ and the outside is ___." "The inside and the outside are both ___" vocabulary in one-on-one conferences

Figure 4.2 Target Assessment Planner

goals and assessments. Heidi's target goals for her second-grade geology unit are supported by a variety of assessment sources that include summative and formative assessments linked to each goal of the unit.

These two samples are simple but efficient tools that ensure instructional planning for inquiry includes assessment planning as well.

GATHERING EVIDENCE

Assessing the science knowledge and competency of young children can pose quite a challenge given the unique cognitive abilities of this age group. Since young children's reading and writing skills are just emerging, we need to think more broadly about how to gather evidence of learning and evidence of the practices of science. Richard Duschl makes the following recommendation:

> *Teachers need to begin listening to inquiry and then develop and apply criteria that engage learners in deciding "what counts" as evidence and as explanations.* (2003, 45)

If we listen to inquiry, as Duschl suggests, we can take advantage of a variety of strategies for capturing the children's theories and questions as they observe, use hand lenses, construct models, and record data.

We need to watch children engaged with materials, listen to their conversations, and ask about their drawings and science notebook entries. Early childhood classrooms offer so many authentic opportunities for children to demonstrate what they know and how they think. The evidence sources that provide rich science assessment data include products, observations, and conversations. Each is necessary, and they often overlap.

Products are an obvious resource, but with young children, it's important to include the child's description or comments so that we can understand the meaning behind the construction or drawing. Without that data, we might miss the deeper understandings or misunderstandings.

The observational drawing in Figure 4.3 suggests many possibilities, but when I asked this child to tell me about his drawing, he responded, "It's the guinea pig, his fur." Now the details are unmistakable: the round shape of our classroom guinea pig, with what may be eyes and

Figure 4.3 Four-year-old's scientific drawing of a guinea pig

mouth or nose, and the long hairs that stick out every which way. The boy's scientific drawing is quite detailed and accurate, but I wouldn't have known this if he hadn't told me. Additional product-oriented sources to consider include the children's writing, science notebook entries, movement (acting out an idea), and models they construct.

Observations of children provide us with evidence about their skillfulness with the practices of science and can reveal their proficiency in manipulating a hand lens, how they work in partnership with their group, how successful they are at predictions or raising questions and reporting findings to a group. Documenting these observations with photographs of the children doing science can provide records of problem solving, persistence, and collaboration. Capturing the accompanying dialogue enriches the evidence of learning that photographs can provide.

Conversations can include science talk (comments, questions, observations, wonderings) that happens during science activities, an interview, informal observations, or discussions in small groups or in large-group science meetings. It's natural to think of the dialogue that occurs in the more formal settings for discussion: children's response to a nonfiction read-aloud, participation in a group discussion, replies in an interview, or comments related to the KLEW charts. But we can also learn from the more informal contexts for conversation: the three children who are trying to figure out how to make a shadow larger as they play on the playground or the children at the snack table as they compare the bubbles they are blowing in their milk. As we become attuned to these less obvious assessment moments, we increase our opportunities for authentic evidence gathering.

Acknowledging that children's discourse is an important source of assessment evidence implies added assessment challenges. How can we document children's conversations and discussions? And how can we find the time to analyze and interpret that information? To tap into children's dialogue as a routine assessment practice, we need to devise efficient systems for recording and reviewing these dialogues.

We can start with simple anecdotal notes of conversations we pick up on that have a connection to the concepts of the inquiry unit we are teaching. I used to keep index cards or sticky notes in my pocket just for this purpose. I would quickly scribble off the date, then record the children's statements using my own invented shorthand (initials for children's names and recording mostly nouns and verbs). This is how I collected the data for the chrysalis conversation I mentioned earlier. (See Figure 4.4.)

At the end of that day, I reread my brief notes, and realized that I needed to come up with additional activities to take the children deeper into an understanding of the changes occurring in the chrysalis. As I became more reliant on children's discourse for assessment, I found a more efficient tool, which Christina Ryan devised for her kindergarten science assessment. (See Figure 4.5.)

Christina wanted to make sure she was thinking about her goals for the content and practices of science, so she added them to her form, but left large blocks of space open so that she could record the children's language. The design, similar to materials used in writing workshop, can be easily revised to match the goals of whatever science unit we are teaching. The simplest design provides space for recording the context and the child's language and space for reflecting on that

9/26/11

EU - Lk -chrysalis
R - dead = leaf
EV - Where's caterp.?
P - In chrys.
R - No, butterfly is waiting in chrys.
P - Where's caterp.?
EU - Dead?
P - Isn't it in chrys.?

Figure 4.4 Raw notes jotted down in the moment

Observation Record for Science

Which senses can we use for observing leaves?

What do you notice about the leaves' colors?

Activity Context/Setting: Autumn Observation Drawings

What do you notice about how the leaves smell and feel?

What are you wondering about this leaf?

Name Date	Uses tools correctly	Identifies Describes Senses	Draws representationally to best of ability	Quotes and Comments (seen and heard)
Kavali 10/26	micro ✓		✓ orange circle many lines	"I made these lines for these parts."
Niloe w/26	mag ✓	feel sight	✓	"I want to write more about it." "It feels hard. It has bumps." ↓ HD ↓ BMPE
Isaac 10/26	✓ micro	sound sight	✓ chooses approp. colors, shape in leaves difficult	"I hear something ... it's like water ... knock knock."
Lucy 10/26	✓ micro		✓	• writes LEF (leaf) • "leaves are outside"

Science Inquiry Skills:
-Collects data, uses senses and tools
-Uses language to communicate findings

-Engages, notices, wonders, questions
-Records/represents experience through drawing, movement, etc.
-Shares, discusses, collaborates, and reflects with group

-Begins to explore, investigate, test predictions
-Reflects on experiences, makes predictions and generalizations
CREATED BY CHRISTINA RYAN

Figure 4.5 Christina Ryan's science assessment template

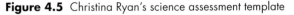

data or connecting it to a goal. For example, in the Pet Inquiry assessment tool found in Appendix 10, the concepts and science practices for that particular inquiry are listed at the top of the form, followed by open boxes for recording the children's statements or questions. Having this information right at hand helps the teacher, paraprofessional, or student teacher concentrate on the goals, but it doesn't constrict the depth of information the way a checklist would. This template allows us to attend to deeper understandings that emerge from the children's talk. The simple structure of the document makes it easy to record and to review the data for planning and for evaluating science learning and skill development.

A comparable tool can be designed to assess the products that children create, particularly observational drawings and models. Children's competency in producing observational drawings or models, as well as entries in science notebooks, develops through experience and through supportive feedback and scaffolding. There are several identifiable criteria that we can use to review the quality of a product and use as benchmarks for our instruction. The Science Notebook Assessment Guidelines in Figure 4.6 (also in Appendix 1) offer a comprehensive list of criteria for assessment. These guidelines are quite extensive and would be most useful in the primary grades. Teachers of younger children will want to condense them and emphasize the skills that are appropriate for their class. This tool could be used several times during the year to assess children's progress and provide a structure for providing feedback to them.

PROVIDING FEEDBACK

Providing feedback to children about their work is an essential piece of the formative assessment process. Children want to know what makes a good observational drawing or a credible science notebook entry. Teaching science in these early years is an exceptional opportunity to help them develop foundational skills in observation and data collection. Our assessment and accompanying feedback give children the information they need to move forward on a continuum of progressive proficiency in recording data. (See Figure 4.7.)

It's important that we use comments that are descriptive and meaningful and that promote children's engagement rather than stifling it.

Nonjudgmental feedback gives information and focuses on the task, not the person; encourages children to think about the work, not about their

Name _____

	Date: Observation	Date: Observation	Date: Observation
Organization Includes date, location Title			
Observational drawings Accurate colors Includes details Size, scale are proportional Magnified view Shows motion, movement Corrects, revises			
Written notes, dictation Makes predictions Includes questions Compares, measures Notes similarities, differences Patterns Makes corrections, revises Uses scientific vocabulary Includes T-chart, Venn diagram Moves from labels to descriptive sentences			
Artifacts, photographs Dated, labeled accurately Captions Descriptive data: context, location Questions			
Understandings Makes connections to evidence Change in understanding Suggests appropriate fair test			

Figure 4.6 Science Notebook Assessment Guidelines

Figure 4.7

feelings or ability; provides comments on what to do next and ideas about how to do it. (Harlen 2001, 129)

If we look at assessment and feedback as teaching more than appraising, this notion of "nonjudgmental feedback" begins to make more sense. When we adopt this style of using meaningful comments, we are compelled to slow down and really think about what the children are doing or saying so that our comments or questions will carry some weight. In some classrooms, feedback is given informally; in others, teachers plan a notebook review session two or three times a year. In either case, the thoughtful nature of the comments help children understand what they do well and what they can do next time to improve their work.

- "The way you shaded the light beam really helps me see where the light traveled."
- "Your drawing shows all the guppies in the tank, but when I read this sentence, 'I noticed the guppies wag their tails when they swim,' I knew that you were watching how they moved."
- "I'm curious about why you decided to cross out that first sketch of the pipes."

- "I can see that you paid close attention to the patterns on the lizard's back."
- "When you added the arrows I could tell how the water traveled through the tubing."
- "You've written `It's cold and windy,' but what do you notice about your drawing?" (The drawing shows the sun, the school, and a tree.) "How can you make the drawing match your observation?"

Even without the actual student work sample it's easy to see how instructive these comments are. Once we become accustomed to the habit of providing rich feedback like this, those almost automatic, empty comments "Good job" and "Awesome" fade away from use.

THE ROLE OF DOCUMENTATION IN ASSESSMENT

Another essential piece of the assessment process is documentation. Documentation—often referred to as making learning visible—evolves from three basic steps:

- Collecting transcripts, work samples, and photographs of the children at work
- Reflecting on those pieces and what they speak to in terms of children's learning
- Organizing and displaying a segment of this information that reveals the children's understandings, theories, and questions

In short, documentation is about reflection and communication. When teachers compose a documentation board, they present a concrete model of the learning process. Mounting documentation in the classroom or hallway gives children, parents, and teachers the chance to read about and see evidence of science understandings, which leads to conversations and more reflection.

The documentation board in Figure 4.8, from Boston University's Early Childhood Learning Lab, chronicles the preschoolers' worm study. Captions for each of the photos describe what the children were learning. For example, the caption under the top right photograph of Iris holding a worm reads:

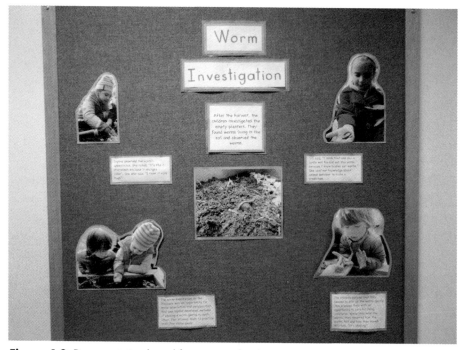

Figure 4.8 Documentation board from a preschool worm inquiry

Iris said, "I think that one day a birdie will fly and eat this worm, because I know birdies eat worms." She used her knowledge about animal behavior to make a prediction.

In Figure 4.9, kindergartners and their teacher gather around the documentation their teacher assembled after they planted seeds. The children's answers to the question, "What are you thinking?" are in dialogue bubbles mounted above their pictures.

Will my seed be good? Will it be beautiful?
Do we need to take home plants for the weekend?
I am worried that if we water the seeds too much, the seeds can rot.
How big is my plant going to be?

The range of questions and responses provoked more discussion and more questions in addition to giving the teacher evidence of the children's work as scientists. This is the real contribution of documentation—taking us beyond the obvious into a richer understanding of how children use the practices of science to understand the world around them.

Figure 4.9

FINAL THOUGHTS

Approaching assessment with the investigative mind-set of a teacher/researcher allows for many possibilities beyond a checklist approach. Assessment is a type of inquiry and requires us to shift gears from a focus on products to a focus on process and the importance of really listening, not just at the end of a unit but throughout, so that we can adjust our plans and instruction to meet the learning needs of the children. The following suggestions may be useful to you as you think about refining your assessment beliefs and systems to focus on assessing for learning and understanding:

- Start with content and process goals. Ask yourself what it is you want the children to learn.
- Make assessment part of the planning process. Expect children to demonstrate their knowledge in many ways: conversations, acting out, drawing, writing, science notebook entries, and photographs. Include the children's words, descriptions, and dictations with any

products.

- Gather data over time; check in regularly, using anecdotal notes, assessment templates, and photographs for documenting children's learning. Devise or revise templates that make information gathering simple and efficient.
- Take time to reflect on the data you've gathered; connect the evidence to your science content and practice goals.
- Apply what you've learned from your reflection to your instruction by adding new lessons or activities to reteach, or by providing more challenging extensions to lessons to develop deeper understandings.
- Use documentation to enrich your understanding of the children's thinking, and to communicate the children's learning to their peers, to their families, and to the larger school community.

Chapter 5

Designing an Inquiry Unit

The *National Science Education Standards'* emphasis on in-depth coverage of science topics is especially relevant for early childhood teachers (National Research Council 1996). I think we, as teachers, often fall into the habit of planning many short units, which leaves us feeling frustrated when we have to move on to the next topic and results in a scattered, superficial approach to teaching science. The NSES recommendation to delve deeply into a few topics for an extended time reflects the real work of scientists and leads to a different approach to planning science units. The welcome emphasis on deep study of fewer topics has created a need for a more thoughtful approach to the design of worthwhile science units that provide children with opportunities to do science in the context of investigating interesting content or topics.

WHAT IS AN INQUIRY UNIT?

There is no singular design for an inquiry unit, but there are some basic attributes that characterize one.

- An inquiry unit is a deep study of a science topic or theme that leads children to an understanding of the world around them.
- An inquiry unit is derived from conceptual knowledge. It begins with the questions, What are the important ideas about this topic? What are the connections that can be made to this topic? This is very different from starting with the question, What can children do to learn about this topic?
- An inquiry unit can be seen as a framework for the investigation, a flexible framework that is modified and adjusted as children's theories and questions surface.
- An inquiry unit merges content (activities that teach about the topic) and the practices of science (observing, predicting, questioning, carrying out investigations, inferring, communicating, collaborating, interpreting and gathering information).

The process for designing an inquiry unit begins with the decision about the topic and moves through topic research, brainstorming, generating concepts, identifying activities and assessment strategies, identifying and planning the activities, and designing an implementation plan. Each of these steps and accompanying instructional supports are described in detail in this chapter. An inquiry unit on pets and other partial inquiry units provide some context for understanding the nuances of this approach.

DECIDING ON A TOPIC

An inquiry unit topic can come from a variety of sources: something the children are interested in, a unique event connected to the classroom, a district requirement, or kit-based materials. It was a combination of our children's interest and a unique event that led my coteacher Christine and me to mount an inquiry unit on pets for our mixed-age preschool class of children from two years and nine months to five years of age, including children with special needs and English language learners. (See Appendix 3 for a detailed, complete plan for this pet inquiry unit.)

During the first month of school, we noticed that the butterfly habitat and larvae in the science area received much attention, as did the nearby fish tank. When the butterflies emerged from their chrysalides, the children were glued to the habitat hoping to see them sip nectar from the sugar water the children had put into the habitat. The fish tank was the first stop each morning for two of our new boys, one of whom had just arrived from Korea and spoke no English. We also noted that many children visited the tank throughout the day to observe and talk about the algae eater and the goldfish and that the job of "Fish Feeder" was a highly sought after position.

We were struck by the children's interest in and eagerness to care for the fish and the butterflies. We noticed lots of pretend pet play outside and in the dramatic play area, with children taking on the roles of pet owners and mostly kittens and dogs as pets. Also, several of the children asked if we could get more fish for the tank. All of these observations led us to the decision to follow the children's interest in pets and design an inquiry that would lead to the acquisition of another classroom pet. Our plan was to design a unit that would give the children a chance to research a variety of pets and, ultimately, apply that knowledge to the choice of a new classroom pet.

You might ask, "Where is the science in a pet study?" and that would be a logical question. We returned to the guiding criteria for a worthy inquiry topic discussed in Chapter 1 to answer it. Figure 5.1 sums up the results—a pet investigation was an appropriate and meaningful topic for this group of children.

As we considered a pet inquiry, one big question concerned us: What about pet allergies? We wondered whether a rabbit or hamster might be problematic and, if so, how we would handle that with the children. After speaking with Jim, our local pet-store owner, we learned that there were many types of pets we could consider that would not cause allergic reactions. We also decided that learning about people's allergies to pets might be a worthy aspect of a pet study, if there were children in our group who had them. Because we could work with the allergy problem if it arose, we felt confident that we could move forward to plan our pet study.

topic concerns

Our next step was to gather information about our topic so that we could develop a set of questions and concepts that would frame our inquiry.

RESEARCHING THE TOPIC

As my coteacher and I brainstormed about the understandings we wanted children to consider, we realized that we had differing understandings and beliefs about pets, so we both did some background reading and talked to Jim, the pet-store owner. Our sources were mainly nonfiction books gathered from the children's rooms of our local libraries. We were surprised at how much we didn't know about pets! Jim proved to be an especially helpful expert, not only for us, but for the children as well.

Criterion Question for Inquiry Topic	Response
Why is this topic especially worthwhile for *this* group of children?	Observed interest in the fish tank and butterfly life-cycle activities; pretend play around pets
Is this a topic that children can explore in depth over several weeks?	Yes, because we will research several types of pets to make a decision about a new class pet.
Can children actively explore this topic through their senses, close observations, and investigations they plan?	Yes, observation will be a constant. Children will be watching, holding, and caring for pets during the inquiry. They will be part of research groups to study different animals.
Can children use science practices (observation, prediction, interpretation, questioning, investigation, communication, collaboration, and using the tools of science) in their study of this topic?	Yes, the children will be part of research groups and small- and large-group discussions. They will observe and record information and apply that information/evidence to choose an appropriate classroom pet.
Do I have access to resources (books, experts, materials, artifacts) to support an inquiry on this topic?	Yes, we have a local pet-shop owner, and there are several families and a student teacher who have pets that we can study. We will expand our collection of books by gathering more from the library.
Does this topic relate to the national and local standards?	Yes, to the state and national science standards on biology (living things).

Figure 5.1 Does a Pet Study Meet the Criteria for a Worthy Topic of Inquiry?

ORGANIZING THE BIG IDEAS

From our reading, we were able to generate some basic understandings about pets. We decided to make a rudimentary web to help us determine what the big ideas were. (See Figure 5.2.) Our leading question was, "What do children need to understand about pets?" From that broad question, we generated several additional questions that all contributed to the overarching ideas about pets and the relationship among those ideas.

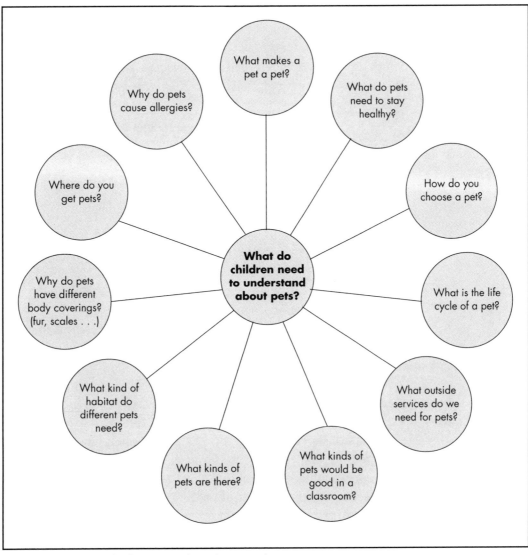

Figure 5.2 Initial web of questions about the topic of pets

We talked about the ideas behind the questions and moved to write a set of concepts that would form the big ideas of our unit. The first list of concepts seemed overwhelming and too oriented toward disconnected facts. We wanted the unit to offer the children opportunities for making connections and to recognize the similarities between different pets and their needs. So we talked some more, looked back at our web, and produced another draft. We also returned to our state standards to make sure we weren't overlooking any important science understandings.

Massachusetts Science and Technology/Engineering Curriculum Framework, Life Science Learning Standards (PreK–2)

1. *Recognize that animals (including humans) and plants are living things that grow, reproduce, and need food, air, and water.*
3. *Recognize that plants and animals have life cycles, and that life cycles vary for different living things.*
4. *Describe ways in which many plants and animals closely resemble their parents in observed appearance.*
8. *Identify the ways in which an organism's habitat provides for its basic needs.* (Massachusetts Department of Education 2006, 44-45)

Our original web of questions was helpful in that it gave us a sense of the broad possibilities for the investigation, but once we started to develop the concepts, we realized that there were some questions we would not explore:

- What pets cause allergies? Since no one in our class had a pet allergy, we decided not to include that aspect.
- What is the life cycle of a pet? We decided to eliminate this question and focus more on the habitat and care of pets.

Our decision to jettison those two questions was based on our intention to design an in-depth study that would enable the children to use the practices of science to make connections about pets, their needs, and their care.

With each draft, the language of our concepts became more clear and more exact. We both agreed that the clarity of the concepts made a huge difference in our teaching. We avoided jargon and used simple, direct sentences, without a lot of adjectives or phrases.

> **Concept 1.** Pets are animals that are cared for by people, usually in homes and schools.

Subconcepts expanded on the main idea, but again we kept to a precise vocabulary and brief statements.

> **Concept 1a.** When people care for pets, they feed the animals. Some animals also need grooming, exercise, and affection.

One challenge we faced was deciding on which pets to study. The diversity of pets was something we wanted the children to learn about, but we felt we needed to choose some examples of pets to begin with, so that we could gather materials and, we hoped, the actual animals as part of our study. One of our student teachers had a speckled newt, so we included that, and since we had the fish tank, we included fish.

> **Concept 2.** Some common pets are cats, dogs, fish, turtles, guinea pigs, hamsters, newts, and geckos.

We knew the animals listed in this concept would probably change based on the information and suggestions provided by the children once they became involved with the unit's varied activities. We were prepared to rethink the other concepts, as well, once the unit began. In this way, we could honor what Eleanor Duckworth refers to as "the having of wonderful ideas" where "the unexpected is valued" (1996, 8). This approach allows teachers to balance the planned concepts of the unit with the questions and ideas the children bring to the investigation. This is quite different from a commercial curriculum that has a predetermined, rigid set of goals and activities.

With our "final draft" in place, we felt confident about what we wanted to teach and comfortable about altering our path given the input of the children.

Pet Inquiry Concepts
1. Pets are animals that are cared for by people, usually in homes and schools.
   a. When people care for pets, they feed the animals. Some animals also need grooming, exercise, and affection.
   b. Pets require special food.
   c. Different pets require unique kinds of housing and equipment (e.g., cages, tanks, collars, tags, toys).
2. Some common pets are cats, dogs, fish, turtles, guinea pigs, hamsters, newts, and geckos.
   a. Different kinds of pets have different kinds of physical characteristics.
   b. Different pets move in different ways.
   c. Different pets make different sounds or no sounds.
3. People can get pets from pet stores, breeders, friends, and animal shelters.
   a. Pet stores sell many types of animals and the food and equipment people need to care for their pets.
4. Veterinarians are doctors who care for pets.
   a. Veterinarians have special instruments they use to examine pets.

The concepts were explicit and thorough. They answered our initial questions, and they provided a research agenda for choosing an appropriate pet for the classroom. The time we spent revising the concepts was well spent. We really knew what we would be teaching.

ACTIVITIES AND ASSESSMENTS CONNECTED TO THE CONCEPTS

Once we had our conceptual framework in place, we could begin planning activities that would teach the concepts and provide the children with opportunities to do science through observing, discussing, questioning, investigating, collecting data, interpreting data, connecting to expert sources, collaborating, and sharing information.

While many of these activities were typical of early childhood instruction, we also relied heavily on the inclusion of KLEW charts, research groups, research trips, expert interviews, and a culminating activity to enrich the science and science practices of inquiry. A brief description of each of these instructional tools follows.

KLEW Charts

The four KLEW charts are a useful tool for promoting inquiry and organizing children's understandings:

What do we think we **know?**
What did we **learn?**
What is our **evidence?**
What are we **wondering?**

Derived from the work of Hershberger, Zembal-Saul, and Starr (2006), the KLEW charts are used during science meetings and then displayed in the classroom to document the ongoing investigation. We presented the first chart, "What do we *think* we know about pets?" at the beginning of our unit so that we could gauge the children's ideas about the new topic. The language used for that prompt was especially effective. Rather than the traditional dogmatic "What do we know about . . . ?" prompt, the speculative, more uncertain use of *"think* we know," illustrates the reflective, evolving nature of science. Responding to "What do we think we know about . . . ?" also provides the children with a safe query that does not pressure them for the "right" answer. Their responses become useful assessment data as well as clues to the prior knowledge that they bring to the investigation.

The **L** ("What did we learn?") and the **E** ("What is our evidence?") charts are usually presented together so that children can practice using evidence to support their claims. It's not uncommon to go back to the original "What do we think we know?" chart and cross out a statement that has been disproved over the course of the investigation. This kind of discovery can be so exciting for the children. It confirms their work as scientists who observe, interpret, carry out investigations, collaborate, question, and use evidence. (See Figure 5.3.)

The final chart, the **W** ("What are we wondering?"), is meant to capture questions that the children have raised throughout the unit that might be investigated at another time or that might be woven into the current unit. I often jot down questions that children raise during their science work, when they are observing or talking. I can't list all the questions they raise, so I explain to them that I'm keeping a record of their questions and will list the ones that might impact future inquiry about this topic.

The KLEW charts are a useful reference tool for science meetings, but they also serve another purpose. In one second grade I visited, the charts

Figure 5.3 Sample KLEW chart from a kindergarten plant inquiry were displayed at the children's eye level near the entrance to the classroom. They created a real buzz around the inquiry unit on light that was underway in the classroom. The KLEW charts become a resource for conversation among children, their parents, and other visitors, as well as a source of information for the children's science notebooks.

Research Groups

It might be surprising to see research groups listed as a tool for pre-K and primary grade levels, but these small groups became a mainstay of our inquiry unit design.

The idea for research groups grew out of our frustration with the limitations of our large-group meeting as a venue for entertaining the children's many ideas and questions about the pet study. Can you imagine trying to conduct a productive planning session with twenty-two colleagues? Many of our children were truly interested in participating in the discussion, but since that large forum didn't always support rich conversation, we decided to move to small groups of four to six children that would allow for more balanced participation and collaboration. These research groups, scaffolded by us, worked together to develop questions or to gather information on a question or topic, and then they reported back to the whole class and shared what they found.

For our first pet inquiry, we chose four of our older children (four-and-a-half- to five-year-olds) to be in the research group; two boys and two girls, one of whom spoke mainly Korean. The research group met right at the beginning of our choice time. The children understood that that meeting would only last for a portion of it, and when the meeting was finished, they would be free to choose another activity. At our first research group meeting we talked about what the children knew about pets. Then I spread out a broad selection of nonfiction books on a variety of animals, and the children spent some time browsing, talking, and pointing to photos. Once everyone had a chance to look at and talk about the animals in the books, we shifted to a discussion about what pets they would like to investigate for our classroom. They listed their choices on a piece of chart paper and the next day, presented this list to the class.

Each meeting had a purpose; we planned each of these research group meetings and explained the purpose to the children so that they knew what we would be doing and why. The initial meeting probably lasted no longer than ten minutes. A follow-up meeting that included browsing through nonfiction books about a variety of pets and talking about what the chil-

Figure 5.4 Newt Research Group reporting to their class

dren noticed extended to almost thirty minutes because the children were so involved in the task. We found these research groups to be much more focused and much more efficient than a large group for discussions and for raising new ideas and questions. Since the group reported back to the full class, it wasn't necessary for every child to be in a research group, so we were able to schedule the group meetings within choice time. Our input in the research group varied depending on the task and the group; initially, we scaffolded heavily, other times the children worked quite independently. (See Figure 5.4.)

Two components contribute to the success of these groups: the composition of the group and the task presented to the group. When organizing these research groups, it is essential to consider the social-emotional *and* the cognitive skills of the children. We took a lot of time to balance these groups: matching competent, independent children with less skilled peers; English language learners with children who are strong in discourse; children who can read and write with children whose literacy skills may be more limited; personable, socially adept children with quieter, less vocal peers; and children with similar interests. A reasoned and thoughtful approach to combining skills and personalities contributes to the quality of the research group experience.

Research group tasks can vary from simple to complex, but there will most likely always be two charges to the group: gathering information and reporting out to the rest of the class. The logistics of the research groups vary, depending on who is in the group and what they are researching. In Ms. Jennings' first-grade ocean habitat inquiry, there were five research groups, each focused on a topic that came from the unit concepts and from the KLEW charts. One group studied the ocean as a habitat, two groups studied fish, another group focused on mammals, another on crustaceans, and another on scientists who study the ocean. Each small group contributed to the whole group's knowledge base through their collaborative work and their shared presentation of new information.

Success with research groups requires planning and an open mind. One challenge is to keep the group task interesting and meaningful. The other is to find ways to manage and scaffold these groups while the rest of the class is working on other tasks. Colleagues who incorporate research groups met this challenge by involving their classroom assistants, student teachers, parents, and even eighth graders. These teachers comment on how important these research groups are to all the children—whether they are engaged as researchers or as the audience. They come to appreciate both roles because they are truly working as scientists sharing findings, discussing these findings, raising questions, and sometimes disagreeing.

Research Trips and Expert Interviews

One of the recommendations of the *National Science Education Standards* states that teachers should "identify and use resources outside the school" (National Research Council 1996, 23). Somehow the term *field trip* does not convey the appropriate depth of learning that should be connected to this type of experience. When the term *research trip* is substituted for *field trip*, the event carries a very different meaning: a purposeful event connected to the unit's concepts and the practices of science. For example, each research group met before their visit to the pet shop to generate questions they would ask the owner. We typed out the questions on strips so that each child could read his or her question to the owner at the pet store. With the right amount of planning, research trips can be an integral piece of the learning plan exposing children to the world around them. Decisions about the actual site and timing of the trip depend on the teacher's goals and, of course, the resources for transportation and fees.

For our pet unit, an obvious research trip was a visit to a pet shop. We were lucky to find a small pet shop less than a mile away and accessible by public transportation. As we reviewed our concepts and talked about a trip to the pet store, we realized that it would have to happen right at the beginning of the unit and probably include two more visits as the unit unfolded. Initially, the children would need to gather information about what animals would be good choices for a classroom environment, and later they would need to acquire items for the chosen animal's habitat and care. These successive visits also allowed us to take small groups (our research groups) rather than the whole class. This was especially effective because the six children in each of the groups were all actively involved—they could see and ask questions freely. The groups then reported back to the rest of the children during our science meeting, so that the whole class had access to the new information gained from the research trip. Over the course of the pet unit, we took three different groups to visit the pet store. This worked out fine for us because it was close by and we could use public transportation. We also had enough adult support to make these repeated trips.

Given the very tight budget situation in many schools, research trips can be more of a challenge if school buses and admission costs are required. When these limitations arise, creative alternatives may be necessary. When Cynthia, a kindergarten teacher, was unable to find funds for a bus to the county fair as part of her study of farm animals, she visited the fair and videotaped the adult and baby animals the children were studying. Thoughtful use of quality Internet sites and visits to the classroom by experts also provide children with opportunities for accessing primary sources of information.

When children have the opportunity to interview experts—to see their tools, their notebooks, and their instruments—they can better understand how the world works. Experts can be found by contacting relatives, other teachers, and professionals. The grandfather who grows vegetables in pots on his third-floor porch, the school maintenance man who knows all about the pipes in the building, the university professor who studies insects, the eighth grader who builds robots, the teacher's neighbor who is a lobster-man, all share a special understanding of their area of expertise that can greatly enrich an inquiry.

During our pet study, we had several experts visit the class: Jim, the pet-store owner; Tracy, a veterinarian from the ASPCA; and the children, parents, and student teachers who brought their pets to our class to visit for the morning. When we introduced science notebooks, one child's mother who was a biologist brought in hers to share. The visit was a short one, just a few minutes at morning meeting, but the children were able to see how a real scientist keeps notes, draws diagrams, and even crosses out incorrect information in her science notebook.

Inviting experts into an early childhood classroom requires the same vigilant planning and organizing that research trips require. In addition to linking the visit to specific learning goals, we tried to make sure that each guest knew what to expect. We found that working with the experts before they came to visit made for a more successful presentation and that the guests were more relaxed and more effective if they had a good sense of what our goals were, what the children might ask, and how long they should present. They all appreciated the cues we suggested for interacting with young children (i.e., use simple language, show items/artifacts as you talk about them, have multiple items to pass around, and follow the teacher's lead when managing the group's interactions). We prepared the children in the same way so that they would be ready to interact productively with the expert visitor. In our pet inquiry, we met with the children before the visits from the pet owners and the veterinarian to develop a list of interview questions for our expert visitors. We were able to include questions from our KLEW chart and questions the children raised in our meeting. We listed the questions on a chart, so that the children could read their questions to the visitor.

Documenting the experts' visits and the research trips with photographs and video gave us extended opportunities for revisiting the experience. For example, English language learners could look at the photographs with a teacher who would scaffold their observations with gestures and simple language that might help expand the children's understanding of the visiting expert's presentation.

Culminating Activity

When children are so intensely involved in this kind of inquiry-based science, they become experts on the topic they are investigating. A culminating activity provides the children with an opportunity to apply this knowledge and to demonstrate what they have learned in a practical application. This idea is also supported by the learning goals listed in *Taking Science to School.* These four goals or strands answer the question, What do children need to do to be proficient in science?

Students who are proficient in science

1. *know, use, and interpret scientific explanations of the natural world;*
2. *generate and evaluate scientific evidence and explanations;*
3. *understand the nature and development of scientific knowledge; and*
4. *participate productively in scientific practices and discourse.*
   (Duschl, Schweingruber, and Shouse 2007, 36)

The culminating activity connects all these goals through an authentic demonstration of knowledge. This is a class project that encompasses the concepts and practices of science embedded in the unit in an explicit and meaningful way. For example, the class might write a field guide for the school yard for a unit on plants; they might narrate a series of videos about insects they have studied for a unit on life cycles; they might design and staff a museum for a unit on simple machines, or, as in our unit, they might purchase a class pet and develop a how-to book on choosing and caring for a pet. The variety of situations and styles in which these culminating activities can occur give all the children, especially English language learners and children with special needs, a broader context for demonstrating their understandings. For each child, the application of knowledge in the culminating activity is what really makes it such a significant piece of the inquiry process.

PLANNING THE UNIT ACTIVITIES

In addition to the KLEW charts, research groups, expert visits, research trips, and a culminating activity, children take part in a variety of activities precisely planned to teach the concepts of the unit and provide opportunities to use the practices of inquiry. This part of the unit development is always exciting, especially when working with colleagues. In our pet inquiry, we had many activities to consider, but our planning was quite streamlined thanks to the set of concepts we had developed. We would read the concept and ask ourselves, "How can we teach this? What activity will take the children inside this information?" Thinking about the instruction also got us thinking about assessment. So another question figured into our planning, "How can we tell if the children understand each concept?" This led to the design of a simple, three-column planning worksheet (Figure 5.5) beginning with concepts, followed by activities, and then assessment opportunities. We listed each concept, added the activities that might be effective, and listed the various ways we could assess that concept. These planning worksheets were the foundation of our unit plan.

The activities were not just science activities; our intent was to integrate literacy, math, and social studies whenever it made sense, but the concepts were the guiding force. The activities listed in Figure 5.5 are just a sample of the variety of experiences we included. (See Appendix 3.) At one point, we had listed thirteen activities for Concept 1; they included experiences in the domains of science, literacy, social studies, and mathematics, but with a

Concepts	Activities	Assessments

1. Pets are animals that are cared for by people, usually in homes and schools.
  a. Some animals also need grooming, exercise, and affection.
  b. Pets require special food.
  c. Different pets require unique kinds of housing and equipment (e.g., cages, tanks, collars, tags, toys).
	• K chart of KLEW—"What do we think we know about pets?"
	• Nonfiction book display in library
	• Field trip to pet store
	• Scientific drawings
	• Pet props for house area
	• Pet props for outdoor play area
	• Making dog and cat tags
	• Cleaning the aquarium
		• K chart of KLEW with children's initials
		• Observations/anecdotal notes
		• Conversations during cleaning and set up of aquarium
		• Science notebooks
		• Class book

Figure 5.5 Sample Planning Worksheet

decided focus on science. We gathered resources from all the likely places: our teaching files, colleagues, curriculum books, the library, and the Internet.

Sometimes we got off task and started to list activities we thought the children might like, but the framework of the concepts kept us focused. The concepts were our filter. If the activity or book or song didn't connect to the concept, then we eliminated it.

We had no trouble finding nonfiction books that were not only accurate and age appropriate but written in an engaging style with excellent photographs and drawings. We did eliminate several fiction picture books because they were not scientifically accurate. For example, we considered some for read-alouds, but when we looked at the text and the illustrations, we noticed that the pets were presented with human traits. *Harry the Dirty Dog* (Zion 1984) and *Clifford the Big Red Dog* (Bridwell 1997) were two books we chose to eliminate because they did not present accurate information about the animals and they did not reflect the information outlined in our concepts. This isn't to say that we would never read these stories; but in this context, in a conceptually designed science inquiry unit, they did not support the science learning of the children, so it didn't make sense for them to be part of the unit.

Other fiction picture books were included. For example, *Whistle for Willie* (Keats 1964) and *Hemi's Pet* (De Hamel 1985) were used as read-alouds for Concept 1 (Pets are animals that are cared for by people, usually in homes and schools), because they were accurate and their stories reflected the ideas embedded in that concept.

Since our intent was to integrate science wherever it made sense, our planning also included a look at the activity centers in our classroom and on the playground as well. We tried to imagine what the children might do in those areas—art, library, drawing and writing, dramatic play, and blocks—that would help them understand the concepts of the unit. Several ideas came to mind for Concept 2's focus on physical characteristics, including making paper-bag pet puppets in the art area and sculpting pet figures from clay. When we considered the block area, we didn't come up with any possibilities to link to our unit, but the children did! We noticed that when they took the stuffed pets out for a walk, they entered the block area and proceeded to build enclosures, houses, and even ramps for the cats to slide on—all elements of Concept 1. So we followed the children's lead and added stuffed dogs, cats, and guinea pigs to the block area.

The richest activity center connection was the dramatic play area. We had initially planned for this area to evolve from a house (Concept 1) to a pet store (Concept 3) to a veterinarian's office (Concept 4). We quickly realized the house area could not give way to a pet store because the children would need a place to care for the pets they purchased and, likewise, they would need a place to care for them when they returned from the veterinarian's office. Consequently, throughout the whole pet study, we had two dramatic play areas: a small house area and an area that was either the pet store or the veterinarian's office. (See Appendix 3.) This design enabled the children to play out each of the concepts in a logical way.

As we listed these activities on our worksheet, it became apparent that several of them taught more than one concept. For example, we planned to have small groups of children research or study a particular pet, and the information would be used to make the decision about which kind of pet would be the best choice for our classroom. The data that each of these small research groups gathered would apply to the first three concepts:

Concept 1. Pets are animals that are cared for by people, usually in homes and schools.

Concept 2. Some common pets are cats, dogs, fish, turtles, guinea pigs, hamsters, newts, and geckos.

Concept 3. People can get pets from pet stores, breeders, friends, and animal shelters.

There were several activities like this that we purposefully listed under each concept: the KLEW charts, read-alouds, class book. It may seem redundant, but, actually, it helped us recognize the importance of revisiting ideas and the depth of the concepts and the understandings we wanted to teach.

Since assessment and curriculum planning go hand in hand, we made notes on how we would assess the children's understandings as we generated the activities. Ongoing assessment is fundamental to inquiry. We needed to find out what the children understood, and what they misunderstood, so that we could adjust our teaching to meet their needs. Throughout the unit, we tapped into many "windows"—combinations of sources, methods, and contexts—for our assessment of the children's knowledge and their thinking (McAfee and Leong 2011, 48). We listened to children's conversations as they observed the gecko and the hamster. We looked at their observational drawings. We observed their play and listened to their discourse as they pretended to care for pets in the veterinarian's office. One morning on the playground, I noticed three children playing out a scenario about a pet tiger. Abigail was on all fours, growling and lashing out, while Malika held her leash and Owen commanded her to sit and come. This happened midway through the unit, so I was somewhat surprised that a wild, jungle animal was considered a pet, when we had focused on domestic pets that are cared for in the home. Clearly, these children had a different understanding. This observation prompted us to add some additional activities and books that expanded the discussion about Concept 1.

We also wanted to know how skillful the children were becoming with the practices of science. As children had more scaffolded experiences observing the animals, we heard comments such as, "He's so cute. I love the gecko" change to, "Look, she swims with legs, feet, neck, and tail." The children were also raising important questions that connected to the concepts, as evidenced by the list they prepared for Jim, the pet-store owner: "What are the kinds of furry pets you have? What does a fish eat? Would a dog or cat be too wild at school? How do hamsters make nests?" Initial observational drawings of the guinea pig that included fanciful hearts and a big smile, eventually gave way to accuracy in coloration and body details. We paid close attention to these drawings and what the children said about them, so we could scaffold in a timely and appropriate way.

Summative assessment came from a culminating activity, a how-to book on choosing and caring for pets. It also came from the information presented by the research groups and the children's decision to purchase a guinea pig. The animals the children originally suggested for a potential pet included: cat, dog, parrot, hamster, guinea pig, newt, and rabbit. The children learned through books, visits to the pet store, interviews with experts (pet owners, veterinarian, and pet-store owner), discussion, observation, and reports from research groups that certain animals make better pets than others, especially for a classroom. The class agreed on a guinea pig for all the right reasons, and that was strong evidence that they understood the conceptual ideas that drove this investigation.

IMPLEMENTING THE UNIT

When we felt that we had amassed enough activities to teach the concepts in a variety of ways, we needed to map out a plan for implementing the unit. We decided to plan in two-week cycles, adding, deleting, and repeating activities in a deliberate plan to build on the children's knowledge. (See Appendix 3.)

We started by sending a letter home to families to familiarize them with the big ideas the children would be investigating, and to request classroom visits from family pets. (See Appendix 4.) About a week before the start of the unit we arranged some interesting information books about pets for browsing. Since the pet unit was the centerpiece of our curriculum, there were activities related to it every day in a variety of areas of the classroom. Because we had such a diverse group of learners, we made sure that the children had plenty of time to engage with the activities and had access to the materials. For example, when we introduced the materials for making dog or cat tags, several of the older children dove in with a fury, making a series of tags that included pet names and owners' phone numbers. Almost a week later, after they noticed the pet tags on the stuffed animals, three of the younger children decided to make their own. The materials were still in the literacy center, so they were able to do this independently during their choice time.

The timing of the research trips to the pet store and the visit from a veterinarian was important because these events would provide foundational information for the children's understanding of the variety of pets and their care. The research trips were taken early on, and the veterinarian visited midway through the unit, so the children could make connections and build their knowledge over time.

Deciding when to end the unit can vary from topic to topic and class to class. Our class was totally engaged in this unit for more than a month. Publishing the class book, reading it to the class, and sharing it with the families was the last official activity, but the big ideas of the unit continued to be played out with the ongoing care of our fish and guinea pig.

LOOKING BACK

The pet inquiry was an exciting learning event for children and teachers alike. The time and effort that we put into planning enabled us to be closely engaged in the children's learning. We were able to watch, to listen, and to provoke learning because we were comfortable with our background knowledge and we were open to the children's ideas. The following year, the pet inquiry was introduced again, with the same concepts and many of the same activities, but without the focus on purchasing a new pet. It was fascinating to see how the new mix of children were as intrigued as the previous group and to see what new ideas they brought to the investigation.

SUMMING UP THE STEPS OF INQUIRY UNIT DESIGN

1. Decide on a topic.
   a. Make sure it is relevant and meaningful to the children's understanding of the world around them.
   b. Make sure children can engage in active exploration of the topic.
   c. Decide whether it meets district standards or curriculum goals.
2. Research the topic.
   a. Develop your background knowledge about the topic through resource books and nonfiction trade books.
   b. Read, connect with curriculum support people. Learn as much as you can about the topic.
3. Brainstorm; organize key ideas.
   a. Decide on the essential questions that will guide this unit.
   b. Consider the learning standards that support this topic.
   c. Develop a concept map or web of key ideas or essential questions.

4. Develop concepts.
   a. Think about the big ideas that children can take away from this study.
   b. Decide what connections you want children to make among these big ideas.
5. Generate activities and assessment opportunities.
   a. Collect teacher resource books and articles. Connect with museums, experts in the field, field-trip sites, and parents.
   b. Include large- and small-group activities that enable children to construct their learning in an active way, supported by opportunities for raising questions and sharing information.
   c. Consider opportunities to integrate math, literacy, and other curriculum domains. Think about how to integrate these subject areas in ways that make sense.
   d. Consider activity centers and daily schedule when thinking about teaching the concepts: blocks, water table, dramatic play area, literacy center, art center, outside, morning meeting.
   e. Consider including some of the following typical activities that might occur in an inquiry unit:

KLEW charts or concept map	Science notebooks
Observations	Investigations planned by
Observational drawings	the children
Interactive displays	Research groups
Research trips	Class books
Science meetings	Visits by experts
Read-alouds and browsing	Dramatic play
sessions with information	Culminating activity
books and related poetry	
and literature	

   f. Make sure that assessment opportunities are continuous, occurring in the context of children's reflections, discussions, products, demonstrations, interviews, and imbedded activities (anecdotal notes, science notebooks, document of children's comments, questions, KLEW charts, assessment template).
6. Design implementation plan.
   a. Decide how the unit should unfold and how long each activity should run.

Chapter 6

Teachers Talk About Inquiry-Based Science Teaching

Whether you are new to inquiry-based science teaching or you are fine-tuning your practice, the support of colleagues in the field who have walked the same walk can stimulate and strengthen your resolve to teach inquiry-based science. The personal anecdotes shared here by three experienced teachers provide practical ideas as well as inspiration.

Lauren Roby, a pre-K teacher in a suburban independent school, has worked with her coteachers to design and implement inquiry-based science units that reflect the children's interest. Because she is a preschool teacher in an independent school, she does not have to deal with district curriculum demands that Christina Ryan and Lindsay Barton face. Christina, a kindergarten teacher in a large, urban school, has been refining her inquiry-based practice for several years. Her classroom environment teems with interesting things to study and reflects her passion for science. Christina weaves science, mathematics, and literacy into her daily schedule so that children read, write, count, measure, and talk about science in a meaningful context. Lindsay Barton also teaches in an urban school. For several years, she has taught a combined first- and second-grade class in which she deftly incorporates inquiry, above and beyond the district science topics required for her grade level.

Each of these teachers has confronted the challenges that inquiry-based science teaching presents, from lack of time and resources to instructional demands that crowd out science. And as you'll see in the comments that follow, they have found ways to make science the center of their classroom and are convinced that the intellectual and social benefits that children derive from inquiry-based science are well worth their efforts to sustain this kind of learning environment.

WHAT SUGGESTIONS CAN YOU OFFER A TEACHER WHO IS JUST BEGINNING TO TEACH INQUIRY-BASED SCIENCE?

Lauren Roby (Pre-K): Before you begin an inquiry unit, take the time to learn as much about the topic and plan as much as you can, but don't wait too long. Even if you don't feel completely confident with the subject matter or the plan for the inquiry, get started with something to keep the children interested. Inquiries often start from a spontaneous event like finding a seed in a piece of fruit, so if you don't build on this momentum, their interest may dwindle. Still, planning is key. As much as the children drive the learning, the teacher still needs to spend time creating activities that will help the children discover information and the answers to their questions. It won't happen on its own.

Don't be afraid to abandon a topic if it's not taking off. After a pet inquiry, we thought the children were becoming interested in food, but when we asked the children what they wanted to know about food, most of their questions involved eggs and which animals are born from eggs. As we listened to their conversations and observed their interactions, we realized they were still very much interested in animals, so we abandoned the food topic and changed the focus to animal life cycles.

Christina Ryan (K): Be full of wonder, just as your young students are. Engage in inquiry yourself. Think about something you enjoy—exercise, cooking, music—there is bound to be some science behind it. As you engage in those activities, think about how you can go about gaining deep understanding of the science; it is probably not from just reading about it! For example, you might follow a recipe, but something does not come out right because of your oven temperature, or a substituted ingredient, or too much stirring. Even as an adult, you gain your deepest understandings from a combination of experiences and content knowledge. The same is true, even more so, for young children.

As teachers, we need to have the content knowledge behind what we teach our students, but we need to use that content to guide their experiences toward discovered understanding, rather than just feeding them facts.

Lindsay Barton (1st/2nd): Start off slowly. As you plan your lessons, you might notice a question that comes from the children. In addition to our big units of study, we try to take the time to follow that question. For example, we have a gecko in our class, and as ideas and questions have come up about the gecko, we've followed up on those questions during our morning meeting. This isn't a high-pressure inquiry unit, but a topical study that the children are curious about and that we can explore in a more informal way.

HOW DO YOU MANAGE TO FIT SCIENCE IN WHEN THERE ARE SO MANY OTHER DISTRICT/SCHOOL DEMANDS?

Lauren Roby (Pre-K): Because I work in an independent school, I have the freedom to teach what I want without many school demands. This makes it easier to include science as a significant piece of the curriculum, but even in classrooms that have multiple curriculum requirements, an integrated model is still doable. Literacy and math are naturally a part of science, so the children can learn many of those literacy and math skills through the inquiry-based science activities.

Christina Ryan (K): Science can be easily combined with literacy centers or with math centers. A principal who observed me working with a small group on a science activity noted to me that there was an organic transition between the time when the children were "doing the science" and the time when the children were "recording the science." Working in their science notebooks was both a science and a writing activity. The children were highly engaged and motivated to write because they wanted to record the results of their investigations. There are many meaningful connections with mathematics, as well; math is a tool for scientists. For example, my students have learned to use tables to organize data while observing gerbil behaviors. Another example occurred when the kindergartners were convinced that weight alone influenced whether an object would sink or float. They compared objects using a balance scale and found that there was not a direct link between weight and sinking. They also weighed the individual objects using base 10 blocks as their unit of measurement, which encouraged counting by tens and counting on.

Having a science center that is a well-maintained, a well-stocked, a respected, and an engaging part of the classroom is key. If you are comfortable hosting live organisms (both plants and animals), you will be providing the children with a context that encourages and supports observation, data collection, observational drawing, predicting, experimentation, and many other inquiry skills. In this way, the environment keeps science alive every day in the classroom, even if the teacher does not lead a specific science lesson.

Lindsay Barton (1st/2nd): One thing I've found incredibly useful is to integrate science with literacy. Writing is a big part of science. Scientists need to write down questions, predictions, observations, and the data they collect. Occasionally, I use literacy times to do this science writing in our science notebooks. The new Common Core's emphasis on nonfiction and persuasive writing supports this integration. Reading is also a place to integrate. Creating text sets that are connected to your inquiry topic with levels that are appropriate for your students creates opportunities for reading-to-learn science.

My classroom's design is based on learning centers that children cycle through during the week. One of my centers is science. Each week students engage in a planned science activity that usually includes some writing or recording to complement the activity. The students rotate through this activity all week long, so that everyone has a chance to do it. At the end of the week, we have a whole-class discussion on that activity. The children report on their findings, and we all discuss what we've learned and what we are wondering about.

Aligning science, mathematics, and literacy has become part of our schoolwide curriculum model. Our school is in the process of designing projects or expeditions in which science, math, and literacy are all integrated. For example, one of the inquiry units my class will be studying is living things. Both our reading and writing units will support our science work by focusing on the genre of nonfiction and developing nonfiction writing skills.

WHAT IF I DON'T HAVE A STRONG BACKGROUND IN SCIENCE?

Lauren Roby (Pre-K): I definitely feel like I don't know enough about science, but I take the time to do some research about the topic to gain a basic understanding. For example, I knew next to nothing about tools and building, but I spent part of the summer gathering information and materials to prepare for an inquiry unit on tools. I talked to people who knew how to use tools, and I collected tools at yard sales. My coteachers and I spoke with some parents and school facilities workers who offered additional expertise about the types of building we could do with the children. By the fall I felt confident enough to introduce the unit. Using a variety of resources—experts, books, and materials I had practiced with—unfamiliar topics become manageable, and I gained the confidence to teach.

I'm also comfortable admitting to the children that I may not know the answers to their questions. Because of the nature of inquiry, finding the answers to the children's questions without knowing the answers yourself makes the inquiry even more authentic and provides the children with a model of an adult using resources to find answers.

Christina Ryan (K): Although I had a few biology classes with an extremely engaging teacher in high school, I had horrible experiences with science in college. Since I've been teaching, I've been fortunate to find interesting courses and professional development opportunities that have enriched my understanding of content and inquiry. For instance, a summer university course on optics helped me design an investigation of light that I implemented with my kindergartners.

I hope I know enough to take responsibility for how I guide my students' learning, but I have also learned that if I don't know something, the best answer is, "I don't know. Let's find out!"

Lindsay Barton (1st/2nd): One of the great things about teaching inquiry-based science is that you are doing *the science* with your children. Before I begin a unit, I do a lot of research to build up my background knowledge. Still, there will be questions and ideas that the children bring up that I may not know about. This is true inquiry; I'm learning right along with my students. Of course I can't possibly know everything that will arise during our science study, but this gives me the opportunity to model for the children how to do science in an authentic way.

WHAT EXCITES YOU MOST ABOUT TEACHING SCIENCE TO YOUNG CHILDREN?

Lauren Roby (Pre-K): It's exciting to see children enjoy learning, especially when I see them becoming really interested in investigating a science topic, raising questions and finding the answers to those questions, and demonstrating that they can use problem-solving skills in authentic situations. When I hear them talking like scientists—saying, "I wonder what would happen if . . ." or raising a question, "Do you think we should do an experiment?" or using scientific terms like *observe, investigate,* and *predict* in their work—I know that the children are truly doing science.

Teaching science excites me most when the children can identify a real problem or question and then think of possible ways to solve the problem or find the answer. This happened during our tool inquiry when the children noticed our classroom workbench was wobbly and the top was cracked. These preschoolers wanted to find out how to fix the workbench. They generated a long list of ways to fix it including: use duct tape, tighten the bolts, secure it to a wall, take it apart, get a new one, and ask the Director of Facilities (who had given a small group a tour of the school's workshop) for help. Many children participated in the inquiry process as they tested their hypotheses to find out how to fix the workbench.

Christina Ryan (K): Young children remind me to stop and ponder the world in an uninhibited way. Case in point: as we were walking in from recess today, I was slightly annoyed that my line of kindergartners was breaking up. The reason for the unruly line: the children were staring in awe at a patch of dirt with hundreds of ants at work. Of course those ants would distract a group of five-year-olds; the ants were fascinating! Now I want to go back and see if they are still there so we can plan to observe them tomorrow.

Lindsay Barton (1st/2nd): One of the exciting things about teaching science to young children is the exploratory nature of the work. There are so many interesting things about the world to discover and learn, things that we adults don't even notice. For example, a few years ago I was required to teach a unit on balls and ramps. This topic was not very interesting to me. However, as we started to dig into the unit, the children's questions and observations amazed me. I discovered so many ideas I hadn't even considered. I was able to connect to their way of seeing the world, which enabled me to open up to a new way of thinking about a common topic that previously held little interest for me.

Science is also exciting because it's a place where students get to do "real work." By that I mean they are using a lot of other skills, including literacy, mathematical, speaking, and listening, to explore their ideas. So much of the science work can also be connected to real-world experiences outside of the classroom, making the work children do even more meaningful.

Lastly, it's fun! Supporting students as they wrestle with these ideas and questions about the world around them is exhilarating.

WHAT ARE SOME OF THE CHALLENGES YOU FACE TEACHING INQUIRY-BASED SCIENCE? ANY SOLUTIONS?

Lauren Roby (Pre-K): I think one of the biggest challenges of teaching inquiry-based science is deciding what activities make sense for preschool-aged children, taking into consideration their developmental skill level and the broad range of questions and ideas they bring to the table. It can be tricky to create experiences for them that are simultaneously child directed, developmentally appropriate, and authentic. We need to plan and scaffold the experiences that enable the children to actually do the science.

Christina Ryan (K): Inquiry-based science does not require a lot of materials, but it does require thoughtful planning, the ability to guide children's thinking and discern the understanding in children's talk and recordings, the skill of creating productive questions that will lead to investigations, and the forethought to know where an investigation leads so that children can reflect and make meaning from experiences. Many of the activities that early childhood teachers are comfortable doing are engaging introductory experiences and help children gather ideas and figure out how materials work. The problem is when teachers stop there and either don't discuss what children have learned or simply give them answers verbally or through books. Teachers need to consider what content can be made accessible to young children by forming questions (with or without children) that they can test and answer through their own investigations. Teachers also need to make the time for whole-group discussions so that children can share ideas that answer those questions and make meaning of their results.

Another challenge is having too many topics to cover and not enough time. A solution is to look at one's science standards for the entire year and consider what can be grouped together; testing a variety of objects to discover whether they sink and float necessitates that children describe the objects in terms of size, weight, material, texture, and so forth as they ponder which variables have an impact. Another solution is to consider which topics lend themselves to longer investigations at a particular grade level and which are more exploratory and can be set up in the science center. For example, part of my current science standards include studying magnets; the science content behind magnets is not accessible to five- and six-year-olds, but they can certainly explore and test magnets independently at a center.

Lindsay Barton (1st/2nd): Time is a big challenge in my classroom. I've found that planning and organization help a lot. I need to decide which of the questions that the children raise are worth digging into and balance those questions with the goals I've set for the unit. Over the years, I've spent time looking at the packaged curriculum that comes from our district, and I've revamped that curriculum to accommodate a more inquiry-based focus.

Developing a culture that supports rich discussion is another challenge. A huge part of my inquiry teaching revolves around student talk. The quality of talk the students are engaged in is crucial to developing their thinking, so I spend a lot of time modeling and teaching the "talk strategies" and the skills associated with productive discussions. I begin with basic group social skills, teaching children how to be part of a group conversation, how to respond to each other instead of being called on by the teacher. Through consistent modeling, practice, and supportive feedback, the students gradually develop as active discussion participants.

WHAT DO YOU WANT OTHER TEACHERS TO KNOW ABOUT YOUR EXPERIENCE TEACHING INQUIRY-BASED SCIENCE?

Lauren Roby (Pre-K): Teaching inquiry-based science keeps every year fresh and exciting. As a teacher, you have to remain open to what the children are interested in and to learning about something you don't know much about. Even if two classes study the same topic, it is different each time because the children will steer it toward whatever aspects of the topic they are particularly interested in. You also have different resources to draw on each time depending on the expertise of the families or the connections they might have. The more you teach inquiry-based science, the more you learn from past experiences and figure out better ways to approach a topic. Also, teaching inquiry-based science is so much more rewarding for the teacher than traditional science instruction, because the problem-solving skills and the disposition toward learning that the children gain will be with them for much longer than the facts they might only remember for a short period of time.

Christina Ryan (K): Science is important for its own sake, but it is also a context to integrate social skills and many other academic content areas—writing, reading, math, drawing, and so forth. Science is extremely interesting to every young child; even the most reluctant learners will observe a bearded dragon lizard, play with water, and be excited to see their little seed start to grow. We teachers need to take advantage of this keen interest to engage our students in processes that could be more challenging and demanding, such as writing, drawing, and working cooperatively. In this way, science is a teaching tool for all kinds of learners.

Lindsay Barton (1st/2nd): It's worth it! Take the time to make yourself feel comfortable with inquiry-based science. I wouldn't say I was excellent at teaching science my first year, but each year as I've chipped away at it, my work has become more coherent, thoughtful, and meaningful for the students. If you make inquiry-based science an integral part of your teaching, you will help your students develop a way of thinking. The idea of understanding not just science content but science methods or practices is powerful and will impact your students' lives and academic careers.

Chapter 7

The Conversation Continues

Teaching inquiry-based science is a continually evolving process for us as teachers, just as it is for the children we teach. That's why teaching science can be so intriguing and so perplexing. The payoff, of course, is the effect of inquiry-based science on children's understanding of science, their ability to make connections and recognize patterns, and their skill in the practices of science. It's difficult to convey the reality of that impact in a book like this. You may have already experienced this in your own classroom or you may have observed it in a colleague's room. Whatever the case, I offer this final image of Nicholas, Maxwell, and Harry as an example of what inquiry is all about. (See Figure 7.1.)

As you look at this photograph, you can't hear them shout, "We did it!" but you can see the triumph in their faces as they deliver this large pumpkin to their classroom on a skateboard. Where is the science in this photo? It began with the inquiry unit on simple machines that was in process in their classroom that fall. One of the concepts their teachers had included in the unit was that simple machines make work easier. The children had been learning this big idea by working with a variety of simple machines; by researching their questions about screws, wedges, and wheels; and by

107

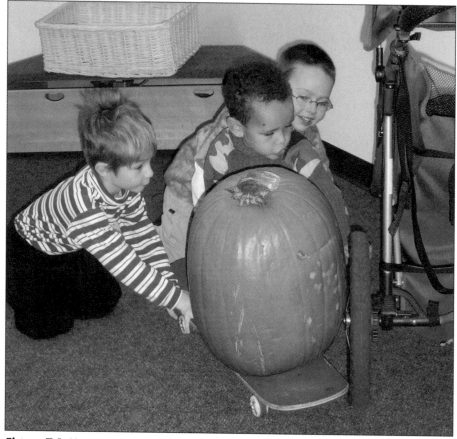

Figure 7.1 How to move a very heavy pumpkin

making their own simple machines. When a friend dropped off some very heavy pumpkins at the entrance of the school, the children's teacher, Jane, recognized an opportunity for applying the children's growing knowledge about simple machines. So Jane posed a question at morning meeting, "How can we get those very heavy pumpkins back to the classroom?" There was much discussion, and the children had many suggestions. Some thought about rolling the pumpkins down the hall, some asked about bringing in the wheelbarrow from the playground, but Nicholas, Maxwell, and Harry were convinced that the skateboard in the science discovery area would accomplish the job. Working together, they successfully maneuvered the pumpkin into the science area using a simple machine. Why was this such an effective, albeit unplanned, inquiry-based science experience? First, the children were ready for science—they had the content knowledge, and they had the confidence to work together, to raise an idea and test it. Their teacher was also ready for science—she had learned about simple machines and planned reasonable concepts to teach, and she was sensitive and open to opportunities for engaging the children in the practices of science. Put this altogether and you can experience the effects of inquiry-based science.

So think about the experience that these children and their teacher had as you develop your plan for infusing inquiry into your teaching. You will have many questions, but you know that's part of the process. These last suggestions should help you begin your journey:

- Start small, but go deep. Choose a topic or a unit that you are knowledgeable about and move it toward inquiry by determining the big ideas or concepts and then structuring experiences that enable children to do the science.
- Be flexible and open to ideas and questions you haven't planned. Take the time to really listen to the children, to be open to their theories, and to be confident in your ability to scaffold their learning.
- Make yourself an expert in one piece of the inquiry process before taking on another. Decide what you want to know more about: observing and documenting the children's learning, developing effective questioning, scaffolding discussions, integrating literacy, assessment. Practice and refine your skills in that one area, and then move on to another.
- Seek out colleagues who are also interested in inquiry and set up a study group. Teachers who have been bitten by the inquiry bug are always eager to share ideas and questions. University partners, museum educators, and web-based connections such as NAEYC's science interest forum can offer a variety of supports.
- Advocate for professional development sessions on inquiry-based science. The research has documented that most professional development funding is directed primarily to literacy and mathematics. By the time this book reaches you, the Next Generation Science Standards (http://www.nextgenscience.org/next-generation-science-standards) will be in place in most states. Your districts will be in the process of aligning their curriculum to the core ideas, practices, and crosscutting concepts of these standards. The timing couldn't be better for a push for training and support for inquiry-based science education.

And, finally, approach science as a "grand adventure," with the curiosity and delight that Nobel laureate Richard Feynman describes:

> *With more knowledge comes deeper, more wonderful mystery, luring one on to penetrate deeper still. Never concerned that the answer may prove disappointing, but with pleasure and confidence we turn over each new stone to find unimagined strangeness leading on to more wonderful questions and mysteries—certainly a grand adventure.* (1999, 144)

Appendix

APPENDIX 1 SCIENCE NOTEBOOK ASSESSMENT GUIDELINES

Name _____

	Date: Observation	Date: Observation	Date: Observation
Organization Includes date, location Title			
Observational drawings Accurate colors Includes details Size, scale are proportional Magnified view Shows motion, movement Corrects, revises			
Written notes, dictation Makes predictions Includes questions Compares, measures Notes similarities, differences Patterns Makes corrections, revises Uses scientific vocabulary Includes T-chart, Venn diagram Moves from labels to descriptive sentences			
Artifacts, photographs Dated, labeled accurately Captions Descriptive data: context, location Questions			
Understandings Makes connections to evidence Change in understanding Suggests appropriate fair test			

APPENDIX 2 CLOSE-UP PAGE FOR SCIENCE NOTEBOOK

This is a close-up of

_____

_____

_____

APPENDIX 3 PET INQUIRY UNIT

This unit is designed to engage children in choosing a new pet for the classroom. The concepts support the children's understanding of what a pet is, what kind of care is required, and what types of pets are typically available. If you are not interested in acquiring a new pet for your classroom, the concepts that drive this inquiry unit can still be used for an in-depth study of pets. Keep in mind that the concepts are a framework to work from, but the children's questions and ideas may move the inquiry in a different direction.

This appendix is set up so that you can view the unit concepts, activities, and assessment strategies in two different formats: the Pet Inquiry Unit Overview and the Unit Plan.

The Pet Inquiry Unit Overview (see Figure A3.1) provides a comprehensive look at all of the concepts, how the information or concepts can be taught, and how the children's understanding and engagement with science skills can be assessed. You'll find the concept listed in column one, the activities that teach that concept in column two, and the suggested assessment strategies for evaluating the children's understanding of that concept in column three. The activities in the overview are specific to our classroom unit and the purchase of our class guinea pig.

Concepts	Activities	Assessment
1. Pets are animals that are cared for by people, usually in homes and schools. a. When people care for pets, they feed the animals. Some animals also need grooming, exercise, and affection. b. Pets require special food. c. Different pets require unique kinds of housing and equipment, (e.g., cages, tanks, collars, tags, toys).	• Book display—nonfiction books (see the Children's Books section of the Bibliography) • KLEW chart K—What do we think we know about pets? • Read-alouds: *Whistle for Willie* (Keats), *Hemi's Pet* (De Hamel), *The Cat Barked?* (Monks), *My Dog Rosie* (Harper), *My Pet Hamster* (Rockwell) • Introducing new fish • Cleaning aquarium, hamster, and guinea pig cages • Pet props for dramatic play area: stuffed cats	• Observations • Anecdotal notes from the children's conversations and discussions • K chart with children's initials • Dictations, writing, and scientific drawings in science notebooks • Interview questions for pet research groups *continued*

Figure A3.1 Pet Inquiry Unit Overview

	and dogs, leashes, food bowls, food boxes, toys, collars, and tags • Book browsing (see the Children's Books section of the Bibliography); generating questions for pet-store owner; visit to pet store; preparing information sharing; sharing pet-store information at group time	
2. Some common pets are cats, dogs, fish, turtles, guinea pigs, hamsters, newts, and geckos. 　a. Different kinds of pets have different kinds of physical characteristics. 　b. Different pets move in different ways. 　c. Different pets make different sounds or no sounds.	• Humane Society website for information and video about pets children want to research • Classroom pet observations and pet care: newt, hamster, fish, guinea pig • Scientific drawings of animals • Field trip and video of visit to the pet shop • Making dog/cat tags • Making play-dough dog bones and chewy toys • Pet play on playground • Poem "I Am a Baby Porcupette" and discussion about which animals make good pets and which do not • Graphing suggestions for guinea pig's name • Book on caring for guinea pig • Organizing guinea pig's habitat, feeding and cleaning schedule • Another small group goes to pet shop for food, bedding • Read-alouds: *I Love Guinea Pigs* (King-Smith), *My Pet Hamster* (Rockwell), *Let's Get a Pet* (Ziefert)	• Observations • Anecdotal notes from the children's conversations and discussions • KLEW chart with children's initials • Dictations, writing, and scientific drawings in science notebooks • Pet clue cards • Class book *continued*

Figure A3.1 Pet Inquiry Unit Overview *(continued)*

	• KLEW charts • Pet matching/ concentration game • Pet floor puzzle • Puzzles of pets and animals that would not be pets • Pet display board with documentation text of children's comments about pets • Pet paper-bag puppets • Video of trip to the pet store • Classroom pet observations and care: newt, hamster, fish, guinea pig • Humane society video on pets in winter • Documentation of newt observations • Pet clue cards • Pet pasting pages • Water table for lizard, newt, snake, turtle, hermit crab, frog, fish play • Class book—research chapters on different types of pets	
3. People can get pets from pet stores, breeders, friends, and animal shelters. a. Pet stores sell many types of animals and the food and equipment people need to care for their pets.	• Research group for pet • Read-alouds: *Pets Without Homes* (Arnold), *Let's Get a Pet* (Ziefert) • Visit to pet store • Classroom pet store (see Appendix 5 for list of props) • Purchase of new guinea pig and equipment • Set up cage, feeding, and cleaning schedules • Video of pet-store visit • Class book • Research group for supplies	• Observations • Class discussions • Class book

continued

Figure A3.1 Pet Inquiry Unit Overview *(continued)*

Starting with Science: Strategies for Introducing Young Children to Inquiry by Marcia Talhelm Edson. Copyright © 2013. Stenhouse Publishers.

4. Veterinarians are doctors who care for pets. a. Veterinarians have special instruments they use to examine pets.	• Read-alouds: *My Mom's a Vet* (Horenstein), *Dr. Friedman Helps Animals* (Flanagan), *Animal Hospital* (Walker-Hodge) • Question list: What do you want to ask the veterinarian? • Veterinarian visit and examination of guinea pig • Vet's office in dramatic play area (see Appendix 6 for list of props) • Class book—chapter on veterinary care	• Observations of play in vet's office • Veterinarian clinic worksheets • Anecdotal notes of vocabulary used during play • Class book

Figure A3.1 Pet Inquiry Unit Overview *(continued)*

This is a major inquiry unit spanning at least four weeks. The concepts and activities engage children in a rich and lengthy investigation. If you are just beginning to work with inquiry units, or if you find that you can't do a month-long unit, you can easily adapt this unit to meet your needs. Just make sure that you start with the concepts and then select the activities that will teach those concepts and will work for your class. This layout of the Unit Overview provides a "big-picture" view of the unit.

The Unit Plan layout is more detailed and shows how the activities might unfold over a period of four to five weeks. The learning experiences are divided into three categories:

- *Large-group meetings.* Every classroom has a different daily plan, but typically the whole class comes together a few times during the day for morning meeting, science discussions, or mini-lessons that precede an activity. Most of the lessons or activities in this section have to do with discussion and instruction. Some of these large-group meetings introduce children to the concepts that will be explored in the small-group activities that follow, and some of these large-group meetings provide a forum for thoughtful discussion in which the children share observations, raise questions, report information to the class, and offer opinions and hypotheses.

- *Small-group activities.* These activities are designed to give the children many opportunities to learn the big ideas about pets and to practice the skills of science both inside and outside the classroom. Young children learn by involving their senses, their bodies, and their minds, so learning science needs to happen through activities that involve movement, painting, drawing, touching, listening, and playing. The arts, literacy, and mathematics are woven into the activities. Most of the unit's small-group activities are designed for a group of four to six children, so these activities would be scheduled over the course of several days to ensure that every child in the class has the opportunity to participate. Doing the activity is just one piece of the learning; the conversations that occur during the activity are also central to the learning. For example, making clay models of pets is one of the activities that help children learn how pets move in different ways and that pets have certain body parts to help them move (Concept 2). In this activity children construct models of a pet's body using play dough, air-dry modeling material, or clay. If children are making models of a newt, for example, they need to consider the contours of the long, narrow body and tail, as well as the short legs and interesting feet. As they manipulate the clay to add tiny pads to the feet or a long thin tail, they talk about how these parts of the newt help it move, balance, and climb up vines or the walls of the tank. So the actual activity combines the content knowledge with discussion, questions, sharing of information, and making models—the practices of science. All of the small-group activities have an active, playful but scientific focus.

- *Read-alouds.* These include nonfiction and fiction trade books that can be read to the whole class or to small groups either during the daily read-aloud segment or to introduce a discussion or a small-group activity. These books are an essential piece of teaching both content information and higher-level vocabulary. There should be a mix of fiction and nonfiction. Sometimes a book is read cover to cover; another time, particularly with the nonfiction books, only a few sections are read, with more time given to conversation about the big ideas embedded in those sections. In both cases, the book is linked to the concepts to build new knowledge, provoke questions, or validate prior knowledge. These books would be placed in the library area and displayed throughout the classroom for the children to use in their observations and play. You might place a selection of animal information books such as *Turtles* (Stevens 2009), *Guinea Pigs* (Evans 1992), and *Your Pet Iguana* (Landau 1997) in the veterinarian's office, or *A Pet's Life: Goldfish* (Ganeri 2009) might be propped up next to the fish tank. More detailed information about teaching through nonfiction texts can be found in Chapter 3.

Is it necessary to do each and every activity? You are the best judge of what works for your class. Your decision about which read-alouds, discussions, and small-group activities to include will be based on what you think it takes for your children to understand the concepts. Because every class is different, it's expected that you will fine-tune these lessons and activities to meet the needs of the children in your class.

The important thing to remember is that children need to *do* the science: to engage with materials, observe, question, predict, collect data, talk about the data, work together, and share their ideas with each other. The variety of experiences provided in this unit will give you a working plan to meet that goal.

PET INQUIRY CONCEPTS

All of the concepts are listed here so that you can easily refer back to them when they are mentioned in the Unit Plan descriptions of the large-group meetings, small-group activities, and read-alouds.

1. Pets are animals that are cared for by people, usually in homes and schools.
   a. Some animals also need grooming, exercise, and affection.
   b. Pets require special food.
   c. Different pets require unique kinds of housing and equipment (e.g., cages, tanks, collars, tags, toys).
2. Some common pets are cats, dogs, fish, turtles, guinea pigs, hamsters, newts, and geckos.
   a. Different kinds of pets have different kinds of physical characteristics.
   b. Different pets move in different ways.
   c. Different pets make different sounds or no sounds.
3. People can get pets from pet stores, breeders, friends, and animal shelters.
   a. Pet stores sell many types of animals and the food and equipment people need to care for their pets.
4. Veterinarians are doctors who care for pets.
   a. Veterinarians have special instruments they use to examine pets.

UNIT PLAN

The week before the unit is introduced, do the following:

● Display five to ten information books about pets. See the suggested titles in the read-aloud section for Week One. Join the children as they browse through these books to get a sense of their ideas and questions about pets.

Starting with Science: Strategies for Introducing Young Children to Inquiry by Marcia Talhelm Edson. Copyright © 2013. Stenhouse Publishers.

- Read *My Pet Hamster* (Rockwell 2002). Build the discussion around the children's ideas about pets, with a focus on Concepts 1 and 2.
- Send a letter to parents to introduce the pet inquiry. (See Appendix 4 for a sample letter.)

Week One
Large-group meetings (morning meetings and science meetings)

- Introduce KLEW charts. (**K**—What do we think we *know* about pets? **L**—What did we *learn* about pets? **E**—What is our *evidence*? **W**—What are we *wondering*?) Use the K chart to record a few of the children's ideas about pets. Post the chart so that you and the children can revisit it as the unit progresses.
- Discuss types of pets to research for the classroom. Generate a survey list from the children's ideas headed by a question, such as What kind of pet do you want for our class? See Appendix 7 for a sample list.
- Use the Humane Society information and video clips to research pets mentioned by the children: http://www.humanesociety.org/animals/pets/.
- From the survey, develop a chart for group input. Questions to consider: What do we want for a pet? What can we do with a pet? What kind of habitat will a pet need?
- Hold a discussion about pet visits. Explain how family and friends will be coming to the class to introduce their pets. Some of these pets will stay in the classroom for several days so that the children can observe the animals, help care for them, and—if it's feasible—play with them. Have children place sticky notes on the calendar to show when each pet will visit.

Small-group activities

- Pet survey. Assemble clipboards with survey, checklist of children's names, and pencil on a string. Have volunteers survey children during outdoor play or activity time and check off child's name and pet choice. Use results for whole-group discussion and set up of research groups.
- Dramatic play/house area. Add pet props (stuffed dogs and cats, leashes, food boxes, bowls). Model use of props; focus on needs and care of pets and their similarities and differences. Read directions on food boxes.
- Literacy area. Set up materials for making pet tags for collars for stuffed pets and for children to use in their dramatic play. Arrange oak-tag shapes, pencils, markers, hole punch, and twist ties. Have samples available showing pet's name and owner's telephone number, along with a list of the children's names and telephone numbers (in case they want to copy their phone number).

- Pet floor puzzle.
- Library area. Children browse through new pet books.

Read-alouds

These books provide background information and opportunities for discussion about Concepts 1, 2, and 3.

- *Guinea Pigs* by Mark Evans
- *A Pet's Life: Goldfish* by Anita Ganeri
- *Hemi's Pet* by Joan De Hamel
- *The Cat Barked?* by Lydia Monks
- *My Dog Rosie* by Isabelle Harper
- *My Pet Hamster* by Anne Rockwell
- *Whistle for Willie* by Ezra Jack Keats

Teacher Question:
I don't have any of these titles in my collection. Can I substitute books that I already have?

Answer:
This isn't a problem as long as the books you choose connect to the concepts and are scientifically accurate. Make sure that the selections include some nonfiction titles. Your school and local libraries as well as science museum libraries can be very helpful in finding and lending nonfiction titles. Also, keep in mind that quality nonfiction texts should be included even if the readability seems a stretch for your class. You don't need to use the entire book. A college-level text on guinea pigs was one of the nonfiction books most sought after by my preschoolers (see Chapter 3). I presented it to them during morning meeting, and instead of reading directly from the text, I pointed out the details in the life-size line drawings of the guinea pig, along with X-rays of the animal and its various body parts. These pages were marked with sticky notes, and the book was displayed on a table next to the science notebooks. You may also have access to books that may not be useful for a read-aloud but, with thoughtful planning, may be inspiring and interesting to the children in your class.

Week Two
Large-group meetings

- Host pet owner and visiting pet. Owner talks about pet's care and needs. Children ask questions. Before visit, provide owner with a list of questions or information related to the concepts so that owner can be prepared to present to the group.

- Introduce pet research groups. Using the data collected from the pet survey, set up a chart that lists the pets to be researched and the names of the children in each pet research group. Prompt children to raise questions to research about each pet listed.
- Revisit KLEW charts. Update information.
- Show samples of children's scientific drawings of the animals. (See the small-group activity for science notebooks in next section.) Have children talk about their drawings, and prompt them to make connections to the big ideas (i.e., body parts and how pets move).
- Have pet research groups report to the whole class and take questions from the group.
- View and discuss Humane Society video clip on caring for pets in winter: http://www.humanesociety.org/animals/pets/.
- Introduce a pet store setup in the dramatic play area. Show children a few props from the pet store. Ask for their ideas about how they would play in the pet store.

Small-group activities

- Pet research groups. Give the children time to browse through the books about different pets. Facilitate a discussion about what the children noticed about the different animals, what they are thinking about for a classroom pet, and what they would like more information on. Take notes; list questions the children generate.
- Pet visits/observations. Small groups will care for (feed, clean habitat), observe, and talk about the visiting pet. Have information books and websites about the animal set up.
- Water table. Set two clear tubs in the water table with buckets of water for the children to make their own aquarium. Let children choose from colored gravel, clear stones, a variety of plastic fish, and aquarium accessories. Encourage conversation about what fish need in both their natural habitat and aquarium.
- Science notebooks. Children will make scientific drawings of the visiting animal and add comments and questions. (See Figure A3.2.)
- Pet visit documentation. Photograph the children's observations of each animal, mount their observational drawings, and set up a panel/bulletin board with the photos, transcripts of the children's conversation, and space for the children to add drawings, comments, questions. (See Figure A3.3.)
- Pet-store visits. Research groups visit pet store separately with questions they have generated about the pet they are studying.

Figure A3.2 Making a scientific drawing of a visiting pet

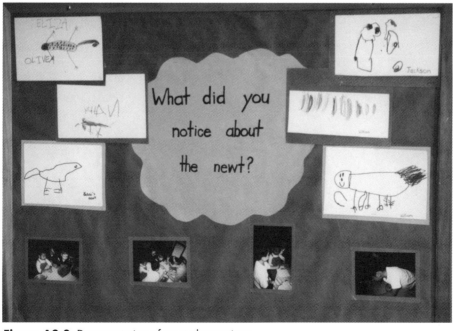

Figure A3.3 Documentation of newt observations

- Clay animal models. Set up clay or air-dry modeling material next to whatever animals are in the classroom. Display photos or pictures in books of other pets the children might want to represent.
- Play-dough bones and chewy toys. Make play-dough bones and toys for pretend pets. Label containers to hold the items, and place in dramatic play area.
- Classroom pet store in dramatic play area. (See Appendix 5 for a list of props to include.) Set up a small house area in another part of the room so the children can play out the whole scenario of purchasing the pet from the store and caring for a pet at home. (See Figure A3.4.)

Read-alouds

- *"Let's Get a Pup!" Said Kate* by Bob Graham
- *I Love Guinea Pigs* by Dick King-Smith
- *Rabbit* (See How They Grow series) by Barrie Watts
- *Your Pet Iguana* by Elaine Landau
- *Keeping Unusual Pets: Hermit Crabs* by Tristan Boyser Binns
- *Turtles: Pet Care for Kids* by Kathryn Stevens

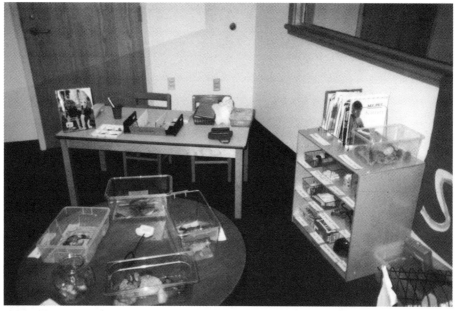

Figure A3.4 Pet store

Week Three
Large-group meetings

- Host pet owner and visiting pet. Owner talks about pet's care and needs. Children ask questions. If possible, pet will remain in the classroom for a few days, so the children can study it. (See the pet visit/observation activity in next section.)
- Facilitate discussion about veterinarian visit. Set up chart "Questions for Dr.———" and list children's questions. Keep chart available so children can add questions. (See Figure A3.5.)
- Introduce veterinarian. (Prior to the visit, ask the veterinarian to bring instruments, X-rays, a scale, an animal's chart, and photos or videos of her or his office.) During the veterinarian's presentation, have the children read him or her their questions from the chart.
- Read *My Mom's a Vet* (Horenstein 1994). Discuss veterinarian's role and highlight tools.
- Discuss how to set up a veterinarian's office. Have children list their suggestions for the office on a chart and mount it where they can continue to add ideas.
- Read the poem "I Am a Baby Porcupette" by Joyce Sidman (2010), and discuss whether porcupines would be good pets.

Figure A3.5 List of questions the children prepared for the visiting veterinarian

Starting with Science: Strategies for Introducing Young Children to Inquiry by Marcia Talhelm Edson. Copyright © 2013. Stenhouse Publishers.

- Research groups report to large-group meeting each day.
- Set up "What does a pet need?" chart. Columns might include: type of pet, habitat, food, special information, questions. After research group presents information, fill in the chart.
- Revisit KLEW charts. Update information on **K** (What do we think we know about pets?) and link **L** (What did we learn about pets?) with **E** (What is our evidence?)
- Introduce a survey/vote chart: "Do you think a _____ would be a good pet for our class?" with yes and no columns. Children sign sticky notes and place in the column of choice.
- Discuss the survey/vote results. Have children tally votes and identify an animal for class pet. Ask children for their ideas about how to proceed with the purchase and setup of the class pet.

Small-group activities

- Pet visits/observations. Small groups will observe and talk about the visiting pet. Information books and websites about the animal will be available. Children can complete a "What does a _____ need?" chart or page that will be used for later discussion on choosing a classroom pet.
- Classroom pet store in dramatic play area. Continue this activity with small house area in another part of the room. Ask children for suggestions for additional materials.
- Block area. Add, bowls, leashes, tags.
- Science notebooks. Children make scientific drawings of visiting pet and include questions, comments.
- Blank pet books. Staple a few sheets of paper into a book—some blank and some with the title *My Pet*. Prepare a reference list of words the children may want to use for labels (e.g., names of pets being observed—*gecko, salamander, guinea pig*; body parts—*fur, whiskers, scales*; habitat accessories—*gravel, exercise wheel, bowl*). Display word list in plastic frames or laminate copies and place in writing center and science center.
- Literacy center. Using the pet photos that families have provided and photos from pet visits to the classroom, invite children to write captions about the pet. Prompt children to include information about the pet's needs and care.
- "What Pet Am I?" Children make pet clue cards to use for next week's meeting. Two or three clues related to Concepts 1 and 2 are written on the outside of a file folder. A small dot of Velcro seals the folder closed to hide the photo or drawing of the animal in question.

- Outside area. Take pet props outside so children can pretend to be pets and pet owners. Ask children for ideas about how to set up a dog park or dog-training class.
- Pet/habitat matching game. Make two sets of cards, one with the animal's photo and label; the other with a picture of the appropriate habitat for that animal.

Read-alouds

- *Owning a Pet Cat* by Ben Hoare
- *My Mom's a Vet* by Henry Horenstein
- *Animal Hospital* by Judith Walker-Hodge
- *Dark Emperor and Other Poems of the Night* by Joyce Sidman

Weeks Four and Five
Large-group meetings

- Play "What Pet Am I?" with the clue cards the children made last week. Provide support to a child as he or she reads the clue, picks children to respond, and opens the folder to confirm the answer.
- Focus on making the connections between the **L** (learning) and the **E** (evidence) in the KLEW charts.
- Introduce veterinarian's office. Ask children to explain how they will use the office, what roles are necessary (e.g., pet owners, veterinarian, assistant, receptionist). Continue to keep a small house area open so that children can take the sick pets home and care for them.
- Introduce chart for choosing class pet's name. List children's suggestions under the heading "Choose a name for the _____" and explain that they can vote during the day by signing a sticky note and placing it on the line next to the name they choose. Have children tally the votes the next day. (See Figure A3.6.)

Figure A3.6

Small-group activities

- Veterinarian's office in dramatic play area (replaces pet store setup). (See Appendix 6 for a list of props to include.) Support children's exploration of the different roles and use of materials in the veterinarian's office. (See Figure A3.7.) When necessary, model each role:
  - Pet owner—filling out information form (see sample in Appendix 8), talking about the reason for bringing the pet (checkup, shots, illness)
  - Receptionist—making appointments, preparing charts, reading and writing information on diagnostic forms
  - Veterinarian—examining pets, reading information sheet, weighing pet, viewing X-rays, looking at reference books, and filling out the diagnostic form (see sample in Appendix 9)
- Pet-store trip to purchase animal. Photograph or videotape to show the rest of the class.
- Pet-store trip to purchase accessories. Photograph to use for class book.
- Habitat setup. Children help to set up habitat for new pet. Photograph to use for class book.
- Class pet care. Teacher models and supports children as they learn how to hold and care for their new pet. (See Figure A3.8.)

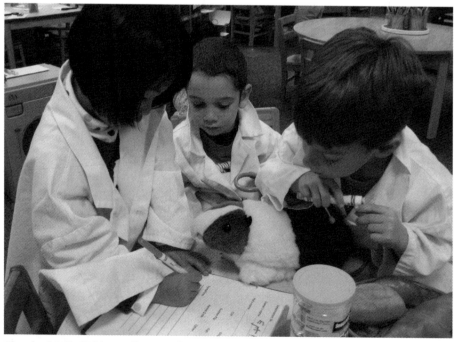

Figure A3.7 Children collecting information about a sick guinea pig

Starting with Science: Strategies for Introducing Young Children to Inquiry by Marcia Talhelm Edson. Copyright © 2013. Stenhouse Publishers.

Figure A3.8

- Science notebooks. Scientific drawings of new pet, with written or dictated questions, comments. Include close-up page. (See Appendix 2 for sample.)
- Class information book. Make available a sample nonfiction book that the children used during the unit (e.g., Landau's *Your Pet Iguana*), a sampling of photos, and charts and documentation of the unit. Have the children decide what the book should be about. For example, they may want to write a how-to book on choosing a class pet or on caring for the pet they chose. Use the table of contents from the sample book to help the children decide what they want to include. During the week, invite children to write captions and illustrate the contents. Include relevant photos of the children—modeling how to hold the pet, how to clean the cage and measure food, and so forth. (Stress accuracy of information.)
- Brochure or video of how to care for the pet at home. If the classroom pet can travel (e.g., gecko, guinea pig, Madagascar hissing cockroach), then families can care for the pet on weekends and during school vacations. Children can design and prepare a brochure or video for the families that explains the proper care of the animal.

Read-alouds

- *Dr. Friedman Helps Animals* by Alice Flanagan
- *ER Vets: Life in an Emergency Room* by Donna Jackson
- *What Does a Veterinarian Do?* by Felicia Lowenstein

Teacher Question:

I'm a first-grade teacher who has very little time to teach science. We have a turtle in our classroom that hardly anyone notices, so I would like to put together a short pet inquiry about our turtle. My question is, How can I shorten this unit so that it would only take a couple of weeks?

Answer:

Your idea to build the children's interest and understanding about the turtle is a good one. Your first step would be to decide what concepts to teach. It seems like Concepts 1, 2, and 3 would be most appropriate for your purpose—understanding what pets are, what their needs are, and how to take care of them, specifically a turtle. Your next step would be to look over the activities listed in the Unit Overview and choose a selection that will give children the opportunity to observe, talk about, and raise questions about the necessary care that pets require and the variety of pets that are available. As I look over the activities linked to the concepts, I would want the children to understand the broader ideas about a pet's needs and how we care for pets, so I would still include some of the read-aloud selections under Concept 2, but I would also narrow the focus of some of the activities to turtles. For example, the class book might end up as a how-to nonfiction piece on caring for a pet turtle.

TEACHER RESOURCES FOR PET INQUIRY UNIT

Humane Society of the United States. "Pets." http://www.humanesociety.org/animals/pets/.

Kneidel, Sally. 1993. *Creepy Crawlies and the Scientific Method.* Golden, CO: Fulcrum.

Lott, Kimberly, and Sylvia Read. 2012. "Is a Mealworm Really a Mealworm?" *Science and Children* 49:47–51.

Meadan, Hedda, and Brinda Jegatheesan. 2010. "Classroom Pets and Young Children." *Young Children* 65:70–77.

Melson, Gail. 2001. *Why the Wild Things Are: Animals in the Lives of Children.* Cambridge, MA: Harvard University Press.

National Science Teachers Association. 2008. Position Statement: Responsible Use of Live Animals and Dissection in the Science Classroom. Arlington, VA: NSTA. http://www.nsta.org/pdfs/PositionStatement_LiveAnimalsAndDissection.pdf.

Nestor Elementary School. "Classroom Animals and Pets—Amphibians, Newts." http://teacherwebshelf.com/classroompets/amph-newts.htm.

Rud, Anthony, and Alan Beck. 2000. "Kids and Critters in Class Together." *Phi Delta Kappan* 82:313–15.

Sandstrom, Susan. 1999. "Dear Simba Is Dead." *Young Children* 54:14–15.

Wickless, Mimi, David Brooks, Amiad Abuloum, Brian Mancuso, Tiffany Heng-Moss, and Lois Mayo. 2003. "Our Zoo to You." *Science and Children* 41: 36–39.

Young, Terrell, and Lynda Paznokas. 2003. "Classroom Pets: Books About Animals in the Classroom." *Book Links* 13: 53–58.

APPENDIX 4 PET INQUIRY SAMPLE LETTER TO FAMILIES

Dear Families,

You might notice some interesting new books about pets in our library area this week. These books are the beginning of our next inquiry unit on pets. We would like to add a new pet to our classroom. For the next 4–6 weeks, the children will be reading, observing, questioning, and gathering information on pets so we can use this new knowledge to choose the best kind of pet for our classroom. We'll begin our pet inquiry with these big questions:

- What is a pet?
- What do pets need to grow and be healthy?
- What are the different kinds of pets available?
- What kinds of pets are best for a classroom?

Of course, the children will be raising more questions that we will follow up on as the study progresses.

There are a few things you can help us with as we begin the unit. We know that some of you have pets at home, and we hope you'll be willing to bring your pet for a visit during the unit. More information and sign-up sheet will follow. We'll also be collecting photos of pets your child is familiar with (i.e., a pet that belongs to a neighbor, friend, grandparent). Please write any identifying information on the back of the photo, and drop it in the envelope on the bulletin board

This should be a great learning opportunity for all of us. Thanks for your support.

APPENDIX 5 PET-SHOP SETUP

This is a general framework for a pretend pet shop. The ideas your children provide, the space you have in your classroom, and the materials you have on hand will all affect your classroom pet shop design.

Design/Organization of the Pet Shop
- Cashier's table
- Display area for pets and pet supplies

Store Props
- Variety of stuffed animals—cats, dogs, parrots, guinea pigs, mice—displayed in cages made from boxes or plastic crates
- Variety of plastic reptiles, amphibians, and fish—snakes, turtles, lizards, geckos, frogs, hermit crabs, goldfish—displayed in appropriate habitat
- Pet equipment stored on labeled shelves:

*Cages	Plastic "tanks"
Fish bowl	Dog, cat bowls
Leashes, collars	*Dog, cat tags
*Bones, chewy toys	Brushes
Variety of pet foods	Nets
Rack of pet-care books	

- *Posters of pets
- *Signs: name of store, open/closed
- Aprons or shirts for pet-store workers
- Name tags for pet-store workers

Cashier Props
- Money drawer/cash register
- *Money
- *Receipts
- *Pet care instructions filed according to pet type
- Telephone
- Bags
- Pencils, paper

---

*Asterisk indicates items made by the children.

APPENDIX 6 VETERINARIAN'S OFFICE PROPS

Organization
- Waiting-room space and reception desk
- Doctor's office

Waiting-Room Props
- Chairs
- Magazines and books about animals
- Cup of pencils
- Clipboards with diagnostic forms
- Mounted and labeled photos of pets
- Open/closed sign

Receptionist's Props
- Table, chair
- Pencils, pens
- Message pads
- Date stamp and pad
- Appointment book
- Business cards
- Charts for pets (file folders with information and diagnostic forms)
- Telephone
- Pad of paper
- Calendar

Doctor's Office Props
- Operating table
- Lab coats, scrubs, gloves, hats
- Blank name tags (Dr. — —)
- Stethoscopes
- Flashlight
- Tongue depressors
- Gauze
- X-rays
- Paper copies of X-rays
- Pencils, highlighters
- Scale
- Reference books on animals
- Cages

APPENDIX 7 SURVEY FORM

What kind of pet do you want for our class?

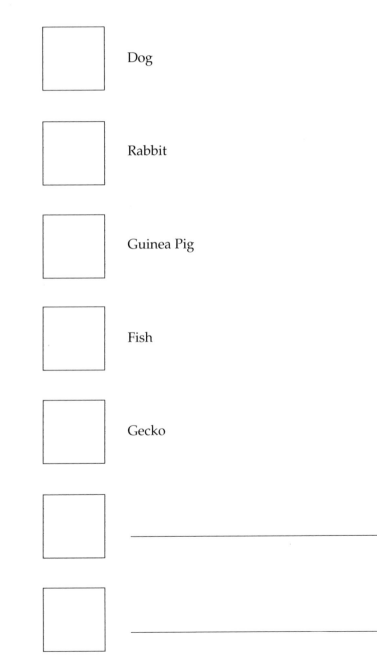

Dog

Rabbit

Guinea Pig

Fish

Gecko

_____

_____

APPENDIX 8 INFORMATION FORM

Dr. _____ 's Office

Name of owner _____

Name of pet _____

Age of pet _____

Cat   Parrot

Dog   Turtle

Guinea Pig   Snake

_____

_____

_____

_____

APPENDIX 9 DIAGNOSTIC FORM

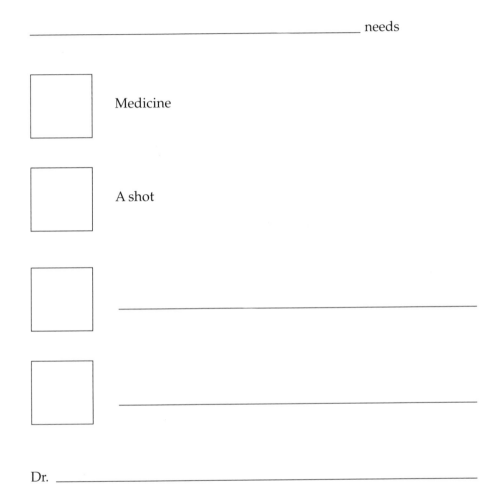

_____ needs

☐   Medicine

☐   A shot

☐   _____

☐   _____

Dr. _____

APPENDIX 10 ASSESSMENT TEMPLATE

Inquiry Unit: Pets

- Science practices: observing, predicting, questioning, planning investigations, inferring, collaborating, communicating, interpreting, and using tools to gather information
- Inquiry unit concepts:
  1. Pets are animals that are cared for by people, usually in homes and schools (care, food, housing).
  2. Some common pets are cats, dogs, fish, turtles, guinea pigs, hamsters, newts, and geckos (characteristics, movement, sounds).
  3. People can get pets from pet stores, breeders, friends, and animal shelters (food, supplies).
  4. Veterinarians are doctors who care for pets (instruments).

Name/Date	Observation notes	Thoughts, questions

Bibliography

PROFESSIONAL RESOURCES

American Association for the Advancement of Science. 2009. *"Benchmarks for Science Literacy."* American Association for the Advancement of Science.http://www.project2061.org/publications/bsl/online/index.php?home=true.

Anderson, Ronald. 2002. "Reforming Science Teaching: What Research Says About Inquiry." *Journal of Science Teacher Education* 13: 1–12.

Bransford, John, Ann Brown, and Rodney Cocking, eds. 2000. *How People Learn: Brain, Mind, Experience and School.* Washington, DC: National Academies Press.

Campbell, Brian, and Lori Fulton. 2003. *Science Notebooks: Writing About Inquiry.* Portsmouth, NH: Heinemann.

Canfield, Michael R. 2011. *Field Notes on Science and Nature.* Cambridge, MA: Harvard University Press.

Carson, Rachel. 1999. *The Sense of Wonder.* New York: HarperCollins.

Chalufour, Ingrid, and Karen Worth. 2006. "Science in Kindergarten." In *K Today: Teaching and Learning in the Kindergarten Year*, ed. Dominic Gullo. Washington, DC: NAEYC.

Committee on Science Learning, Kindergarten through Eighth Grade. 2009. *Taking Science to School: Learning and Teaching Science in Grades K–8,* ed. Richard A. Duschl, Heidi A. Schweingruber, and Andrew W. Shouse. Washington, DC: The National Academies Press.

Copple, Carol, and Sue Bredekamp, eds. 2009. *Developmentally Appropriate Practice in Early Childhood Settings Serving Children from Birth Through Age Eight.* Washington, DC: NAEYC.

Doris, Ellen. 2010. *Doing What Scientists Do.* Portsmouth, NH: Heinemann.

Duckworth, Eleanor. 1996. *The Having of Wonderful Ideas.* New York: Teachers College Press.

Duke, Nell, Anne-Lise Halvorsen, and Jennifer Knight. 2012. "Building Knowledge Through Informational Text." In *Knowledge Development in Early Childhood*, ed. Ashley Pinkam, Tanya Kaefer, and Susan Newman. New York: Guilford.

Duschl, Richard. 2003. "Assessment of Inquiry." In *Everyday Assessment in the Science Classroom*, ed. J. Myron Atkin and Janet Coffey. Arlington, VA: NSTA.

Duschl, Richard, Heidi Schweingruber, and Andrew Shouse. 2007. *Taking Science to School.* Washington, DC: National Academies Press.

Early Childhood Science Interest Forum. n.d. http://ecsif.blogspot.com/.

Feynman. Richard. 1999. *The Pleasure of Finding Things Out.* Cambridge, MA: Perseus Books.

Gandini, Lella. 1998. "Educational and Caring Spaces." In *The Hundred Languages of Children: The Reggio Emilia Approach—Advanced Reflections*, 2nd ed., ed. Carolyn Edwards, Lella Gandini, and George Forman. Greenwich, CT: Ablex.

Geiken, Rosemary, Beth Dykstra Van Meeteren, and Tsuguhiko Kato. 2009. "Putting the Cart Before the Horse: The Role of a Socio-Moral Atmosphere in an Inquiry-Based Classroom." Childhood Education 85: 260–263.

Harlen, Wynne. 2001. *Primary Science: Taking the Plunge.* Portsmouth, NH: Heinemann.

Hawkins, David. 1974. *The Informed Vision Essays on Learning and Human Nature.* New York: Agathon.

Hershberger, Kimber, Carla Zembal-Saul, and Mary Starr. 2006. "Evidence Helps the KWL Get a KLEW." *Science and Children* 43 (5): 50–53.

Massachusetts Department of Education. 2006. *Massachusetts Science and Technology/ Engineering Curriculum Framework.* Boston, MA: Massachusetts Department of Education. http://www.doe.mass.edu/frameworks/scitech/1006.pdf.

McAfee, Oralie, and Deborah Leong. 2011. *Assessing and Guiding Young Children's Development and Learning.* Upper Saddle River, NJ: Pearson.

Michaels, Sarah, Andrew Shouse, and Heidi Schweingruber. 2008. *Ready, Set, Science!* Washington, DC: National Academies Press.

National Research Council. 1996. *National Science Education Standards.* Washington, DC: National Academies Press.

National Science Teachers Association. 2013. NSTA Blog: Early Years. http://nstacommunities.org/blog/category/earlyyears/.

Next Generation Science Standards. 2013. Public draft of Next Generation Science Standards. http://www.nextgenscience.org/next-generation-science-standards.

Project Zero and Reggio Children. 2001. *Making Learning Visible: Children as Individual and Group Learners.* Reggio Emilia, Italy: Reggio Children.

Smith, Nancy, and the Drawing Study Group. 1997. *Observation Drawing with Children: A Framework for Teachers.* New York: Teachers College Press.

Vygotsky, Lev. 1986. *Thought and Language*, ed. Alex Kozulin. Cambridge, MA: MIT Press.

Weller, Diana, and Carla Finkelstein. 2011. "From 'Adding Inquiry' to 'Doing Science.'" *Science and Children* 48: 49–53.

Winokur, Jeff, and Karen Worth. 2006. "Talk in the Science Classroom: Looking at What Students and Teachers Need to Know and Be Able to Do." In *Linking Science and Literacy in the K–8 Classroom*, ed. Rowena Douglas, Michael Klentschy, and Karen Worth. Arlington, VA: NSTA.

Worth, Karen, and Sharon Goldman. 2004. *Worms, Shadows and Whirlpools: Science in the Early Childhood Classroom.* Portsmouth, NH: Heinemann.

CHILDREN'S BOOKS

Adamson, Heather. 2004. *A Day in the Life of a Veterinarian.* Mankato, MN: Capstone.

Arnold, Caroline. 1983. *Pets Without Homes.* New York: Clarion.

Barretta, Gene. 2009. *Neo Leo: The Ageless Ideas of Leonardo DaVinci.* New York: Holt.

Bell, Simon, and Alexandra Parson. 1991. *What's Inside? Small Animals: A First Guide to the Wonders and Workings of Small Animals.* New York: Dorling-Kindersley.

Boyer Binns, Tristan. 2010. *Keeping Unusual Pets: Hermit Crabs.* Mankato, MN: Heinemann-Raintree.

Branley, Franklyn. 2006. *Air Is All Around You.* New York: HarperCollins.

Bridwell, Norman. 1997. *Clifford the Big Red Dog.* New York: Scholastic.

Bulla, Clyde Robert. 1994. *What Makes a Shadow?* New York: Harper Collins.

Burleigh, Robert. 2003. *Into the Woods: John James Audubon Lives His Dream.* New York: Atheneum.

De Hamel, Joan. 1985. *Hemi's Pet.* Cambridge: Houghton Mifflin.

Ehrlich, Amy. 2008. *Rachel: The Story of Rachel Carson.* New York: Harcourt.

Evans, Mark. 1992. *Guinea Pigs.* New York: Dorling-Kindersley.

———. 1992. *Kitten.* New York: Dorling-Kindersley.

———. 1992. *Puppy.* New York: Dorling-Kindersley.

Flanagan, Alice. 2000. *Dr. Friedman Helps Animals.* Danbury, CT: Children's Press.

Ganeri, Anita. 2003. *A Pet's Life: Guinea Pigs.* Chicago: Heinemann Library.

———. 2009. *A Pet's Life: Goldfish.* Chicago: Heinemann Library.

Gibbons, Gail. 2002. *Tell Me, Tree: All About Trees for Kids.* New York: Little, Brown Books for Young Readers.

Graham, Bob. 2001. *"Let's Get a Pup!" Said Kate.* Cambridge, MA: Candlewick.

Harper, Isabelle. 1994. *My Dog Rosie.* New York: Scholastic.

Head, Honor. 2001. *My Pet Kitten.* New York: Raintree Steck-Vaughn.

Hernandez-Divers, Sonia. 2010. *Keeping Unusual Pets: Geckos.* Chicago: Heinemann Library.

Hoare, Ben. 2005. *Owning a Pet Cat.* Danbury, CT: Franklin Watts.

Horenstein, Henry. 1994. *My Mom's a Vet.* Cambridge, MA: Candlewick.

Jackson, Donna. 2005. *ER Vets: Life in an Emergency Room.* Boston: Houghton Mifflin.

Keats, Ezra Jack. 1964. *Whistle for Willie.* New York: Penguin Books.

King-Smith, Dick. 1994. *I Love Guinea Pigs.* Cambridge, MA: Candlewick.

Landau, Elaine. 2006. *Your Pet Iguana.* New York: Scholastic.

Lowenstein, Felicia. 2006. *What Does a Veterinarian Do?* Berkeley Heights, NJ: Enslow.

Macaulay, David. 1983. *Underground.* New York: Houghton Mifflin Harcourt.

MacAulay, Kelley, and Bobbie Kalman. 2005. *Rabbits.* New York: Crabtree.

Markle, Sandra. 2001. *Outside and Inside Rats and Mice.* New York: Simon and Schuster.

Miller, Michaela. 1998. *Cats.* Des Plaines, IL: Heinemann Interactive Library.

Monks, Lydia. 1998. *The Cat Barked?* New York: Dial Books for Young Readers.

Parker, Steve. 1990. *Fish.* New York: Alfred A. Knopf.

Rockwell, Anne. 2002. *My Pet Hamster.* New York: HarperCollins.

Sidman, Joyce. 2010. *Dark Emperor and Other Poems of the Night.* Boston: Houghton Mifflin.

Simon, Seymour. 2011. *Butterflies.* New York: HarperCollins.

Stevens, Kathryn. 2009. *Turtles: Pet Care for Kids.* Mankato, MN: Child's World.

Walker-Hodge, Judith. 1999. *Animal Hospital.* New York: Dorling–Kindersley.

Watts, Barrie. 1992. *Rabbit.* (See How They Grow series.) New York: Lodestar Books.

Wick, Walter. 1997. *A Drop of Water.* New York: Scholastic.

Ziefert, Harriet. 1993. *Let's Get a Pet.* New York: Penguin Books.

Zion, Gene. 1984. *Harry the Dirty Dog.* New York: HarperCollins.

Index

A

activities, assessments, 82–89
  KLEW charts, 82–84
  research groups and, 34–36
  research trips, expert interviews
    and, 86–88
American Association for the
    Advancement of Science, 13
assessments, 61–63, 92
  activities and, 82–89
  conversations and, 66
  curriculum planning and, 62
  documentation and, 71–72
  feedback and, 68–71
  formative, 62
  gathering evidence and, 65–68
  nonjudgmental feedback and, 70
  planning for, 63–64

product-oriented culminating
  sources for, 66
  worksheets and, 63–64
assessment template, pet inquiry
  unit, 138
attitudes, 61

B

Barton, L., 97–98
  fitting science in, 100
  science background and, 101
  suggestions, 99
  teaching science, challenges of
    and, 104
  teaching science, excitement of,
    102–103
  what teachers need to know and,
    105

Bredekamp, S., 13
Bulla, C. B., *What Makes a Shadow?*, 11–12
Burleigh, R., *Into the Woods: John James Audubon Lives His Dream*, 52

C
Carson, R., 4
Chalufour, I., 14
children's conversations, assessments and, 63
classroom organization, 26–32
    displays and, 29
    labels and, 32
    laboratories and, 31
    living things and, 29–29
    science centers and, 26–27
close-up page, science notebook, 113
collaborating, 9
Committee on Science Learning, *Taking Science to School*, 14
communicating, 10
competence, children's, 12
content, 12–15, 61
Copple, C., 13

D
diagnostic form, pet inquiry unit, 137
discussions, conversations and, 53–59
    meetings and, 54–59
displays, 29
documentation, assessments and, 71–72
documentation board, 71–72
Drop of Water, A (Wick), 52
Duckworth, E., 2, 81

Duschl, R., 65

E
Ehrlich, A., *Rachel: The Story of Rachel Carson*, 52
expert interviews, 86–87
    sources for, 87–88

F
feedback, assessments and, 68–71
Feynman, R., 110

G
Gandini, L., 28

H
Harlen, W., 2, 21, 70
Hawkins, D., 2
Hershberger, K., 82

I
implementation, inquiry units and, 93–94
information form, pet inquiry unit, 136
inquiry, defined, 5
inquiry-based science, 5–6
    content, processes and, 6
    elements of, 15–17
    hands-on approach, versus, 18
inquiry units
    activities, assessments and, 82–89
    culminating activity and, 88–89
    defined, 75–76
    implementation, 93–94
    planning sheet, 63–64
    planning unit activities and, 89–93
    research and, 77
    research groups and, 84–86

research trips, expert interviews
and, 86–88
steps of, 94–95
topics and, 76–77
interpretation, information and, 10
Into the Woods: John James Audubon Lives His Dream (Burleigh), 52
investigating, 8–9

K
KLEW charts, 82–84

L
Leong, D., 92
literacy
comprehension, meaning making and, 48–50
discussions, conversations and, 53–59
nonfiction read-alouds and, 50–53
science and, 33
literacy skills, science notebooks and, 38
pictures to words, 45–48
writing prompts, 47

M
McAfee, O., 92
Macaulay, D., *Underground*, 52
Massachusetts Department of Education, 80
modeling disposition, practice of science and, 24–26

N
National Association for the Education of Young Children, 13
National Research Council, 5, 11, 22, 86

National Science Education Standards, 22, 86
National Science Research Council, 22, 53
Next Generation Science Standards, 109
nonfiction read-alouds, 50–53
suggestions, 51–52
notebooks. *See* science notebooks

O
observation, 6–7
observational drawings, 38–45
materials needed for, 40–41
supportive environments for, 40–42
worksheets and, 42
writing prompts and, 47
organization
ideas and, 80–82
web of questions and, 79

P
pet inquiry unit, 114–119, 138
assessment template, 138
diagnostic form, 137
information form, 136
large-group meetings and, 117
overview, 114–117
pet inquiry concepts and, 119
pet-shop setup, 133
read-alouds and, 118–119
sample letter to families, 132
small-group activities, 117–118
survey form, 135
teacher resources, 130–131
unit plan and, 119–130
veterinarian's office props, 134
pet-shop setup, pet inquiry unit and, 133

planning unit activities, 89–93
  sample worksheet for, 90
practices, science, 61
predicting, 7

Q

questioning, 7–8, 21–24
  effective, 23
  strategies,
  types of, 21–24

R

Rachel: The Story of Rachel Carson
  (Ehrlich), 52
read-alouds, 118, 121, 124, 127, 130
  nonfiction, 50–53
research groups
  activities, 84–86
  composition, task of group and,
  85–86
Roby, L., 97
  fitting science in, 99
  science background and, 101
  suggestions, 98
  teaching science, challenges of
  and, 103
  teaching science, excitement of,
  102
  what teachers need to know and,
  104–105
Ryan, C., 97
  fitting science in, 99–100
  science background and, 101
  suggestions, 98–99
  teaching science, challenges of
  and, 103–104
  teaching science, excitement of,
  102
  what teachers need to know and,
  105

S

sample letter to families, pet
  inquiry unit and, 132
science, practices of, 6–12
  collaborating and, 9
  communicating and, 10
  information tools and, 10–12
  interpretation of information
  and, 10
  investigating and, 8–9
  observation and, 6–7
  predicting and, 7
  questioning and, 7–8
science notebooks, 34–50
  assessment guidelines and, 112
  best types of, 36–37
  close-up page for, 113
  comprehension, meaning making and, 48–50
  defined, 34–36
  literacy skills and, 38
  observational drawings and,
  38–45
  pictures to words and, 45–48
  styles of, 37
Starr, M., 82
strategies
  classroom organization and,
  26–32
  modeling, science dispositions
  and practice, 24–26
  questioning, 21–24
  watching, listening, 19–21
survey form, pet inquiry unit, 135

T

Taking Science to School (Committee
  on Science Learning), 14
tools, information gathering and,
  10–12

topics
    organizing big ideas and, 78–82
    researching, 77–78
    selecting, 76–77

U
Underground (Macaulay), 52
unit plan, pet inquiry, 119–130

V
veterinarian's office props, pet
    inquiry unit and, 134

W
watching, listening, strategies and,
    19–21
What Makes a Shadow? (Bulla),
    11–12
Wick, W., *Drop of Water, A*, 52
Worth, K., 14

Z
Zembal-Saul, C., 82